L

MW01090008

"*Lobster Wars* is a fast-paced satire that exposes the crazy effect of reality TV on otherwise sane people. Mark Greene's muscular writing style and crafty storytelling grab you on page one and never let you go. Could not put this down."

—Bill Jemas, Former Marvel Publisher and Chief Operating Officer

"Chaotic, fast-paced, enthralling, and full of surprises—a tangled plot that twists, turns, rises and dips like the waves of a restless sea. . . . You'll never look at lobster the same way again!"

—Steve Jam, Author of *A Seventh Sense*

"With razor-sharp satirical humor, insight, and superb dialogue, Mark E. Greene's *Lobster Wars* is a literary gem of a boat ride—from its hilarious and engrossing plot turns to the colorful characters that will stay with you long after you've read the novel. Imagine if Damon Runyon was transported to a Maine fishing village and given carte blanche, and you can let your imagination go from there."

—Thomas H. Carry, Author of *Privilege*

"As someone who knows next to nothing about New England, fish, or sailing, this book was fantastic! The setting of a small town hosting a reality show is unique. I could feel and smell the locations, and the competing interests and insanity as the town grapples with exploiting their fame before it fades were as intriguing as any TV drama could hope to be. Loved it!"

—Tracy Salzgeber, Author of *The Girl in the Gun Club: My Time As One of the Few Good Men*

*Lobster Wars*

by Mark E. Greene

Published by

**◪ köehlerbooks**™

3705 Shore Drive
Virginia Beach, VA 23455
800-435-4811
www.koehlerbooks.com

# LOBSTER
## *Wars*

### A NOVEL

# MARK E. GREENE

VIRGINIA BEACH
CAPE CHARLES

For Kirby

*If only there were enough cranes*

# SEASON ONE:

# The Finale

**ON-SCREEN IMAGE:** Long shot of a line of weather-beaten lobster boats chased by dipping, banking seagulls as they steam out of the harbor into the cold sunrise. Dark-green waves break over the boats' sharp bows. Red channel buoys rock and clang. Surf crashes on a rocky shoreline in the distance.

**VOICE-OVER:** It's late September on the coast of Maine. A high-pressure system has settled over New England, and the water temperature is dropping. For the lobstermen of Tranquility, little time remains before the lobster migrate from the shallow inshore waters to the deeper ocean. Only days from now, the season will come to a close as the lobstermen race to haul their final traps, hoping to bank enough money to see them through Maine's long, cold winter.

**CUT TO:** Connor Nichols, a big man, faded yellow storm bibs over a gray hoody, the suspenders stretched across his thick shoulders, steps out of the cramped wheelhouse of a lobster boat. He points a long-handled metal hook at a string of orange-and-black buoys marching off into the distance, bobbing and ducking on the green swells. "Those aren't mine. Mine are red and white." Connor slams the boat hook against the wheelhouse and tosses it on the deck, scowls into the camera—bright blue eyes, black shadow of beard on a square chin.

"I set ten traps here yesterday. Now they're gone. Every single one. Vanished. I'm running out of time, and they're still screwing with me."

He steps back into the wheelhouse, puts the boat in gear, and begins to motor off. "The worst part is the money; at eighty bucks a trap, I'm out eight hundred dollars. Which . . . I . . . don't . . . have. Plus ten fewer traps really cuts into my catch—even more money lost."

"Oh, well." Connor shrugs, waves a hand at the gentle rollers, the craggy Maine shoreline. "This is why I came back to Maine. It sure beats the hell out of spending your life chained to a desk. Way better. I love being on the water and I like the work, even though it's hard. But it's tough to earn a living when the other guys are always messing with me. I knew it wasn't going to be easy. I didn't exactly grow up in a lobster fishing family. But I'm starting to get the hang of it." He pauses, stares into the camera. "I've always liked a challenge."

CUT TO: The deck of an old but neat gray boat, riding the swells. Wade Baxter, heavyset, orange bibs, tangled gray-and-brown beard, holds a huge, dripping lobster. Its giant claws snap the air while its tail tucks and curls. He cracks a yellowish smile. "Ayuh, now there's a keeper. Probably go two, maybe three pounds. That makes about nine hundred pounds total. Not bad for late season. And the prices stayed up all summa, so I've managed to make a few bucks this year."

Wade drops the lobster into a large tank, baits the trap, and tosses it back into the water, followed by an orange-and-black buoy. "Lobstah fishin's hard work, but I make it look easy 'cause I been at it most of my life. Not like some folks, think they can just take a bunch of Daddy's money and figure it out. There's no room here for outsiders, for rich boys wantin' a hobby."

**CUT TO:** Connor leans over the side of the boat and snags the red-and-white lobster buoy with his boat hook. He loops the line over the block and then around the hauler, starts the hauler spinning, and watches the line draws tight. He relaxes against the bait station, smiles into the camera. "At least this string didn't disappear. But you only get one hundred and fifty traps on a first-year license. And now I'm ten traps short. No way I can cover my expenses without replacing them."

The trap breaks the surface, water cascades off its green wire frame. Connor frowns as he stops the hauler, grabs the trap, and heaves in onto the gunwale-mounted platform. "Not again."

**ZOOM IN:** A large wet rock about the size of a melon.

He pulls the rock from the trap and, with a flip of his wrist, lobs it into a round plastic tub with several others.

"The bait's gone, too."

He quickly re-baits, tosses the trap, line, and the red-and-white buoy over the side. Grabs the wheel, throws the motor in gear, and moves into position to catch the next float.

And another big, slick rock flies into the tub.

His blue eyes squint into the camera. "Well, boys and girls, some of the other fishermen are playing a little prank on good old Connor. I'm always up for a good joke, but it's time to put a stop to this shit."

**CUT TO:** Dock, pilings, other lobster boats lined up in their slips, stern in.

Steadicam follows as Connor heaves the rock-filled tub onto the dock and jumps over. He motions toward the camera with one finger. "Always remember, safety first. We're licensed professionals. Never try this at home."

He grabs the rope handles and lifts the tub and makes his way down the dock. Seagulls pop off the pilings and wheel out of his way.

Steadicam pans ahead to the gray-hulled *Sweet Tail* tied in its slip.

**CUT TO:** Connor drops the tub. "Hey, Wade, you

in there?"

Wade comes out of the small forward cabin. "I'm busy, college boy. What do you want?"

"With all your experience I thought maybe you could give me some advice." Connor plucks a rock from the tub, holds it up. "Does this look like a lobster to you?"

Wade snickers. "Ayuh, rock lobstah. Much easier to catch than Maine lobstah. Most rookies do real well with them."

"Boy oh boy, that's for sure. Because I caught about eight. What do you think they're worth?" Connor shot-puts the rock. Wade flinches as it barely clears the *Sweet Tail's* wheelhouse, splashes into the harbor.

Wade edges behind the lobster tank. "No idea. Why don't you take 'em over to the co-op and ask them, instead of wasting my time."

"Now, there's a thought. But I bet they'd just laugh at me and ask a bunch of stupid questions, like what did I use for bait, how long do you have to boil them, how do they taste dipped in butter." Connor throws another rock. It just misses Wade's head as it sails over the cabin.

Wade dives behind the lobster tank. "Ayuh, you're fu-*beep*-ing crazy."

"What I find interesting is that rocks can't swim. But they managed to get in my traps anyway. Being an expert and all, I thought maybe you could explain how that happened." Connor picks up another. "But I can see you don't have much interest in helping me."

Wade peeks out from behind the lobster tank. "Careful you don't start something you can't finish."

"Don't worry, Wade. I plan on seeing this deal to the end." Connor sails the rock over the *Sweet Tail*.

Wade ducks. "Piss off."

"Stay away from my traps. Stay away from my boat. Stay away from me. Last warning." Connor picks up the tub and dumps the remaining rocks into the stern of the *Sweet Tail*. He turns to the camera, winks. "Let's see if he gets the message."

**CUT TO:** Long shot of lobster boats chased by dipping, banking seagulls as they race toward the harbor and the red-streaked sky of a setting sun.

**VOICE-OVER:** Will Connor, the rookie, the outsider, make it as a lobsterman? Will Wade and the other old-timers back off? Join us next season for *Lobster Wars*, reality TV's hottest new show.

Connor watched from the back of the room, leaning against the wall, hand wrapped around a beer, wondering if he was going to have to fight his way out. One week until Christmas, and almost the entire town of Tranquility had crowded into the Elks Lodge to watch the season finale of *Lobster Wars*. He wasn't particularly worried about the shopkeepers, real estate agents, bankers, or the old retired couple

who owned the town's four B and Bs. It was Wade and the other
lobstermen. The same guys who had fucked with him all summer
were now jammed up against the bar, congratulating themselves and
pounding down shots of whiskey with beer chasers. Connor knew a
volatile situation when it was staring him in the face. But Phil Pratt,
Tranquility's first selectman, local muckety-muck businessman and
the prime motivator behind the show, had insisted he attend. And
now here he was, questioning his own judgment for accepting the
invitation.

Everyone in Tranquility knew everyone's business—or at least
thought they did. The way it is in a small town. So when Connor
moved there last spring and bought a lobster boat, word spread.
Several months before the season started, Phil came to him about the
TV show. Of course, Connor had already heard about the show from
practically everyone in town. They were rabid over the opportunity.
Phil sat in the cramped kitchen of Connor's trailer and with a straight
face called it an "important documentary" about life in a small
lobster fishing village and how the good people of Tranquility had
an obligation, almost a patriotic duty, to help these TV folks record
a sacred way of life—especially the new people. Like Connor.

Phil had slid the production company's release across the table
and offered his pen. "They plan to start production in June. So just
sign and date. It means a lot."

Connor fingered the document. "What's in it for me?"

"Uh, what do you mean?"

"The last new boat in Tranquility sunk after two weeks. Word
around town is that the other lobstermen aren't too happy about my
plans to fish."

"I might have heard that, too." Phil shrugged. "But them boys is
just cranky. Doesn't mean anything."

"I'm not looking for trouble. I bet if the first selectman really wanted this TV thing to go forward, he could have a friendly chat with the other lobstermen and convince them not to screw with me when the season starts." Connor picked up the pen. "You know, for the good of the town."

"I don't know. Them boys is a hard bunch. I don't have much sway with 'em," Phil looked like he was going to cry. "But I guess I could talk to 'em."

"The concept's simple; go along to get along."

"I'll try my best, promise."

"No problems? No pushback?" Connor uncapped the pen.

Phil held up his hands in surrender. "Okay, okay."

"Then we've got a deal." Connor scribbled his name on the release.

Connor kept an eye on Wade and the boys as Phil turned off the TV and waved the crowd into silence. "Okay, okay. Now, everyone listen up. I talked to the production company, and they said the network is happy with the ratings. The plan is same as last year. They tape the show all summa and then run the new episodes next fall. But this time, instead of eight, they'ah planning to shoot ten, maybe twelve episodes. In the meantime, they gonna rerun the show from now until next summa."

The crowd cheered and clapped.

Phil continued, "Opportunities like this don't come along every day. That show put Tranquility on the map. They'ah gonna be a lot more tourists. And we don't have much time between now and next summa. But what everyone needs to think about is how to cash in. I'm gonna expand the store. The rest of you got to think of somethin', you want in on this."

Wade shouted from the bar. "How about the TV people pay us

more money for being on the show? Especially me, seein' as how I'm the big star."

A few of the other lobstermen booed and hissed.

Phil swallowed hard. "I, uh, asked. The producer didn't seem too happy with the idea but said she'd think about it. Said most people get a small bump after the *second* season. We'll just have to wait and see when the new contracts come."

As the crowd thinned, Connor held his position while Phil made his way over. "I heard your boat's dry-docked in Camden. You just havin' some work done for next season?"

Connor finished off his beer. "They're working on the engine."

Wade stepped up, shot glass in hand, nodded at Phil, leaned into Connor, crowding him. "Ayuh. Good idea. Put a little money in it and you'll get a better price come spring."

"You want to buy the *Nu B*?" Connor tensed.

Wade threw back the shot and grinned. "Ayuh, that's all I need— another fuckin' lobstah boat."

"But, Connor, you're coming back for next season?" Phil asked. "I mean with the show and all . . ."

Connor pushed off the wall. He smiled at Wade and Phil. "I had such a great time last summer, why wouldn't I come back for more?"

# CHAPTER 1

Connor's plan was simple. Buy a boat. Buy traps. Set traps. Catch lobster. Sell lobster. Pay off debts. Have a life—on the water. From the time he put his name on the wait list for a license, he had thought about his plan. Now he was right where he wanted to be, leaning against the captain's chair in the wheelhouse of the *Nu B*, one hand resting on the throttle as he guided his boat through the placid green swells toward the mouth of Tranquility's harbor. The spring air had that familiar salty tang, and waves broke white and foamy on the rocky shore in the middle distance. Perfect.

He wasn't naive. Of course it wasn't going to be easy. There was a big difference, a huge difference, between running a handful of traps for friends and family and the life of a professional lobsterman. The work could be brutally hard and sometimes dangerous.

Plus these inbred jerkwads in Tranquility had an industrial-strength hard-on for anyone without ten generations of headstones in the local cemetery.

So his first season was even more difficult than he imagined. He had started with a nice little cushion from his logging job, but last year's learning curve was steep, and his expenses were killer, and now his cushion was a thin, hard pad. In fact, he was upside down on this whole lobster fishing business. Not even close to making his nut.

The *Nu B* was a classic Maine lobster boat—thirty-six feet long, eight feet wide at the transom, a high, flared bow for taking rough seas, a cramped V-berth and small forward wheelhouse, more for protection from the elements than for comfort. She was a sweet boat, solid and stable, but needed work. During the winter, he had sent her to the boatyard in Camden, ten miles to the south. Overhauling her engine had practically sucked his wallet dry. But now he had her back, and Maine's stingy spring weather had finally granted him a rare, calm, sunny day for the two-hour run of open water. Despite last season's bullshit with the locals and the stupid TV show, Connor had decided to give it one more shot.

This year, he would figure out how to make it pay.

Had to figure out how to make it pay.

No problem.

He steered into the channel and throttled down the big diesel from a roar to a throb, keeping enough speed to maintain steerage. The harbor's opening was wide, but the navigation channel was deceptively narrow; a set of jagged rocks lurked barely beyond the red right-side markers. At high tide, some boats would cut the corner, saving time and fuel, but once the tide turned, the shortcut became a guessing game. A game Connor had tried a time or two until he learned that the rocks had won so many rounds the locals had nicknamed them "Jaws."

In the harbor proper, where the broken land dropped down to meet the shore, a small, weathered town huddled along the water's edge—bleached cedar shingles and sprung clapboard siding out of plumb, salt stained and working class and too coarse for tourists. It suited Connor fine.

Up ahead, he spotted a young guy in a yellow sea kayak, sunlight glinting off his wet paddle blades. It looked like fun, and he sure understood the attraction, but the guy was paddling his way directly across the busy boat channel. Not a good idea in a working harbor like Tranquility. Gaining on the kayaker, Connor slowed to shout a warning before one of the other lobstermen turned the guy into sushi.

The loud *BLATT, BLATT, BLATT* of an air horn jolted Connor, and he glanced over his left shoulder to see Wade Baxter bearing down on him at full throttle in the *Sweet Tail*.

The *Sweet Tail* drew even, forcing Connor toward the red channel markers, toward Jaws.

Wade leaned out of his small cabin and gave Connor a nasty smile, shouting over the engine noise, "Heard you gave up after last year."

Connor poured on the power, matching Wade's speed. "You heard wrong."

But Wade held position, driving Connor closer and closer to the hull-gouging rocks. Dead ahead the kayaker was now windmilling furiously to clear the channel ahead of the racing lobster boats.

Wade drank from a can of Miller. "Easier to sell a boat this time of year. Unless it's got a big goddamn hole in it."

"What about the lobster fishing business? What about the TV show? What would I do for fun?" Connor eyed the kayaker. The poor bastard was paddling for his life. No need for a warning now.

"This ain't no hobby. The sooner you learn that, the better for everyone." Wade crushed the beer can and tossed it on the deck. He pointed at the kayaker. "You and that kid. Leave the water to professionals."

Wade leaned his thick frame forward, peering out of the speeding F150's windshield into the night. "Fog's so heavy I can't see squat. I can't make out the numbers, and the road's slicker than gull shit on a wet dock. Damn it, Kent, slow down."

Kent Baxter resettled his grease-smudged Evinrude cap and tapped the brake, slowing the pickup into a turn. "Haven't you screwed with this guy enough? You cut his traps. You pissed in his gas tank. I got things to do besides running you around in the middle of the night, looking for trouble." Kent peered into the fog and jerked the wheel. He steered with one hand, the other resting on a quart bottle squeezed between his legs.

Wade looked at his younger brother in the thin blue light of the dashboard. Kent reminded him of a clean-shaven, leaner version of their father—a grass-is-always-greener kind of guy, with thick, calloused hands and work-stained clothes and never more than a wrinkled twenty in his pocket.

Their father, Lloyd, had been a lobsterman, as was his father and his father before him. It seemed like the whole damn Baxter family was nothing but a bunch of smelly fisherman, going back generations. And lobster fishing was a fickle enterprise. If the haul was bad, prices stayed up and you sold your catch for big money, but your numbers were low. If the haul was good, everyone fished hard, often flooding the market and driving down the price. Plus your operating costs always went up, never down. About twenty years ago, after one particularly bad season, Lloyd announced that they were busted but that he had secured a berth on a big-time fishing boat out of Juneau, Alaska, and he was heading down to Logan for a flight out tomorrow. He promised a better life. He promised to send money. They never heard from him again.

"Gimme the vodka." Wade reached for the bottle. "The season's starting, and them TV people gonna be here any day. I saw him running his boat yesterday. I got to make sure he don't set no traps. Got to send a message." Wade tilted the bottle to his lips.

"I don't know. The TV people must like him. They got him in practically every show. It's like he's the star," Kent added. "Maybe cause he's telegenic."

"Tele-what?" Wade snorted.

"It means he looks good on TV. Like Brad Pitt or George Clooney."

"Hell, I'm telegenic," Wade replied.

Kent laughed out loud. "I beg to differ."

Wade wiped his mouth with the back of his hand, smoothing his tangled beard. He stared at his brother. "I love it. You sell one piece of that scrap metal shit to some rich twat from Camden and start talkin' like a sissy."

"My sculpture's not scrap metal shit," Kent sniffed. "It's working man's art. It's conceptual."

"Yeah right. You come home from the boatyard, get hammered on cheap vodka, weld up a bunch'a rusted boat parts, and call it art."

"*Conceptual* art," Kent added.

"Always lookin' for something better," Wade snorted. "Just like Dad."

"Shit, like most everyone," Kent replied. "Why not me?"

Wade shot back, "Just don't expect anything."

Growing up in a place like Tranquility, it felt like you had only two options. Haul traps in the season, or get up every morning at the crack of dawn, drive to one of the fancy towns, like Camden, and work the summer catering to rich tourists. But when the lobster moved to deep water and the tourists went home to Boston or New York, you spent the winter trying to make ends meet.

At least the tourists were reliable. But who wanted to make beds and clean toilets for minimum wage? Waiting tables paid better, and you could always serve a spitter to that snotty bitch from Greenwich who sent her salad back because you forgot "dressing on the side."

Their mother, Alice, worked all kinds of crazy hours at the White Swan Inn, complaining every single day. Kent mined the middle ground, working as a boatyard mechanic, making his living off both the fisherman and the wealthy summer boaters with their precious toys. Wade fished; it was all he really knew.

"Well, it's going into her gallery. She's even planning a show. 'Kent Baxter: Gears of the Ocean.' Says the summa people'll buy it for sure." Kent snatched the vodka bottle away from his brother. "All's I'm saying is, for once, things are going okay for me, for us. Maybe you don't want to start with this guy right before the TV people get here."

"That's the whole point, little brother. Get him to pull out now. Phil keeps talking about cashing in, and I'm thinking maybe I could get me some kind of deal, make some dough on the side. You know, like a TV commercial or something. But with Nichols around, they might go to him instead."

"I don't know," Kent replied. "It seems like he's kinda important to the show."

"Fuck him. He shouldn't even be here. We never let a new guy in. When was the last time some outsider set traps in our waters? I don't know how he even got a license. His rich daddy probably pulled strings." Wade started for the bottle. "There's only so many lobstah. We got a right."

Kent slapped his brother's hand away. "You had your share. Last bit's mine."

Wade got his big hand around the bottle's neck and tried to wrench it from Kent's grip. "You've drunk up most of it. Give it here."

"No way, Wade." Kent twisted the vodka bottle. The pickup shot forward, fishtailing on the slick dirt road.

"Watch the ditch." Wade jerked the bottle away.

Kent clutched the wheel with both hands. "Foot's caught on something." He worked at the wheel, overcorrecting as the truck spun off the slick road. "Can't get my boot loose."

"Watch the trees, asshole." Wade laughed and pointed at a stand of big pines rushing toward them, tilting the vodka to his lips, bracing one hand against dashboard.

A few minutes later, Wade stood up from in front of the truck. "You got lucky again. Front end's resting on an old stump. Too dark to tell for sure, but looks like the truck ought'a run, we get it down."

Kent sat on the ground next the open driver's door, poking at an angry red bump on his forehead. "Where's the damn vodka?"

"How the hell should I know?" Wade wiped his hands on his jeans. "Bottle went flying when you hit that stump. I'll get the come-along and chains. We'll pull her off." As Wade circled around to the truck's bed, he spotted a rusted mailbox nailed to a tree next to an overgrown dirt driveway. He stared at the number painted on the box. "I'll be damned, Kent, you found it after all."

"Huh? Found what? The vodka?"

Wade grabbed a gas can and a handful of rags out of the truck's bed. "You get her off the stump and on the road. I'll be back in a few minutes."

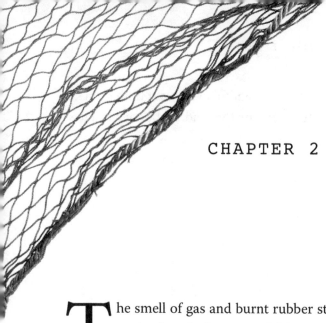

# CHAPTER 2

The smell of gas and burnt rubber still in his nose, Connor trudged up the long gravel driveway. He had snagged a ride from Tranquility, but the house was still almost two miles from the hardtop. Of course, he would have preferred to drive his own truck. But late last night, some asshole had sent a message, and now his Dodge Ram was a smoldering heap of metal and plastic.

His shoulders sagged when he spotted his mother's silver Audi A8 parked in front of the cedar-shingled Cape. She was usually gone by now. His plan was to slip in, leave a note, and borrow his dad's truck. The house had been his family's summer retreat for as long as he could remember. Remolded and expanded, it sat on six carefully tended waterfront acres in Camden, Maine. And the four-car garage held just what he needed.

He elected not to use his key, rang the bell, and waited. Time to shake off last night's insanity and focus on the task at hand. Brooke could be a handful. But when it came to his mother, a little honey never hurt.

Brooke opened the door. "Oh, Connor. My always entertaining youngest progeny." Her blue eyes were bright and her speech was crisp. "What a nice surprise. I was expecting—"

"Good morning, Mom." Connor scooped her up in his arms, spun her around in a full circle, and planted a big, loud kiss on her cheek.

"Connor, my hair. You're wrinkling my dress," Brooke giggled and swatted at his arms. "I was expecting the caterer. I need to show her where to place the tents. I didn't hear you drive up. Where's your truck? And why do you smell like gasoline?"

"Little problem with the truck." Connor held her hand and followed her inside. "Caterer? A party?"

"Later this week." Brooke led him to the kitchen. "Sylvia Meyers claims to have found the next major artist. A real talent. Or so *she* thinks. From the indigenous population. If you can believe *that*. She's going to feature him in her gallery and asked me to host a pre-opening cocktail party."

"But I thought you loved the local art—glass float lamps, wooden lobster trap coffee tables, driftwood sculptures. So rustic. So crafty. So quintessentially American."

Brooke shuddered. "Stop making fun. It's ghastly detritus for tourists and only good for the local economy, and you know it." She gestured toward a small watercolor propped on the kitchen's gray, granite center island. "In fact, this arrived only yesterday. I met the artist in France last year—Xavier Merratt. Aren't the colors amazing? Look at the depth, the contrast, the composition. He's a masterful colorist."

Connor pointed. "His shading does add a strong sense of space."

"I'm glad you agree." She picked up the little frame and held it at arm's length. "A truly wonderful artist."

"Maybe that's who Sylvia's discovered," Connor offered. "A *wonderful* artist."

"Oh, Connor. Please. One does what one can for one's friends. I'm only throwing this party as a favor to Sylvia. After all, we're co-chairing the Camden Arts Council this year, so it's best she owes me one."

Brooke poured herself a drink from a large, iced pitcher. It looked like orange juice, but she didn't offer him one. He grabbed a Coke from the Sub-Zero and settled onto a stool at the kitchen island. "I thought you swore you'd burn the Wyeth before chairing the arts council again."

"We had a minor disagreement over a trivial matter and patched things up." Brooke paused. "What else would I do here all summer?"

"How about your poetry? A little iambic pentameter? A sestina or a sonnet? I can't remember the last time I saw you write anything other than a shopping list."

Brooke had won the National Book Award for a collection of poems she published when she was only twenty-five. Three short but acclaimed collections followed. Then she had married his father, Edwin, and had raised a family and managed a household while Edwin jetted around the world, building his business. Now in her early sixties, she wrote sparingly, publishing very little in the past twenty years, mainly spending her time collecting art and hosting charitable events and fundraisers.

"Veal chops and arugula aren't suitable for a sestina. Which you should know from your excellent education. Despite the fact that you appear determined to throw it away," Brooke replied.

"But don't you miss writing?" Connor asked. He liked her poetry. Brooke used simple language to convey subtle, sometimes wry situations. "Plumbing the dark recesses of the human soul? Revealing the ironies of contemporary life?"

"Now that you mention it, yes. I do."

"So, Mom, blow off the arts council and spend the summer writing. Isn't that what this house is all about?"

"It was. Once." Brooke looked around the kitchen, sighed. "But it's not that easy. I have responsibilities. Priorities. Especially where your father is concerned."

"Maybe Dad shouldn't get a vote." Connor tapped the Coke can on the counter.

"True. Your father always resents the time I spend writing. Calls it 'going into my black hole of distraction.'" Brooke shrugged, sipped her drink. "Help me hang this watercolor before you leave. And what happened to your truck? You didn't tell me. Did you think I was going to forget asking?"

"Truck needs a few repairs. Where *is* the big cheese?"

"He's visiting his factories. First China, then Thailand." Brooke paused to take another sip of her drink.

"That's Dad. Making the world safe for *component* parts," Connor quipped. Edwin Nichols—inventor, engineer, and hard-charging entrepreneur. It wasn't that Connor and his father had a bad relationship. But Edwin—no one called him Ed, including his family and friends—was a bit of a control freak. Borderline obsessive. Maybe over the border. Edwin had a plan for everything. Micromanagement was a key ingredient to Edwin's business success, but it got a little tedious when it came to his family.

"His itinerary is around here somewhere," Brooke said. "Do you really care?"

"Of course I care. I need to borrow the Toyota."

"Seriously," Brooke scoffed.

"Only for a few days."

"Why don't you just help yourself to his MG?"

"I would, but my head sticks over the windshield." Connor circled his fingers and held them to his face. "I don't like to wear the goggles."

"Oh, Connor. I'm concerned about you. Lobster fishing and that ridiculous TV show. I heard about it from all my friends. It makes you look something of a boob. A handsome boob, but a boob nevertheless. Whatever made you agree to do it?" Brooke asked.

"You raised us to appreciate the arts," Connor protested. "We practically grew up in museums."

"By anyone's definition, reality TV is *not* art."

"I think of it more like a documentary. Plus it might lead to an acting career." Connor held his head in profile. "What do think, leading man or character actor?"

"I've watched several episodes, and quite frankly, I'm worried you're going to end up in the medical center." Brooke leaned forward and put a hand on Connor's shoulder.

"That's just the way they edit the show. You know, to highlight conflict, just like any good drama."

Brooke fixed Connor with a frank stare. "Don't BS me. I'm more in tune with how the locals operate than you might think. Sometimes, I fear you are your own worst enemy."

"Okay, yeah, I'm getting some pushback. But nothing I can't handle. And as for the show, I'm not even certain I'm going to do it again."

"But why don't you find . . . another job? Something more suitable." Brooke sipped from her orange drink.

Connor replied, "I've invested a lot of time and money to get to this point. I'm not going to bail now."

"That sounds like an excuse, not a reason," Brooke observed.

"This is why I moved back to Maine. Besides, lobster fishing is more than a job. I'm running my own business. But starting a new business takes a little time. I was working out the kinks last season. This year, smooth sailing."

"Do you need to borrow some money?"

Connor shook his head. "No. I'm fine. Everything's on track. Besides, every time you and Dad bail me out, I have to hear one his lectures."

"Despite his hectoring delivery, your father is right. You should be using your brains, not brawn—"

Connor cut her off. "To build factories in China where children work twelve-hour days?"

"My God, Connor, you ran rings around your brother. You even outscored Joanna on, well, virtually everything. It's not too late. Finish your degree. We'll find you a graduate program, and then you can have a real career."

"Ah, the Nichols Family Plan for Success," Connor said. He had coined the term during one particularly argumentative family Thanksgiving dinner. The one where he announced his decision to leave Bowdoin for trucker school.

"Let's not open old wounds," Brooke replied.

"Okay, say I finish my BA. Then what?" Connor asked. "MIT? Harvard MBA? Dad practically cloned Daniel. Or slog through UVA med school like Joanna and spend eighty hours a week cracking chests for a living. Yuck. No thanks."

Brooke stifled a laugh. "There are some elements of all jobs, or *businesses*, which are distasteful. But you're almost thirty-five. You need a plan."

"I have a plan."

"Do tell." Brooke crossed her arms over her chest.

"Simple." Connor smiled. "Avoid artificial light at all costs."

After a moment, Brooke shook her head. "I'm sorry, but that plan sounds a little vague."

"It's in its early stages." Connor drummed his fingers on the counter. "I'm still formulating some specific ideas. Entertaining various opportunities. Evaluating several scenarios."

"I see. And those early stages would include learning several trades." She ticked off her points on her long fingers. "First a truck driver, then an electrician, followed by roughneck, and now lobster fishing."

"You forgot logger." For as long as he could remember, Connor felt out of sync with the family agenda. He knew that the Nichols Plan did not include any dirty-fingernail, calloused-hand vocation, no matter how satisfying or successful.

Brooke replied, "Ah, yes. Your Paul Bunyan phase."

"Believe me, properly sharpening a chain saw is a lot more satisfying than writing papers on the postcolonial significance of Melville's multiethnic characters in *Typee* and *Moby Dick*." Connor sipped his Coke and grinned. "Plus, think of the job security. No one will ever get their tree topped by a call center in India."

"How comforting." Brooke gave a sly smile. "Where exactly does 'reality TV character' fit into the mix of the 'various opportunities' you're entertaining?"

"I'm a reality TV *star*. In some circles I'm considered a true

Renaissance man." Connor winked. "Except I don't speak French. Or fence."

"A Renaissance reality TV star who fishes for lobster. This is your plan?" Brooke asked. "Because, quite frankly, it doesn't appear very marketable."

"What about Snookie? The Kardashians?" Connor replied.

Brooke gave him a blank stare and shrugged.

"Never mind. It's too bad my plan doesn't fit the family program. But at least I'm happy with what I'm doing." He kissed her cheek. "Now I need to borrow the FJ for a little while."

"You weren't joking? Your father's FJ? His precious truck?"

"Think of the look on his face when he checks the odometer." Connor smiled.

"Well . . ." Brooke winked. "As you know, I have absolutely zero knowledge of mechanical devices." She placed a hand on Connor's shoulder. "But please be careful."

"Don't worry. I'll take good care of father's beloved toy."

Father's beloved toy was a fully restored, white, two-door 1965 Toyota FJ40: tall and boxy, with knobby tires, four-wheel drive, and a bumper-mounted winch—very helpful in case you got stuck in the mud. Not that this particular truck ever saw mud. Most of the year, it sat in a spotless garage, next to a pristine, black, 1951 MG. Only occasionally driven. Slowly. Over dry roads. For short distances. Because his father was, well, his father was Edwin Nichols. Not Ed.

An hour later, as he slowed the truck to stop by his mailbox, Connor caught his reflection in the rearview mirror. Only his mother's bright-blue eyes staring back at him convinced him that he hadn't been switched at birth.

The big rusty mailbox was unexpectedly full. Connor did a quick driveway sort and immediately spotted a nasty-looking notice from the bank. Then several catalogs and what looked like a fan letter. Smelled like one too—cherry or raspberry. When he turned back to the Land Cruiser, a glint of litter by the side of the road caught his eye. He picked up an almost empty plastic bottle with a plain white paper label, black lettering: *W-o-d-k-a*. He tossed it into the Cruiser and headed down the driveway to his house trailer and the still-smoking hulk of his truck.

He kept his overhead low by renting a trailer parked in a quiet stand of birch trees on the forgotten backside of a hundred-acre blueberry farm. Nothing fancy, it was an old-style single-wide—kitchen at one end, solo bedroom at the other, with a small living area and bathroom squeezed in the middle, the whole thing sheathed in white-and-turquoise aluminum scabbed together with rust-leaking pop rivets. Simple, private, and remote. Until last night.

As he pulled the Land Cruiser around his trailer, Connor spotted a blue-uniformed state trooper inspecting the remains of his Dodge Ram. "Hello there, Officer. If you're here for the barbeque, we're fresh out of hot dogs. But I could make s'mores if you brought marshmallows."

"I'm Trooper Mack." The trooper, short and wide and sporting a brush-cut mustache, glanced at his clipboard. "You the owner? Connor Nichols?"

"Yeah. Are you the rapid response to my 911 from *last* night?"

"Your call was passed to me by the trooper on night duty. He didn't have time to come by and take a statement. Car hit a moose on the interstate—double fatality."

Connor pointed. "Some asshole toasted my truck. How about that for a statement?"

Trooper Mack nodded. "Well, I guess that sums it up pretty well. You sure it was arson?"

"I heard someone last night. Came running out here. The fireball wasted my vision, but I think heavyset guy, beard, plaid shirt."

"Well, that describes about half the men in Maine." Mack scribbled some notes. "You look familiar. How long have you lived in Tranquility?"

"Going on two years."

"Before that?"

"Oregon."

"What do you do, Mr. Nichols?"

"Lobsterman."

The trooper chuckled. "No, really."

"You want to see my license?"

"You didn't grow up here? Move somewhere and come back recently?" Mack lowered his clipboard. "You're from *away*?"

Connor shrugged. "Yeah, from *away*. But I live here now."

"How'd you even get a license?" Trooper Mack asked.

"Got lucky, put my name on the wait list early on. What about my truck?"

Trooper Mack looked at the blackened chassis. "Let me make an educated guess: this isn't the first time you've had, um, an issue?"

"The locals have been screwing with me since the day I started hauling traps."

Trooper Mack nodded. "I was born and raised in Maine, transferred to this area from Rangeley. We've lived just up the road in Rockport six years now, and my neighbors still don't talk to me."

Connor pointed at the smoldering remains. "This isn't exactly the same as not inviting me to their Fourth of July clambake."

Trooper Mack peered at Connor. "Wait a minute. I knew you were familiar." The trooper grinned and banged the clipboard against his leg. "You're on that TV show. You're the rookie college boy. My wife loves that show. She tries to tape it for me because I pull a lot of night shifts. So I've only watched it a few times. That one show with the rocks was hilarious."

Connor sighed, "Right. A real laugh riot."

"That Wade Baxter seems like real piece of work. At first I thought it was just how they do the show, but my shift captain remembered him from when he was kid." Mack shook his head. "Says he was always a prick."

"Maybe you should talk to him."

"About what?"

Connor waved at the smoldering Ram. "Arson?"

Trooper Mack took a deep breath and stared up at Connor. "Listen, Mr. Nichols. I don't see any forensic evidence, which doesn't mean it wasn't arson. But let me give you a piece of advice. Don't take matters into your own hands."

"I would never do that. I hate violence. I don't even like to throw rocks. I'm practically a pacifist." Connor held up his hand, made the peace symbol. "You know, make love, not war."

"That's funny because you look *exactly* like the kind of guy who takes matters into his own hands. Which is a bad idea. These old boys in Tranquility are a hard bunch. Especially the lobstermen. Hell, they can barely stand each other."

Connor scratched his chin. "You should tell that to the chamber of commerce so they can update their brochure."

"The only police coverage for this town is state troopers like me, and we're spread pretty thin. No local cops, no sheriff. The fire department is volunteer. How long did it take *them* to respond?"

"Three hours. When they got here, didn't even bother with the hoses. Just laughed."

"Then you get my point."

"Yeah, stop fishing or buy a big-ass fire extinguisher."

"Well, a home fire extinguisher is always a good idea. But you might consider another line of work if you plan to stay in Tranquility. Meantime, I'll check around, but I wouldn't expect much." Trooper Mack flipped his notebook to a blank page, held out his pen. "Can I get an autograph? You know, for my wife. Make it 'To Trudy—too bad you're already married.'"

"Sure." Connor grabbed the pen and scribbled.

"She'll be tickled I met you." Trooper Mack handed Connor a business card. "Here's my direct number in case there's any more trouble."

Connor pocketed the card. "Thanks. I feel safer already."

He dumped the day's mail onto the kitchen table and tore open the bank's letter. It was a past-due notice on the *Nu B*'s note with the word *REPO* in big, red block letters, plus a lot of threatening legal terms. He was four payments behind, plus accumulated interest. But he had mailed a check only last week. No grace period? What the fuck? He had to get this bullshit straightened out.

Connor grabbed his cell phone, dialed the 800 number on the notice, and went through the voice menu, responding to prompts and pumping in the PIN number and loan codes, finally ending up on hold for a live person.

With the phone wedged between his ear and shoulder, he slit opened the fruity-smelling fan letter and dumped out its contents. Ever since the original eight episodes of *Lobster Wars* ran last fall, he had received a steady stream of letters and emails from old girlfriends, wannabe girlfriends, horny housewives, and hot grannies. Ah, the perks of being a minor reality TV star. This was a short note claiming undying love and promising white-hot sex, plus two close-up photos of a juicy pink example. Connor squinted. Was that tramp stamp a set of instructions?

Connor dropped the letter in the trash with the catalogs and junk mail, then carefully filed the photos in a shoebox with several others. Putting the shoebox on the kitchen counter, he fetched a cold Bud from the fridge and then sipped the beer at the table, listening to the endless elevator music while he stared at the depressing past-due repo notice.

He flipped through his checkbook. He was using his rapidly thinning cash cushion to get ready for the upcoming fishing season— ransoming the *Nu B* from the boatyard and buying more traps, lines, and floats. But he needed to get caught up on his boat payments, and fast, or start looking for a secret spot to anchor the *Nu B*. He had barely enough cash for one or the other, but not both. Not to mention replacing his truck.

Lately, he was even staying away from the ladies. A self-imposed zipped-pants policy. It wasn't an ideal situation, but keeping it parked in his shorts did save money—not to mention cut down on the crazy factor.

However, he did need the occasional release to keep the old engine in tune. A little tug on the starter cord, so to speak. And a face-to-face at the bank might be more effective than arguing this out over the phone. Connor ended the call, finished his beer, and pulled the shoebox from the counter.

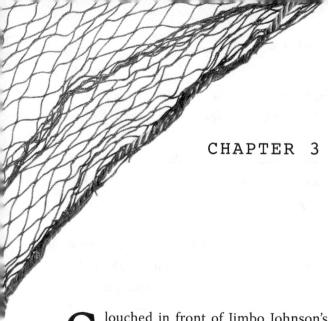

# CHAPTER 3

Slouched in front of Jimbo Johnson's desk in the cramped manager's office, Evan Pratt tugged at his collar, sweating through his uniform shirt so bad he could smell his own stink. Even with the office AC running full blast, he felt like he was baking in a Phoenix parking lot at noon in July. He watched Jimbo's fat finger push the play button. A grainy black-and-white image flickered on the security monitor, and Evan saw himself loading flat-screen TVs into the back of his old Dodge van.

After the loop repeated three times, Jimbo sat back in his chair, lacing his fat fingers behind his head. "Damn, Pratt. For a security guy and convicted felon, you sure are a stupid son of bitch. You have the keys to the surveillance room. Why didn't you just turn off the cameras?"

"Uh, well, I thought someone might notice the blank space." Sweat from Evan's right armpit trickled down his ribs.

"Shit, boy. The blank space is between your ears. No one sees a blank space on those tapes. Least not my uncle." Jimbo's uncle was Big Bob Johnson, owner of Big Bob's Discount TV—with twelve convenient locations throughout central Arizona. "How much you get?"

"'Bout ten grand." Evan relaxed and fixed Jimbo with a sly grin. He really got fifteen, but he had a pretty good idea where this conversation was now headed.

Jimbo tapped the TV monitor. "Looks like you boosted enough of them TVs to clear twenty, twenty-five, easy."

"No way! Big Bob only stocks crap—Emerson, Magnavox, Coby. No LGs. No Samsungs."

"You sell 'em yourself?"

Evan shook his head. "I got a guy, buys the whole load."

"All right, here's the deal. You're gonna pay me twenty-five to keep my mouth shut." Jimbo picked at scab on the back of his hand.

"Shit, Jimbo. The money's gone. That was a one-shot thing to clear some debts." Evan was trying to go straight, he really was, but he needed the money to take care of a little problem that involved counterfeit Harley parts and some bikers with no sense of humor. "I'm on fuckin' parole."

"Exactly. Twenty-five grand, or I show this tape to your parole officer." Jimbo pulled the man's card out of Evan's personnel file. "But since I'm such a nice guy, I'll give you one week to come up with the cash."

Evan's PO would kick his butt right back to the Federal Correctional Institution in Tucson. Working security at Big Bob's sucked, but not as bad as getting cornholed in the showers by some iron-pumping 'roid monster. Evan fingered the big black Maglite hanging from his belt—it held four D-Cell batteries—and thought briefly of bashing Jimbo's fat head to a bloody pulp. Instead, he forced a big smile. "How about eight?"

"Did I say I wanted to negotiate?" Jimbo reached for the phone and started to dial.

Evan needed a drink. Bad. He rooted around in the refrigerator for a cold beer. This situation with Jimbo required some serious thinking. The greedy fuck really was looking for twenty-five K. In one week. If not, Evan believed the guy would turn him in, no question. That meant a fast trip right back to FCI Tucson. It also meant three more years of Mexican Mafia gangbangers, Aryan Brotherhood skinheads, and Crips and Bloods from Phoenix and Tempe. Hell, Evan was basically a businessman, although he wasn't above the occasional act of violence. But only in the line of duty. To the guys in federal lockup, violence was a hobby, a recreational activity to pass the time.

He jerked his head out of the fridge. "Damn it, Darlene. Didn't I tell you to pick up some Bud next time you went out?"

"Haven't been shopping yet," she shouted over the sound of seagulls blaring on the TV. "I was gonna change and head to the Safeway right after this show. Thought you was working the night watch at Big Bob's. What're you doing home?"

Evan found a black cherry wine cooler hiding behind a lidless container of moldy, low fat cottage cheese. He stalked into the next room. "Got the night off. Besides, I might have a little problem with old Jimbo the manager."

"Told you not to mess with those TVs." Still dressed in her Hooter's uniform, Darlene's tight little body was curled on the worn, green-and-tan-striped sofa. She was counting her tip money—a big wad of twenties. "Told you Jimbo's not as dumb as he looks."

Evan knocked back half the bottle. "And I told *you* to pick up some beer."

About a year ago, Evan had sweet-talked Darlene into quitting her pole-dancing gig and moving in with him, convincing her he had a surefire scheme for making some big bucks, put them on easy street. But it was hard to be a successful entrepreneur when you were on fuckin' parole, and lately, her critical attitude was grinding on his nerves, getting in the way of his big-picture thinking.

"And I told *you* I haven't been to the store yet." She folded the stack of twenties. "They's talking about making me the assistant manager."

"Who is? Pete? That horndog what runs the place? Little shit's just trying to get into your shorts."

"No, smarty. An EVP from the head office in Florida spotted me a few weeks ago. Had me take a test, and I did real good and we've been talking. *And* he's a she." Darlene turned her attention back to the big flat-screen perched on two plastic milk crates. "Didn't you say once you was from Maine?"

"Grew up there a long time ago." Evan gulped down the last of the too-sweet wine cooler and wiped his mouth with the tail of his uniform shirt.

Darlene tilted her chin at the TV. "I'm watching this show about lobster fishing in Maine, and it looks awful nice. Maybe you can take me there someday."

"Maine sucks. Trust me. It's really fucking cold."

"I meant, like in the spring or summer. When it's warm and we can see the ocean, maybe go for swim. I've never seen the ocean."

"Shit, the ocean's always cold. You can swim for maybe one or two weeks right in the middle of summer. That is, if the tide don't flush your ass out to sea."

"Okay, so we won't swim. I don't swim so good anyway. But it still looks awful pretty." Darlene fanned the twenties.

"The place is stupid, and the people are stupid, and if you grow up there, all you get to do is fish lobster or wait tables, unless you live up in the woods; then you're totally fucked because all there is for those dumb bastards is cutting down trees. And if your parents drive drunk and hit a moose and die when you're only ten, like me, then you're double fucked. Plus, everyone says 'ayuh,' which don't mean shit, but they think it does, so they say it all the time."

"If you grew up there, how come you don't say 'ayuh'?"

"'Cause I don't want to sound like some dumbass from Maine."

"Well, I want to go to Maine. Eat me some lobster. Ain't never had no lobster. Can we go? Please, it'd be fun."

He slid onto the sofa and put his arm around Darlene's shoulders. Maybe she was a little plain in the face, with a big nose and a left eye that wandered to the right. But the skimpy Hooter's uniform never failed to get his motor started—the white tank top showing off her yummy rack and the orange shorts hugging her curvy ass. Plus, he really needed to relax, and one wine cooler wasn't going to solve the Jimbo problem. Evan unzipped his pants. "Sure, honey. I got some lobster for you right here."

Darlene wrinkled her nose and tried to shrug off Evan's arm. "Pee-yew, your pits stink. Go take a shower while I watch the rest of my show."

"It's mostly commercials." Evan massaged the back of Darlene's neck. He needed immediate relief, and her blow jobs were world class. "If you'll be quick, I'll be quick. Then you can watch the end of your show. After, I'll take you out to dinner."

"Really? We never go out to dinner. Where?" Darlene reached inside his pants.

"There's one of those new Rowdy Robby steak places right by the Wally Mart. Opened the other day. Been hearing the ads on the radio." Evan began to relax.

"You're just telling me so I'll suck you." Her hand worked its magic.

Evan leaned back into the cushions. "Nah, honey. Honest."

"I don't believe you. You always fall asleep right after."

"No, I promise." Evan pointed at the TV. "Better get started—commercials are almost over."

"No. Dinner first." Darlene abruptly pulled her hand out of his pants and scrambled off the sofa, heading for the doorway. "You take a shower. I'm gonna change."

"Ah, come on, Darlene," Evan complained. "That ain't fair."

This was exactly the kind of uncooperative shit she was pulling more and more. But he liked Darlene and wanted her to stick around. Plus he was worried he couldn't do much better, especially with his current money problems. So maybe dinner first.

Evan sat on the sofa, his boner wedged uncomfortably in his jeans, contemplating the merits of jerking off when the commercials ended and Darlene's stupid show about Maine caught his attention.

He leaned forward, staring.

**ON-SCREEN IMAGE:** Long shot of a line of weather-beaten lobster boats chased by dipping, banking seagulls as they steam out of the harbor into the sunrise. Dark-green waves break over the boats' sharp bows. Red channel buoys rock and clang. Surf crashes on a rocky shoreline in the distance.

**VOICE-OVER:** Up and down the Maine coast, there's a tough breed of men who make their living from the sea. They battle the wind and the weather and the tides, and sometimes, each other, to harvest nature's bounty. And the fortunes of one small town rise and fall on the daily labors of these brave men. Welcome to Tranquility. Welcome to *Lobster Wars*.

**CUT TO:** Close-up of spinning hauler, white line snaking onto the deck; a green wire lobster trap breaks the surface, strong hands grab the trap, position it on the worktable.

**CUT TO:** Close-up of Wade's bearded face. "Ten traps, about eighty pounds. Not bad for the first string. It looks easy—just bait a trap and throw it over. But there's a lot more to it, and most guys never get the hang of it. I been at it pretty much my whole life. Same as my dad. And his dad before him. And his dad, too. Ayuh."

**CUT TO:** Wade leans over the rail, snags a float, quickly loops the line over the block and then around the hauler and starts it spinning. "Sure, it's a hard way to make a living. I tried lots of stuff before getting serious about the fishin'. Most guys around here do. Even got into some trouble as a kid. You know, a few scrapes with John Law, but no big deal." Another green wire trap breaks the water's surface. Wade stops the hauler and grabs the trap, steadies himself on the rolling deck, heaves the trap onto the workstation.

"Seas are runnin' about three feet today, but the sky's clear, and it's not too cold. A fine day to work. We'll haul this next string quick, because the tide's turning and I don't want to put my baby on the rocks. Ayuh." He pulls a lobster from the trap, measures it, tosses it into the holding tank. "Most of the other guys fish a sternman, but not me. The last thing I need is some hungover loser getting in my way."

CUT TO: Connor leans against the wheel, stares down into the open engine compartment. "I'm stuck at the dock while the other guys haul traps. The mechanic tells me I've got contaminated fuel. But I buy my fuel the same place as all the guys. Doesn't make sense."

CUT TO: Tranquility Market exterior. Stained, white clapboard siding. Smudged windows. Flashing *Cold Beer* neon sign.

CUT TO: Phil behind the deli counter. "I'm the first selectman. That's same as mayor, so I spend time looking after the town when I'm not here at the market. Tranquility has good people, decent people who work hard and don't expect no handouts. And we're not fancy here, not like some places all they care about is rich `summa people."`

"Wade! That motherfuckin' asshole! I don't believe that asshole's on TV!" Goddamn, Uncle fuckin' Phil!" Evan shouted. "The whole fuckin' town's on TV!"

Then his cell phone buzzed with a text message. He pulled it from his shirt pocket and checked the screen. It was from Jimbo: *25K, one wk, or els.*

Evan jabbed a finger at the TV, hollering into the next room, "Darlene, pack your shit!"

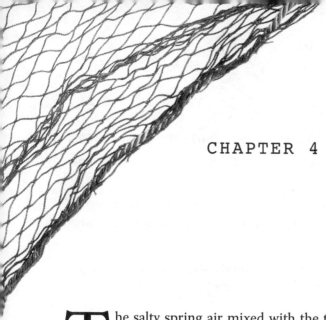

# CHAPTER 4

Then salty spring air mixed with the tangy odor of diesel as Connor carefully guided his boat toward the mouth of Tranquility's harbor. He had taken the *Nu B* out to test the steering linkage and break in the rebuilt motor. And because he could. Connor cut his speed as he negotiated the narrowest section of the inlet's entrance, and within minutes he entered the harbor's main body.

Spending time on the water was like a friendly addiction. A habit Connor had acquired during his summers in Maine. There was always a boat or two tied to the dock at their place in Camden. Of the three kids, it seemed like he used them more than anyone. Connor was always out sailing or using the little Whaler to chase stripers and blue fish or haul his few lobster traps. It was habit he didn't want to kick. He liked the lifestyle, could see it working for him—self-contained, simple and straightforward. Except for a few minor problems—repo notices, boatyard invoices, a toasted truck.

Last winter he had earned extra cash for boat repairs by working as a rough carpenter, framing the interiors of new condos in Freeport— humping two-by-fours and driving a nail gun. It felt good to build something with his hands that would eventually become someone's home. The general contractor had even offered him a full-time job.

The construction work *had* temporarily plugged the hole in his bank account, staving off the dreaded "personal finances" discussion with his parents. Especially with his father, who was always quick to escalate a simple request to borrow a few bucks into a detailed explanation of the Nichols Family Plan—complete with PowerPoint slides if there was laptop handy. Edwin had happily written checks to all manner of overpriced graduate and medical schools for both Daniel and Joanna. But not a dime for learning how to drive the big rigs.

Now Connor needed to get his plan on track.

This year, as a second-year lobsterman, Connor was allowed to set an additional one hundred traps, which would greatly improve his cash flow. But traps cost money—eighty to a hundred bucks each. So he needed at least eight grand plus operating cash to get the season started. His boat payments were fifteen hundred a month. Four months behind meant he owed the bank six grand, not including interest. He had about eighty-nine hundred in his checking account.

Somehow, he'd figure it out.

Up ahead he spotted the same kid in the yellow sea kayak, carefully picking his way through the boat traffic. Avoiding the fishermen. Message received. But when Connor nudged the wheel, adjusting his course, he spotted Wade Baxter in the *Sweet Tail* bearing down on the boy from the opposite direction. Baxter roared past the sea kayaker, barely missing his stern, and the *Sweet Tail*'s two-foot wake flipped the yellow kayak instantly.

Wade leaned out of the wheelhouse and gave Connor a big, nasty smile, shouting over the engine noise, "Some people never learn."

Connor grabbed a handful of dry suit and hauled the kayaker out of the water, dumping him on the deck. But the kayaker wasn't a boy. He was a she. And she was pissed.

"Idiots!" the young woman sputtered and coughed. "This is a no-wake zone. You lobstermen are such idiots." She was thin and plain, and her brown hair, limp with seawater, hung straight to her narrow shoulders. Her big eyes flashed hazel as she stalked around the deck, waving her arms, spacing out her words as if Connor were hearing impaired or a little slow. "No. Wake. Zone. Clearly posted. Why. Can't. You. Honor. Other. People?"

Connor fished out her kayak and paddle.

"I mean, really. Full throttle through the harbor?" She pointed toward Baxter's retreating boat. "Are all you guys brain-dead Neanderthals?"

Connor leaned against the gunwale. "I think the more sensitive Neanderthals would find that insulting." The hazel eyes opened a fraction wider. "Someone needs to defend Neanderthals from inappropriate slurs." Connor shrugged. "It's not like they can defend themselves, being extinct and all."

"It's a big ocean. Why can't you share the water? Is that too much to ask?"

"No . . . but I *was* the one who pulled you out." Connor hoped this bit of logic would calm her down. But it appeared to have the opposite effect.

"I saw you and that idiot playing chicken yesterday." She glared at him. "I could have drowned. My dry suit leaked, and I'm soaked. I still might die of hypothermia."

"Hypothermia? Really? We're only five minutes from the dock."

"I see, you're a comedian and a lobsterman *and* a medical expert, too."

"I'm kind of a seafaring Renaissance man. Only I don't fence." Connor indicated the front of the boat. "I've got some clean, dry sweats in the V-berth. Guaranteed to prevent hypothermia." He started to lead the way.

"Don't go all nautical on me. I know where the V-berth is. I grew up around boats." She made her way forward and down the stairs, slamming the door behind her.

Connor sat in the captain's chair, drinking a cold Bud. By now, surely his sea kayaker had felt the boat stop moving and the engine shut down. But almost forty minutes after he'd tied to the dock, the young woman had yet to emerge from the forward berth. Was hypothermia actually a possibility?

He stooped into the passage, slipped quietly down the steps, and listened at the door. Nothing. He knocked lightly. No answer. He knocked harder. Still, no answer. Maybe she was unconscious. He turned the latch, opening the door. She was lying on the small lower bunk, curled under an old blanket, softly snoring.

Connor cleared his throat to get her attention. "Uh, miss?"

No response.

He gently poked her shoulder. "Uh, miss? We're at the dock."

Her hazel eyes popped open, and she sat up abruptly, looking around the cabin. "Sorry. I must have fallen asleep."

"That's a symptom of hypothermia. Should I call 911?"

"Very funny."

"I've got things to do. I can't wait any longer."

She yawned and slipped back under the blanket. "Just give me five more minutes."

"But I'm leaving. Now."

"It's okay. I'll show myself out." She rolled over, facing away.

"But . . ."

"I'm so tired." She held up a hand, waving her fingers. "Just five more minutes. Please."

Connor backed out of the small cabin. When she didn't emerge five minutes later, he checked his lines, pocketed the engine key, and headed into town for something to eat. She'd be gone by morning.

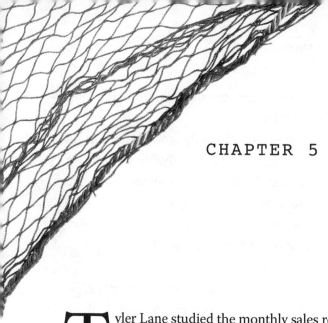

# CHAPTER 5

Tyler Lane studied the monthly sales report while he took his customary position at the head of the long table. Last month's numbers were off. Not by much. A few points. He focused on the document, ignoring the churning activity in the room. Growth was slowing. Profits? *Well,* he chuckled to himself, *Rowdy Robby Steak Houses are a profit machine.* But when growth slowed, profits weren't far behind, as the know-it-all Wall Street analysts were only too happy to point out. Now his board of directors was getting restless; there was even some whispering about a forced early retirement. He had made these guys a buttload of money. *Where's the patience? Where's the loyalty? Answer: what's your stock price today?* Tyler needed a big win, a big idea, or the circling sharks would begin to feed.

Senior executives from Operations, Product Development, Quality Control, and Marketing and chefs and servers with various assistants scurried in and out, preparing for the boss's quarterly tasting.

The room filled with the savory aroma of grilled meat, fry grease, and cream sauces as covered dishes lined both sides of the table. One assistant carried in a large trash can and positioned it by Tyler's side. A stack of white cloth napkins, a bin of silverware, and a pitcher of sparkling water were placed on the table within Tyler's easy reach.

Ronald, Tyler's executive assistant, stood with his hands on his hips, impatiently tapping his suede loafer. "Come on, people. Mr. Lane has a plane to catch."

"It's okay, Ronald. I think the plane will wait for me." Tyler set aside the report and smiled at the room.

Ronald clapped his hands. "Everyone. The food's getting cold, and Rowdy Robby number 2512 opens tonight at 5 PM sharp."

Tyler turned to Fred Wilson, head of Rowdy Robby's product development. "Okay, Fred. Where do we stand?"

"We've made some tweaks since your last tasting, and we need your final approval for three dishes."

Tyler frowned. "I thought our goal for this quarter was to introduce *four* new entrees into regional test." Tyler held up the monthly sales report. "We missed our target by 2.5 percent."

Suzanne Fournier, EVP, Marketing, jumped in. "We began the year with a total of thirty-seven new concepts. What you're tasting today are the only dishes that consistently scored top-two-box on the Consumer Entrée Approval Test."

"So, what's the bottom line?" Tyler asked.

Fred shrugged. "C-EAT methodology is flawed?"

"Excuse me?" Suzanne turned on Fred. "Maybe you need to go back to the kitchen and come up with some recipes that will move the needle."

"There's nothing wrong with my recipes."

"There is according to the five hundred people on my C-EAT panel," Suzanne quipped.

Tyler held up his hands. "Let's not make this personal. We knew this wasn't going to be easy. With the exception of our Southern fried chicken, Rowdy Robby customers love us for our steaks and ribs. In some ways, we're our own worst enemy."

"Our steak and rib positive association numbers *are* consistently over ninety-eight percent." Suzanne leaned back in her chair, crossing her arms over her chest.

Tyler looked at Suzanne and Fred. "Assuming C-EAT isn't flawed, it sounds like we need to up our game for new concept development. Let's take that discussion off-line and get on with the tasting."

Ronald pointed, and the first dish was placed in front of Tyler. The chef adjusted his tunic and rested his hand on the cover, waiting for a signal from the boss.

Like a surgeon, Tyler held out his right hand, palm up. "Fork."

Ronald slapped a silver fork into Tyler's hand. "Fork."

Tyler nodded.

With a flourish, the man whisked away the silver dome and said, "Boneless beef short ribs wrapped in hickory smoked bacon, simmered in a cream butter sauce, served over a bed of sour cream mashed potatoes."

Tyler speared a tiny taste and chewed thoughtfully. "The bacon is a new addition?"

"Yes, sir. It increased consumer approval by five points," the chef answered with obvious pride.

Tyler pulled a small piece of bacon free and held it to his nose. He rolled the bite of food in his mouth. "There's something else. Not just hickory? Another type of wood?"

"*Applewood*," the chef answered.

"Nice combination." Tyler spit into the waste bin and handed the used fork to Ronald, then took a sip of sparkling water to clear his palette. "Excellent. Increase the portion by one rib. Include Applewood in the dish's name. Next."

The second chef nervously stepped up. "Good morning, Mr. Lane, sir." He slipped his offering in place and waited.

"You look familiar." Tyler accepted a clean fork from Ronald.

"Six years in Accounting. But I've always wanted to cook. I'm in the company's Follow Your Dreams program."

"Proceed."

The man carefully lifted the cover. "Chicken fried steak, smothered in sausage gravy with buttermilk biscuits."

Tyler leaned over the dish and inhaled. "Fennel?"

"Yes, sir. I switched to a different type of sausage."

Tyler dragged a bite of chicken fried steak through the gravy and placed it in his mouth. He sat back, slowly working his jaw. "I like it. The fennel really intensifies the gravy, and that balances nicely with the steak. Did you change the ratios?"

The chef from Accounting puffed out his chest. "I added seventeen percent more sausage to the gravy."

"Perfect. Approved." Tyler turned to Ronald. "Have HR increase the budget for cross-training by ten percent. You never know where the next winner will come from. In fact, I hear there's a guy in Distribution who's won three chili cook-offs. Check it out."

"Yes, sir." Ronald snapped his fingers at the next chef, then typed a note into his iPad.

The man described his offering. "Osso buco braised in a red wine reduction, served with mushroom risotto and sautéed asparagus."

"Osso what?" Tyler demanded.

A few anxious snickers escaped from the onlookers.

"Osso buco. It's—"

"I know what the hell it is." Tyler impatiently drummed his fork on the table. "You think any of our customers know what it is?"

Suzanne spoke up. "Tyler, that's not the name we tested."

The chef stood his ground. "I know it's not the name we tested, but I thought we could educate—"

Tyler cut him off with a wave of his fork and sampled the dish. He closed his eyes, concentrating on the flavors. "This *is* delicious."

"Thank you, Mr. Lane."

Tyler spat into the trash can and wiped his chin with a clean napkin, then reached for his water. "How did it test?"

"Very well." The chef paused, shrugged. "Somewhere in the high nineties."

The room fell silent. Ronald's head snapped up from his iPad. The remaining chefs fidgeted nervously.

"The *high* nineties?" Tyler leaned in. "Ninety-six? Ninety-seven? Ninety-eight? Ninety-nine? Feel free to stop me when I guess the score."

"Well, uh, Mr. Lane, but—"

Tyler cut the man off. "People, come on. I'm trying to run a business here. Suzanne, give me a number, please."

"Ninety-seven point five."

"Thank you." Tyler turned to address the room. "Everyone. Why do we care about consumer approval ratings?"

They shouted the answer in unison. "A satisfied customer is a loyal customer!"

"And how do we satisfy customers?" Tyler demanded.

Now they chorused the Rowdy Robby slogan. "*Good Food and Plenty of It!*"

Tyler glared at the chef. "That's better. Never bring me a dish without knowing the exact approval rating. Understood?"

"Yes, sir."

"All right. I like it, but we need to make some changes. We'll call it 'veal shank with mushrooms and rice.'" Tyler paused. "And deep-fry the asparagus."

Tyler relaxed in the back of his G4, sipping a Booker's and water, looking forward to tonight's opening and trying to decide who among the board of directors was the real troublemaker and who was the weak link.

Suzanne swiped at her iPad. "I'm still hearing rumblings that one of the network news shows is researching a story on the restaurant industry and its impact on obesity, and we're the main focus."

"Shit. That's all I need. The stock price will tank, and the board'll have my ass. If our customers don't care, why should a bunch of kale-munching liberal journalists care? They don't eat at Rowdy Robby anyway." Tyler adjusted the window shade. "What are we doing about it?"

"I know the heads of most of the big network news organizations, so I'm trying to find out who's doing the story. Then maybe we can offer our side, you know, try to shape the narrative—let them look at some of our research, talk to our staff nutritionists."

"Good luck with that. Those pinheads don't like facts to get in the way of a good hatchet job. Make sure your PR people are prepared and have a way to spin this so it doesn't become a runaway disaster."

Suzanne replied, "I'll call them as soon as we land and get them going on a plan."

"I also want an analysis from finance on how it might affect our stock price."

"I'll handle that." Ronald nodded.

Tyler took a swig of the Booker's. "Three out of four meals are eaten at home. Why don't the news guys focus on the boys from Kraft or Nestlé or General Mills? Why pick on Rowdy Robby?"

"Kraft buys a lot more ad time than we do?" Suzanne shrugged as she kicked off her heels and stretched in her seat.

Tyler's eyes tracked from her feet, over firm calves, to the edge of her navy skirt. "You're telling me. How about personal responsibility? I guess they can't haul every fat-ass in America in front of the camera and ask them why they eat so goddamn much."

"Well, it would get complicated." Suzanne winked, folding her legs under, tugging at the hem of her skirt.

"We're not selling cigarettes or drugs. It's only food. People have to eat. They go to restaurants to enjoy themselves, for the experience. We're just giving them what they want. Rowdy Robby's success proves it."

"Almost like a public service," Ronald added.

Tyler squinted at his assistant. "You screwing with me, boy?"

"No, sir." Ronald focused on his iPad.

Hiring Ronald had been HR's idea. After two divorces and three paternity suits, the head of Human Resources made an oblique suggestion that Tyler might be better off with a gay executive assistant rather than the steady stream of former University of

Texas cheerleaders that Tyler favored. He had to admit, Ronald was efficient, even if he pulled the occasional snit.

Tyler swirled the ice cubes in his glass. "We going to have any problems tonight?"

"You mean with Rowdy Robby himself?" Ronald asked.

"No, I meant with the air-conditioning," Tyler replied, mimicking Ronald's catty sarcasm.

"No, sir. We flew him in from his ranch this morning. And he's already stashed at a local hotel. Dried out and ready to go."

Tyler rolled the glass between his hands. "I feel a certain obligation to Robby for his contributions to the business, but goddamn, between the cost of lawyers and rehab, that boy's becoming a first-class pain in my ass."

When Tyler was thirty, he had owned Tyler's T-Bone, a struggling steak house in Dallas, Texas—a very tough town to sell grilled meat if you weren't a former Dallas Cowboy or well-known oil man. One night, the reigning world champion bull rider, Rowdy Robby Clifton, celebrated his eighth consecutive belt buckle by hosting a drunken party at Tyler's place. The damage was spectacular. Every stick of furniture was reduced to scrap wood. Not one plate, bowl, whiskey glass, or beer mug remained. To make matters worse, Rowdy Robby had a bad case of the shorts. So instead of filing a complaint and turning him over to the sheriff, Tyler made Robby an incredible offer. He would agree to forget the damages if Rowdy Robby let Tyler name the restaurant after him.

"You mean like we's partners?"

"Not exactly. But I'll pay you a percentage of the cash register."

"What have I got to do? I can't cook worth spit."

"Nothing. Stand by the front door, dressed in your best cowboy duds, this year's belt buckle, and greet the customers."

"Well, *shee-it*. I can do that. Gettin' older. Not much future ridin' bulls anyway."

"Then we've got a deal."

Tyler's attorney wrote up a licensing agreement, which Rowdy Robby happily signed without the benefit of corresponding counsel. Rowdy Robby's name and oversized personality attracted the customers, giving Tyler the opening he needed. Twenty years later, Tyler Lane was now the CEO of one of the most profitable restaurant chains in the world—Rowdy Robby Steak Houses.

Tyler's formula for success was simple: combine Rowdy Robby's star power with a keen understanding of what made diners happy— big portions of taste-bud-tickling food served in a down-home setting with a touch of Texas twang. The Rowdy Robby slogan said it all: *Good Food and Plenty of It.*

Tyler crossed his legs, admiring the perfect crease in his charcoal-gray suit pants and the shine on his black boots. When he took Rowdy Robby Steak Houses public ten years ago, he had dropped his Texas cowboy businessman look for something more Wall Street. No more string ties, ten-gallon hats, or giant silver belt buckles. Now his suits were custom tailored on Savile Row. His two lingering concessions to Texas were his love of cowboy boots—hand stitched by a cobbler in Austin who had a two-year waiting list—and the nickel-plated Colt .45 Auto that his grandpappy carried when he'd been a Texas Ranger. Tyler liked to wear it in a fast-draw shoulder rig.

"How about the special interests?" Tyler asked. "Think any of those wackos will show? They almost spoiled the last opening."

"Right now, it only looks like a couple of the splinter groups— Americans Against Lard and maybe the Overeaters Coalition." Suzanne glanced at her notes. "Possibly the Vomitistas, but they're not really organized yet. They still might target the fashion industry or Hollywood."

"Crap, I hate those Lard fuckers." Tyler took a hit of bourbon, shot another look at Suzanne's legs. "We got the local cops on alert?"

She smiled. "I sent two hundred pounds of ribs, fifty fried chickens, and twenty gallons each of three different side dishes over to the local police station. No protesters within a hundred yards. Guaranteed."

# CHAPTER 6

Connor was hungry, with a big growling hole in his stomach, from a long day of running his boat and rescuing angry, stubborn, sleepy sea kayakers. What could have made her so tired that she would fall asleep on some stranger's boat? Maybe he could ask her if he saw her paddling in the harbor again, which wasn't likely after her encounter with Wade. He guessed he would never find out. Not that it mattered; he had plenty to keep him busy. The water temperature was almost perfect, lobster were moving inshore, and he still needed to round up some more traps, lines, buoys, and couple dozen bait bags before he could start hauling.

He angled the Toyota toward the center of town, which consisted of one small bank branch, a real estate office, the Elks Lodge, a tired prefab municipal building, and the Tranquility General Market, the town's only store. But not for long. One restaurant, two gift shops, and some kind of antique store were all in the final stages of construction, all straining to open their doors in time for the expected crush of new tourists and their money.

He pushed through the market's entrance to find Phil behind the deli counter, slicing bologna for Stubs Williams, a retired lobsterman and one of the few guys in town who tolerated Connor. When no one was looking, he had even given Connor some tips on where to set his traps last year. Stubs gave Connor a silent nod, and when Phil turned his back to wrap the bologna, Connor asked, "How's retirement working out?"

"Not bad," Stubs replied. "Got me some repair jobs, a little carpentry up to Camden. Keeps me from spending all day at the Elks. But I do miss the water."

"You wouldn't have any traps you're looking to sell?"

Stubs glanced around the store before whispering out the side of his mouth, "Ayuh. Got about a hundred and seventy-five left. They're in pretty good shape. You stop by one night, I'll make you a deal."

"Thanks." Connor almost grinned. His luck was changing.

When Phil handed over the bologna, Stubs walked away without another word.

"Sausage-and-pepper grindah? Made the sauce fresh this morning." Phil held up a hunk of bread.

Connor nodded. "I'm starving. Can you throw on some extra sausage?"

"Sure thing." Phil waved a hand toward the back of the market. "Finally got the expansion finished. You should check out the new gourmet section. We got a bunch of fancy cheeses and wines and cookies. Had to take out a second mortgage, but I think it'll be worth it come summa. Going to take a lot of business away from Camden. What do you think?"

"Looks nice. The Camden crowd, huh?" Connor could just see his mother taking a selfie down at the docks or cruising the aisles of Phil's market, looking for an aged Gruyère and a crisp Pinot Gris.

"Ayuh. No question. I think those people been watching *Lobstah Wahs* all winter and can't wait to come visit our pretty little town, see where it's filmed, maybe meet some of the lobstermen, eat a grindah made by old Phil Pratt himself."

Connor's mouth watered at the smell of the sausage as Phil wrapped the grinder, the greasy sauce instantly staining the paper. "Well, you do make a pretty mean grinder."

"Listen, the producer's assistant called and left me a message that she hasn't got your signed contract. Since I'm looking out for things up here, she wanted me to check with you. You mailed it, right?"

Connor shrugged. "I'm still thinking it over."

"What's to think over?" Phil's voice jumped a register as he talked over his shoulder while he bagged the grinder. "Sign it, send it back, and get ready to cash in. Opportunities like this don't come along every day."

"I don't know. I'm not sure it's worth the effort. We didn't get much of an increase, hardly enough to cover the new fuel prices."

"The show itself ain't gonna make you rich." Phil gestured at his market. "You got to make out on the exposure. You must be getting lots of calls. You know, opportunities. T-shirts. Autographs."

"I'm entertaining a few proposals." Connor thought about the instructional tramp stamp. "Nothing's come into focus yet. Besides, no one seems to want me around, especially Wade and his buddies. It's going on my second year, and they're still screwing with me."

"Ah, they're just pulling pranks. No big deal."

"Setting my truck on fire is your idea of a prank?"

Phil grimaced. "I heard about that."

"So, what happened to our agreement?" Connor asked.

"What agreement?" Phil placed the grease-stained bag next to the cash register.

"Go along, get along. Remember?"

"Yeah, but—"

"In fact, the town busybodies told me that the production company only agreed to do the show after I moved to town and bought a lobster boat. Wonder why that is?"

"Ayuh, I don't know anything about that—must be a coincidence."

Before Connor could respond, the loud voices of Wade and Kent Baxter arguing filled the store. When Wade made eye contact with Connor, he gave his brother a shove and walked over to the deli counter while Kent headed for the coolers in back.

Wade grinned through his beard. "You fish out that dumbass kayaker?"

"The one you almost sliced into chum?" Connor asked.

"Hell, if the kid can't handle a little wake, he's got no business on the water in one those things. Now that I think about it, I'm surprised more of them don't get swamped, clogging up the harbor every summa. Makes it tough on the working boats."

"Hey, Wade." Phil nodded. "You ready to start hauling?"

"Ayuh, just waiting on the lobster," Wade replied.

Phil said, "I been talking to the TV folks about putting cameras in town hall. They like the idea. It'll let them show me doing my selectman job *and* running the store."

Wade laughed, "Good idea. Then the whole world will know that our first selectman is the nose picker behind the deli counter making grindahs with his bare hands. That'll help the town's image."

Phil winced. "Damn, Wade. Why are you always such an asshole?"

"Yeah, Wade. Why are you always such an asshole?" Connor handed over a ten and picked up the bag. "You should treat our first selectman with respect. He works hard looking after everyone's welfare. Like trying to keep the TV show on track. Making sure the production company is happy and the lobstermen don't have any problems that could keep us from working." Connor turned to face Wade. "Such as a lack of transportation. *You* heard about my truck, right?"

"Everyone's heard. Too bad, but those things happen." Wade suppressed a small grin. "One time I had an old outboard go up in flames for no reason at all."

"Spontaneous combustion. There's an interesting theory." Connor paused. "I'll have to mention it to the police."

"Cops got any idea?" Wade scratched his beard.

Connor nodded. "The trooper told me they'd solve it quick."

"Ayuh?" Wade's eyes cut to the back of store.

"He already seemed to have a pretty strong lead."

"Bullshit. State troopers are only good for speeding tickets and clearing dead moose off the highway."

"Trooper Mack seemed pretty sharp," Connor said.

"Ayuh?"

"Said there were plenty of clues. Said the guy who did it wasn't very clever."

Kent appeared, cradling two six-packs of Busch and a bottle of Wodka. "Hey, got our sandwiches done? I'm starving." He gave Connor a stiff nod.

Wade ignored his brother. "Sounds like cop bullshit to me."

"Maybe. But I have a feeling it won't take much detecting." Connor studied the bottle in Kent's arms.

Wade followed Connor's gaze. "No?"

Connor tapped the bottle with a thick finger before taking his change from the counter. "That's the beauty of a place like Tranquility. Everybody knows the screwups because they never stop screwing up."

After Connor left, Phil leaned over the counter and said to Wade. "You better back off messing with that guy."

"What are you talking about?" Wade asked

"Setting his truck on fire. The whole town knows it was you."

"The whole town don't know shit." Wade snapped. "Could have been anyone. He's got no business here."

"If he walks, we'll lose the show, and then we're screwed," Phil said. "I pitched the idea for three years, and the TV people only agreed to shoot the first eight episodes when I told them about Connor—a rich kid from away, with a new license, buying a boat, planning to fish."

Wade replied, "Bullshit. The show's not just about him."

"I don't know, Wade," Kent said. "He's telegenic."

Wade swiveled his head from Phil to Kent and back. "People watch 'cause of the hard time I been giving him. They like the rough stuff. That's what sells."

"Just don't give him such a hard time that he quits." Phil started working on their sandwiches.

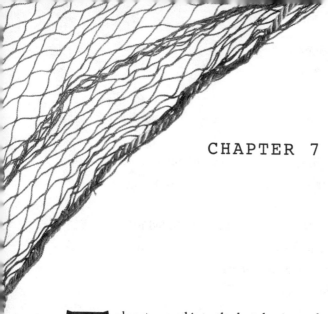

# CHAPTER 7

Tyler stormed into the hotel suite and stripped off his suit coat, balling it up and tossing it into the corner before resettling his shoulder rig. "Brand-new suit and now it's ruined. I'm going to sue those Lard fuckers. Disrupting our opening, pouring chicken fat on me." He turned on Ronald and Suzanne. "I thought we had the local cops in our pocket? No protestors within a hundred yards?"

Ronald rolled his eyes toward Suzanne.

Tyler stood at the bar, pouring Booker's. "Come on, Suzanne. Your job is to make sure things like this don't happen."

"Before we panic, let's see if we can get an idea of the damage. The news guys don't usually pay attention to the Lard people, too fringe." Suzanne scooped up the TV remote and started channel surfing. "The local news has already run. Let's hope national didn't pick it up"

Tyler sipped his bourbon and checked his reflection in the mirror behind the bar. Globs of chicken fat clung to his close-cropped gray hair and ran down his neck, soaking his shirt collar. Then, in the mirror, he saw Rowdy Robby's image on TV. "Shit!"

Tyler watched as Rowdy Robby—white cowboy hat cocked sideways, big drunken grin plastered across his face—cut the ribbon and then shook hands with the mayor. Next came a disturbance in the crowd as the Lard people pushed past the cops, flinging ladles of chicken fat on everyone. The cops regrouped, drew their nightsticks, and surrounded the protestors. The scene settled. But a brawl erupted when Rowdy Robby, bellowing like an angry bull, charged past the cops and dove into the Lard people. The scene ended with the cops handcuffing Rowdy Robby and dragging him away.

Ronald asked, "What do you want me to do about Rowdy?"

"Eight weeks in rehab out in Malibu, and he shows up smashed out of his gourd. Leave his ass in jail." Tyler slumped into a chair, spilling bourbon on his slacks.

Suzanne put the TV on mute and sat glumly on the sofa.

Ronald leaned against the bar, munching on a strawberry from the hotel's complimentary fruit platter.

"I can't believe that made the national news." Tyler gulped the last of the Booker's and held out his glass for a refill.

"Oh, this isn't good." Suzanne poured generously.

"No shit." Tyler glared at her. "That's all you've got to say?"

Before Suzanne could respond, Tyler's cell chirped. He slipped it out of his shirt pocket and checked caller ID. It was Ernie Peltz, one his board members.

Tyler thumbed the little green icon. "Yeah, Ernie. Of course I saw it. Yeah, Ernie. We're discussing it now. No, it just happened, but don't worry . . . What do you mean next week? That's not on the calendar . . . Okay. Yeah, I'll call when I get back." Tyler broke the connection and said, "Fucking board wants a meeting next week. *Emergency* meeting to discuss the future of Rowdy Robby."

"I thought Ernie was a friend?" Suzanne said.

Tyler nodded. "I've made him a millionaire ten times over. Hell, together we even have controlling interest, and he's always voted with me. Never asked any questions. But now he claims he's getting pressure from the other members, the new ones, the outsiders we put on the board because it would look better to Wall Street. Spineless little shit."

Then Suzanne's phone went off. She looked at the screen. "No name, but it's a New York number. I better take this."

Tyler waved his hand and went back to his drink while Suzanne answered.

"Suzanne Fournier . . . Yes, I see. No, not at this time. He's unavailable at the moment, but we'd be happy to offer some . . . I see. When exactly . . . Okay. Can I get back to you at this number? Great." Suzanne clicked off and stared at Tyler. "That was the executive producer of *Sixty Minutes*."

"Well, I guess we know who's doing the story," Tyler said. "How bad?"

Suzanne sucked in air between clenched teeth. "This could get ugly. Scott Pelly has taken a personal interest in the obesity issue. They're willing to listen to our side of the story but only if he gets you on camera for an interview."

"I built this business from nothing. I'm not going to lose one point of market share because some blow-dried talking head thinks my restaurants are responsible for obesity."

"It could be worse." Ronald picked up the remote.

"How exactly?"

"At least they aren't talking to Rowdy Robby."

"Robby's nothing more than a whiskey-soaked pitchman. They'd get more information interviewing fucking Roy Rogers. They know who runs this business." Tyler slapped the chair. "I want ideas. Fast. And they better be good."

Suzanne shrugged. "Well, we need an initiative. A message we can spin to our advantage. Something to preempt the potential damage."

"But what else can we do? Fund another study on obesity? Donate more money for gastric bypass surgery? Liposuction?" Tyler threw up his hands. "What?"

"It has to be something directly related to how *we* do business. Like announcing a shift in our core strategy."

Tyler blanched. "You want me to change the Rowdy Robby formula? We're number one for a very simple reason—we give people what they want. Our customers love us. Satisfaction scores are off the charts."

"Then how about a significant adjustment to acknowledge the

obesity issue?" Suzanne asked. "Offer some low-calorie meals, more salads and greens. Smaller portions. Healthy alternatives."

"Hell, you remember what happened when we tried salad bars. Total bust. Rowdy Robby customers don't eat salad. The shit just sat there rotting."

"How about fish?" Ronald pointed at the TV while he increased the volume. "Everyone thinks fish is healthy."

**ON-SCREEN IMAGE:** Long shot of a line of lobster boats chased by dipping, banking seagulls as they steam out of the harbor into the cold sunrise. Dark-green waves break over the boats' sharp bows. Red channel buoys rock and clang. Surf crashes on a rocky shoreline in the distance.

**VOICE-OVER:** Only a few weeks into the new season, and the lobstermen of Tranquility are hard at work to make their numbers. Even the new guy, Connor Nichols, has managed to haul some traps.

**CUT TO:** Wade steps out of the wheelhouse and grabs the boat hook. "Already hauled three strings. About two hundred'n ten, twenty pounds. I never seen a season start off better than this one. Like free money. Hope the price stays up. But with all the guys haulin' traps, well, shit, you can't never tell what the market will do."

**CUT TO:** Wade leans over the rail, snags a float, quickly loops the line over the block and then around the hauler, and starts it spinning. A green wire trap breaks the water's surface. Wade stops the hauler and grabs the trap, heaves it onto the workstation. "Damn. Another full one. Like takin' candy from babies."

**CUT TO:** Connor rocks, unsteady on the *Nu B's*

deck, baits an empty trap, flips it over the side, quickly sidesteps the line just before it snags his leg. "I left college a year before graduating. I was damn bored, and the next step was grad school, so only more of the same. In fact, that road led to a whole lifetime of the same. As a kid, I'd watched these guys for years—running their boats, out on the water, on their own, no boss telling them what to do. Looked sweet." Connor leans over the side, makes three attempts to snag his buoy with the boat hook, finally snatches the line with his bare hand and loops it over the block and around the hauler. He fumbles with the lever, then gets it spinning. The trap surfaces, he slams it up on the gunwale-mounted workstation. "At least that's what I thought."

CUT TO: Close-up of trap—empty.

CUT TO: Tranquility Market exterior. Stained, white clapboard siding. Smudged windows. Flashing *Cold Beer* neon sign.

CUT TO: Phil behind the deli counter, wraps a steak and, with a wink and big smile, hands it across to a female customer. "That's the special rib eye I been tellin' you to try. You like it, let me know and I'll get it for you anytime you want. It's kinda my specialty."

CUT TO: Wade points across the water at Connor's boat, the *Nu B*. "That college boy won't last the month. He'll either fall overboard and drown or just plain give up. Who knows? Lobster fishin's dangerous work. Guys get hurt all the time."

CUT TO: Connor struggles to loop his line around

the hauler, finally gets it set, and starts the
hauler spinning. "I know they're all watching
me, thinking I can't cut it. I guess I'll have
to prove them wrong."

"What is this?" Tyler leaned forward, interested.

Suzanne responded, "A hot new reality TV show about a lobster
fishing town in Maine."

"Who's the tall guy?"

"Connor something. One of the stars."

"One of the stars?" Tyler gestured at the screen. "Doesn't look
like he knows what he's doing."

"It's in reruns. That was an early episode. He stuck it out and
even started to get the hang of it by the end of season."

"That's it?" Tyler shrugged.

"Viewers find that *very* appealing." Suzanne pointed. "Plus he's
good looking if you like those rugged outdoor types."

"Don't most women?" Tyler asked.

"Duh, like all."

"He does have a certain attraction," Ronald said. "You know, to
women."

Tyler arched an eyebrow at Ronald but focused on Suzanne. "You
like this stuff?"

"It's my job to stay on top of media trends."

"How big are these shows?" Tyler asked.

"You're kidding?"

"Other than sports and Bloomberg, I don't have much time for
TV."

"Huge. Cheap production costs, a limitless pool of people who
see it as a path to fame and fortune, and a public who loves the
spectacle."

Tyler sipped his bourbon. "Maybe—"

"Actually, now that I think about it, lobster are crustaceans, not fish," Ronald said.

"Fish, lobster, crustaceans, whatever." Suzanne waved at Connor's image. "He's right. Seafood is healthy. We could re-field C-EAT and include some seafood dishes, get some good top-line scores. I could spin that."

"We tried seafood. Deep-fried catfish. Couldn't give it away. I'm not screwing with the Rowdy Robby formula. I've got a better idea. Bigger. Much bigger." Tyler gulped the last of his Booker's and jumped out of the chair. "Ronald, get off your ass. Call the pilots."

# CHAPTER 8

With the approach of summer, the sun was climbing a little higher in the sky each day, but the early April mornings were still cold as swirling pockets of mist skittered across the harbor's placid surface. Connor admired the yellow-streaked sunrise as he strolled down the dock toward the *Nu B*. He would pick up a load of traps in Camden and, if there was time, swing by the bank to sort out his note before the situation got totally out of hand. A busy day working his agenda, but time alone on the open water was the reward.

Connor stepped across the opening between his boat and the dock and into the wheelhouse. He keyed the diesel to life, set down his coffee cup, and unwrapped his egg, bacon, and cheese breakfast sandwich on the console, carefully smoothing down the wrinkled paper. The wheelhouse filled with the aroma of hot coffee, fried bacon, and eggs. He checked the oil temperature and pressure gauges as he slipped into the captain's chair, letting the diesel warm, feeling its insistent rumble, intent on enjoying the first few peaceful minutes of his day. He took a bite of the sandwich. Delicious. As Connor was raising the coffee to his lips, the V-berth door flew open, and he jerked, spilling hot coffee in his lap.

"Good morning!" the kayaker sang.

"Goddamn it!" Connor vaulted from the chair. Hot coffee soaked his jeans. "Ahh shit!"

She covered her mouth, eyes wide, staring, while Connor danced from foot to foot, tugging at his crotch.

"Not funny. You almost gave me a stroke." He bucked his hips and pulled at his jeans. "I think I scalded my junk."

"Sorry," she replied. "I didn't mean to scare you."

"What are you even doing here?"

She poked at his sandwich, wrinkling her nose. "Bacon? Dead pig. Yuck. You're not going to eat that, are you?"

"What? Huh? Of course I'm going to eat it."

"It's your funeral." She gestured toward the boat's tiny berth. "Let me make you some oatmeal."

"Oatmeal? Are you my mother? Who the hell are you? What are you doing on my boat?"

"My name's Crystal." She smiled and held out her hand. "Pleased to meet you."

Connor stared. Her shoulder-length hair, now dry, was light brown, almost blond, and framed a finely boned face with those bright, hazel eyes that had caught his attention yesterday. Standing barefoot, still dressed in Connor's oversized sweats, she had a dancer's supple build.

Crystal wiggled the fingers on her outstretched hand. "This is the part where we shake hands and you tell me *your* name."

"Uh . . . Connor." Her grip was firm and her hand very warm, almost hot.

"Well, pleased to meet you, Connor."

"Did you sleep here?" Which was more troubling—this strange woman sleeping on his boat without permission, or not noticing yesterday how pretty she was?

"Yeah, sorry. I kind of passed out. Hope you don't mind." She turned and headed down the steps into the small forward berth.

Connor ducked and followed. His little cabin had been transformed. A colorful patchwork quilt covered the lower bunk. Small squares of bright tie-dyed cloth hung over the two portholes, like curtains. His extra clothing and the gear he usually carried were neatly folded and piled on the top bunk. A six-inch bronze Buddha statue rested on a little cooler next to a hot plate. She waved at the space as she climbed onto the bottom bunk, crossing her legs lotus style. "I made a few changes. Really brightens the place up. Don't you agree?"

"You said 'five more minutes.' That doesn't mean all night." Connor hunched in the doorway.

"You *did* leave me here. You weren't being very nice yesterday. Practically rude."

"Me?" Connor sputtered. "I pulled you out of the harbor."

"I didn't think you'd mind. It's just a stinky old lobster boat. I didn't hurt anything. And you weren't using it." She waved at his size. "You can't even stand up down here."

"So, you're a stowaway."

"That's being a little judgmental."

"Not according to maritime law."

"That's a very narrow-minded interpretation. Especially for a Renaissance man."

"I have to pick up traps and gear, and I don't have time to debate you."

"I don't have anything to do today, and I always enjoy a boat ride. I'll come along and help. I can be your first mate."

"Stowaway."

"Very judgmental." Crystal frowned.

Connor looked at his watch. "I'm casting off in five minutes."

After a ninety-minute run, Connor throttled down the diesel, letting the wind push him into the floating dock anchored to his family's property. A few weeks after his father had shuttered the family's house in Camden, marking the end of last summer's season,

Connor had piled all of his lobster traps, buoys, and lines on a remote corner of the property, out of direct sight of the house and above the high-tide line. Storing everything for the winter next to his trailer in the woods made more sense, but his landlord had been whining over past-due rent, and Connor was worried about a hasty exit. He planned to retrieve the traps today and the rest of his gear tomorrow. Together with what he was going to buy from Stubs, he would have enough to start the season—at least until they started cutting his lines.

He was about to leave the wheelhouse to tie off when Crystal emerged from the V-berth, dressed in a gigantic yellow storm bib over his old Bowdoin hoody, and marched right past him. "I've got it, Captain."

He watched as she positioned the bumpers and then quickly tied off the boat on the dock's cleats, handling the lines and scampering around the slick deck with the poise of an old salt.

Connor stepped onto the dock. "Wait here."

"Aye-aye, Captain." She stood at attention and snapped a salute.

"Very funny." He turned to survey the back of his family's house where a crew of workmen were busy erecting a white-and-blue-striped tent while several others unloaded chairs and tables from a delivery van. Martini glass in one hand, Brooke stood in a small knot of people, waving and gesturing, obviously upset about something. Connor remembered his mother's plan to help Sylvia Meyers launch her newly discovered local artist.

"Oh boy. A party," Crystal said. "Are we crashing, or do you know these people?"

"It's my parents' summer house." Connor started up the dock. "I'll be back in a minute."

Crystal ignored his instructions and followed. "Nice place. Good energy. What's with all the junk in the yard?"

Between the back of the house and the water's edge, Connor counted eight separate piles, or maybe towers, of oddly configured, rusty boat parts. One was an old engine block standing on end, wrapped with a drive shaft, topped with a bent and twisted propeller. He saw that each had a small white placard fixed to a stake in the ground.

"I think it's 'art.'"

"Well, eye of the beholder and all that." Crystal shrugged. "But it *does* look like stacks of rusted trash to me. Although I prefer not to judge."

"I'll be sure to keep that in mind." Connor paused. "Didn't I tell you to wait on the dock?"

Brooke spotted them, separated from the cluster of people, and, balancing her drink, threaded her way between the rusted mounds.

"My darling boy. Since I didn't schedule a lobster delivery"—she pointed in the direction of his traps and gear—"I assume you've come to remove that pile of flotsam."

Connor kissed her cheek, smiled. "Good morning, Mom. You look lovely."

"Don't change the subject, Connor. My party is tomorrow, and you know I like everything to look perfect. Your equipment might confuse some of the less sophisticated guests. They could mistake it for art."

"Don't worry; it'll all be gone before the first air-kiss."

"Thank you," Brooke sighed. "But what possessed you to leave it here in the first place?"

Connor replied, "A few issues with my landlord. Besides, the house sits empty all winter."

"Thank God your father's not here. You know how particular he is about the property." Brooke paused to sip her drink.

Connor tapped one of the rusted heaps with the toe of his boot. "What would Father say about this stuff on his lawn?"

"Your father might not appreciate the creative process, but he understands the *commerce* of art." Brooke appeared to notice Crystal for the first time. "And you are . . . ?"

"Crystal." She smiled and held out her hand. "I'm Connor's first mate."

"I see." Brooke sipped her martini. "Nautical or biblical?"

"Purely nautical."

"She's a stowaway," Connor added.

Crystal smiled. "We're having some issues with the interpretation of maritime law, but I prefer first mate."

"Until my son adds maritime lawyer to his Renaissance resume, I prefer your definition." Brooked sipped her drink with a grin. "Besides, you're far too pretty for 'stowaway.'"

The day had warmed nicely, and a flat, calm sea allowed Connor to cut thirty minutes off the return trip to Tranquility. He would have time to grab the Land Cruiser and stop by the bank, plead his case for more time and less repo. The rocky shore sliding by on his port side, he was angling for the harbor entrance when Crystal emerged from the V-berth and handed him a steaming mug.

Keeping his eyes focused on the water, he held the cup to his lips but paused before taking a sip. "This isn't coffee."

"Of course not. Herbal tea. Clover, dandelion, ginger. Better for you than coffee." She leaned against the console.

"Thanks for helping with the traps. I was hoping my mother wouldn't be home."

"You two seem to have an interesting relationship."

"Mostly we get along just fine, except when it comes to little issues like lifestyle choices."

"Yours or hers?"

"Good question." Connor tasted the tea and winced. "How can you drink this stuff? It tastes like lawn trimmings." He flicked the mug, sending its contents overboard.

Crystal sipped her tea. "It cleanses your system of toxins. And from the looks of what you ate for breakfast, your system could use a major cleaning."

"My *system* is just fine, thank you."

"I bet you've never even had your colon purged."

"A couple of guys tried in logging camp one night, but I've always preferred to keep a tight seal on my O-ring. Call it a personal policy." Connor checked the tach and made a small adjustment to the throttle. He pointed toward shore. "We're almost at the dock. I've got to run an errand. Where do you want me to drop you? I'm sure you need to get home."

"How about I stay here?"

"Here? As in, here on my boat?" Connor shook his head. "I don't think so. The season's starting."

"Only for a couple of days. I'm new to the area and don't know anyone."

"Why would you want to stay on my 'stinky old lobster boat'?"

"My legs," Crystal replied.

Connor glanced down. "Your legs look fine to me."

"I've been living on a sailboat for the last year, and I've gotten so used to being at sea I can't seem to get my land legs back. Last night was the first time I've slept in a week."

"Then why not sleep on your own boat?"

"It's up in Camden at the boatyard. They're working on the diesel, so I've been staying at an inn called the White Swan. But they should have it done in a few days, week at the most. They promised."

Connor shook his head. "No. Find another boat."

"But I've unpacked already."

"Lobstering is tough work. The traps are heavy, even empty." Connor pointed at her. "And you're barely a hundred pounds soaking wet."

"I'm a lot stronger than I look. I'll make a great first mate."

"We call it 'sternman.'" Connor nudged the throttle. "Anyway, I can't afford the split."

"Oh, I don't need money. In fact I'll pay *you*, just like the inn."

Connor looked at her. "I'm listening."

"How about seventy-five a day?" Crystal said.

Connor thought about his visit to the bank and the going rate for a room at the White Swan. "Two fifty."

Crystal rolled her eyes and pointed at the cabin. "We're not talking the Saint Regis. I'll go one hundred. Take it or leave it."

"Done." Connor held out his hand, and once again, her grip was firm and her hand very warm, almost hot.

"But I don't like the word *stern*." Crystal frowned. "Too negative. First mate sounds more positive."

Connor glanced over. "You're a stowaway until your check clears."

Head pounding, stomach churning, Wade trudged down the dock toward his boat. When they got home from the market last night, Wade and Kent had killed the entire bottle of Wodka. Plus both six-packs of Busch. Then Wade watched his brother stumble around the house, wearing one those faggot French artist hats—a fucking beret of all things. He was celebrating his big art party that some stupid Camden bitch was throwing for him. At least Kent had bought the booze. But damn, Wade was paying for it this morning.

As he approached the *Sweet Tail*, seagulls popped off the pilings, beating the air, squawking. He squinted, shielding his eyes against the harsh morning sun glancing off the green water. It looked like someone was on his boat. Wade hoped it was a Wodka-soaked mirage. No, the image was real. Evan Pratt, wearing a jean jacket over a Harley T-shirt, greasy hair tucked behind his ears, was on the deck of Wade's boat, arms folded, leaning against the gunwale. His old running mate. Wade hadn't seen the little shit in almost ten years. About the amount of time it took for people to forget all the trouble they had caused. Not forget, exactly—no one in Tranquility ever forgot—but at least stop talking about it every fucking day.

Wade steadied himself against a piling. The salt air was flavored with bile. "The fuck you want, Pratt?"

"Not much of a greeting for an old friend. Thought you'd be happy to see your old pal and new sternman." Evan patted the gunwale.

"Shit. You know I don't fish no sternman. Never have. Never will."

"That's 'cause you was always too big a douchebag; no one will fish with you."

"Get the fuck off my boat." Wade pointed at the parking lot.

"This is how you treat old friends now that you're a famous TV star?"

Wade stepped down onto the deck. "I should have known. Another piece of trash washes in on the tide."

Evan smiled. "I'm happy to see my old buddy doing so well. I just thought you might want to share your good luck. Considering as how I spent three years in Maine Correctional but never said shit about how *we* skimmed fifty thousand off the co-op's retirement fund. Which, the way I figure, was my time and yours both."

"You mean the fifty thousand you took out to Vegas and blew in three days?"

"Well, that *was* a pretty bad run of luck, now that you mention it." Evan shrugged. "Tough to concentrate when the cocktail waitress is smokin' your joint under the blackjack table."

"Ayuh. While you were partying out in Vegas, the cops were hauling my ass in for questions every other day. Made my life pretty miserable. I could have turned you in, but I kept my mouth shut. Turns out I didn't need to. You screwed up and got caught on your own."

"Yeah, maybe giving those hookers Uncle Phil's credit card was a bad idea. Shit, I didn't know those dumb whores would try to buy a Cadillac." Evan sat on the gunwale, feet dangling. "I wonder why no one in town has said anything to the TV people about their big star being implicated in a felony."

"Everyone knows to keep their mouths shut. They want this show to happen. Besides, I was never charged, so you're just pissin' in the wind. Phil's the big wheel when it comes to the show. You want in, go talk to him."

"Funny, he didn't mention anything last night when I got here. But you and me, we go way back, and honestly, I'm in a jam."

"So, nothin's changed." Wade edged close, staring down at the smaller man.

"Well, what's changed is that my good friend Wade Baxter is a now big TV star." Evan spread his arms wide, grinning. "I'm just looking for a little taste of the action."

"Taste this." Wade drove his forearm into the side of Evan's head, flipping him over the side and into the cold water with a loud splash.

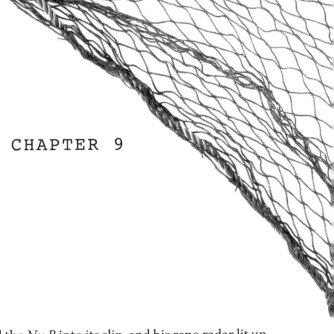

# CHAPTER 9

Connor backed the *Nu B* into its slip, and his repo radar lit up when he noticed a tall, trim man with neat gray hair pacing on the dock. He wore a well-cut, navy-blue suit, white shirt with French cuffs, and dark-gold necktie. Not exactly Connor's image of nautical repo wear, especially the shiny black cowboy boots. Obviously a banker. But definitely not from the local branch.

While Crystal raced around the dock, securing the boat, the man shot Connor a big friendly smile and waved. "Howdy. You must be Connor Nichols. I'm Tyler Lane."

Connor looked up from the deck. "I mailed a check last week. At most, I'm only three payments behind, Mr. Lane."

"Tyler, please. May I come aboard?" Despite the slick-soled boots, he had no problem scampering down onto the boat's deck.

Connor waved at the parking lot. "Better idea. Why don't you go back to the bank and tell them the check's in the mail."

"Bank?" Tyler asked, tugging on his lapels, settling his suit coat. "I'm the CEO of Rowdy Robby Steak Houses."

"I guess that explains the boots." Connor relaxed. "What can I do for you?"

Tyler replied, "I flew all the way to Maine to discuss a business proposition."

"A business proposition? I can't imagine what we have to talk about." Connor looked the man over; that was no off-the-rack suit. The guy reeked of money. "But I'm an open-minded guy, and since you took the trouble, go ahead."

Tyler said, "Rowdy Robby is the world's biggest steak house chain. I'm sure you've dined with us."

"Afraid not." Connor shook his head.

"You're kidding? There's one in Portland." Tyler patted his breast pocket. "I'll give you a coupon. As I was saying—"

Crystal stepped over to Connor's side. "I can feel my arteries hardening just thinking about eating there. Giant portions of saturated fat and calories. Very toxic."

Tyler grimaced. "Are you Mrs. Nichols?"

"No, I'm the first mate."

"Well, young lady, I don't want to stand here and debate you. But I've got an idea to change all that, and it involves Connor here."

Connor stepped between Tyler and Crystal. "Listen, Mr. Lane, Tyler, I don't know anything about restaurants."

"Not a problem, because I do."

"Okay. So what's your big idea?" Connor asked.

"I'm staying in a town called Camden, at the White Swan Inn. It's not far. Here's my card. Join me for dinner tonight at seven, and I'll explain everything. It's a win-win situation. Possibly a very lucrative win-win. Trust me, you won't be disappointed. I promise. At the very least you'll have a nice meal. I understand they have an excellent chef." Tyler smiled at Crystal. "And bring your pretty first mate. I'm sure they serve something low fat."

After Tyler left, Connor checked his watch—barely enough time to get to the bank. If he put it off until tomorrow, he could take another run through his numbers, come up with an explanation that might get them to back down. Buy some more time. But he didn't want to take the chance and find the *Nu B* repoed in the morning. So he had to get moving. Connor turned to Crystal.

"Listen, about that hundred dollars per night—"

"Why would the CEO of a gigantic restaurant chain come to see you?"

Crystal asked.

"Has to be *Lobster Wars*. Can't think of any other reason," Connor replied. "Listen—"

"What's *Lobster Wars*?"

"You don't know about the TV show? I thought everybody knew about it. They've wired up the entire town and most of the lobster boats. Next few days, they'll mount little cameras in these." Connor tapped one the empty plastic brackets the production crew had installed in his wheelhouse. "Last year was the first season, and it was a big hit." He grinned. "I'm sort of a reality TV star."

"How nice for you," Crystal replied. "I spent the last year sailing around the Caribbean. So I'm kind of out of touch. Not that I've ever paid much attention to reality TV."

"It might be *very* nice for me. They're about to start taping the second season, and everyone around here is going a little nuts, thinking they're going to make out, and here comes Mr. Tyler Lane, CEO and apparent rich guy, with a business proposition for *me*." Connor shrugged. "Go figure."

"I don't trust those kind of guys. They always have an agenda."

"It never hurts to listen." Connor picked up his jacket, preparing to leave. "I have to stop by the bank. Think you can write me a check for the first two nights?"

Connor was seated across from his loan officer, Allen York, in the man's small office. Crystal's two-hundred-dollar check had covered the accumulated interest, which made the banker happy.

But he hadn't received Connor's latest payment. So Allen insisted that Connor was four payments behind. And he wanted the money now. But Connor simply didn't have enough cash to get current on the note *and* cover this year's start-up expenses.

Allen tapped his computer screen. "According to our records, you have a little less than nine thousand in your checking account. Enough to get current on your note."

"But I need that money to buy more traps and gear and cover expenses until I start hauling."

"But you really need to get current on your note." Allen tapped his screen again.

"But that'll hurt my operation, and I won't be able to make enough money to pay down the *rest* of the note. I'll be worse off than I am now."

"But you're three payments in arrears." Allen pointed.

"I understand that," Connor replied in frustration. "Once I start hauling with more traps, I'll make more money, and things should work out. So I need some time. Not much. Say, four weeks?"

Allen tapped his keyboard and frowned, shook his head. "Your payment history is substandard. And if necessary, we can invoke a clause in your boat loan that allows us to apply the funds in your checking account to your note."

"Just clean out my checking account?"

"No." Allen clicked his computer mouse. "You'd have about twenty-nine hundred left."

"You might as well repo the *Nu B* now."

"We really favor performing loans."

Connor thought about Phil expanding the market. "You know, a lot of people in town are adding rooms to their B and Bs, updating stores, expanding businesses because of *Lobster Wars.*"

"Uh, that's true," Allen replied.

"I bet you gave out a lot of second mortgages and loans to cover all that work."

"Well, we have been very busy of late." Allen fidgeted in his seat.

"I was thinking"—Connor leaned back in his chair—"if you repo my boat, then I can't fish and star on the show, and people might stop watching, and then maybe it gets canceled. Which would make it tough on everyone, especially the people who borrowed all that money. In fact, they might not be able to pay it back. Which would leave *you* holding the bag on a lot of unpaid debt, way more than my boat loan. If I'm not mistaken."

Allen started to sweat. "But what do I tell the loan committee?"

So Connor bought himself some time, not much. Allen agreed to ten days. Like it or not, Connor needed to find a way to capitalize on the fact that he was reality TV star. *Minor* reality TV star.

Connor climbed the front porch steps of the White Swan Inn. He knew that the CEOs of major corporations didn't personally pitch business propositions unless there was money involved. Serious money. And right now, serious money sounded pretty damn good. So why not listen to Tyler's proposition? Plus, he was hungry.

But when he turned into the dining room, Connor stopped dead in his tracks. There was Crystal, sitting at a large round table with Tyler and two other people. She was wearing black jeans and a black tank top under a military-style, dark-green shirt that made her hazel eyes glow. Her fine features were highlighted by a light brush of makeup.

She smiled and waved him over. "There you are. We were beginning to wonder."

Tyler stood and extended his hand. "Connor, we've been having a very lively conversation with your pretty first mate. I'm glad you decided to join us." He made introductions. "This is Ronald, my executive assistant. This attractive young lady is Suzanne Fournier, EVP of Marketing. Please, have a seat."

Connor shook hands all around, and sat, whispering to Crystal, "What are you doing here?"

"Tyler invited me, remember?"

"Yeah, but I thought you couldn't get your land legs."

"I'm not a mermaid. Plus, I needed to get the rest of my things and settle up with the front desk for my room." Crystal accepted a menu from the waitress.

Tyler studied the wine list, then glanced at the waitress's nametag. "Alice, I think we'll start with a nice white. Give me a 2005 Puligny-Montrachet, Folatieres from Leflaive."

"Wicked good choice, sir. I'll get the wine and then come back for your orders."

Connor noticed that Alice looked a little old and bent for the trendy White Swan; an oversized white shirt and black pants hung on her thin frame. She was also familiar. The individual and the type. Most likely she lived in one of the towns bordering Camden that, like Tranquility or Rockport, supplied the hired help.

Connor said to Tyler, "I appreciate the dinner invitation, but earlier you mentioned a win-win business proposition."

"You do like to get right to the point, don't you?" Tyler replied.

"Time is money." Connor felt like he was channeling his father. Had it come to that? Sad.

"Very true." Tyler paused briefly. "Do you enjoy lobster fishing?"

"Love it. Can't think of anything I'd rather do. Running my boat, out on the open water, my own boss, the fraternity of fishermen," Connor replied. "It's a dream come true."

"Is the dream making you rich?" Tyler asked.

Connor laughed, "No one gets rich lobster fishing. Comfortable, maybe. It's more of a lifestyle choice. Beats driving a desk and racking up frequent flyer miles."

"But what if this lifestyle choice *could* make you rich?"

"This must have something to do with *Lobster Wars*," Connor replied.

"Indirectly," Tyler explained. "As Crystal pointed out this afternoon, we're having a few issues with the Rowdy Robby chain. It seems that a very vocal minority, and I stress *minority*, has a problem with our menu. They claim our food is unhealthy."

"That's an understatement, Tyler," Crystal said. "You're killing people. Admit it."

"You can't substantiate that," Suzanne snapped.

"Explain the national obesity rates. The average calories for a restaurant meal are over four thousand, before drinks and dessert." Crystal's hazel eyes flashed.

Suzanne replied, "Our research has shown no causal link between obesity and eating at Rowdy Robby."

"Of course, *your* research wouldn't," Crystal said with more than a little heat.

"Ladies, please." Tyler held up a hand. "What's important is how we're going to move forward. That's where Connor comes in."

"Yes, *ladies*." Connor shot a look at Crystal. "Why don't we let Tyler explain where I come in."

Suzanne glanced in a folder. "Your Q-score is in the high eighties, which is great considering it's Lobster War's first season. By the end of season two, your awareness should be firmly established in the nineties. Of course, we haven't had time to field an in-depth survey, but your topline likeability rating with women eighteen to forty-nine is eighty-nine percent. Very high for potential endorsement."

"I guess those women don't kayak in a no-wake zone," Crystal offered.

"Your *Davie Brown* Index is lower than I would like, but I think that's attributable to the show being in reruns. Your DBI should bump up significantly when the new season begins."

"We're still going to have to run a background check. You know, make sure there's nothing too nasty in your past." Ronald smiled. "Unless you want to fess up now."

"David Bowie Index? Q-score? Sounds like corporate doublespeak." Connor turned to Tyler. "I still haven't heard anything that sounds like a win-win."

Alice cleared her throat and presented the bottle to Tyler, who nodded. She quickly pulled the cork and poured a sample.

"Don't get carried away, Ronald. I'm sure Connor's background is clean. I have a good feeling about this." Tyler tasted the wine. "Excellent."

Alice circled the table, filling glasses.

When she was finished, Tyler held up his wineglass. "Here's to the healthy dining alternative. The Captain Connor Lobster Shacks."

Connor ducked his head. "The Captain Connor what?"

"We'll start small, maybe one hundred units. You know, until we work out the kinks, finalize the menu. Then, a national rollout. Say, fifty units a month. After that, we go global."

"Lobster shacks? Do you mean restaurants? I told you before, I don't know anything about restaurants." Connor shook his head.

"You don't have to. I do." Tyler leaned forward. "We're a successful company because we give people what they want. But with a chain of lobster shacks, I can also make the case that we're a *responsible* company. Seafood is perceived as healthy. If people want healthy, then we'll give them healthy."

"*And* rake in the money while you're at it." Crystal sipped her wine.

"What's wrong with that? We're a public company, and I'm accountable to our shareholders. What they want is profits—the bigger, the better. If the Captain Connor Lobster Shacks are a big hit, then everyone wins." Tyler tilted his wineglass at Connor. "Including you."

"Say I'm interested." Connor paused, spreading a pat of melting butter onto a warm roll. "What do I win?"

"Simple. I'm offering a licensing deal. Similar to what we have in place with Rowdy Robby. In exchange for your name and likeness and certain responsibilities, we'll give you a small up-front payment, salary, and a royalty tied to sales."

"So far, so good. But can you be a little more specific, you know, about the numbers?" Connor asked.

"I'd rather get an agreement in principal, then have our legal team put everything in writing. That way we can iron out the details. But you can count on at least a five-figure signing bonus. Let's say fifty thousand?"

Fifty grand would solve all his problems. Boat. Truck. Gear. Plus put some padding back in his cushion. Connor chewed the roll and held his glass while the waitress poured more wine. "But what do I do, exactly?"

Suzanne replied, "You become the friendly, fit face of a new restaurant chain. Appear in ads, go to openings, special events."

"Sounds like a big commitment. What about my day job?"

"Fishing, the TV show, and the restaurants all dovetail perfectly. Each promotes the other. Lots of synergy"—Tyler paused, winked—"*and* lots of money."

Connor studied their faces. "So, let me get this straight. I'd do the same thing as this Rowdy Robby guy?"

"Same as Rowdy Robby." Ronald smirked. "Only without rehab."

Crystal asked, "You realize what they're asking, don't you?"

"What do you mean?" Connor replied.

"It's more than a big commitment." She pointed at Tyler. "They would own your identity. Own *you*."

Tyler leaned in. "You make it sound like a one-way street. My company would allocate significant resources to making this a success. Time, money, people."

"And if it doesn't work?" Crystal asked. "You fold your tent and go on to the next big idea."

"I think we're getting ahead of ourselves." Tyler turned to Connor. "What do you think? What's your gut telling you?"

"I *am* very busy. The season's starting. Taping for the show." Connor picked up his menu. "But it does sound interesting. I'll have to run it by my advisers."

"Can we at least get the paperwork going?"

"Sure, why not." Connor shrugged.

Tyler leaned in. "I'm getting the feeling that you're on the fence."

"Well, the TV show taking off has created a lot of buzz. I'm considering a number of lucrative propositions."

"Anything I can offer to nail this down?" Tyler asked.

"I could use a new truck."

Connor settled behind the wheel of the Land Cruiser. He grinned. Tyler was talking significant money. Not coffee mug or autographed-poster money. Phil did say he should cash in. Maybe this TV gig wasn't such a bad idea. Fame. Fortune. Practically the Nichols Family Plan.

He was fantasizing about trim options for his new truck when Crystal knocked on the passenger window and opened the door. "I need a ride back to Tranquility."

"How did you get here? Don't you have a car?"

"Rental car. But I turned it in." She quickly hoisted two big duffels into the Toyota's rear compartment, then plopped into the passenger seat. "Plus, I don't think I should drive. I may have had a little too much."

"How much did you have?"

"Two glasses."

"Two whole glasses?" Connor chuckled as he pulled away from the curb. He'd had at least a bottle, maybe more. Good stuff, too. Plus a pretty tasty grilled rib eye. "Crack the window. The fresh air will clear your head. Don't puke on the seats. My dad would stroke out."

"I think they should recheck your likeability rating."

"I hope not. If they do, it could lower my Q-*whatever* and screw up my David Bowie Index, and then no more Captain Connor Lobster Shacks."

"Q-*score*. It measures familiarity and appeal. And it's *Davie Brown*, not David Bowie. That measures influence and purchase intent. They're trying to figure out if you'd make a suitable spokesperson."

"You know this stuff?"

"I know how corporate America operates. Bigger is always better, you cut costs no matter what, and don't worry if product quality suffers. Seafood is healthy, until you deep-fry it in lard or drown it in mayo. Or cover it with MSG. Which is the only thing Mr. *Rowdy Robby* Tyler knows. Trust me."

"That's an awfully bitter interpretation of the business world."

Crystal stretched in her seat. "I started in advertising in New York. Art director. Hated it. Corporate politics. Infighting. Blame. So I quit and opened a yoga studio. I wasn't making nearly as much money, but I was happy, and over time, I developed a real nice following. Then one of my clients—a high-pressure Wall Street type—talked me into letting him invest so I could expand. Next thing I know, I'm managing twelve studios, dozens of instructors, worrying about things like class schedules, attendance counts, and unhappy clients, and I'm more stressed out than my Wall Street guy. And all he cared about was *return on investment*."

"Tyler didn't come all the way to Maine because he's got a minor problem. Otherwise, he would have sent some low-level flunky. No. He's dealing with a serious issue."

"But what's that have to do with you?" Crystal asked.

"Serious problems are solved with serious money."

"You weren't joking back there?" Crystal worked the window crank. "You're actually considering their offer? What about your lifestyle choice? Or was that all BS?"

"I love this lifestyle, but I'm getting pretty tired of people setting fire to my stuff," Connor replied.

"Fire?"

"Yeah." Connor explained about the harassment. The cut trap lines. The contaminated fuel. The toasted Dodge Ram.

"Have you considered giving up? Moving? Sometimes walking

away is your best option. Believe me, I know. That's why I sold out."

"And spent the last year sailing around the Caribbean." Connor glanced over. "Sounds like *you* did okay. In fact, it sounds like you did more than okay."

"All right, I made some money. No question. But the point is, I wasn't willing to stick with the business just *because* of the money, not when it was making me so unhappy."

"I've tried a lot of different places, and I had some good jobs. Interesting jobs. Jobs where you felt a sense of accomplishment at the end of the day. But something was always missing. This place is a good fit. And I thought they'd eventually get tired of screwing with me, that it was only a matter of time before I was accepted."

"You mean by guys like that butthead who almost drowned me?"

"Wow. Not very compassionate for someone who carries around their own little bronze Buddha."

"He did that on purpose. And it was very irresponsible and dangerous. I was terrified." Crystal leaned against the door, curling her legs on the seat.

"The town's crazy about the TV show and the possibilities of cashing in. Everyone's scheming and angling to make a buck, and this just falls in my lap. If I take Tyler's deal, it will drive the locals nuts. Especially that butthead who almost drowned you. It might be worth it just for payback."

"Um . . . payback"—Crystal yawned—"usually backfires."

A few minutes later, Connor slowed as they rolled into the small parking area for the docks. "Okay. We're here."

No answer. He stopped the truck and looked over. Her hazel eyes shut, Crystal was snoring with her mouth open. At least she hadn't puked.

When Connor gently lifted Crystal from the truck—she was light, no more than 110, 115 tops—she looped her arms around his neck, leaning her head on his shoulder. He flipped the door closed with his foot and headed toward the docks.

"Sorry, too much wine," she mumbled, half asleep.

"No problem. Happens to the best of us. Even hard-drinking sternmen."

She was very warm, and he felt the firmness of her body in his arms, and her hair smelled like flowers, possibly jasmine or lavender.

When he reached his slip, he stopped. "Hang on; I'm going to step over."

Without saying a word, she adjusted her hold on his neck and relaxed into his chest. He crossed over to the deck and carried her down the steps and into the small cabin and arranged her on the lower bunk, covering her with the quilt. "Big day tomorrow. Another run to Camden."

Crystal snuggled under the quilt. "Don't forget my duffle bags."

As Connor swung the Land Cruiser down the driveway, the truck's lights filtered through the birch trees, splashing across his trailer, finally outlining the melted hulk of his Dodge Ram. *Message received.* But that didn't mean he was going to quit. Edwin and Brooke Nichols didn't raise a quitter. They might have raised a stubborn, impulsive hardhead who occasionally made questionable choices, but definitely not a quitter. In fact, with Tyler's deal staring him right in the face, just the opposite. No fishing meant no TV show, which meant no endorsement deal. More importantly, no fifty-thousand-dollar signing bonus.

But something that Crystal had said stuck in his mind: they would own him. Was that so bad? Sure, Tyler would call the shots on the Lobster Shack deal. But Connor could always walk away, couldn't he?

Lobster fishing was about freedom. You existed in your own little self-contained bubble of industry—run your boat, haul your traps, sell your catch. Connor considered himself lucky to be living out one of his childhood fantasies. Way better than fireman or policeman.

Kind of like a seafaring cowboy.

Connor's dad had always preached about the advantages of self-employment, endlessly mocking the soul-sucking existence of the cookie-cutter corporate lifestyle. So while Edwin might not agree with his son's choice of vocation, he couldn't argue with Connor's goal.

He stood in the dark, looking at the remnants of his truck, thinking about Crystal's warning, and he caught a faint whiff of her scent on his shirt. Growing up, most of the women Connor met seemed to fall into one of two categories. They were either highly educated, hard-charging career women intent on building impressive resumes or highly educated, hard-charging mommies-in-waiting intent on building impressive families. He hadn't had much success relating to either group. As he drifted around the country, sampling different jobs, he had made do with one-night stands and women with certain *professional skills*. Not very fulfilling, but effective.

Crystal came across as something of a hippie-chick nature girl with a Midas touch. So he wasn't sure where she fit into the mix. But he wouldn't mind having her around for a few days, despite the fact that she had turned the *Nu B* into a floating hotel for bendy girls on the run from their yoga empires.

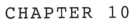

# CHAPTER 10

S quinting at the faded mailbox numbers, Evan guided his van down the narrow gravel road, trying to avoid the brush-choked ditch. Almost fifteen years, but nothing much had changed. "Don't know why he's back living at home with his crazy-ass mother."

"I'm cold. Turn up the heat," Darlene whined.

"You're the one wanted to see Maine." Evan twisted the heater knob, trying to coax some warmth out of the old Dodge van. It belched out a feeble stream of tepid air.

"July, August maybe. I thought we was gonna eat some lobsters and see the ocean. Instead we end up in your uncle's house the whole time. And he don't even want the company, you ask me. Why don't we check into a motel?"

"Motels cost money. Besides, Uncle Phil's happy to see us. He just don't go on about it." Evan banged on the heater control.

Darlene hugged herself. "Yeah, that's why he answered the door with a shotgun."

"Ah, he was being careful, is all. Never know who's gonna knock on your door in the middle of the night."

"How come he didn't put it down when he realized it was you?" she asked. "And now we're going to visit someone who already threw you in the ocean."

"Harbor. Big difference."

"Seems to me like the people around here aren't all that happy to see you."

"I was kind of a wild kid. But that was a long time ago. You know how hard I've been tryin' to straighten out my act. I'm working a few things gonna make us some big money. That happens"—Evan snapped his fingers—"easy street."

"Uh-huh. Just like the flat-screens?"

"Fuckin' Jimbo and his goddamn security cameras." Evan thought about the steady stream of threatening text messages from Jimbo looking for his money.

"How about those motorcycle parts? Even I know there ain't two Rs in Harley."

"Well, shit. You could have said something before I unloaded all them gas tanks and mufflers." Evan was getting tired of Darlene's willingness to trot out his fuckups for no reason.

"Tried to, but you said mind my own business. Said you knew what you was doing. Said if I stopped dancing, you'd take care of me." Darlene paused. "Now I don't even got that Hooter's job."

"Like they was gonna make *you* assistant fuckin' manger," Evan snorted.

"The lady from the main office said my test score was one of the highest she'd ever seen. Said I was real management material."

Evan stopped the van in front of a small, gray-shingled Cape. The yard was littered with rusted boat parts, and the battered house squatted in the weeds like it was hiding from something. "Here it is. Grab that bottle of Stoli. And Darlene, for once, try to work with me here. Okay?"

Wade opened the front door with a scowl. "You again. The fuck you want this time?"

Evan held out the Stoli. "Brought you the good stuff. Maybe we got off on the wrong foot."

"You bring her for me too?" Wade eyed Darlene as he accepted the peace offering and stood aside, letting them in.

"This is Darlene. Say hi to Wade Baxter."

"Hi, Wade Baxter. I seen you on TV." Darlene smiled. "You're famous."

"You better believe it, honey."

Evan thumped Wade's shoulder. "You're lookin' at the best goddamn lobsterman in Maine."

"We here to eat lobster?" Darlene asked.

"Shit. I hate lobster." Wade turned, carrying the bottle toward the kitchen in the back of the house. He cracked the seal and made three drinks, straight Stoli over ice, nodding toward the table. "Move that junk out of the way and sit down."

The table was covered with piles of T-shirts, coffee mugs, and posters, all bearing the likeness of Wade's boat, the *Sweet Tail*.

Evan held up one of the shirts. "What are you doing with this crap?"

"Looking to make some money." Wade handed Darlene a drink.

"Selling fuckin' T-shirts and coffee mugs? What about the TV show?" Evan tossed the T-shirt on the pile.

"Tried to tell you. The show don't pay shit. Last year was a hundred and fifty an episode. They made eight shows, so I made twelve hundred bucks. Barely pays for a week's fuel." Wade took a big hit of Stoli and smoothed his beard with the back of his hand. "Got alimony could choke a horse. Why the fuck you think I'm living here?"

"All that work and that's all they pay you?" Darlene asked.

"What work? They put tiny little cameras everywhere, and I go about my business like usual. After a while, you just forget about 'em. Hell, don't even know if they're on half the time."

"What about TV commercials and shit like that?" Evan asked.

"Nothing yet." Wade shook his head. "Shit, I'm the star, and your uncle Phil's gonna make out better than me, expanding that goddamn store."

"Maybe Phil and I need to have a chat." Evan topped off his drink. "Kent on the show?"

Wade snorted. "You mean my brother, the famous artist?"

"Famous what?"

"He's working days up to the boatyard in Camden. Then spends all night drinking and welding his masterpieces. Surprised he's not here now; he can smell Stoli a mile off."

"Masterpieces?" Evan asked.

Before Wade could explain further, his mother, Alice, appeared in the doorway, dressed in an oversized white shirt and black pants— her waitress uniform. She looked a little unsteady on her feet. "Evan Pratt. Phil said you was in town."

Evan held up his drink. "Mrs. Baxter. Good to see you too. Join us."

"Ayuh. I could use another drink." Alice made straight for the vodka. "Who's the girl?"

"I'm Darlene."

"Sure you are," Alice grunted.

Evan moved his chair, making room at the table. "We were just talking about how to make some money from this TV show."

"We?" Wade asked.

Alice knocked back a big slug of vodka, her eyes watering. "Money, huh? You should'a been at the goddamn Swan tonight, you want to talk about money. They was this—"

Wade cut her off. "Evan and Darlene don't want to hear you complain about the Swan's shithead customers."

Alice glared at Wade. "I'm not talking about getting stiffed by some yuppie from Bahston on a two-hundred-dollar check."

"They serve lobster at the Swan?" Darlene asked.

Wade placed a hand on Alice's shoulder. "Why don't you get some sleep?"

She shrugged him off and hit the vodka again. "Goddamn it, I'm workin' two jobs—waiting tables at night and cleaning rooms during the day—while you're screwin' around with that stupid lobstah boat, thinkin' you can make a livin'. And your dumbass brother spends all his time out in the shed, welding up rusted junk. The two of you, just like your dad. But at least he had the good sense to get out of here." Alice waved one of Wade's coffee mugs. "Three dollar coffee mugs. Donald fucking Trump."

Evan refilled Alice's drink. "It's okay, Wade. Let Alice tell us what happened at the Swan."

When Alice finished describing Tyler's offer to Connor, the room was dead silent.

Wade spoke first. "Motherfucker."

"Who the fuck is this Connor guy?" Evan asked.

"Some rich kid from away," Wade complained. "Trying to run him out of town since last spring."

"He's cute," Darlene said.

"Why don't you kick his ass?" Evan gulped some Stoli. "Then see how cute he is."

"Evan!" Darlene shot him a nasty look.

"I have to be careful." Wade paused, reached for the bottle. "Everyone in town knows it's me and him. Plus, some people, like Phil, think he's important to the show."

"This restaurant guy staying at the Swan?" Evan took the bottle from Wade and tipped some more vodka into Alice's glass.

"Ayuh. Him and his people took a whole floor."

"What's that, like six, seven rooms?" Evan asked.

"Same as the TV folks." Alice replied with a sloppy grin. "Who're comin' in three days."

"Okay, we have to think this through," Evan said.

"The fuck you mean *we*?" Wade grumbled.

Evan slopped more Stoli into Wade's glass. "Meantime, I've got to come up with some cash. Getting tired of Phil looking over my shoulder."

"We're going to a motel?" Darlene asked hopefully.

Alice finished her drink and stood to leave. "The Swan's catering some big fancy party for this rich Camden bitch tomorrow. Help's tight. They need bartenders and servers. Pay's okay. Good tips. I can't work it, but I could fix up you two with the manager."

Wade wanted Evan to leave. Not just his house or the town, but the entire state of Maine. He had worked hard to put the bad old days behind him and clean up his reputation, which was tough to do in a gossipy town like Tranquility. Having Evan around would only get people talking and maybe lead to some new bad old days. He needed some space to think over the implications of Connor getting a deal from this restaurant guy—exactly the kind of thing he had been worried about. But instead, Wade spent the next thirty minutes getting grilled, the little shit always looking for an edge.

Meanwhile, Darlene watched TV on mute, working the clicker. Shortly before midnight, Kent stumbled into the kitchen through the mudroom. Wade watched his brother's bleary gaze slide back and forth between Evan, Darlene, and the almost empty bottle of Stoli.

"A little party, huh? Didn't get no invite." Kent grabbed a glass and helped himself to some vodka. He asked Evan, "When you get back in town?"

"Couple of days ago. This here's Darlene."

"Kent." He saluted with the glass.

Darlene smiled. "I like your hat."

"Thanks. It's a beret."

"Where the hell've you been?" Wade asked.

"Worked late at the boatyard. All the summer people want their boats in the water yesterday."

"Wade says you're an artist. I like art." Darlene sipped her drink. "Tried to learn how to paint, once. Signed up for a class in junior college. Turns out the teacher was more interested in having me pose naked than teaching me how to paint."

"I don't paint. I weld." Kent gestured toward the shed in the backyard. "Wanna see?"

"Sure," Darlene replied.

"Good, you go look at Kent's *art*. Wade and me got some high-level business to discuss," Evan said.

After they left, Wade split the rest of the Stoli with Evan. "Where the hell'd you get her?"

"She was pole dancing in some shithole in Reno. I had a little business filling them condom machines. You know, the ones you see in truck stops, bowling alleys, titty bars. I was getting the rubbers real cheap from this old Jew, had a wholesale operation. Them rubbers was all dried out and cracked. That's why they was so cheap. But who gives a shit? Serves you right for screwing some lot lizard in the back of your Peterbilt."

Evan paused and combed his hair back with his fingers. "Anyway, I guess old Darlene took a liking to me, coming in her club all businesslike, filling them machines so the girls wouldn't get no diseases. You know, a regular professional, not some drunken scuzzball sticking dollar bills in her twat."

"What's wrong with her eye?"

"Yeah, kind of hard to tell where she's lookin." Evan gulped some Stoli. "But the girl can suck a doorknob through a keyhole."

Wade leaned back in his chair. "Always good to have a skill."

"Anyway. That was a sweet gig while it lasted. But I'm about broke, and if I don't get liquid soon, she might walk. And I like her. Plus I got this asshole back in Arizona puttin' the arm on me for twenty-five K or he's gonna get me sideways with my parole." He rolled the glass between his hands.

"So you loaded up all your problems in that piece-of-shit van and brought them back to your good buddy in Maine?"

"Listen, Wade, we've always watched out for each other. It's not like I want to screw things up for you by talking to the TV people about your little run-in with John Law."

Wade leaned forward and grabbed a handful of Evan's shirt. "Are you threatening me?"

"No way." Evan held up his hands. "Listen, I'm just in a bad spot is all, and I think with this TV show and these restaurant people, there's a shot at making some real money."

Wade opened his hand and settled back in his chair. "I don't know about you, but first thing tomorrow, *I'm* gonna see this Mr. Lane. Explain the difference between a real lobstahman and some pussy college boy. Besides, I got a feeling Nichols may decide to pull out next time he runs his boat."

"Good. Should have done something the first day he ran a string. Maybe I should come with you in case this Lane guy don't get the point."

Wade shook his head. "No. You hang back."

"You mean, kinda go undercover?"

Wade rolled the glass in his hands. "Let Alice fix you up with that fancy party job."

"Good idea. That way, you need me, he won't see me coming."

"You got it."

Evan held up his glass. "Well then. Just like old times."

"Ayuh." Wade stared hard at Evan over the rim of his glass. "Just like old times."

# CHAPTER 11

The next morning, Connor joined the line of fishermen, boatyard workers, and contractors crowding the Tranquility Market's deli counter, shouting their orders while they grabbed coffee and a newspaper. Phil was in his usual place, frying eggs, bacon, and ham for their breakfast sandwiches. Everyone was in a big hurry to get their day started, including Connor, who needed to retrieve the rest of his gear before Brooke's party—otherwise he'd never hear the end of her complaining.

"Come on, Phil, don't got all day. Those eggs ain't gonna climb on the roll by themselves."

"Yeah, Phil, once they take that bacon off the pig, it can't walk. Throw it on my roll and let me get to work."

Phil spun away from the griddle, waving his spatula in frustration. "You want fast, drive out to the damn McDonalds. Otherwise, shut up and wait your turn."

"Wow. Old Phil's cranky this morning, boys."

"Getting his period, sounds like."

"Or Mrs. Phil's getting hers and he ain't getting squat."

"If your wives would drag their lazy asses out of bed and make you guys breakfast, you wouldn't have to come in here and bother me." Phil shoved an armload of sandwiches across the counter. "Now get out of here. All of you."

When Connor stepped aside for the departing crowd, one of

the other lobstermen on the TV show, Eddie, hung back. He was a serious fisherman and longtime resident. He spoke to Connor without making eye contact. "Heard you might need some buoys. Got a couple dozen extra. Might have some line, too. I'll let it go cheap. Stop by one night."

"Uh, sure, thanks," Connor replied to Eddie's back as he walked off.

"See, not everyone hates you." Phil rested his hands on the countertop. "Running low on bacon. How about ham?"

"I'm pretty hungry; better make it two." Connor sipped his coffee. He could sure use the buoys. "Those guys don't usually rattle your cage. Something bothering you?"

"My nephew and his girlfriend showed up a couple of days ago. Evan's parents died when he was ten. The only thing they left him was a run-down lobster boat with a big bank note. We took the boy in and raised him. The little dirtball had a real wild streak, and we worked hard to straighten him out. I even thought one day he'd take over the market."

"He didn't like that plan?" Connor asked.

"Told me he was cut out for better things, and no way he was gonna spend his life slicing bologna."

Connor chuckled, "Don't feel bad. Sometimes kids have to figure it out for themselves."

"Ayuh. Well, he ain't no kid now. Going on forty. I believe he's running from some trouble out West. He used to pal around with Wade Baxter, and it seemed like the staties had my address memorized." Phil cracked four eggs onto the griddle.

"I've got to tell you, Phil, I'm not feeling the love from Wade. And no one's stepping up about my truck. I'm very disappointed. Don't forget our deal."

"I know. I know. I've talked to him, might need to again," Phil replied over his shoulder. "But he's a stubborn SOB."

"So am I," Connor said.

"A couple of the TV people rolled in late last night. They're beginning to put the cameras in place. The rest of the crew should be here by end of the week. Most every place is booked for the whole summa." Phil dropped two slices of ham, sizzling onto the griddle. "Can't wait. I'm tired of suckin' hind tit to Camden."

"And you have a plan for cashing in."

"Damn right." Phil handed over two breakfast sandwiches. "And I hear you had a pretty good meetin' up to the Swan. Looks like you figured out your angle."

"I may have, Phil." Connor winked. "I might even get a new truck out of the deal."

Connor stopped short, stared at the *Nu B*, and the idea of a peaceful breakfast vanished. A thin rope cord stretched from the top of the wheelhouse forward to the bow, and a second back to the stern. Both were adorned with brightly colored Tibetan prayer flags flapping gaily in the early-morning sunshine. Prayer flags on a lobster boat? Just what you need when you're trying to keep a low profile and fit in.

When he stepped across and dropped down to the deck, he noticed a male figure moving around in the cramped wheelhouse. It was Jeff Russell, head cameraman from the production company.

Russell, squat and solid, dressed in jeans and a navy hoody, popped out of the cabin, laughing. "Hey, Connor. Nice to see you again. Like what you've done with the boat."

"I'm going for the floating monastery look. I might even shave my head and wear a saffron robe."

"Excellent visual. But the shaved head would drive the executive producer crazy."

Looking around, Connor held his hand about five feet above the deck. "You see a small girl, sandy hair, green eyes?"

"Your first mate?" Russell grinned. "Boy, she's a hottie."

"Yeah, but not really my type."

"That's what she said about you."

"She's into all that health and wellness stuff. Got the holier-than-thou thing going on. Plus, I like them a little more, you know . . ." Connor cupped his hands in front of his chest.

"I'm not that picky," Russell replied.

Connor peered into the wheelhouse. "She in there?"

"Left about thirty minutes ago."

"She have all her stuff with her?" Connor asked.

"Stuff? What stuff?"

"Clothes, blankets. *Stuff,*" Connor explained impatiently.

"No. She went off with the other cameraman to get supplies. Said something about your colon." Russell snickered. "I didn't know you were having a problem with your colon."

"I'm not, unless you're planning to put a camera up there."

"It depends on the ratings. So, where'd you find her?"

"Floating in the harbor."

"No. Seriously."

"She kind of found me."

Russell chuckled. "You big-time TV stars."

"Yeah, maybe." Connor rapped his knuckles on the console. Why was he now worried that she had cleared out? She was only going to stay a few days, until her boat was fixed. And he was certainly better off without the distraction.

"Well, the camera's going to love her. Good move. Come on, I'm almost finished. Let me show you what I've rigged up for this season."

Inside the small cabin, Russell pointed to a tiny camera attached to the plastic bracket bolted onto the console. "Same basic setup as last year. One camera in here. One outside, covering the deck. Everything's still line of sight. Only this year we have a bigger budget, so we upgraded to remote control. All the cameras have adjustable focus and tiny servo motors so we can track you from the production van."

Connor nodded, wondering if it was bad karma to cut down prayer flags.

"I'll be installing all the cameras and running tests for the next few days, so if you see the little sucker move, don't worry; that's me," Russell continued. "The other camera guy is going to wander around with the Steadicam and get some B-roll. You might bump into him."

"As long as he doesn't get in my way. I'm going to start hauling tomorrow."

Wade's voice rasped from the dock. "Jeff Russell, you dickhead, why're you wasting your time on this piece-of-shit boat?"

Both men stepped out of the wheelhouse. Russell replied, "Nice to see you too, Wade."

"You coming down to work on the *Tail*?"

"Soon as I finish up here," Russell replied.

"Better hurry up. I got to run her today."

Connor looked up at Wade. "Jeff here was telling me they have a special camera for you this year."

Wade looked with interest at Russell. "No shit. It's about time. Where you gonna put it?"

Connor said, "It's colon mounted."

"Fuck you." Wade turned and stalked down the dock.

Connor grinned at Russell.

Crystal, her arms filled with grocery bags, shouted from the dock, "Hey, how about one of you guys giving me a hand?"

"Maybe I should put a camera in your V-berth," Russell chuckled.

Connor fired up the diesel, letting it warm while urging Russell to finish his work. Brooke might complain about the arts council, but Connor knew that his mother took her social events very seriously, and with today's wind, the run to Camden was going to be at least two hours, maybe longer. Finally, twenty minutes later, the cameraman gathered his tools and equipment and headed down the dock to the *Sweet Tail*.

Crystal had disappeared into the cramped berth. Now she was banging pots and pans, cooking something that smelled like rotten seaweed at low tide. Connor glanced at his watch and then quickly dug one of his breakfast sandwiches out of the paper bag and unwrapped it, placing it on the console. The smell of fried eggs and ham battled with the funky odor wafting up from the galley. He took a big bite.

Crystal appeared, carrying a steaming bowl. "Not those grease bombs again. They're poison. Here, try this."

Chewing the bite of sandwich, Connor looked in the bowl and wrinkled his nose.

"Chinese congee," Crystal explained. "My own special recipe. Very good for digestive health and restoring balance."

Still chewing, he rolled his eyes, pointed a finger straight up.

"The prayer flags? I didn't think you'd mind. Aren't they beautiful? And from what I've seen around here, you need the peaceful energy."

Connor tapped his watch, gestured toward open water. Finally, he swallowed the bite and replied. "No time to discuss your belief system. The check cleared."

"So, I'm your first mate? Uh, sternman?" She smiled, set the bowl on the console, and clapped her hands together.

"Keep writing checks, and no more health food." Connor nodded. "Cast off."

"Aye-aye, Captain."

Crystal darted out of the cabin to wrestle with the lines and bumpers while Connor settled into the captain's chair. When she moved to the stern, he opened the wheelhouse window and flicked the bowl's contents into the water.

The spring sky was clear, with small white clouds scudding along on the stiff breeze. The open-water run to Camden was going to be a

bitch. Standing at the wheel, Connor estimated the wind at a steady
ten to fifteen knots, with gusts to twenty. As he cleared the harbor's
entrance, the seas were running a good three feet, and the surf was
crashing hard against the rocky shore.

"Pretty rough out here," Crystal said.

Connor pointed. "If you get sick, puke over the side."

"You spend a lot of time worrying about people puking on your
stuff."

"Just lightweight sternmen who can't hold their liquor."

"I grew up in Annapolis and sailed the Chesapeake from the time
I was in diapers."

"This ain't the Chesapeake." Connor waved to the east. "Next
stop is England."

"But why not wait for a better day?"

"No one messes with my mom's party plans. And I need to move
the rest of my gear so I can start hauling tomorrow. Two birds, one
stone."

"I understand the gear part. But with your mom, is it really about
the party? Or a bigger issue?"

"Like what?" Connor asked.

Crystal replied, "She's probably unhappy that you're a lobster
fisherman."

"How did you figure that out?"

"Well, people who host catered art parties at their perfectly
tended summer houses on the water in Camden, Maine, don't usually
send their children to lobster fishing college."

"There's no such thing as lobster fishing college." Connor made
a small course correction.

"My point exactly."

"Let's just say that my family and I don't always agree on how I
live my life."

"But it's *your* life."

Before Connor could respond, the boat began to shake from a

loud metallic banging. Next came the wail of the fire alarm as heavy, acrid black smoke began pouring from below the deck.

Connor threw the throttle into neutral and killed the ignition, but the smoke continued to engulf the boat.

He grabbed Crystal. "Here, take the wheel. Try to keep us pointed into the wind."

Fighting the urge to panic, he darted forward, jerked the fire extinguisher from its bracket, and turned to the engine compartment.

Thick smoke seeped from around the hatch's lip. He choked on the harsh fumes, eyes stinging and tearing as he wrestled with the hatch's chocks.

Holding the extinguisher in both hands, he kicked the hatch open with his foot. A rush of hot flame and smoke erupted, driving him back. Connor held his breath and scuttled forward, keeping low to the deck. He aimed the extinguisher's nozzle and squeezed the discharge lever.

A jet of fire retardant whooshed out of the extinguisher. Connor advanced, directing the nozzle, filling the compartment and covering the engine. The flames quickly died, smothered under the white foam.

When he was certain that the fire was out, Connor stood straight and released his breath. Hands shaking, he peered into the dark hold. A mixture of slick white chemicals and oily diesel clung to everything. No way to see how the fire started or the extent of the damage.

"Hey, Captain!" Crystal shouted, waved, and pointed to starboard.

The stiff onshore breeze and hard-running seas were pushing the *Nu B* shoreward.

They were almost on the rocks.

Connor kicked the engine compartment in frustration, thinking about the small ten-horse motor he usually carried clamped to a drop-down bracket on the boat's transom. Emergency backup if the big diesel ever crapped out. Like now.

Unfortunately, the outboard was in the bed of his Ram. Melted down to slag.

He waved Crystal away from the controls. "Got to try and restart the engine. Life jackets in the cabin."

Two shitty options—burn to the waterline or wreck against the rocky shore. Connor pursed his lips and turned the key. The diesel coughed, belched black smoke, but caught, ticking away on idle.

He looked over his shoulder.

The smoke had cleared. No signs of fire.

But they were almost in the surf.

He gingerly advanced the throttle, hoping for the best. At around 1200 rpm, the *Nu B* finally dug in, barely holding position against the stiff rollers. He nudged the lever, going for 1800. Slowly the boat gained momentum, bucking and diving against the three-foot waves. When the rpm's hit 2000, the loud banging returned and smoke poured from the hold. He quickly backed off and the engine quieted, the smoke stopped.

Crystal handed him a life jacket. "Which way?"

Connor shrugged into the jacket and buckled it with one hand, keeping the other on the wheel. "The wind's shifted. It's out of the northeast. I don't have the power to turn around and run against this mess all the way back to Tranquility, and I don't know how long the engine's going to hold out. Another mile and we can cut southwest toward Camden harbor. Then we'll have the wind on our stern."

"Anything I can do?" Crystal asked quietly.

Connor focused on her for the first time since the fire. She had that spooked-fawn look but was working hard to keep it together. Maybe she *was* tougher than she looked. "Yeah. Find some better prayer flags."

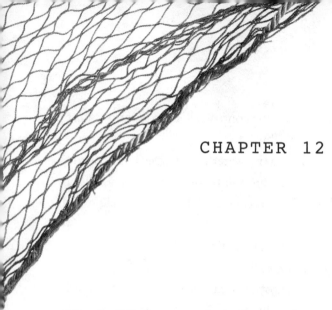

# CHAPTER 12

**W**ade smoothed the tangles out of his beard and straightened his worn Cat hat before knocking on the door to suite 210. According to Alice, this Tyler Lane and his people had taken over the White Swan's entire second floor, all six rooms. Big bucks. Some of the guys from Tranquility occasionally hit the Swan's bar, acting like rough and tough seaman, bullshitting about boats and fishing, getting the rich banker pussies from Boston to buy them beers and shots, but Wade had never even stepped foot in the place before now.

He was about to knock again when a good-looking, dark-haired woman opened the door. "You're not room service." She looked past him down the hall. "We ordered breakfast twenty minutes ago. You'd think they could find their way to the second floor." She stared up at him, blocking the doorway. "Can I help you?"

"Ayuh. I'm here to see Tyler Lane," he said, looking the woman up and down. She wore some kind of businesswoman outfit—cream-colored blouse and straight dark skirt. A little prim and proper for Wade's taste, but she did have a nice chest and shapely legs. "Shit, honey. You his secretary?"

"EVP Marketing."

"Well, I'm Wade Baxter."

She moved back from the doorway. "Greasy Cat hat, scraggly beard, dirty Carhart jacket, and rubber boots. *Lobster Wars*, right?"

"Damn right." He sauntered past her into the suite.

Two men were seated at a small round table in front of the window. The younger guy, light-blue dress shirt open at the collar and navy slacks, was hunched over a small laptop, pounding on the keys. The older man peered at a document through small half-glasses perched on his straight nose. He had neat gray hair and wore a white dress shirt and solid, dark-gray tie that matched his gray slacks. And black cowboy boots.

The look said money, even if Wade wasn't too sure about the boots. He cleared his throat.

The younger guy kept typing.

The older man kept reading.

Wade cleared his throat again.

The good-looking woman stepped up. She gave Wade a nasty smile.

Wade fingered the zipper on his jacket, shuffled his feet, and coughed into his fist.

"Tyler?" she asked.

The older man continued to study the document. "It's about time." He waved at a table on the other side of the room. "Suzanne, have him put the breakfast over there."

"It's not room service, Tyler."

Tyler lowered the document and peered at Wade over his glasses.

Suzanne giggled, "Tyler Lane, meet Wade Baxter. Lobster War's *other* star."

Tyler dropped the papers on the table. "Pleased to meet you, Mr. Baxter. How can I help you?"

"I catch more lobstah than any fisherman in Tranquility."

"Well, good for you. This is important to me how?"

"My family's fished these waters since the town was founded."

"Ronald, what time is our appointment?" Tyler studied his watch.

"The real estate agent will be here in ten minutes. We have three locations to visit." The young guy continued typing.

"And after that?"

"You had expressed interest in the art exhibit that the manager mentioned."

"Yes. Schedule that, please." Tyler turned to Wade. "I'm very happy that you're such an accomplished fisherman. Professional competence is important. Especially in this day and age. Not to mention that you're clearly proud of your family's heritage. I've always believed that strong family ties are the cornerstone of our society." Tyler paused, glanced at his watch. "But what *exactly* do you want?"

"Well, uh . . ." Wade thought it was obvious.

Suzanne came to Wade's rescue. "If I had to guess, I would say that Mr. Baxter is here because of our offer to Connor."

Tyler asked, "How would he know about . . . ?"

"Small town," Suzanne replied. "Word spreads."

"Is that why you're here?" Tyler leaned back in his chair.

"Uh, well, uh . . . yes."

"I see. Suzanne, do we have any numbers on Mr. Baxter?"

Suzanne plucked a file off the table. "His Q-score is almost as high. But likeability with our target audience is below fifty percent."

"Q-score? Likeability? What the hell are you people talking about?" Wade asked.

Tyler walked over to a dark leather briefcase resting on a coffee table. "I'm afraid we don't have time to explain."

"But I'm the *real* star of the show. Not that asshole college boy."

"Maybe so, but there's a big difference between starring in a reality TV show on cable and having the image it takes to support the launch of a new restaurant chain," Tyler replied.

"What's that supposed to mean?" Wade asked.

Ronald closed the laptop. "Customers might want to get drunk with you, but they don't want you touching their food."

"Let's just say that you're not a suitable spokesperson," Suzanne said.

"What exactly would make me *suitable*?"

"See a dentist, shave the beard, lose thirty pounds, wash your clothes," Ronald snickered. "And clean your fingernails."

Tyler opened the briefcase, pulled out a shoulder rig, and slipped it on. Wade glimpsed the butt of a big .45.

Tyler shrugged into his suit coat. "Thanks for stopping by, Mr. Baxter."

"*You* didn't answer my question." Wade pointed at Tyler.

Tyler buttoned his coat. "Well, let's just say that Mr. Nichols is our first choice and leave it at that."

"There's no changing your mind? You know, something that might get you to reconsider?"

"I don't see why we would. But thanks for your interest. Ronald, do we have some coupons for Mr. Baxter?"

"You always wear a gun?" Wade asked.

"I'm a big fan of personal security." Tyler handed two coupons to Wade and escorted him to the door.

"It loaded?"

Tyler smiled his big CEO smile. "I'm from Texas, Mr. Baxter."

Two hours later, Wade opened his front door, expecting Evan back for more scheming. After his disappointing trip to the Swan, he was worried that the guy's ideas might even start to make sense. Instead, Phil stood on his front step, holding a package wrapped in butcher paper.

"The fuck you want?" Wade growled.

"I know your mother likes rib eye." Phil offered the package. "We need to talk."

Wade turned toward the back of the house. "You say so."

The two men settled in the kitchen. Wade placed two cans of beer on the table and waved at Phil. "So talk."

"I thought you agreed to back off on Connor." Phil opened his beer. "And now I hear someone set fire to his boat."

"Uh . . ." For a second, Wade was caught off guard. How did Phil hear this shit so fast? Wade knew that Phil was the town gossip, but he must be plugged into the best grapevine in Maine "Don't know anything about that."

"Don't bullshit me, Wade. If Connor walks, we're all screwed."

"Then you must'a heard about the restaurant guy. So you know college boy ain't gonna walk."

"Listen, Wade. You don't seem to understand. Connor don't need to fish, and he don't need to be on the show, and I bet my ass he don't need no deal from some restaurant guy. But *we* need him. The show wasn't going to happen until he came along."

Phil's words triggered a long-simmering resentment. Wade leaned forward, pointing a finger. "You're always in that store, *nice and safe* behind the counter, making sandwiches, taking money from the guys that go out every day getting their asses kicked. We've never let in someone from away, but now you're okay with it because *you* got that new addition, thinkin' you're gonna make out from all the extra summa people. But what do I get? A lousy extra fifty bucks a show."

"I hear you on the money, but you got to be patient. So Connor gets the first deal. Now he's off the board. The next company that comes callin' will look at you."

Wade thought about the business chick describing him as *not a suitable spokesperson*. "When did you become such a fuckin' expert on getting deals?"

Phil held up his hands. "Okay, okay, I'm no expert. But it stands to reason. You *are* one of the show's stars."

"Ayuh. And what happens if *I* decide to quit? How many people you think want to watch a TV show about slicing bologna and making grindahs?"

"All I'm asking is to take it easy on the guy. I mean, for Christ's sake, setting his boat on fire?" Phil drained his beer.

Wade chuckled. "No proof it was me."

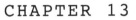

# CHAPTER 13

Evan tucked his hair behind his ears and wrestled the too-big white shirt back into the waistband of his black pants. First thing that morning, Alice had introduced him and Darlene to the White Swan's manager. The horny fuck took one look at Darlene and hired them both on the spot. Now here he was, dressed like a jerkoff waiter, stashing bottles of beer and white wine on ice—for two dollars over minimum wage, plus tips. The whole gig had felt like a big waste of time. Until he saw the inside of this house.

He had never set foot in a house like this before. Everything was so clean. There were so many rooms, and each one was filled with stuff, and it all looked expensive. Not just expensive. What was the word Darlene used? *Tasteful.* Yeah, that was it. Everything looked tasteful. Like in those magazines and catalogs she was always reading.

There were paintings and statues and all kinds of bowls and plates and stuff. Tasteful *and* expensive. He just had to figure out which one of these tasteful pieces of shit was worth the most money, and no more Jimbo problem. Maybe even put him and Darlene on easy street. But one thing he had learned in prison from the B and E guys: never boost anything the same day you work a place. They always suspect the help. He would have to figure a way to come back.

Evan was opening another case of wine in the foyer when Darlene walked in with her arm around Kent. She giggled, "Evan, do you know who this party is for?"

"Think the manager said some faggot artist or something. Don't know. Don't care." He looked around, then said under his breath, "Did you see the shit in this place?"

"The party's for Kent, dummy." Darlene did a little hop and tugged playfully on Kent's sleeve. "Those are his sculptures out in the yard."

Evan stammered, "You shittin' me? Those piles of rusted boat parts out back? They're throwing you a party for that crap?"

"The exhibition is called Gears of the Ocean." Kent angled his beret. He was dressed in clean jeans and a tan canvas vest over a long-sleeved black T-shirt.

"Goddamn. It looks more like stripped gears of a drunk welder, you ask me."

"Well, no one asked you," Darlene said. "Kent knows all about sculpture and painting and arty things."

"Is that so?" Evan pointed to small statue of a cowboy on a bucking horse; the dude looked like he was about to get his ass kicked. "You know what this is?"

"Of course. It's a Remington," Kent replied.

"You mean like the gun?"

"Spelled the same. Frederic Remington was an artist back in the 1800s, early 1900s. He died in 1909."

"Damn, you do know this shit. Uh . . . what's something like that worth? Can't be much—it ain't all that big. Any idea?"

Kent shrugged. "Might sell for a hundred grand."

Evan whistled, grabbed Kent by the arm, and ushered him toward the living room. "I'm really liking this art stuff. Tell me about some of this other crap."

They stood in the living room as Kent tried to explain that, unlike flat-screen TVs, the size of art did not equal value. He pointed at a painting barely a foot square. "I know it's not big, but it's a Wyeth. See the colors and textures. The way—"

"Yeah, yeah, whatever. But how much is something like that worth?"

"Oh, no idea. I'm not that good with paintings. But a lot more than the Remington."

Before he could respond, Evan watched two women descend on Kent. One was rawboned and horsey and dressed in a dykey tweed jacket and wrinkled khaki pants. The other was tall and thin, with black hair and bright-blue eyes. Evan thought she looked pretty damn good for her age, all decked out in a snug black dress with white pearls around her neck and a martini glass in one hand. Definitely MILF material.

"There you are, my dear." The horsey broad grabbed Kent by the arm. "I want you to meet Brooke Nichols, your hostess."

Kent grinned like a fool and pumped the MILF's hand. "Pleased to meet you. This means a lot to me."

"I'm only glad I could lend my modest home." Brooke waved her glass. "Sylvia's the one to thank. *She* really believes in you."

"Well, Brooke, you know how I enjoy discovering new talent."

"His work does have a raw energy," Brooke conceded. "I did notice how he uses the medium to create a certain dynamic tension."

Evan tried to follow the conversation, his attention split between the valuable artwork and thoughts of a quickie with the hot MILF.

"I think we might have a serious new artist on our hands," Sylvia gushed.

"One can always hope." Brooke paused and then eyed Evan curiously. "Are you new?"

"Huh?" Evan's mind drifted back into focus.

Brooke sighed, "Finding help this time of year is such a challenge."

"What?" Evan mumbled.

She handed him her empty glass. "Vodka martini, straight up with an olive. And try not to spill on the Persian. Anything for you, my dear? Kent?"

"White wine," Sylvia said.

"I'll have a beer, my good man," Kent chuckled and winked. "Make it a Heineken."

Evan was about to tell Kent where he could stick his goddamn Heineken when the hot MILF gasped and pointed at the windows. "Now, this is the last straw."

Holding the martini glass, Evan watched a lobster boat, trailing a huge plume of black smoke, bucking and diving on the rough seas, about to collide with the Nicholses' dock.

# CHAPTER 14

With a little less than two miles to go to the boatyard, the banging and black smoke had started again. Backing off on the throttle helped at first. But when Connor reached a point where he had little forward power, he decided that his family's dock was the closest and safest option.

While he babied the engine and steered, Crystal got ready to handle the lines. Once he was certain of making the dock, he cut the power and drifted. Crystal scrambled with the bumpers, and then tied off the bow and stern.

After one final shot from the fire extinguisher, Connor slammed the engine cover and climbed out of the *Nu B*. Crystal was admiring a gleaming, black-hulled boat tied to the other side of the dock.

"Is this a Hinckley?" she asked.

"Yeah. Dad's newest toy. They must have just brought it down from the boatyard. He's out of the country. I don't think he's even seen it yet."

"I'm partial to sailboats, but it looks like the world's most beautiful lobster boat."

"You mean the world's most expensive lobster boat." Connor waved at the Hinckley. "You're looking at thirty-six feet, eleven inches of fiberglass, carbon fiber, and Kevlar—a rich guy's fantasy of an inshore workboat. My dad ordered six hundred horsepower. Not to mention a rainforest's worth of hand-fitted teak."

"Oh boy." Crystal pointed. "Here comes a lot of negative energy."

Connor clenched his jaw, watching as his mother emerged from the house, followed by a small gaggle of people. The little troop threaded its way through the sculptures. "Great. Exactly what I need."

"What choice did you have?"

"Let the *Nu B* burn and swim to shore." Connor trudged up the dock to meet his mother.

"My seafaring son. That is quite the dramatic entrance. I assume your boat doesn't typically resemble a floating smudge pot. Is there a problem?" Brooke paused. "You do realize my affair begins in thirty minutes?"

"Good morning, Mom. You look fetching. Love the dress. Love the pearls." Connor smiled. "I'm still hoping for that invitation."

"Stop trying to change the subject. If you dirty your father's new Hinckley, he'll have a stroke."

"I'm afraid the *Nu B*'s stuck here until it's repaired or towed to the boatyard."

Brooke sputtered, "Please tell me you're joking."

"There's nothing funny about what happened." Connor looked past Brooke at Kent. "We could have died."

"Well, I certainly hope *that's* not part of this supposed plan you're formulating."

Crystal added, "We caught fire and the wind drove us toward shore. We nearly smashed up on the rocks."

"Ah, the first mate." Brooke squinted in the direction of the prayer flags.

Connor jabbed a thick finger at Kent. "He works at the boatyard; maybe he can fix it. I'm sure he knows what caused the problem."

"Kent is showing today. He doesn't have time. This will have to wait," Sylvia said.

"I didn't touch your boat," Kent said.

"Good, then you can tell me what happened." Connor snatched a handful of Kent's vest and dragged him toward the dock. "You've got thirty minutes."

"Okay, okay." Kent held up his hands. "I'll take a quick look."

Crystal trailed behind, shaking her head. "Very bad energy."

Sylvia followed after them. "Connor, please don't get him dirty."

As the little group reached the dock, Sylvia put a soothing hand on Brooke's shoulder. "Dear, don't get upset. I think Connor's boat provides some authenticity to the show's theme."

Brooke turned toward the house and almost bumped into the bartender. "Where's my martini!"

Connor leaned against the gunwale and watched the top of Kent's beret as he did the math on his finances, doubting his cushion had enough padding to cover the repairs, afraid Tyler's deal was his only salvation. Crystal, complaining about the "super bad energy," had gone to inspect the Hinckley.

Kent climbed out of the engine compartment, wiping his hands on a rag, his vest and shirt streaked with grease. He pushed the beret back with his forearm and said, "The four bolts holding the fuel pump were loose. That's the banging you heard. The smoke and flames were from raw diesel spilling on the hot manifold. You'll need a new fuel pump, new lines, maybe replace the manifold. Couple of days to clean up and fix."

"How much?" Connor asked.

"Don't know for sure." Kent shrugged. "Parts and labor, maybe two, three grand."

"I put in a rebuilt motor last winter, and that included a new fuel pump. You telling me the boatyard screwed up?"

Kent avoided Connor's stare. "I'm not telling you nothing. The four bolts were pretty loose, that's all."

"Worked themselves loose, huh? You ever seen a boat burn? I have. Up in Alaska. Two halibut fishermen, barely had time to jump overboard. You guys have fucked with me for the last time."

"Listen, I know you've been getting a hard run." Kent stabbed a greasy finger at the engine. "But *I* didn't do *that*."

"Yeah, who then?" Connor demanded.

"I don't know."

"Wade?"

"Could've been anyone." Kent jutted his chin over his shoulder at the immaculate house. "I didn't know Brooke was your mom. That's a nice place your family's got. Real nice. Our dad disappeared and left us with nothing. I'm trying to make something of myself. It ain't easy. But family's family. Nothing you can do about it."

"I'm familiar with the problem," Connor sighed. "But if you want to be an artist, you're in with the right crowd. Just stick to your welding, and make sure that when Wade goes down, he doesn't take you with him."

Kent dabbed at a stain on his vest and shook his head. "Shit. The showing's about to begin and I'm covered in grease."

Connor smiled. "Don't worry, the grease will lend authenticity to your work."

With the party guests arriving and the commotion of finding clean clothing for Kent, his mother didn't notice when Connor backed his father's MG out of the garage. Eyes watering, the wind whipping his face, Connor squinted as he drove the tiny sports car from the Camden boatyard toward the White Swan Inn. He was too tall to drive it with the top up, and with the top down, his entire head poked above the windscreen.

The boatyard was crazy busy, everyone wanting their boat fixed and in the water now. But Connor had pushed the issue of a loose fuel pump on a newly rebuilt motor, and the manager, clearly worried about liability, promised he would get to the *Nu B* as quickly as possible—one, two days at the latest. The repairs would kill any opportunity to catch up on his note. Repo might hurt less. The deal with Tyler was looking better every second.

Connor parked by the curb in front of the Swan and jogged up the steps. He was crossing the lobby when someone in the bar called his name.

"Connor, join me." Jeff Russell, the cameraman, held up a beer.

"Maybe a quick one. I've got a very tight schedule." Connor accepted a cold draft from the bartender, who turned back to watching a Cubs game on the TV hanging over the bar. "How's the work coming?"

"Everything's installed, tested, and ready to go. I can relax, take turns with the Steadicam, get some B-roll." Russell clinked his glass against Connor's. "They promoted me to assistant producer."

"Is that good?"

"Hell yeah. Now I get to boss the other guys around." Russell drained his glass and signaled the bartender for another.

"You'd like my father," Connor mumbled.

The bartender placed a fresh beer in front of Russell, squinted at Connor, and then grabbed the TV remote, surfed through the channels, finally stopping on a rerun of *Lobster Wars*. He waved the remote from the TV to Connor and grinned. "That's you."

Connor stared at his own image. "I guess you want my autograph."

The bartender pointed at Russell. "Yeah, on *his* tab."

Laughing, the man walked down the bar to take an order from a waitress.

Russell saluted the TV with his fresh beer. "This is episode six. The one that got me the promotion. Watch this next part."

**VOICE-OVER:** Late August and tensions on the dock are spilling over into the quiet town of Tranquility.

**CUT TO:** Connor stands in the parking lot of the

Tranquility Market, faces Wade, both surrounded by a loose circle of men. Connor jabs a thick finger into Wade's chest. "When I pulled into the dock, I saw you screwing around next to my truck."

Wade pushes Connor's hand away and steps forward. "So what. Didn't hurt your truck. Free country."

The circle of men tightens. Connor points at Wade. "Same goes for the ocean."

"You think?" Wade snarls, crowds Connor.

**CUT TO:** Side door of the market bangs open, and Phil, wearing a butcher's apron, rushes into the parking lot, shoulders his way through the circle. "Not here! Not here, god-*beep*-it! Take it down to the docks!"

Connor and Wade separate. Wade grins at Phil. "What's the matter, Phil, afraid of a little blood in your parking lot?"

"You mean a lot of blood," Connor snaps at Wade.

"Ayuh. If you got it to lose," Wade replies, turns, and heads out of the parking lot, followed by the other men.

Connor turned to Russell. "You got promoted for *that*?"

"It was my idea to follow you around with the Steadicam and get some B-roll. The producer loved it. Which reminds me, Phil mentioned that you didn't sign your release and contract for this year, and I'm in charge of that stuff now."

"Yeah, they're somewhere on my kitchen table."

"Is there a problem? Because if I don't have them before the producer and the rest of crew shows up, she's going to chew a new hole in my ass."

"Some more money would be nice."

"Uh, dude. Phil's been banging that drum since last year. The next person who asks the producer for more money most likely will get killed. And I mean, like, dead killed. Not just dropped from the show killed."

"Where is the foul-mouthed little munchkin?" Connor asked.

"Big last-minute meeting in New York at the mother ship. But she's on the way." Russell shrugged. "So we're a few days late. No big deal. My apartment in Park Slope looks like a rat's nest compared to this place. Actually, it is a rat's nest, now that I think about it."

"Shit, I live in a thirty-year-old trailer out in the woods." Connor watched Russell's reaction. "And no, you cannot put a camera in my place."

"I'd be happy with your V-berth," Russell replied. "Which reminds me, the producer's very excited about your first mate. But I have to get her to sign the papers, too. So really, where did you find her?"

"Wade was running the *Sweet Tail*, drawing a huge wake, and flipped her kayak; I pulled her out of the harbor and now she's camped out on the *Nu B*."

"Is she from around here?" Russell signaled for two more beers.

"I think she was a big-deal yoga person in New York. You've never heard of her?"

"Do I look like someone who does yoga?" Russell patted his gut. "What's she doing here?"

"She's on some kind of extended road trip. More of a cruise. Which seems to be stalled in my V-berth." Connor drained his beer. "Thanks for the brews. Gotta run."

"Where to?"

"Going to a business meeting upstairs." Connor shot a quick glance at his watch. "Then couples counseling with Wade. We need to work out a few issues."

Connor rapped on the door to suite 210. Ronald, a cell phone pressed to his ear, opened the door and motioned him inside. Connor followed him through the suite. It was a very nice suite, perfect for a reality TV star, even a minor one. The trailer was only supposed to be temporary, cheap and easy until he got the lobster fishing gig up and running. But its monkish decor was getting a little old. Not to mention the molten yard art.

Ronald barked into the phone. "Okay, I'll repeat it one more time. Mr. Lane wants all three sculptures at his summer house before he opens it for the season. Is there a problem?" Ronald rolled his eyes at Connor, pointed at the phone, and then gestured to the sofa while he continued.

The same episode of *Lobster Wars* was playing on the suite's TV, the sound turned down very low.

**CAMERA FOLLOWS** as Phil, a full head shorter than Connor, leads him from the parking lot through the side door into the market.

**CUT TO:** Interior of the market. Phil hands Connor a cup of coffee. "You can't be squaring off with that guy. Especially with all his friends around."

Connor sips the coffee, smiles. "What's the matter, Phil, you don't think I can handle six on one? Worried about some bad press for your store?"

"None of that. I don't want to see you get hurt."

"Yeah?" Connor drains the cup and tosses it in

the garbage. "But think of the ratings."

Connor muted the sound and watched as Ronald paced the room, hammering the poor soul on the other end of the conversation. He thought about Tyler's offer and the slim chance that the *Nu B*'s fire was an accident. *Lobster Wars* was like an amplifier, wired right into both his problems and opportunities.

"Yes, I know where the sculptures are now. Yes, I know that's a long way from Bozeman. Yes, I know that crating and shipping take time. That's why Mr. Lane pays you guys a premium. So get it done or we'll find someone else." Ronald broke the connection, smiled, and sat down next to Connor. "Why hello. Nice to see you again. I've been watching some reruns of *Lobster Wars*. You look great on the show."

"Thanks," Connor replied. "Mr. Lane around?"

"Tyler's out." Ronald scooted closer. "Think I might get a ride? I mean, on your boat?"

"I wanted to talk to him about his offer. Get a handle on the specifics. Did he get the paperwork going?" Connor asked.

"Yes, of course."

"Good. He mentioned the up-front payment but nothing about the other details."

Ronald said, "He instructed our legal people to put everything in writing. It takes a few days."

"There's that much to it?"

"Oh, yes." Ronald nodded. "These licensing deals are very complicated, and Tyler likes everything clearly spelled out so there's no misunderstanding."

A little green-eyed warning bell sounded in the back of Connor's head. "How complicated?"

"Oh, very. But not to worry; it's just standard legal stuff. I'll even help you through it. Now, how about that ride?" Ronald asked.

Connor replied, "It can get pretty rough out there. You might not like it."

"That's okay. I like it rough."

"You could take a real pounding. My boat's not very big."

"I'd be surprised if it wasn't large enough." Ronald ran his hand up Connor's bicep. "Just relax."

"That's what the guys in logging camp said." Connor grabbed Ronald's hand, squeezing his fingers.

"Ow, ow, ow!" Ronald pried his fingers loose and jumped to the opposite end of the sofa.

Just then, the suite's door opened, and Suzanne walked in. "Hello, Connor. I see you and Ronald are playing nice."

Connor stood. "I was asking Ronald here about the deal. When the paperwork might be ready."

"Our legal guys are working on the documents." Suzanne smiled. "Why don't I give them a call and check on the status, find out when you can see something? Give me your cell number."

"That would be great." Connor held up his phone so Suzanne could copy the number. "About the up-front payment Tyler mentioned. When do you think I could have it?"

"We usually have the payment ready for when someone signs a contract."

"Soon?"

"Absolutely. We're very excited about this concept." Suzanne playfully took Connor's hand and walked him toward the door. "And once we're finished with the paperwork, you and I can focus on making you a first-class spokesman."

"It's that simple?" Connor asked.

"Easier than you think. It's what I do."

"Think I can get a certified check?"

# CHAPTER 15

Wade and Evan sat in Wade's small kitchen, working a fresh bottle of Stoli. For the last forty minutes, Evan had yammered on in a vodka-fueled account of the day's events. Clearly, the little shit was working an angle. Wade had zero interest and wanted to tell the guy to take a hike, but Evan kept bringing up their past like Wade owed him or else.

Evan sloshed more Stoli into their glasses. "Goddamn, to hear your brother, there's millions in art and shit, just sitting there."

"Forget it," Wade said. It was like Evan had a little window in his head and Wade could watch the gears turn.

"Ah, Wade. Don't be so quick to walk on a good thing. I don't see anyone makin' you rich."

"Goddamn. I knew that asshole Nichols came from money, but shit," Wade said. "Why would he want to fish lobster he has a loaded family? Don't make no sense."

"Maybe Daddy cut him out the will, maybe he took too many drugs fried his brain, maybe he just likes to stink like fuckin' bait. How the hell should I know?" Evan did a shot of Stoli, wiped his mouth with the back of his hand. "But your fuckin' brother sure knew what he was talking about."

"All this time I thought Kent was jerkin' off. Reading them books and taking art classes up to the community college. Shit, I wish I could have seen the look on his face when that asshole accused him of rigging the fuel pump."

"You was the one fucked up his engine. Right?" Evan asked.

"Ayuh." Wade threw back a hit of vodka, and his eyes teared as he smoothed his tangled beard.

"Well, Kent said only a day or two to fix. Guess you didn't do such a good job."

"I wasn't trying to kill the bastard. Just send him a message. Fuck, the TV people are already here. And they're gonna start taping next week. If I can get him to pull out, I still might get that restaurant deal." Wade drained his glass. "But as long as Nichols is around, that restaurant guy won't even talk to me."

Evan's skinny arm snaked out, grabbed the Stoli, and tilted another slug into Wade's glass. "Blew you off, huh?"

"Said I'm not a 'suitable spokesperson.' Whatever the hell that means. I'm sick of fuckin' rich guys always calling the shots."

"Speaking of rich guys, this one dude shows up, buys three pieces of Kent's junk."

"You shittin' me?"

Evan replied, "I heard the manager say the dude was staying at the Swan."

"Short gray hair, rich-guy clothes, black cowboy boots?"

"Yeah, yeah, yeah. You know him?" Evan began to raise his glass.

"You dumbass. That's the guy."

Evan froze, glass halfway to his lips. "Huh? What guy?"

"*The* guy. The fucking restaurant guy." Wade slapped the table. "Mr. Tyler *fucking* Lane."

"Well, let me tell you, when he whipped out his checkbook, I thought they was gonna crap their pants. Your brother practically had a stroke; the old dyke tried to act cool, like it was no big deal, but I know it was, 'cause your boy's mommy practically humped the guy's leg. But hey, I'd tap that. She's a total MILF."

"This sucks."

"Shoot the fucker."

"Who? The restaurant guy?" Wade asked, trying to keep up with Evan's twisted commentary.

"No. Nichols," Evan replied.

"Are you crazy? The whole town knows I've been screwing with him. Who do you think the cops will come after first?" Wade smoothed his tangled beard. But it did suck.

"I don't know about no restaurant deals, but I need to get back in that house," Evan said.

Wade leaned forward, could see it coming. "What the hell are you talking about?"

"Five, ten minutes in that place and I'm set." Evan snapped his fingers. "I get Jimbo off my back. Make Darlene happy—"

Wade cut him off. "Count me out."

"And I'm gone." Evan smiled.

The swaybacked old house looked like scrap wood waiting for one final storm. Connor slotted the MG next to Wade's truck and scrubbed the bugs from his eye sockets. Go along, get along wasn't working. Wade had finally taken things too far, and it was time to get some clarity on the situation. Eyes watering, he pounded on the warped front door of the gray-shingled Cape.

Wade jerked open the door. "The fuck you crying about, Nichols?"

"We need to talk."

"Make it quick. I'm busy."

"Wade, I'm very disappointed. Well, more than disappointed. You might even say upset. It's our relationship. I feel like we're stuck. We're simply making no progress."

"Relationship?" Wade edged forward. "The fuck you talking about?"

"Someone messed with the fuel pump on the *Nu B*. Fixed it so the engine would catch fire."

Wade snickered. "No shit."

"That's what I thought." Wade might outweigh him by twenty pounds, but Connor had learned a valuable lesson in logging camp—serve first. So he slammed his big fist on the point of Wade's chin. The man sagged against the doorframe, his legs buckled, and he slid to the ground. Connor grabbed a handful of Wade's shirt, dragging him to his feet. "This is exactly what I'm talking about. I come here to have a friendly discussion. Air our differences. Find some common ground. But you show complete disregard for my feelings, and that's very hurtful."

Wade's head bobbed on his neck, his eyes rolling and blinking.

Connor led him into the weed-choked yard. "Wade? Wade? Can you hear me?"

"Uh . . . uh . . . uh . . . ayuh."

"Good." Connor leaned him against a dead birch tree, propping him up with his left hand. "Try to concentrate. This is important. I hate to repeat myself."

"Concentrate? Important?" Wade's response was distant and dreamy.

"Wade, the last time I checked, the ocean's open to the public, and I'm not going to stop lobster fishing. I'm not going to quit the show. I'm not going to leave Tranquility. Do you understand me?" Connor tapped his forehead.

Wade straightened and tried to push Connor's hand away. "I fuckin' hear you."

"I know you can hear me. But do you understand me? There's a big difference."

"Screw you, Nichols."

"Ah, now we're getting to the nub of the problem. Which is why we're having this friendly chat. First my truck. Now my boat. Not to mention all the shit you pulled last season. You've screwed with me long enough, and now you're going to stop. Because if you don't, I'm—"

"Fuckin' college boy."

"Wade, interrupting someone when they're speaking is such bad manners."

"Screw you, Nichols."

"Now you're just repeating yourself, Wade. I'm worried that you don't understand me. I don't want to have to do this again."

"Fuck you, Nichols."

"You're really making this hard." Connor pulled back his right arm, about to give Wade another shot, when he caught a blur of movement to his left. For a split second, he wondered why the bartender from his mother's party was swinging a rusted car muffler at his head.

# CHAPTER 16

"You sure we didn't kill him?" Wade knocked back a shot of Stoli.

"The fuck you care? He was kicking your ass." Evan stood at the kitchen sink, washing blood off his hands. "You should thank me."

"What if the guy bleeds to death?"

"Head wounds bleed like a bitch. He ain't gonna die."

"Like you're some expert?" Wade's own head pounded, his jaw swelling and getting stiff. The boy packed some muscle. It was a good thing that Evan's move with the muffler saved him from a second shot.

"I seen a lot'a guys hit on the head. Stabbed, shanked, cut, too. You only got to worry when the blood's spurting. That means you hit an artery. Then you're fucked. Shit, he'll have a big-ass headache is all."

"Maybe now he'll finally get the message." Wade reached for the Stoli, but just then, Kent appeared in the kitchen doorway with Darlene.

"What message?" Kent asked.

Wade squinted at his brother. "Where the hell you get them clothes?"

Kent was dressed in neatly creased khakis and a pale-blue button-down with a tiny pony embroidered on the breast pocket. But his beret was smudged with grease. "Mrs. Nichols loaned them to me. Pretty nice, huh? I might buy some of my own."

"Don't he look great? Like some rich guy going to play golf or out to dinner," Darlene said.

"Yeah, like those scuzzballs used to stick dollar bills in your crotch," Evan sneered. "Where the fuck you been?"

"What do you care? You've been ignoring me the whole trip. I thought we was going to a motel."

"First, Wade and I got to take care of some business."

"I was helping Kent move his sculptures over to the gallery. And Sylvia, the lady that owns it, said she might give me a job." Darlene smiled and fluffed her hair.

"Yeah, a tongue job," Evan grunted and reached for the vodka.

"Don't be so nasty," Darlene replied. "Sylvia said I have a nice way with people, same as that EVP from Hooter's."

Kent headed for the back door, said to Darlene, "Let me get my portfolio and we can go."

"Now where the hell you think you're going?" Evan whined.

Darlene said, "Mr. Lane invited Kent to dinner at the White Swan and said he could bring someone."

"Who said *you* could go?" Evan demanded.

"Who said I need your permission? You don't own me. Besides, they got lobster."

"That art gallery dyke gonna be there? 'Cause you better watch your pussy," Evan laughed.

"Of course. And Brooke and Kent and me."

Evan's head snapped up. "Brooke Nichols, Connor's mom?"

"Uh-huh." Darlene nodded.

"What time's dinner?" Evan asked.

"Seven o'clock."

Kent appeared with a large vinyl binder. "Okay, ready."

Darlene shot a snotty look at Evan, hooked her arm through Kent's, and they disappeared toward the front of the house.

After the front door slammed, Evan grinned at Wade. "Now we know where Brooke Nichols is gonna be tonight, and it ain't at home."

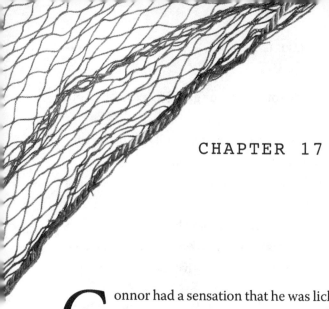

# CHAPTER 17

Connor had a sensation that he was licking an old boot. Then his eyes focused. His face was pressed against the MG's passenger seat, his tongue dragging on the musty leather. The left side of his head throbbed as he pushed himself upright and looked around. The tiny car was wedged in a stand of spruce just off a dirt road.

Remembering the skinny guy with the rusty muffler, he gently probed the spot under his ear, and his fingers came away sticky with blood. Connor sat up and tried not to puke, waiting for the pain to recede, collecting his thoughts. Which were a tad scrambled.

Lobster fishing. The TV show. Phil and his agenda. Green-eyed Crystal decorating the *Nu B* with prayer flags. Wade and his bartender friend. And finally, the Captain Connor Lobster Shacks—possibly the best or worst idea in the world. Too many tangents. Too many loose ends.

Connor reached forward, his fingers scrabbling over the dashboard, searching for the ignition key. Gone. He looked around the interior. Maybe it was on the floor. Nope. No key. The shitheads probably threw it into woods.

No problem.

He shoved his hand into the nest of wires under the dash. One good thing about his father's love of antique sports cars—a little kid could hotwire them. Something he figured out when he was only fourteen.

Forty-five minutes later, his head clearing, he bumped down the long driveway to his family's house, the MG's weak lights leading the way.

Brooke's Audi sat in the turnaround, but the house was dark. She was out for the evening. Good. Connor was in no mood to explain the MG's blood-soaked seats to his mother. Maybe in the morning.

The conversation with his father would come later. But Connor vaguely remembered something about a three-year search for the perfect leather. His dad might very well stroke out right in the garage.

He searched some storage boxes on a back shelf and came up with an old black hoody, then retrieved a first aid kit from the laundry room. In the kitchen, he packed a ziplock with ice from the Sub-Zero's freezer. Holding the ice pack against the side of his head with one hand, he filled a canvas boat bag with the makings of dinner—cold cuts, cheese, bread, pasta salad, fruit. Then he grabbed a bottle of wine and headed down to the dock. He wanted to check out his dad's new boat, relax, drink a little wine, and figure out how his life got from a simple point A to a complicated point B.

Crystal emerged from the Hinckley and greeted him as Connor stopped on the dock's edge. She held her hand to her mouth, hazel eyes big. "What happened? You're covered in blood."

"A minor disagreement during couples counseling." Connor tugged at the collar of his bloody T-shirt. "Someone got carried away trying to make a point."

"Your shirt's soaked. I'd say you need a new counselor."

"I can't afford the one I have." Connor waved at hand at the Hinckley bobbing quietly on the side of the dock. "That's going to cost you two hundred a night."

She wrinkled her nose. "The *Nu B* stinks like burnt diesel."

He climbed onto the Hinckley. It reeked of oiled teak and freshly stitched canvas and fine craftsmanship and a touch of salt spray. Connor slipped into the captain's chair and studied the controls; there were only two hours on the Hobbs. Then he noticed a small door on the console. He popped the latch. Inside were the owner's log and the key.

He fit the key into the ignition. "Let's see what all the fuss is about."

The Hinckley felt solid yet nimble as it surged through the light chop. The jet drive handled with a precision unlike any propeller boat Connor had ever captained. He could easily get accustomed to this, spoiled even. Maybe obsessive wasn't so crazy after all.

While he minded the wheel, Crystal inspected his wound before dressing it with a small bandage. "The cut's not too bad, but you've got a pretty big lump on your head. Possibly a concussion."

"I was only out for a few seconds. So if I have a concussion, it's minor."

"Minor's still bad. What did he hit you with?"

"Rusted muffler."

"Then you probably need a tetanus shot." Crystal tugged off his canvas jacket. "Put your arms up; we have to get you out of this T-shirt."

Connor raised his arms. "I think the little weasel that hit me is a friend of the guy who almost sliced you into sushi."

Crystal pulled the shirt over his head. "What are you going to do, beat him up?"

"Philosophically speaking, I'm opposed to violence. You know, 'Turn the other cheek.'"

"Well, your philosophy and actions aren't very consistent. You come across as more of an eye-for-an-eye type."

"What can I do? These guys aren't singing from the same hymnal."

"I unilaterally oppose all forms of violence. Negative energy only begets more negative energy." She leaned close, helping him pull the old hoody over his head without bumping the wound.

"But what happens if someone attacks you?" Connor asked, realizing that he'd started it. Sort of.

Crystal shrugged. "Those are my beliefs."

Connor held the ice pack to his head while he steered a southerly heading. "There's a cove up ahead. We can drop anchor and discuss your beliefs."

Seal Cove was wooded on all sides, dark and private. A bald eagle perched on a high branch, scanning the water's calm surface for diner. The Hinckley rode placidly at anchor as the final shards of daylight drained from the spring sky.

Crystal arranged the food on the table in the small galley while Connor opened the wine and poured. They sat side by side on the padded bench. She said, "This is nice. Have you been here before?"

Connor nodded. "When we were kids, we'd anchor here and party."

"So, it's like your version of a make-out spot." Crystal ignored the cold cuts, concentrating on the cheese and fruit.

"I'm not sure how much *making out* we did, but I guess we tried." Connor sipped his wine. "Why, did you want to make out?"

"No, thank you."

"Good, me either," Connor said. "Listen, as soon as my boat's fixed, I'm moving it back to Tranquility, and you might want to go back to the Swan. I'm expecting a shit storm with the locals."

"I'm a big girl. I can take care of myself."

"I'm sure you can," Connor replied. "But I don't think you understand the kind of guys I'm dealing with."

"You mean the kind of guys who almost drowned me and then set fire to your boat?" Crystal asked. "And hit you over the head."

"Exactly."

"It's okay. The boatyard called. The part they've been waiting for finally came in, and they should have my boat ready in a day or two."

Connor had totally forgotten about her sailing trip. "Where are you going?"

"My plan was to explore the coast of Maine for the summer, maybe head up to the Maritimes in Canada. That's why I sold out and went sailing—clear my head, regain my center." She shrugged. "And who knows, maybe come up with another business idea. But one that's even more consistent with who I am."

"You don't miss your yoga empire?" Connor asked.

"Twelve studios wasn't exactly an empire. Not like I was running GE. But I do miss the people and the practice. It was the business part that I had trouble making peace with."

"Sounds like you were pretty good at the business part."

"I was, and that's part of what's bothering me."

"Russell thinks you'd make a great addition to the show."

"Why in the world would I want to be on reality TV?" Crystal asked.

"Fame, fortune." Connor shrugged. "I don't know."

"You're cute." She smiled, reached up, and kissed him full on the lips.

Connor kissed back. "So, you do want to make out."

"Don't get the wrong idea. That was a thank-you kiss for letting me stay on your boat. I'm not looking to hook up. You're cute but clueless."

"What's that supposed to mean?"

"I don't want to hurt your feelings."

"Maybe you already did," Connor protested.

"Sorry. Let's just say you're not my type."

"Well, you're not *my* type." Connor realized that he sounded like a petulant child.

"I'm glad we cleared *that* up." Crystal smiled. "Besides, you need a good night's sleep more than you need to get laid."

"Isn't that the captain's decision?"

"Not tonight." Crystal stood and pulled him to his feet and gently pushed Connor toward the forward cabin. "I'll take the first watch. Get some rest."

Connor sat on the edge of the bunk, staring at the closed cabin door, thinking about his zipped-pants policy. That single kiss had stirred up the little guy in his lap, who had a much more flexible definition of *type*. Which was one of the key reasons Connor had instituted the policy in the first place. Wasn't the idea to formulate a plan during calm times, with a clear head, so he knew exactly what to do in an emergency? Wasn't this better than winging it, making it up as he went along? Hadn't that usually led to disaster?

He opened the cabin door and peeked out. Crystal, wrapped in a blanket, was sitting, legs crossed, on the bench. Connor cleared his throat. "So, I was thinking . . ."

She opened one eye. "Forget it. Not going to happen. Ever."

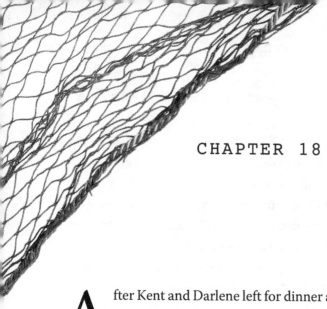

# CHAPTER 18

After Kent and Darlene left for dinner at the Swan, Wade and Evan sat working the Stoli in the kitchen, Evan pitching his plan. Selling hard, but with an edge of threat.

"All we need is ten, fifteen minutes to grab a couple of things. Shit, there's so much good stuff in that fuckin' place might be weeks before she realizes anything's missing," Evan said. "We'll split it fifty-fifty and you'll never see me again."

"Ayuh. Go ahead. You don't need me."

"Then lend me the *Sweet Tail*."

"The fuck you talkin' about?"

Evan explained the layout—long private driveway, big property, deepwater dock well clear of the house. If Brooke showed up early or the cops came, Evan's van, parked in the driveway, filled with all her valuable shit, would be a little hard to miss. But with the boat, he could pull away in the dark. It was perfect. A seagoing version of slipping out the back door.

"No fuckin' way you're taking the *Sweet Tail*," Wade snorted. "It's almost two hours of open water, and you don't know squat about running a boat."

Evan smiled. "Okay. Then you drive."

But by the time they reached Camden harbor, Wade's boat-handling skills were shit. After finishing the Stoli, they had hunted up a fresh bottle of Wodka hidden in Kent's studio. Now the Wodka was half gone, and Wade worked hard to keep it together while Evan swaggered around the deck, imitating a fucking pirate.

Wade banged the *Sweet Tail* into the dock. He gunned the diesel and slammed against the wooden pilings, wrestling the wheel, laboring to keep position. Forgetting the bumpers, Evan stumbled forward, struggling with the lines, finally tying off after several tries and nearly falling overboard.

Wade stood on the *Sweet Tail*'s deck, admiring the house. "I can't believe fuckin' Nichols came from this."

"Yeah, yeah, yeah. Rich asshole, blah, blah, fuckin' blah." Evan took a hit of Wodka. "Stop whining."

"What about an alarm?" Wade asked.

"No alarm I could see. Besides, by the time any police drive all the way out here, we're gone. Smooth sailing all the way, matey." Evan climbed onto the dock.

"Cut that fucking pirate shit. This ain't funny."

Evan started toward the house. "Come on, we got to get moving."

"Not me." Wade shook his head. "I'll stay with the boat."

"Ah, shit, Wade. That means I got to carry everything myself."

"Just take what you want. Nothing for me."

"You sure?" Evan asked. "May not get another chance like this."

"Hurry up, before someone sees us."

Evan pointed a finger at Wade. "Just don't leave me."

"Ayuh. Don't worry," Wade replied. "Just be quick."

Evan hurried up the sloping yard to the house, and Wade heard the faint tinkle of breaking glass. Ten minutes later, Evan walked back down to the dock, carrying a small painting.

"That's it? Tiny little painting?" Wade asked.

"Kent said this is worth way over a hundred K." Evan handed it over to Wade and turned back to the house. "Don't you fuckin' leave me."

Wade worked his aching jaw and thought about the fancy house. Rich people liked their comforts. No doubt the medicine cabinets would yield some leftover painkillers. He called after Evan, "Search the bathrooms. Find some pain pills. And get another bottle of vodka, too."

Evan had already scoped out most of the house during the party, pretending he was lost. Unfortunately, he hadn't had enough time to rifle the drawers, really look hard.

But he *had* spotted a jewelry box half hidden in the master bedroom closet. And even if Wade changed his mind and asked for a cut, this was small stuff he wouldn't have to share. After all, the whole plan *was* his idea. Wade could never think up something this slick on his own. Evan had a gift, criminally speaking.

Before heading upstairs to the master bedroom, he stopped at the bar and grabbed a fresh bottle of Kettle One, breaking the seal and hitting the juice as he walked up the stairs.

He flicked on the closet light. The box was gone. He pushed aside a rack of clothes, and right there, set into the wall, was a safe. Locked. Shit. Evan backed out of the closet and quickly searched the rest of the room—nothing.

He needed to grab at least one more goodie on his way out, but if he didn't find some pills for Wade, the guy would complain all the way back to Tranquility. So he moved to the bathroom and searched the cabinets. Personally, he'd never had much use for drugs. A little pot, some cocaine when it was around, but he was mostly a booze guy. He studied the label on a small brown bottle—Percocet. That sounded familiar; he slipped it into his pocket.

Evan closed the toilet lid and sat down, sipping the Kettle and thinking about what next. He tried to concentrate, running through the mental list of stuff Kent had pointed out. Then he remembered a heavy glass bowl sitting on a small table near the bar. Kent had a name for it: Stumpy, or Stubby . . . *Steuben*—that was it.

He was about to raise the bottle to his lips when he heard the crunch of tires on the gravel driveway. He crossed over to the window. A long black limo circled the drive and pulled to a stop. The driver popped out and smoothly opened the passenger door. Brooke emerged, followed by that Tyler guy. Arm in arm, giggling and laughing, they headed for the front door.

In a panic, Evan slipped out of the bedroom, down the hall, and froze. He held his breath and peeked around the corner. They were already coming up the stairs. Not exactly *up* the stairs, more like *on* the stairs.

Evan retreated a few steps and listened.

"Oh, Tyler, right here?"

"Why not? We can do it in bed later."

"Later?"

"That's why they make Viagra."

"You're awful," Brooke giggled.

"We'll see, little lady."

"My, what a big gun. Very impressive."

"Thank you. I'm very fond of it."

"Do all Texans have one?

"If they're lucky."

Evan retreated to the master bedroom, searching for a way out. He checked the windows. Two stories and a steep pitch on the roof, no handholds, and a hard drop to the ground. Plus, he could see the fucking limo driver leaning on the car, smoking a cigarette in the dark, obviously waiting while his boss knocked off some quick after-dinner tail.

He decided to hide in one of the other bedrooms and sneak past when they came up for their second round on the giant four-poster bed in the master suite. Evan walked down the hall, slipped into another room, and sat on the bed, sucking the Kettle, waiting for the moaning to stop.

Evan tried to follow the conversation on the stairs. They giggled about Tyler taking his *medicine* before a second round while Brooke said she wanted a nightcap, and they worked their way from the stairs to the bar to the kitchen. Not ideal, but okay. He would give them a few minutes to get settled and then sneak down the stairs and out the back door.

He waited ten minutes and then worked his way down to the first floor, across the foyer, and toward the back of the house. When he drew even with the small table next to the bar, he spotted the Steuben, sparkling in the half-light coming through the windows. Evan wrapped a hand around the heavy glass piece.

Brooke must have chosen this moment to freshen her drink. "Excuse me. May I help you?"

Evan froze.

There was a look of shock and curiosity on her face. She stepped back. "You're the waiter from my—"

Evan hit her in the head with the bowl.

Brooke squawked and folded to the floor.

Tyler emerged from the kitchen. "What the hell?"

Evan calmly raised his arm, about to smash the big glass chunk across Tyler's head, when he saw the man drop his drink and, in one swift movement, reach under his arm.

Evan's vodka-soaked brain worked in slow motion. Was that nickel plating? He threw the Steuben at Tyler and sprinted toward the door.

Clear of the house, Evan was moving pretty goddamn fast, or so it felt until he heard a loud, booming crack and tripped. He landed facedown in the damp grass, scuttled along on all fours, fighting to get his balance. He finally pushed himself to his feet, but his left leg wasn't working very well.

He was almost at the dock, practically dragging his leg, when Evan chanced a quick look over his shoulder.

There was an eye-searing flash of light, followed by another booming crack.

It sounded like the guy was shooting a fucking howitzer.

Evan ducked and scurried down the dock toward Wade's boat. Which was already pulling away.

"Wait! Wait! Wait!" he shouted over the rumble of the diesel.

At the end of the dock, he launched himself into the air. Arms flailing, he landed hard across the transom, feet dragging in the cold water. With a final heroic effort, Evan levered himself over the transom and crumpled onto the deck.

They were about a half mile offshore, Wade sitting on an empty lobster crate, Evan leaning against the gunwale, whimpering softly while the *Sweet Tail* drifted on a slack tide. The little painting rested on the lobster tank. With no moon and an overcast sky, the only points of reference were the house lights twinkling on the mainland.

Wade popped three Percocet into his mouth and washed them down with the Ketel One. He smoothed his beard with the back of his hand and passed the bottle to Evan. "I can't believe you didn't drop the vodka."

"Yeah, and I can't believe you were gonna leave me on the dock. Gimme those pills; my leg's totally fucked." He chased two Percocet with the vodka.

"Just warming up the engine."

"Shit." Evan put some weight on his leg, winced. "Feels like my ass is broke."

"Maybe you twisted something when you tripped. No big deal." Wade looked hard at Evan in the dark. "You think she got a good look at you before you hit her?"

"Nah. House was pretty dark," Evan replied.

"You think you killed her?" Wade asked. This was potentially worse than any of the shit they pulled as kids.

"Don't know, but she went down hard."

"But what do you think?" Wade pressed.

"Like I said, I don't know." Evan shifted his weight. "Shit, my leg hurts."

"How about Lane, he see you?"

"No, too dark. All I could see was that goddamn gun. Who'd'a figured the bastard would be carrying heat. I thought he was a businessman, for Christ's sake."

"Yeah, but no lights on in the back, and the dock's a good ways from the house." Wade paused, wanting absolute clarity. "I doubt he saw the boat."

"I'm sure he could hear it. But these boats all look the same, especially in the dark. He'd need to see the name."

"Ayuh. You're right, too dark to read the name." Wade began to have a far-off, fuzzy, uncoupled feeling as the painkillers joined the vodka. "Important thing is we got away clean. Right?"

"The fuck you worried about? I'm the one jumped parole. I'm the one robbed the place. I'm the one hit her on the head." Evan handed the Ketel to Wade and twisted around, groping his rear end.

"Ayuh . . . but the TV show . . . the restaurant deal . . ." Wade watched Evan loosen his belt and shove a hand down the back of his pants while the wisp of a foggy idea formed.

Evan probed his ass, grunted, "Fuck the TV show and double fuck that restaurant guy. We get back to shore, I'm gonna fix it so he don't talk. I ain't going back to prison."

"Prison. Shit." Wade sipped the Kettle, the idea starting to take shape. If Tyler didn't see the *Sweet Tail*, couldn't identify it, then Wade should be in the clear. Except for one little problem.

"If she's dead, we're talking big-time incarceration. Maybe life." Evan jerked his hand free and stared, eyes huge. He slumped against the gunwale. "That's blood. I think the fucker shot me."

"We? I didn't have anything to do with it," Wade protested. The little problem was Evan.

"You drove the fuckin' boat. That makes you an accessory, *matey*."

Wade rocked forward, slamming the vodka bottle into Evan's chest, flipping him over the side and into the water with a splashing gurgle. Problem solved.

Wade's jaw was still stiff, but at least the pain was manageable. In fact, he was having a tough time remembering why it hurt in the first place. Something to do with setting fire to Nichols's boat? Or was it college boy's truck? Maybe both?

He sipped the Kettle and tried to concentrate as he leaned hard on the throttle, pushing the *Sweet Tail* toward the mouth of Tranquility's harbor.

With Evan out of the picture, his only concern was whether or not Tyler could identify the *Sweet Tail*. And even if he could, there was no proof that Wade was driving it. Lobster boats got "borrowed" all the time.

Wade peered through the windscreen, trying to get his bearings—a few lights winking in the distance were his only guide in the flat, moonless dark. Jaws lurked right in the mouth of the harbor. But he'd run the channel hundreds of times, maybe thousands. He could practically find his way with his eyes closed. Drunk or sober.

Feeling light and free, he hit the vodka again and made a small course correction, lining up to run the narrow cut into the harbor. But there was a nagging twitch at the base of his skull. He shook it off, took another hit of Kettle. But the feeling kept coming back. Evan? Tyler? Brooke? He had it all worked out. Didn't he? What was he forgetting? He squeezed his eyes shut for a second, trying to concentrate.

Nothing.

*Oh, well, screw it. Not important.* He grinned and raised the vodka to his lips.

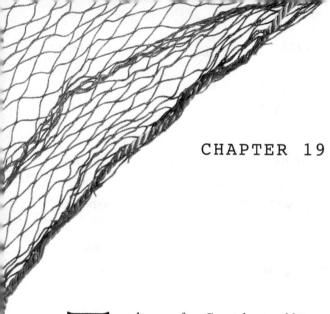

# CHAPTER 19

Two hours after Crystal vetoed his proposal, Connor walked out of the forward berth into the small cabin. With no moon, the cove was inky black, but he felt the boat swinging gently on a firm anchor, pointing into the ebbing tide. He checked his watch; dead low in about two hours, but he knew that the cove was deep enough to safely float the Hinckley.

Crystal had spread the blanket on the deck and was holding a yoga pose. She looked up. "Tide's heading out. We going to move?"

"Jet drive, no propeller, no rudder. This thing doesn't need much more water than a canoe. We're fine here."

"Good. I like it here. Very peaceful." She finished her pose and joined him on the bench. "How's your head?"

Connor replied, "I only see double when I open both eyes."

"Concussions are nothing to joke about. You should see a doctor."

"No time. My payback list is getting longer by the second. Too much to do. Invitations need to go out. Arrangements made."

She inspected the bandage. "What are you really going to do about those guys?"

"Serious injury, dismemberment, unmitigated pain and suffering." Connor smiled, pointed at the cove. "We live right on the ocean, so maybe waterboarding."

"I can't tell when you're serious or joking."

"Sometimes, neither can I. But if it's good enough for the CIA .

. ." Connor shrugged. "You want to help me?"

"Not if that includes hurting people. Why don't you move your boat to Camden, tie up at your parents' dock? Much less confrontation."

"My license is for the waters off Tranquility. The extra running time doesn't make economic sense." Connor paused. "Plus, in case you didn't notice, I'm experiencing a smidgen of family friction."

"Because you've chosen a lifestyle they don't like? That seems a little rigid and unforgiving."

"Talk about rigid. My older brother, Daniel, is the chief operating office of Dad's company. And my sister, Joanna, is a surgeon. They never had a chance."

"I don't know about the rest of your family, but I think there's something more going on between you and your mother. Not just your lifestyle choice. Something deeper."

"Are you a yoga teacher or a therapist?" Connor asked.

"Stop mocking."

"It's ancient history."

"Sometimes better understanding your history helps you cope with the present."

"Not in my family. But if you insist." Connor sighed. "Mom *was* a serious artist. A pretty big-deal poet. But her work really slowed down when we were still kids, right about the time Dad's business took off. Hardly writes anything now. I can't remember the last time she published."

"And?" Crystal prodded.

"I was an English major. Thought I might teach. Maybe write. So I started with a few short stories. Pretty mediocre, actually, but she was very excited, really wanted me to pursue the writing." He tugged at the logo on his sweatshirt. "But I got bored with the whole Bowdoin thing and split before graduation."

"That could explain a lot."

"I wasn't into the liberal arts scene, too squishy. I don't have the patience to teach, and I have zero talent as a writer. But most importantly, I don't belong indoors."

"Sounds like your mom lost her connection to the child she related to most. But at least she's around. You can talk to her, work out your issues."

"*Issues*? You sure sound like a therapist," Connor said. "Believe me, I've tried. But we usually end up arguing."

"You need to try again."

"Maybe someday." Connor settled back on the cushion.

"Don't wait too long. Mothers don't live forever." Crystal leaned back against the cushion. "How old are you?"

Connor replied, "Thirty-four. Why?"

"It seems like you're old enough to have figured out a few things. Like what you want to be when you grow up and how to get along with your mommy."

"I know what I want to be when I grow up," Connor protested.

"Are you sure?"

"Hey, I'm not the one drifting on the high seas."

"I've already built and sold one business and I'm only twenty-eight. But believe me, I understand the idea of finding your way. Everyone's allowed to go down a few dead ends. But not forever. I've had some false starts. So I know what I'm talking about. There was even a time I was thinking of becoming a Buddhist monk." Crystal slipped the blanket off her shoulders and handed it to Connor.

"You know, prayer flags are Tibetan," Connor said.

"I'm still sorting out a few issues with my belief system."

"Why didn't you?" Connor asked.

"Why didn't I what?" She slipped off the bench and raised her arms over her head, rising on her toes, stretching.

"Become a monk."

"I had a problem with the vow of celibacy." Crystal disappeared into the forward berth, closing the door behind her.

The next morning, Trooper Mack was standing on the lawn in the bright sun as Connor gently swung the Hinckley up to the dock. Connor had expected a little friction for "borrowing" Dad's newest toy—not to mention outright indignation over the bloody MG. But was his mother actually spiteful enough to call the police?

"Are we in trouble?" Crystal asked.

"*We?*"

Trooper Mack made his way toward the dock while Crystal tossed out the bumpers. When she threw him the lines, the policeman tied off on the dock cleats.

"Nice boat." Mack admired the Hinckley. "Not exactly set up to fish lobster."

"Belongs to my father." Connor gestured across the dock. "That one's mine."

The policeman tugged at the corner of his mustache, consulted his clipboard. "Then Brooke Nichols is your mother?"

Connor felt the heart-pounding sensation that preceded bad news. "Yes. Why?"

"Your mother is in Penn Bay Medical Center." Trooper Mack read from his notebook. "Apparently, she returned home last night and walked in on a robbery. The robber knocked her unconscious."

"My mom?" Connor stared at the policeman, unwilling to accept what he'd just heard. "This is insane. Why hurt her?"

"Maybe she confronted the robber? Maybe he panicked?"

"Is she going to be all right?" Crystal asked. When Officer Mack looked at her without answering, she added, "I'm his first mate."

"First mate, huh?" The policeman handed Connor a card. "I don't know her status. Penn Bay's number is on the back of my card. You can call and get an update. Listen, I have to ask, where were you last night?"

Connor explained, "We left about six, anchored overnight in Seal Cove. Just got back."

"No one was here when you left?"

"Mom was already out." Connor looked at the card, still trying to process the idea of his mother injured and in the medical center.

"They got away on a boat." Trooper Mack pointed. "Your boat here all night?"

"My boat's down for repairs. Someone set fire to the engine."

"Arson? Did you call it in?" the trooper asked.

"It happened on the water, and I was a little busy saving my life."

"You should have called it in. We'll talk about that later." Trooper Mack made a note on his pad. "I understand your mother hosted a party yesterday afternoon? Lots of people coming and going?"

"Yeah, her art crowd. Friends, people she knows," Connor replied

"Do you know a Mr. Tyler Lane? Texan. Money."

"Yes, why?"

"Apparently, he was here at the house with her when this happened."

"You think he did it?" Crystal asked.

"Not likely. He called the ambulance and was about to give us a statement. Then his people showed up, running interference, and now he's referring calls to his lawyers. But according to his limo driver, there was gunfire. So we still don't have the whole story."

"He'll talk to me," Connor said.

"Excuse me?" Mack asked.

"Nothing. Forget it." Connor held up the card. "I want to call the medical center."

"Of course." The policeman gave a sympathetic smile. "Mind if I check out the Hinckley?"

"Go ahead." Connor and Crystal jogged up the dock toward the house.

"She's in a coma." Connor hung up the phone and forced out a ragged breath. Speaking the words only reinforced the stark reality of the situation. "They think she's bleeding in her brain, but they're not sure. They've called in a neurologist to run more tests. They're talking about transferring her down to Portland or even Mass General. But she's stable for now."

Crystal leaned against the kitchen counter, twisting a hank of hair. "What about your family?"

"Dad's in China with my brother. Their itinerary is around here somewhere."

"Didn't you say your sister is a doctor?"

"I should call her first. This is her thing; she can advocate for Mom." He reached for the phone.

His sister was in surgery, but her service said that they would forward the message as soon as possible. Connor tried his father and brother and ended up leaving his cell number in four different places. With multiple time zones and their crazy travel schedule, he doubted he would hear from either one before tomorrow.

While Crystal went upstairs to take a quick shower, he headed back to the dock to retrieve his phone from the pocket of his canvas jacket. Halfway across the sloping yard, he spotted a bottle lying in the grass. He walked over and nudged it with his toe, turning it so he could read the label: Wodka. Not exactly Mom's brand. Connor was about to pick it up, but he glimpsed Officer Mack standing on the dock, watching him and holding something in his hands.

When Connor approached, the policeman held up a bloody T-shirt and canvas jacket. "You mind explaining?"

Connor touched his bandage. "Hit my head."

"*You* hit your head, or *someone* hit your head?"

"A minor disagreement over something that has *nothing* to do with my mom," Connor replied.

Trooper Mack waved the T-shirt at the Hinckley and then in the direction of the house. "Why would a guy like you want to fish lobster, especially considering the hard time you're getting from those boys in Tranquility? Unless it's all about getting on that TV show."

"Fame. Fortune. Unlimited nooky." Connor nodded. "Same as every guy."

"I don't know if what happened to your mother is connected to Tranquility, but don't forget what I said about taking matters into your own hands." Trooper Mack pointed at Connor's bandage, handed him the bloody clothes, and walked up the dock toward the house.

Connor dug his phone from the jacket as he called after him, "Any chance you found the shitheads who torched my truck?"

# CHAPTER 20

The *Sweet Tail* might have been drifting a half mile offshore when Wade shoved Evan over the side, but at dead low tide, he only had to dog paddle for about three hundred yards. Then he slogged through sucking mud, razor-sharp mussels, and barnacle-encrusted rocks, finally pulling himself up a steep bank and slithering under a split rail fence into the backyard of some rich dickhead's estate.

Shivering and aching, his head foggy from the pills and vodka, Evan hunkered down in a stand of birch on the property's edge, watching the house slowly go dark, thinking he'd swipe a car and make it back to the harbor where he had left his van.

Then go kill Wade.

Maybe that restaurant guy, too.

*Yeah, definitely.*

When all the lights were out, he hobbled along a tall hedge, keeping in its shadow as he worked his way toward the front of the house. Big place like this, rich fuckers, they must have cars out the ass. *Probably leave them in the driveway, keys on the dashboard.*

But when Evan poked his head around the corner of the garage, he was pissed to see that the driveway was empty. He was feeling his away along in the dark, looking for a way to raise one of the garage doors, when he caught his foot on bicycle leaning against the side of the house, crashing it into a row of metal trash cans.

Immediately, a bright floodlight flared. Then all hell broke loose.

What sounded like about a hundred dogs started barking, and then more and more lights came on, bathing the outside of the house in a bright-yellow glow.

Crouched next to the overturned cans, Evan watched as the front door flew open and a pack of baying, howling dogs streamed out into the dark. An old man in a red-and-blue plaid bathrobe, tufts of gray hair dancing wildly on his head, stalked out of the house, waving a double-barreled shotgun and screaming into the night, "Cock-sucking raccoons! Get 'em, girls!"

Evan grabbed the bike, quickly shoved it through the tangled hedge, and jumped onto the seat. Pain shot from his butt up his spine. Grunting and moaning as he peddled away, he heard the old man's shouts of encouragement to the wailing dogs, punctuated by the booming blasts of the shotgun.

The white stripe on the road's edge shimmered in and out of narcotic focus as Evan chased it with his front tire, wobbling along, ass throbbing, peddling with one leg. He heard the pack of dogs wheeling through the thick forest off to his right. At any moment, he expected the snarling beasts to break out of the woods and haul him down like a wounded deer.

Trying to avoid the police, he ditched the bike whenever a set of headlights appeared, diving for cover in the tall grass on the shoulder. Three times, the pack of dogs burst out of the forest only inches from his front wheel, sending him sprawling on the asphalt as they poured across the road in snarling pursuit of something small, dark, and very fast.

Finally, around two o'clock in the morning, Evan dragged the bike up to his van parked near the docks in Tranquility's harbor. He climbed into the back, chewed two more Percocet, choking them down dry, and curled up under some blankets to let the drugs do their thing.

"Darlene! Darlene! Darlene! Goddamn it, where are you?" Evan hollered as he dragged his dead left leg through the front doorway of Uncle Phil's house. No response. His aunt and uncle always left for the market by five thirty. But where could Darlene be at seven o'clock in the morning? Just when he needed her for something important, the flaky bitch disappeared. Typical. He limped into the kitchen and pulled a cold Bud from the refrigerator. Then shook another Percocet out of the little brown bottle and washed it down with beer. He tried to count the remaining pills, but his vision blurred, his concentration splintered.

He hobbled into the bathroom, stripping off his dirty, sodden waiter's shirt. His damp hair was matted and caked with mud; his skinned elbows were raw and bleeding. Both hands were a welted mass of cuts and scrapes. He unbuckled his belt, shoving down his pants. Turning his backside toward the mirror, he craned his neck to see an angry, purple furrow oozing pus and blood. Unbelievable. That Tyler fucker had shot him in the ass.

Evan was fumbling through the medicine cabinet for first aid supplies and more pain meds when he heard the front door bang. "Darlene? Darlene? That you?"

Darlene appeared in the bathroom's doorway. "Holy shit, Evan. What happened to your butt?"

"Fucker shot me. Get the alcohol and bandages."

"You need to go to the medical center."

"Ah, come on, Darlene. Give me a hand here. It ain't that bad. Bullet just grazed me, didn't even go all the way through. Just help me clean it up and slap a bandage on it."

Evan teetered against the sink, his underwear and black pants bunched around his ankles.

"No way, Evan. I don't want any part of what you've been up

to, sneaking around with Wade at all hours." Darlene backed away, shaking her head. "I just come to get my stuff."

"Stuff? What you talking about?" Evan shuffled out of the bathroom and followed her down the hall.

"You and me. We're through." Darlene was in the bedroom, throwing clothes into her bag.

"Because I got shot? That wasn't *my* fault." Evan couldn't understand why people were always blaming him for things he didn't do. Wasn't right.

"No, stupid."

"Because I didn't take you to eat lobster? You patch me up, we can go get lobster for lunch. I promise."

Darlene closed her bag. "I had lobster last night."

Evan noticed the unused bed. "Where the hell were you last night?"

Darlene's eyes cut to the front of the house.

Evan stumbled over to the window, parted the curtains. "That's Kent's truck. You and that retard? Did ya blow him?"

"He's not a retard. He's an artist, and he's gonna to be famous. And he's way nicer to me than you ever was."

Evan pointed at his ass. "Who do you think I've been doing all this for?"

Darlene picked up her bag and edged toward the doorway. "Plus he don't treat me like a damn vacuum cleaner."

Evan hopped forward. "I can do better. Promise."

"You always say that." Darlene inched back, clutching her bag.

"Come on, Darlene. I need you."

"I already wasted too much time on you. I don't know what I was thinking."

Evan lunged, grabbing for her. "Goddamn it, Darlene!" His feet tangled in his pants, and he lost his balance. Arms windmilling, he bounced off the edge of the bed and crashed down hard on his butt. "Agh, shit!"

"Serves you right." She turned toward the doorway.

Evan whined, "Don't do this. Ain't fair."

After Darlene left, Evan used four hunks of gauze and about three feet of white tape to patch up the bloody groove in his ass. He kept thinking about where Uncle Phil stashed his shotgun—just in case Wade needed a little extra convincing regarding the matter of who exactly owned the little painting. Finished with his butt, he pulled on a fresh pair of jeans, a clean Harley T-shirt, dry work boots, and his jean jacket. Then went looking for Phil's Remington.

He sucked on another cold Bud as he limped around the house, on the hunt for the big black shotgun good old Uncle Phil had shoved in his face the night he and Darlene arrived. The old fart was still cheesed about those hookers trying to buy a Cadillac with his Master Card. But family was family, and Evan had finally sweet-talked Phil into letting him and Darlene crash in the spare bedroom.

Now that he thought about it, maybe he was better off without Darlene. Despite her world-class blow jobs, she brought him down with her constant nagging. "Can we stay in a hotel? Can we swim in the ocean? Can we eat lobster?"

*Whiny bitch.*

*Let Kent deal with her.*

Evan jerked open the door to Phil's bedroom closet and spied the Remington propped in the corner. Finally. He grabbed the gun, working the slide to check the breech—empty. Nothing in the magazine. Maybe his uncle had been bluffing.

He pawed through Phil's dresser drawers and found three 12-gauge shells—number 8s, fucking grouse loads—which he slipped into the front pocket of his jacket.

# CHAPTER 21

W ade levered himself upright, squinting in the bright morning sunshine, his brain jackhammering against the inside of his skull. He leaned against a large rock and paused to catch his breath against the thudding pain, trying not to vomit. His beard was caked with damp sand, and his clothing was soaked, but the life jacket was keeping him warm.

He fingered one of the jacket's buckles and looked out over the glinting harbor.

*Life jacket? Why am I wearing a life jacket?*

*Where is my goddamn boat?*

When the answer finally came, he rolled forward with a groan, heaving his stomach contents onto the rocky beach with one huge, sour explosion.

Wade had run Jaws at dead low tide a thousand times. Always at full throttle. Why not? He knew these waters like the back of his hand. Fished them since he was tall enough to see over the bow.

But last night. *Last night. Shit.*

With no moon and a head full of vodka and Percocet, he had lined up a little too far to the right. Not much, maybe four or five feet at most. But that was all it took. Wade remembered the crunching sound of fiberglass on rock as Jaws gutted the *Sweet Tail* like a flounder. The boat lurched and bucked beneath his feet, broke free of the rocks, and then began taking on water. He hit the auxiliary bilge pump switch and paused to think, to sort out the situation.

But his brain was stuck in neutral. Bleak choices. Shitty options. Dumb ideas. *Pick one.* He could beach the fucker, but too many questions. It was only a half mile to his slip. Maybe the pump could keep it afloat long enough to work some kind of patch.

Wade aimed for the docks.

But the *Sweet Tail* only wanted to circle. He wrestled with the wheel, worked the throttle. No good; the rudder was bent. While he fumbled the controls, the boat rode lower and lower in the water, limping in smaller and smaller circles, until finally, the *Sweet Tail* just squatted in the harbor, spinning, gurgling, waiting to die.

Standing on the deck, water sloshing at his knees, Wade had pulled on a life jacket, took one final hit of Kettle, and swam for shore as the *Sweet Tail* slipped beneath the cold surface.

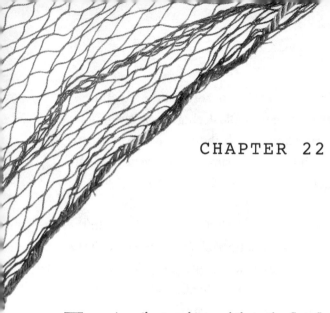

# CHAPTER 22

L ying silent and immobile in the flat, florescent medical center
light, her head wrapped in white gauze, Brooke looked pale
and weak. A nearby monitor beeped and clicked a depressing
vigil. Connor stood next to her bed, feeling anxious and panicky and
out of control, wondering what was happening, trying to remember
their last conversation, afraid he would never get the opportunity to
speak with his mother again.

Crystal stepped up beside him and placed her fingers lightly on his
arm. "I just spoke to the nurse. The doctor should be in any minute."

"I can't believe this. It's like a nightmare." Connor pinched the
bridge of his nose, squeezing the moisture from the corners of his eyes.
"One minute she's busting my stones over a stupid pile of fishing gear,
worried about her party, and the next minute she's . . . she's . . . here."

"Then hold her hand and talk to her, let her feel your presence."
Crystal reached in her bag and removed a small Buddha statue, which
she placed on the bedside table. Then she held up a ziplock containing
several small brown bottles. "Essential oils. They promote healing."

Connor watched as Crystal selected a bottle and placed a few
drops on Brooke's wrists, neck, and forehead. The room filled with
the aroma of lavender.

The doctor walked in, examining a chart. He wore a white lab
coat over green scrubs and had thick, shaggy blond hair and a surfer's
tan that looked out of place in springtime Maine. His nose twitched

as he smiled, extending his hand to Connor. "I'm Doctor Willis. You're Mrs. Nichols's son?"

"Connor. Thanks for speaking with us."

He turned to Crystal. "And you are?"

"Crystal. His first mate."

Dr. Willis nodded. "Lavender is good, but you might also try chamomile. If you have it."

"Good idea." Crystal quickly dug out a different bottle and went to work.

Dr. Willis glanced once more at his chart and then said to Connor, "Your mother has a severe concussion. There was some internal bleeding, but it appears to have stopped. She's stable and her vital signs are good. Now it's just a waiting game."

"What are we waiting for? What's keeping her from waking up?" Connor asked.

"Those are always the questions with a head trauma. The simple answer is that she's suffered a major shock and her body is healing, gaining strength, hopefully preparing to wake up."

Before Connor could ask another question, his cell phone rang. He slipped it out of his pocket and recognized his sister's area code. "Hey, Jo. I'm at the medical center . . . I don't — I'll have to ask the— Slow down and let me . . ."

Finally he offered the phone to Dr. Willis. "My sister's a doctor at Mount Sinai."

"I understand." Dr. Willis took the phone.

Connor listened to the one-sided conversation. It sounded similar to the one he had just had with Willis except for the addition medical jargon.

Finally, the doctor ended the call and handed the phone back to Connor. Dr. Willis said, "Your sister was called into an emergency, but she's on her way and should arrive sometime tonight."

"The state trooper mentioned something about transferring her to another medical center," Crystal said.

"It was an option when we were uncertain about the bleeding. But moving her is not without risk."

"Is there anything else we can do?" Connor asked.

"Medically?" Dr. Willis shrugged. "Nothing really. The best approach is to monitor her and wait." He paused and then winked at Crystal. "But never ignore the spiritual."

# CHAPTER 23

The individual parts and pieces of his grandpappy's .45 were organized on a clean towel. Tyler sipped his steaming coffee, placed the cup on the table, and then calmly went back to work while he replayed the events of last night in his mind. He was pretty sure he had winged the guy, but it was self-defense, so he didn't feel bad. Maybe a little bad. But if you invaded someone's home, you got what you deserved. Especially in Texas. And he had a feeling that the folks in Maine played by the same rules. The police might have an *issue* with the fact that Tyler shot him as he was running away, but he'd let the lawyers sort that out.

He ran an oiled swab through the barrel, held it up to the light, and frowned. "That ammo really fouls the bore. Ronald, there must be a gun shop around here somewhere. Get me a box of the full copper jackets."

Ronald looked up from his laptop. "Which ones?"

"The Winchester, 230 grain."

"Didn't they jam last time?"

"No. That was the Federal. Wouldn't feed worth a damn."

"I'm pretty sure it was the Winchester."

"I didn't know you were such an expert."

"Okay. You're the boss." Ronald's phone chirped; he studied the screen. "It's our legal guys." He pressed it to his ear, turning his back to Tyler as he listened and then spoke into the phone. "What do you mean, don't leave the state?"

Tyler spoke to Ronald's back. "Remind those idiots that I have a federal permit, that it was self-defense."

Ronald waved and nodded. "Did you hear that? Federal permit. Self-defense."

Suzanne was pacing on the other side of the suite, talking into her own cell. "Are you sure? When? Shit."

Suzanne broke the connection. "That was one of my little spies. Someone on the board got word of the *Sixty Minutes* piece and they want to move up the meeting."

"When?" Tyler asked.

"In two days. Thursday," Suzanne replied. "They plan on notifying you tomorrow."

"Ungrateful pricks. Especially that bozo Ernie. You'd think he'd have the balls to call me directly. Two days, huh? Plenty of time to get this deal done. Ronald, tell them I want Connor's contract today. This morning. And the check better be on the way. Also, tell them they've got until Wednesday to clear up this bullshit with the police. No excuses." Tyler squinted through the barrel. "Definitely need the full copper jackets."

Ronald pulled the phone from his ear and said to Tyler, "They want to know if you hit the guy. They're thinking we might need to call in criminal counsel."

"Well . . ."

Suzanne stopped pacing. "Come on, Tyler. This isn't the Wild West. Did you hit him or not?"

Tyler fidgeted with the barrel.

Ronald stared.

Suzanne tapped her foot.

"I think yes. But not the ten ring."

"He thinks yes," Ronald said into the phone.

"Gawd." Suzanne walked over to the window, parted the drapes, and looked out. "That's all we need. Headline: Cholesterol King Plugs

Fleeing Man's Artery. The media could be here any second. They'll have a field day."

"Did we send Brooke some flowers? I should go to the medical center and visit." Tyler fit the barrel into the frame and reached for the slide.

Suzanne said, "I'll handle the flowers. You've already done enough for that *poor woman*."

Her phone buzzed again.

"Yes." Suzanne's face went white. She stammered, "Uh, well, we're happy to, uh . . . But our research shows . . . We'll have an announcement shortly regarding a new— Yes, but— I see. Uh-huh. Let me get back to you. No, really, five minutes. I promise."

She faced Tyler. "That was Scott Pelly's producer."

Ronald barked into his phone, "Call you back."

Tyler snicked the slide in place. "Fuck."

Connor pulled the MG to the curb in front of the White Swan. He had used some ratty old bath towels from the garage to cover the blood-stained seats. The towels wouldn't fool his dad for a second, but they did give the antique a certain used-car-lot charm. He wiped his eyes and turned to Crystal. "I'll be right back."

He was halfway across the lobby before he realized she was right behind him. He stopped short, grabbed her arm, and steered her into the dining room. "I'm hungry. Order us some breakfast."

"I think I should stay with you. You're pretty upset."

"I'm not upset. I'm pissed. There's a big difference."

"I might not approve of Tyler's agenda, but he seems like a civil person, and I'm sure he'll gladly answer all your questions. But you need to calm down and find your center. You need to breathe."

"This shouldn't take long." Connor pulled out a chair. "And don't worry, I won't forget to breathe."

Upstairs, hearing a commotion inside, Connor pushed open the door to suite 210 and walked in. Tyler, Ronald, and Suzanne were crowded around the table, gesturing, waving, talking animatedly.

He cleared his throat to get their attention. "What's everyone arguing about?"

Tyler stood and smiled. "Just business. I'm glad you're here."

"We need to talk. In private."

"Certainly." Tyler pointed. "Bedroom?"

Connor followed, slamming the door behind them.

"I'm very sorry about Brooke." Tyler sat in an armchair. "I can see you're upset."

"What do you expect? My mom's in a coma." Connor perched on the end of the bed.

"What can I do to help?" Tyler asked.

"You can start by telling me what the hell happened last night."

"Uh, on advice of counsel, I'm not supposed to discuss the situation."

"You don't say."

"My lawyers are dealing with the local police. You know, setting the record straight regarding my involvement."

"Really."

"Yes. Meanwhile, I'd be happy to discuss your contract," Tyler offered.

"My contract?"

"It'll be ready this morning. We're very excited about this concept."

"You had mentioned an up-front payment." Connor paused. "But before we talk contract—"

"I'm certain you'll find the terms very generous." Tyler looked at his watch. "The check should arrive any minute."

"I'm thinking a new Ford F250." Connor said. "Now, about last night—"

"I favor the Suburban, being from Texas. However, the F250 is certainly nice."

"They're pretty pricey, especially when you throw in some extras—towing package, heavy-duty suspension, leather." Connor rocked forward. "Listen, I want to know—"

Tyler cut him off, again. "I think this partnership is going to be very fruitful for all parties."

Connor leaned in and poked Tyler's chest with a stiff finger. "There's not going to be a *partnership* if you don't answer my questions."

"Okay. Okay." Tyler nodded, held up his hands. "There's not much to tell. After the party, we all went to dinner. Then I gave your mother a ride home."

"Who was at the dinner?"

"Besides your mother and my staff, that artist, Kent something, his date, and the dealer."

"What happened at the house?"

"Your mother invited me in for a nightcap. Only a nightcap—nothing else. When she went to the bar to freshen her drink, she must have surprised the guy. He hit her with a large crystal bowl. I heard the noise and went to check. He threw the bowl at me and ran."

"The police said there was shooting."

Tyler nodded. "I touched off a couple."

"Did you hit him?" Connor asked.

"That seems to be the question of the day."

"Well?"

"I'm pretty sure I hit him, but he didn't die. At least, not in the backyard."

"Big guy, scraggly beard?"

Tyler shook his head. "No. Medium build. Long greasy hair. White shirt, black or dark-blue pants."

"Like a bartender or waiter?" Connor headed for the door.

Downstairs, Connor found Jeff Russell and Crystal sitting at a small table in the dining room. The stocky cameraman was smiling and laughing as Connor approached. "Mind if I join you?"

"I was afraid you were around here somewhere." Russell frowned and pointed to an empty chair. "Crystal told me about your mother. I hope she's going to be all right."

"Thanks," Connor replied. "Doctor says it's a waiting game."

"Police have any idea who did it?" Russell asked.

"Zero," Connor snorted. "I'll probably find him before they do."

"I think we should follow you around with the Steadicam," Russell said. "You know, for the human interest angle."

"Whatever. Just tell your guy to keep the camera out of my face." Connor grabbed for a coffee mug.

Crystal asked, "How did it go upstairs?"

"Tyler and I have an understanding. He was happy to fill in the blanks."

"Good. See how easy it is when you approach a difficult situation with a positive attitude."

Connor held his coffee mug as the waitress poured. He asked Russell, "Any word from the mother ship?"

"The rest of the crew arrives tomorrow. We'll have a big preproduction meeting, then we'll all get shit-faced and begin taping the next day with massive hangovers. What happened to your head?"

The waitress circled, delivering their breakfasts and filling coffee cups.

Connor scowled at his plate. "What's this?"

"Fresh fruit. Granola. Low fat yogurt," Crystal replied. "You know, a *healthy* breakfast."

Connor poked at the yogurt with his spoon. "Yuck."

"You're welcome."

Russell chuckled and dug into his ham and eggs. "I was wondering where your boat was."

"What do mean?" Connor waved, trying to get the waitress's attention.

"Yesterday afternoon I fired up the whole system and was running through the locations, looking for some good B-roll. Your wheelhouse and deck were both empty, so I panned out and saw what looked like a lawn party at some fancy house. Definitely not the docks at Tranquility."

"It was Brooke's party," Crystal said.

Russell stared. "*That's* your mother's house?"

"Your video system has that kind of range?" Connor asked.

"Even better than last year. We've got a taller receiving mast on the production van. And we got permission to park at the library, which is one of the highest points around here."

Connor grabbed Russell's plate and stood up.

"Hey, I'm eating that."

"Take it to go." He tossed the MG's keys to Crystal. "Don't strip the gears."

Thirty minutes later, Connor leaned over Russell's shoulder as the man positioned himself in front of the console in the production van. Russell flipped several switches, and the TV monitors and computers came to life. Next, he gave Connor a quick lesson on how the recording system worked.

"There's the list of all camera locations." Russell indicated a clipboard attached to the wall. "I knew that you came from money but didn't know you were rich."

"My family's rich. Not me. Big difference."

"What happened? They disown you?"

"Practically. Not much sympathy for the industrial arts. Especially my father."

"Dude, then why bother?" Russell scanned the location list.

"Every family needs a black sheep."

"If you say so." Russell's fingers flew over the keyboard. "Now I punch in the code for the location we want." He hit the enter key. "For example, here's the Tranquility Market."

They watched as Phil, his back to the camera, worked at the sandwich counter while talking over his shoulder to a customer. Russell hit the volume control, and Phil said, "Why don't you get the rest of your groceries and I'll have these lobstah rolls ready by the time you're done shopping."

When the customer moved off camera, Phil picked at a red scab on his neck, examined his finger, and wiped it on his apron before going back to work on the sandwich.

"That disgusting son of a bitch!" Connor wailed.

"Gross, huh? You don't know the half of it. That's why he can't get our catering order," Russell replied, tapping the keyboard. "Let's try the *Nu B.*"

The image jumped to the outside deck of the *Nu B*. Two men in greasy overalls leaned into the engine hatch, tools and engine parts spread out on the deck.

"Those are the boatyard mechanics. They finally showed up to fix the fire damage," Connor said.

"Fire damage?"

"Long story. I need to find Baxter. Can you locate the *Sweet Tail*?"

"Find Baxter?"

"I'm looking for a friend of his."

"Wade Baxter has friends?" Russell checked the list and typed. "So, what's the deal with Crystal?"

"There is no *deal*. As soon as her sailboat's fixed, she's moving on."

"Nothing going on between you two? For real?"

"Nada."

"Well then, think she'd be interested in a short, stocky assistant producer?"

"Not with your diet."

Russell frowned at the monitor. "That's weird. No signal from camera number one." He reentered the code and toggled a switch for the second camera on Wade's boat. "Huh. That one's dead, too."

Connor inspected the master list. "It says here, 'Baxter-Truck.'"

"Yeah, the asshole let us mount a unit on his dashboard. Talk about a DWI waiting to happen." Russell entered the code for Wade's truck.

The monitor showed an image of weeds, rusted boat parts, rotting scrap wood, and the corner of a gray-shingled house.

"Looks like it's parked in a junkyard," Russell said.

Connor studied the screen. "No, that's his house."

Every time this Evan guy popped up, there was trouble, and according to Phil, Evan and Wade were longtime running mates with a pretty sketchy track record. Connor wasn't sure how it was all connected, except for a nagging suspicion that his troubles in Tranquility had spilled over onto his mom. Screwing with someone for hauling traps was one thing. Connor was a big boy, could take care of himself. But putting a guy's mother in a coma crossed the line. Big time.

When Connor knocked, Wade's front door slowly swung inward on creaky hinges. He found the man sitting in the kitchen, shoulders slumped, cradling his head in his hands, staring down at the table. A mug of black coffee sat untouched. An old, faded life jacket lay on the floor.

Wade fixed Connor with a bloodshot stare. "The fuck you want?"

Connor took a seat on the opposite side of the table. "Someone broke into my family's house last night. Put my mother in the medical center in a coma. You wouldn't know anything about that, would you?"

"I ain't no burglar."

"They got away in a boat. Where's the *Sweet Tail*?"

"Asshole swiped it."

"You mean like a pirate?"

"Ayuh, a pirate."

"With an eye patch, peg leg, maybe a hook?" Connor leaned forward on his elbows. "You expect me to believe that crock?"

"Check the docks."

Russell had given Connor a ride from the production van down to the harbor to retrieve the Land Cruiser. Curious about the dead cameras, they had checked Wade's slip—empty. But Connor couldn't imagine Wade Baxter loaning the *Sweet Tail* to anyone for any reason.

"Who? Your bartender friend?" Connor asked.

"That'd be Evan, all right. But he's no friend of mine."

"Not according to Phil."

"Long time ago. He's nothin' but trouble. Been trying to ditch him since he came back to town." Wade wrapped a shaky hand around the coffee mug.

"You know where I can find him? We need to get a few things straightened out."

"Don't know. Don't care."

"I'm sensing a real lack of enthusiasm for this conversation. I hope we don't have to continue it in the front yard."

Wade massaged his jaw. "That didn't work out so well for you last time either. Or your pretty little toy car."

"I don't know about you, Wade, but I think our relationship is in real trouble. We may have to call it quits." Connor stood.

Wade leaned back in his chair, threw up his hands. "You and me, that's just between us. No one else."

Connor grabbed the life jacket off the floor, examined it, dropped it on the table. "If I find out you had anything to do with what happened to my mother, nothing's going to keep your head above water."

Back at his family's house in Camden, Connor walked onto the patio to find Crystal and his sister, Joanna, both down on all fours on yoga mats. His sister, taller than Crystal, had their father's coloring:

blond hair, dark-green eyes, light complexion. As they lowered to the mats, extending their arms, he silently watched, wondering about the incongruity of Joanna—a hard-charging, type-A, cardiothoracic surgeon—doing downward dog with a former yoga mogul.

When Joanna spotted Connor, she jumped to her feet and threw her arms around his waist. "Little brother." She stood on tiptoes, kissed his cheek, and frowned. "Yuck. Forget to shave?"

Connor ran a hand over the blue-black stubble. "It's good to see you too, Jo."

"I guess that look's okay for a rugged TV star, but I'm not sure how it will play in the restaurant business," Joanna said.

"You heard, huh?" Connor cut a frustrated glance at Crystal, who refused to make eye contact as she picked up the mats. He tried to change the subject. "How'd you get here so quickly? It's at least nine hours by car or two flights and then a two-hour drive from Portland. Is that your rental out front?"

"The head of gastroenterology bought a new airplane, and he's always looking for an excuse to fly it. We landed at the little airport outside town."

"Must be good money in that end of the business. Maybe you picked the wrong specialty."

"Doctors and planes. Thought I was going to pee my pants." She shuddered. "Never again. But at least I've already made it over to see mother."

Crystal called over her shoulder as she carried the mats into the house, "I'll make tea while you two talk."

"How is she? Anything new?" Connor asked.

Joanna replied, "She's stable. Vital signs are strong. So we wait. Not much else we can do."

"What about that hippie doctor? What's his name? Willis?" Connor asked. "Should we consider moving her to Portland or Mass General?"

"Willis is from Mass General. He's a fellow in their neuro program. He was on a rotation in Portland and drove up for a consult.

I checked him out; he's a top guy, and he feels we should leave her in the medical center for now."

"I'm glad you're here. You're the only one Dad will trust to make medical decisions."

"As much as he trusts anyone." Joanna gestured toward the house. "I can't believe you've hooked up with Crystal. She's awesome."

"Pardon me?"

"You've never heard of Crystal Yoga? They must have at least a dozen studios in the city. I try to go at least once a week. I even managed to take one of her advanced classes. Better than sex."

"We're not *hooked up*." Connor took Joanna's arm. "And don't get used to her; she's not sticking around.

"Too bad. She would be perfect for you. Just what you need."

"*Your* opinion."

"No, seriously. Perfect," Joanna insisted.

"Great."

As they walked inside the house, arm in arm, Joanna stopped in the living room. "The only thing that seems to be missing is the Wyeth." She pointed at an overturned table. "Mom kept it over there on the wall above that little maple side table. But I'm sure father has a big, fat insurance policy."

"When are you going back to visit Mom?" Connor asked.

"I left a bunch of cases hanging in New York. So I've got to make some calls, check in with my staff. Then maybe head over around lunchtime. You'll come too?"

Connor turned the table upright. "I don't know what good I would do."

"Well, neuro is not my specialty, but I have read some research that indicates coma patients have more awareness of visitors than we previously thought."

"Mom's not too happy with me. Even more than usual."

"You big lug. What did you do this time?" Joanna patted his cheek.

"She's ragging on the lifestyle issue again."

"So what? Ignore her."

"Easier said than done, and *you* know it."

"True. I guess Daniel and I never questioned. But *you*. You bailed on the whole program."

"I never planned to ditch their agenda, but it wasn't right for me. It felt like I was wearing a straitjacket. I'm almost thirty-five. I wish she and Dad would let it go already."

"Forget Dad. We're only talking Mom here. In her own way, she admires you for walking. But it also makes her jealous. Especially as she gets older."

"That would explain a lot," Crystal said as she handed Joanna a mug of tea. "Which is why you two need to talk."

"Says you." Connor frowned.

"Crystal's right. You should listen to her." Joanna paused to sip her tea.

"When did you two become such good friends?" Connor asked.

Joanna continued, "Plus, the longer you take to figure things out, the more concerned Mom becomes."

"Okay. I've had a few stumbles, but I'm on the right track now."

"Lobster fishing or that silly TV show?" Joanna teased.

"All of the above." Connor grinned and placed both hands on her shoulders. "*And* the TV show is creating some opportunities with significant upside."

"*Now* you sound like Dad. But lobster restaurants?"

"Not just restaurants. *Casual dining* restaurants. Second only to fast food in terms of contributing to obesity," Crystal added.

"I'm looking at a lot of money. Big bucks. They're not talking about one lobster shack stuck out on Route 1, but a chain, like hundreds or even thousands. Edwin will be pleased." Connor shrugged. "I even get a new truck."

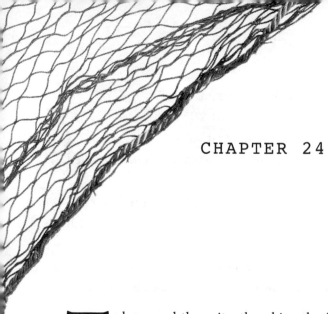

## CHAPTER 24

T yler paced the suite, thumbing the fresh Winchesters into the .45's clip. He clicked the last round into place and said, "We need to get control of this situation before the board overreacts and does something stupid."

"What's the deal with you and Connor?" Suzanne asked. "He seemed pretty upset."

"You guys were making a lot of noise." Ronald grinned. "Did you and Connor get a little rough?"

"Connor and I have an understanding." Tyler jabbed a finger at Ronald. "*You* concentrate on getting me a final copy of his contract. If I don't have it within the hour, things are going to get rough, all right." He turned toward Suzanne. "What did Pelly's producer want?"

"They're moving up the special on obesity. Going to run it this Sunday. Scott wants to include an interview with you, get your side of the story."

"Fair and balanced, huh?" Tyler grimaced. "When does he want to do the interview?"

"His producer said Thursday."

"Hmm. Same day the board wants to meet."

"What are you thinking?" Suzanne glanced down at her phone, quickly tapping an email.

"Not sure. But this could be a great opportunity for us," Tyler said.

Suzanne's head snapped up; she stared. "You're not actually

planning to give Scott Pelly an interview, are you? That would be suicide."

"It's an interesting idea. Meet with the board, tell them about the deal with Connor, and then use the interview to announce it to the public. Turn the tables on *Sixty Minutes.*"

Suzanne froze in place. "Tyler, listen to me very carefully. They have final edit. It doesn't matter how charming you are or what you have to say. You could announce a new promotion to give away a free puppy with every meal, and his producer can still make you look like Jeffrey Dahmer."

"But Thursday's too tight."

"Oh, gawd!" Suzanne waved at Ronald. "Help me out here."

"She's right, Tyler, bad idea. Very bad idea. Scott Pelly might look like a hair-jelled cream puff, but believe me, you don't get to where he is without kicking some serious butt."

"Okay, here's what we're going to do. Tell them I've agreed to the interview . . ."

Suzanne crumpled onto the sofa.

". . . but I'm not available until Friday morning. If they try to schedule it sooner, just make up the usual bullshit—travel, board meetings, corporate obligations. Tell them I'm looking forward to it, anxious to tell my side of the story. I'll even come to New York, do it face-to-face, make it easy." Tyler slapped the full magazine into the .45, racked the slide, set the safety, and nestled the big, silvery gun into his shoulder holster.

"I thought you weren't supposed to leave the state until Legal deals with the police?" Suzanne asked.

"Everything's worked out." Tyler waved a dismissive hand. "Let the pilots know."

Suzanne launched off the sofa and made a hard line for the bar. She poured a straight shot of Booker's and threw it back in one swallow. Eyes watering, she turned on Tyler. "You're completely off the deep end. You do this and the stock price goes right into the tank.

I only have one more year until my options vest."

"You have options?" Ronald's head snapped up from his laptop.

Tyler pulled on his suit coat and gently placed an arm around Suzanne's shoulders. "I thought you had more faith in me."

Suzanne dabbed at her mascara with the heel of her hand. "Huh? What do you mean?"

Tyler handed her his handkerchief. "I have no intention of giving Scott Pelly or anyone else an interview."

"Really?" Suzanne asked.

"Of course not. The more we protest, the more they smell blood in the water. Tell them we'll do the interview, and they back off. Leave us alone. That gives me time to put this deal together and get the board to buy in. Once I've got the board back under control, everything else is just static. We call a press conference, on our schedule, and announce our great new healthy dining initiative— Captain Connor Lobster Shacks."

"But what about his show on obesity?"

Tyler shrugged. "News flash, most Americans *are* fat. There's nothing we can do about that *or* Pelly's show. We've had negative press in the past. The *Sixty Minutes* piece will run this Sunday, and one week later no one will remember it."

Suzanne answered a knock on the door, opening it to a short, round, balding man of about fifty, wearing a stained butcher's apron. "May I help you?"

"I'm Phil Pratt," the man replied and held out a bulging white lunch bag. "I make the best lobstah rolls in Maine."

Suzanne stood back and looked him up and down. "Ah, the deli guy from *Lobster Wars*."

Phil walked into the suite. "And don't forget first selectman."

"We're a little busy. What can we do for you, Mr. Pratt?" Tyler asked.

"I heard you might be looking for someone who knows a thing or two about seafood." Phil offered the bag. "You try one of these and you'll see what I mean."

"This is like an open casting call for a bad Broadway play," Ronald said without looking up from his laptop. He held out his hand. "But I *am* hungry."

Phil dug into the bag and placed a wrapped lobster roll in Ronald's hand, then looked hopefully at Tyler. "Try one?"

"Mr. Pratt. Phil? I'm sure your lobster rolls are delicious. And if you're looking for a cook's position, Ronald will put you in contact with our HR department," Tyler said.

"Cook?" Phil winced. "I'm one of the stars of *Lobster Wars*, and people come from all over to eat my food. You put *my* face on your new restaurants, and you'll make millions. Millions."

"I appreciate your pride in your culinary skills, but we're interested in someone who's a little more . . ." Tyler looked at Suzanne. "How do I say this?"

"Camera ready," she offered.

"Exactly." Tyler gently steered Phil toward the door. "And, Mr. Pratt, we think in *billions*."

Not five minutes later, Suzanne answered another knock on the suite's door and signed for a Fed Ex envelope, opened it, and stared. "It's bank check for fifty thousand but no payee."

"Excellent, right on time." Tyler plucked the check from Suzanne's fingers and slipped it into the inside breast pocket of his suit coat.

"Who's it for, and why is only the amount filled in?"

"It's Connor's advance against licensing fees." Tyler buttoned his suit coat.

"Then why didn't you have the bank fill in Connor's name? That's like walking around with cash. Isn't a wire transfer simpler and safer?"

"Negotiating tactic. Wire transfers are abstract. Contracts are abstract." Tyler patted his breast pocket. "But big-ass checks are real. Watching someone write your name on a big-ass check is *very* motivating."

Wade was having a completely fucked-up dream, more like a nightmare. He was drifting out to sea on a homemade wooden raft, swept away on the outgoing midnight tide. At least he could see what was happening because his hands and feet had turned into flaming torches. Which was interesting and somewhat helpful. But burned like hell. Despite his best efforts, he was completely unable to douse the flames by dunking his fiery limbs in the cool ocean water.

"Wade? Wade? Wade, are you in there?"

Wade tried to roll away from the tapping on his forehead and the annoying sound and concentrate on putting out the fire.

"Wade? Wade? Come on, sleepyhead, time to wake up and tell your matey where you hid the *Sweet Tail*."

Wade again attempted to shrink away from the sound. Evan's voice. Which didn't make sense because he had tossed Evan overboard last night and Evan drowned. But the voice wouldn't go away. And he couldn't move. His arms and legs continued to burn. And his head pounded. So he decided to open his eyes.

"Ah, there you are." Evan's sweat-slicked face loomed over him. He held an empty bottle of Ambien. "Have a nice nap? How many of these little suckers you take?"

Right after that asshole college boy had left, Wade gobbled four of Alice's sleeping pills and staggered off to bed. Now as his eyes finally focused, he tilted his head up to realize with a sickening premonition that he wasn't in his bed and was instead lying on top of the heavy wooden workbench in Kent's welding shed. Not exactly lying, more like pinned. No, not really pinned. Wired. Yeah, wired, his arms and legs pinched in place by four tightly twisted strands of baling wire.

Wade squirmed against the wire cutting into his flesh. "The fuck?"

"Oh, sorry, matey. Let me give you a hand." Evan reached out and twisted the wire holding Wade's right arm.

Wade arched his back and bucked against the slicing pain. "Goddamn! Motherfucker!"

"Oops. Sorry. Let me try again."

"Agh, shit!" Wade thrashed against the bench.

"That still hurts?" Evan paused. "Oh, yeah, it's righty tighty, lefty loosey. Never could keep them straight." He leaned back on a shop stool, draining a can of Bud. "I'd offer you a beer, but that was the last one. I'm going to make a booze run right after we finish. Can I get you anything?" Evan tossed the empty and rolled the stool over to a red metal toolbox. He rummaged through the drawers and pulled out a large pair of metal shears.

"Cut me lose," Wade demanded.

Evan inspected them under the shop's harsh fluorescent light. "Now, there's an idea."

"The fuck you want?" Wade croaked.

"What do you think I want? I want that fuckin' painting. Gonna meet my fence and cash out. And I was even going to cut you in. But now you don't get squat because you tried to drown my ass, which was very rude considering that restaurant guy had shot me and all." Evan rolled over on the stool and rapped the cold metal cutters on Wade's forehead. "So, when I go down to the harbor, looking for the *Sweet Tail*, no boat. Which means no stolen art. Which means you hid it. Which means you need to tell me where it's at. And quick. Matey."

"Boat's gone."

"I know the boat's gone, Wade. That's why I wired your fat ass to the workbench. Which wasn't easy. You need to think about Weight Watchers." Evan fumbled open a pill bottle, shaking one directly into his mouth. He popped a fresh beer and washed it down. "Guess I was wrong on the beer count. But that's definitely the last one." He leaned his elbows on the workbench, his dilated, red-rimmed eyes inches from Wade's face, gesturing with the shears, clacking their blades with each word. "Where. Is. The. Fucking. Boat?"

"Told you, boat's gone."

"Gone. Like how gone? Explain gone."

"It sunk."

"Bullshit."

"Ayuh."

"You expect me to believe that? You love that boat more than your own dick." Evan waved the shears. "Which I just might have to remove, you don't tell me where it's at."

"Missed the cut at low tide. Jaws sunk it right in the mouth of the harbor."

"Oh, Wade, Wade, Wade. You think I'm a retard? You been running that cut since you were fresh out of diapers. The *one* night I score big-time, you tell me you fucked up and sunk the *Sweet Tail*." Evan swiveled around on the shop stool, surveying the shed. He tossed the metal shears on the floor, slid off the stool, and limped over to the corner.

The small shed filled with the sound of metal grating on concrete as Evan pulled and dragged something very heavy.

"What're you doing over there?" Wade struggled against the wire, trying to keep Evan in sight. "Ah, come on, Evan. I wouldn't lie to you about my boat. I sunk her, honest."

"Just be a second," Evan grunted. "I don't understand why your stupid brother doesn't have this on a dolly. Much easier."

"Listen, we can still make out. I'll get another boat." Wade was getting desperate. "Hell, the TV people will probably buy me a new one, they find out what happened. You'll be my sternman."

"Oh, *now* you want a sternman."

"We'll share everything fifty-fifty."

"Fifty-fifty, huh? I thought you told me the show don't pay spit."

"Uh, it don't. But if that Nichols asshole can get a deal, why not us? We just need to come up with something. I bet loads of companies are looking for guys like us."

"Guys like us? You know who comes lookin' for guys like us?

Cops, parole officers, process servers, fuckin' bookies. That's who comes lookin' for guys like us." Evan stopped and scrubbed at the tears leaking down his face. "Not some big-time business dickhead lookin' to make us rich. That's a fuckin' fantasy."

"Yeah, but . . . but . . ." Wade sputtered. Evan was losing it.

"What you gonna do? Cut some deal with Budweiser, suck down their beer on TV, get rich and buy a big house on the water in Camden? Not. Going. To. Happen." Evan finally finished dragging Kent's acetylene torch over to the workbench. "I got to get out of here. I mean, I did smack Nichols's mommy on the head. Might even of killed her, the way she went down. Not to mention violating parole down in good old Arizona. That shit has a way of sticking."

"Ayuh, but—"

Evan put on a welder's helmet, leaving the mask up. "I think it's better we make a clean break. You tell me where you hid the *Sweet Tail*. I get my painting and split."

"Ayuh, but I told you."

"Yeah, yeah, yeah. You sunk it." Evan flicked the striker, and the acetylene torch lit with a dull *whoosh*. Turning the oxygen knob on the handle, he adjusted the fat red flame to a hissing, pinpoint blue. He drained the beer and gave a sharp nod, and the dark welder's mask clunked down to cover his face. Evan hunched over Wade's right foot, his voice muffled. "We'll get this sorted out right quick, matey."

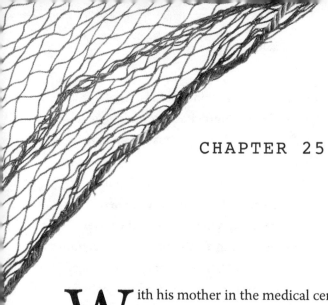

# CHAPTER 25

With his mother in the medical center and his boat stuck in Camden, awaiting repairs, Connor drove the Land Cruiser back to Tranquility. First, he stopped at the market, where Phil told him that Evan's van was gone from the driveway and the scumbag had cleared out of the spare room. Too bad because Connor wouldn't mind getting his hands on the little weasel before the police found him. But he suspected that he hadn't seen the last of Wade's pirate friend.

Next, he drove to his trailer to check his mail and grab some fresh clothes, figuring he would sleep at the family house until things settled down or until his dad arrived and took over. He sat at the table in his small kitchen, sorting the mail, separating bills and past-due notices from junk, taking an occasional peek inside a promising fan letter. One young lady, not much for prose, had managed some pretty persuasive photos. Not bad considering she was holding the camera with one hand. He was carefully slipping them into the shoebox for future reference when his phone beeped.

He checked the display. Tyler.

Connor hit the connect icon. "Nichols here."

"Connor, it's Tyler. I have your contract. I'd like to meet as soon as possible. Where are you?"

"At my place in Tranquility, but I'm leaving for Camden in a few minutes, so if you're at the Swan, we can meet there."

"Excellent. I'll get us a quiet table in the restaurant. We can have bite to eat and go over the documents. You'll be pleased."

"See you in about forty-five minutes." Connor broke the connection.

They were seated in the Swan's small private dining room. Alice, the familiar face from dinner, was clearing plates and refilling coffee cups. Connor fanned the pages of the thick contract and then placed it neatly on the table next to the remnants of his lunch. Even with Brooke's focus on art and culture, money and business deals had always been the number one topic of conversation in the Nichols house. Interested or not, you learned by osmosis. Tyler's offer would definitely put his lobster fishing business on an even keel. Plus some. But he kept thinking about Crystal's warning.

"I guess it looks pretty straightforward."

Tyler sat directly across the table, smiling, offering a black-and-gold fountain pen. "It's a very basic agreement. Very basic." He pulled a check from his pocket and placed it on the table with a flourish. "Plus, once the contract is finalized, I can fill in your name."

Despite the word *repo* echoing in his head, Connor squinted, poked at the check with a finger, and almost without thinking said, "Guess I'll have to pass on the leather interior for the Ford."

Tyler blanched. "That's only the advance against licensing fees. You know, a good-faith payment. Something to show how excited we are about working with you and how very committed we are to this endeavor."

"Connor, that's a lot of money," Suzanne added.

"Don't think I don't appreciate it. Advances and royalties are good, but I was hoping for a deal with more of what you guys call *upside*. After all, you're going to own my identity."

"Uh, what were you thinking exactly?" Tyler asked, screwing the cap onto his pen.

Suzanne tapped her watch and arched an eyebrow at Tyler. "Don't forget the board meeting."

"I didn't see anything in there about options." Connor leaned back in his chair, lacing his fingers across his chest. He couldn't help himself; between his dealings with the bank and now Tyler, he felt like a dormant gene had kicked in. "Options would be nice."

"Options?" Tyler looked confused.

"I'm sure you've heard of them," Connor started to explain. "Stock options are a form of—"

Tyler waved a hand. "Of course I know what options are. I just didn't think—"

"I would know enough to ask?" Connor asked.

"Well, no, it's not that." Tyler paused.

"Why don't you take some time to think it over. I'm not in a hurry." Connor smiled. Tyler's offer was more than enough to square his note with the bank and catch up on his bills and expenses, with plenty left over for a big fat down payment on a very slick new truck. But a deal that included stock options was in a whole different league. "I've got to check on my boat, and then I'm going to the medical center. You can call my cell when you decide."

Tyler frowned. "I guess we *could* discuss some options."

"Excellent. Then it's settled." Connor stuck out his right hand. "I'll let you come up with a number. I'm sure you'll be fair."

"Uh, sure. Of course. Why not?" Tyler shook hands as he worked his smile back into place.

"Great, options for everyone." Ronald frowned.

"Ronald, tell Legal I'm going to call in a few minutes with revisions and then . . ." Tyler turned to Connor.

Connor shrugged. "Send it to my lawyer?"

On the way to Camden, Connor had called Skadden, Arps, the law firm that represented his father's company. His father liked to brag that they were one of the largest and most aggressive corporate law firms in the world, and after a few minutes chatting with the senior partner who represented his dad, the man was only too happy to add a few more billable hours to Edwin's account. Connor would settle with his dad later.

He waved a small slip of paper with the senior partner's name and contact information. "This guy is expecting to hear from you."

Tyler plucked the page from Connor's fingers and handed it to Ronald. "Legal can email the revised contract. Make an appointment for later today, and we can get this wrapped up."

Grumbling quietly, Ronald pulled out his phone and looked at the paper. "Tyler, this is a New York number."

"New York?" Tyler looked at Connor.

"They do a lot of work for my dad's business. I hear they're pretty good. And he said he would get on it right away." Connor sipped his coffee. "I've got to get back to the medical center."

"Well, yes, of course, your mother is the priority. And there's no reason we can't deal with a lawyer in New York, especially if he's ready to get to work."

Tyler paced the suite, fuming. "I can't believe he didn't sign the contract. The big-ass check never fails."

"At least he has a lawyer ready to review the changes," Suzanne said.

"Yeah. Skadden, Arps. Shit. Now we're negotiating. Once those jackals get involved, everything slows down. This could take days, weeks even. We may have to come up with a different approach." Tyler flopped into a chair and stared out the window.

"Does Connor really matter?" Ronald asked.

"What do you mean?" Tyler pulled his attention away from the window.

"Isn't one famous lobsterman just as good as another? I mean, for our purposes."

"Oh no, Ronald," Suzanne sighed. "Are you crazy? I can work miracles. But Baxter?"

"He did have a high Q-score," Tyler said, thoughtfully. "But I don't want to deal with another Rowdy Robby. We'd have to keep him on a short leash."

"He's big-time negative with our target market," Suzanne argued. "He's about as appetizing as salmonella."

"So get your team here ASAP—stylists, makeup, whatever you think you need. Then call our ad agency. I want them to storyboard a simple concept ad we can show the directors. But it needs to be slick so those pinheads will buy it. You might try to find a local production crew." Tyler turned to Ronald. "And find some people who can, you know, *handle* him."

Suzanne continued to protest, "I know *how* to make him over, but not *what* to make him into."

"Lovable lobsterman, loudmouth fisherman, whatever. I'm sure you'll think of something. Just stay on point with our positioning."

Suzanne frowned. "I don't know . . ."

"I thought you liked a challenge?"

"I do, but—"

"If it was easy, anyone could do your job." Tyler stared at Suzanne. "Well, uh . . ."

"My point exactly." Tyler grabbed a copy of the contract and spent several minutes scribbling furiously in the margins before handing it to Ronald. "Run those changes by legal and get me a new version, then figure out where we can find Baxter. We pull this off and you may have earned yourself some options."

Connor was pretty pleased with himself. Tyler's deal was going to put some real money in his pocket. One of the perks of reality TV stardom. *The Nichols family black sheep finally gets with the*

*program*. How could Edwin argue with that?

His main concern now was Brooke. But he couldn't spend every minute at the medical center, watching his mom sleep. Just like he couldn't spend every minute sorting out Wade and Evan. He would deal with them on the go.

The sun was high in a clear sky with a slight onshore breeze, a perfect day to be on the water. A few guys were already setting traps, looking to jump-start the season. Exactly what Connor wanted to do, needed to do. However, until Kent, wedged inside the greasy engine compartment, installed a new fuel pump, the *Nu B* was going nowhere.

"How soon?" Connor asked the back of Kent's head.

"Couple more hours. I get this last line run, you should be able to take it out for a trial this afternoon or first thing tomorrow," Kent replied.

"Any idea where I can find your friend Evan?"

Kent stopped working and straightened, wiping his greasy hands on a shop rag. "Evan's no friend of mine. Ask Wade."

"I did. But your brother seems a little fuzzy on certain details."

"He was staying with Phil and Irene," Kent offered.

"Phil claims the guy cleared out."

Kent pointed at the wheelhouse. "Ask Darlene. She might know."

Connor watched as Crystal and a plain-faced brunette with a lazy eye and a spectacular rack emerged from the forward cabin. "Darlene, huh?"

"She *was* Evan's girlfriend, but she's with me now," Kent said with more than a trace of pride.

"Good for you."

Darlene smiled up at Connor. "Wow, you're even taller in person."

"Editing trick," Connor said, trying to gauge exactly where she was looking.

"Sorry about your mom. I hope she comes out of it soon."

"Thanks," Connor replied. "Any idea where I can find Evan?"

Darlene shook her head. "Nah, he's a loser. I cleared out my stuff.

He wasn't looking so good last time I saw him. Maybe he went back to Arizona. I hope."

"Did he mention anything about what happened here? About my mom?

"No. But the day of Kent's party, he was eyeing the place, really checking it out. So I wouldn't be surprised if it was him."

"You were here?" Connor asked.

"Yeah." Darlene nodded. "The manager at the White Swan hired both of us to work the party."

"If you run into him, tell him we need to have a chat," Connor said, trying to maintain eye contact despite the distraction of her chest.

"Okay, but I hope I never see him again." Darlene looped her arm around Crystal. "It was very nice of your mom to host that party for Kent. He sold a lot of art. Not fair she ends up in the medical center."

Connor looked at Kent. "You sold a lot of pieces, huh?"

"Yeah. It was kind of a big deal for me. Some of the pieces I sold went for over four grand. I really owe your mom. She didn't have to do it." Kent waved at the house. "People like your mom don't usually help people like me."

Connor thought about Brooke's comment that she was only throwing the party to appease Sylvia Meyers. But Brooke had a keen eye for new artists, so he suspected there was more to her agenda. "Don't sell yourself short. If your work wasn't any good, believe me, she never would have given you a second thought. So, now I've got a famous artist working on my boat."

"Shit, I wish." Kent grinned.

Crystal said, "Darlene and I were talking, and it turns out she's had some jobs that require serious people skills, so I suggested that she help manage the business side of Kent's career so he can focus on his work."

"Crystal knows a lot more about business stuff than I do. But I'm going to try. Might even take some classes at the community college," Darlene said.

"I think art buyers would really respond to her," Crystal replied.

"She's got a way with people," Kent added, obviously pleased with his new manager and her appealing assets.

"I'm sure she does." Connor's attention was pulled away by the sight of Trooper Mack making his way across the yard, toward the water.

"I'm looking for Kent Baxter," Trooper Mack called from the floating dock. "The boatyard said I could find him here."

"What's Kent have to do with my mother?" Connor demanded.

Trooper Mack stroked his mustache with a knuckle. "I have no idea what you're talking about."

Connor shot back, "Why am I not surprised?"

"Where were you this morning?" Trooper Mack asked.

"Negotiating. Doing deals. Seeing my people," Connor replied.

"Witnesses?"

"Several. Why?"

Kent climbed out of the engine hatch and walked over to the rail. "I'm Kent Baxter. What can I do for you?"

Trooper Mack consulted a small notepad. "You have a brother named Wade?"

"Yeah."

"Your brother was injured. He's been admitted to the medical center in town, and he gave them your name."

Darlene stepped up to Kent, putting a hand on his arm. "Is he going to be okay?"

"He's not going to die, if that's what you want to know. You are?" Trooper Mack asked.

"Darlene."

"She's my girlfriend," Kent replied. "Mind telling us what's going on?"

"The situation is unclear. That's why I wanted to speak with you. Your brother's injuries are not consistent with an accident, but they're definitely not self-inflicted. And he refuses to answer any questions." Trooper Mack stared at Connor while he addressed Kent. "Any idea who might want to hurt him?"

Connor snorted. "You did meet him, right?"

"Not enough to put him in the medical center," Kent offered.

"Can you tell us how was he injured?" Crystal asked.

Trooper Mack turned to Connor. "You and Wade Baxter aren't exactly buddies. If I recall, you even seem to think he might have had something to do with your truck catching fire. Indulge in a little payback?"

"You told me not to take matters into my own hands. Besides, I'm a pacifist." Connor threw up the peace symbol. "Remember?"

"Some people don't follow that advice. You seem like one of them." Trooper Mack turned to Kent. "Here's the odd part. Your brother has third-degree burns on the big toe of his right foot. Nowhere else. Very concentrated and deliberate."

"Did someone light him on fire?" Crystal gasped.

"No, those injuries would be general and widespread. This was something very hot and concentrated. Like a road flare or blow torch." Trooper Mack paused. "It appears he was tortured."

After the trooper left, Kent packed up his tools and headed to the medical center, promising to return later to finish installing the fuel pump. But Connor had his doubts as he stared into his engine compartment, inspecting the progress.

So, the *Nu B* was stuck at his parents' dock for another night.

Crystal walked up and handed him a steaming mug. "Poor Wade."

"Poor Wade? He set fire to my boat." Connor kicked the engine cowling in frustration. "Goddamn Kent."

"You can't blame him for wanting to go visit his brother. I know you don't like the guy, but who would want to torture him?"

"Did you forget he almost drowned you?" Connor tasted the tea and dumped the mug overboard.

"I've forgiven him. I have to. Holding on to such negative emotions is very toxic."

"Well, *someone's* holding on to some pretty negative emotions. I bet it's that toxic little shit Evan. He's disappeared. Probably in Canada by now."

"It would be much healthier for you, and everyone around you, if you *just let it go*—"

"Maybe I don't want to just let it go," Connor grumbled. Crystal's equanimity toward the situation was starting to piss him off. What was wrong with nurturing a little self-righteous anger?

"Plus, I thought Officer Mack told you to stay out of this?" Crystal replied evenly.

"He did." Connor let out a frustrated breath, glanced at his watch, and climbed onto the dock. "I have to go visit my mother."

"Good idea. She needs you."

"You can stay here, get your stuff organized, pack up your little Buddha. When I get back, I'll give you a ride to the boatyard." With Crystal back on her voyage, Connor could handle his battles without distraction. His way.

"Whatever you say," Crystal replied, following him onto the dock.

"Maybe I can find Kent at the medical center and talk him into finishing today." Connor headed toward the back of the house.

Crystal trailed closely on his heels. "It'll give you another chance to stare at Darlene's boobs."

## CHAPTER 26

**W**ade leaned back against the stiff medical center pillow, sipping ice water through one of those curvy straws the nurse had given him right after she finished checking his dressing. The morphine drip was doing a first-class number on the pain and made him feel pretty damn good about things in general.

His right toe looked like a lump of charcoal. But at least Evan had not used the metal shears on Wade's dick like he had threatened. All in all, it could have been a lot worse. Like the time he almost lost three fingers, getting them caught in the hauler trying to clear a jammed line.

But he was still going to have to kill Evan for good.

Wade was sipping the last of the ice water, distracted by thoughts of grinding Evan into chum, and was surprised when Tyler Lane and his two flunkies from the White Swan—the business girl with the nice legs and the snotty little homo—appeared in the doorway.

Tyler flashed a bright smile. "Mr. Baxter. Mind if I come in? We heard about your accident, and I have something to discuss with you that might make you feel much better."

Ten minutes later, Wade stared at the contract in his hands, trying to concentrate and process his amazing luck. He couldn't believe it. *No way.* "What happened to Nichols?"

"Let's just say that we've re-evaluated the situation. Given the current environment, driven by certain market forces and additional influences, we now find that our goals and objectives align nicely with the concept of *you* as our spokesperson," Tyler replied.

"Huh?"

"You're now our first choice," Ronald said.

"*We* want *you*," Suzanne added. "But with a few changes."

"There are two copies, one for each of us. I've already signed both on behalf of the corporation." Tyler offered his pen. "If you'll just sign on the last page of each, right above your printed name, we've got a deal. Ronald here's a notary, so we're covered."

Wade grabbed the pen and eagerly scrawled his name. "Uh, what's next?"

"We're going to give you a slight makeover. Nothing drastic. You know, smooth off some of the rough edges," Suzanne replied.

"Honey, you can make me over into anything you want." Wade tried to wink.

"Good." Suzanne smiled. "Then we're going to shoot some footage for a concept ad."

"Uh, what's that?" Wade asked.

"Like a TV commercial," Suzanne replied. "Something we can show our board of directors and then use at a press conference."

Wade asked, "Here in the medical center?"

"No." Tyler snapped his fingers. "There's one place that perfectly characterizes this new venture. One place that leverages all the positive qualities we're trying to communicate. One place that says everything anyone needs to know about Captain Wade Lobster Shacks." He pointed at Wade. "The deck of a working lobster boat. *Your* lobster boat."

# CHAPTER 27

Evan's welding session with Wade had convinced him the asshole was telling the truth. The dumb shit had sunk the *Sweet Tail* along with the little painting from Nichols's mommy's house.

Unsure of what to do next, he headed for the White Swan. After all, that Tyler guy had shot him. Maybe he could figure an angle for a little payback, make up for the lost artwork. Not to mention the pus-filled ditch in his ass. No way Evan was coming up empty handed after driving all the way across the country. He had to make some money and get clear of this fucked-up place. Quick.

Evan watched Tyler and his little gang climb the front steps of the White Swan Inn. He had followed them from the Swan to the medical center, and then back to the inn. The guy sure was busy and never far enough from his people to give Evan an opening. Plus he probably still had that goddamn bazooka strapped under his arm.

Evan adjusted his sore butt cheek in the seat, crunched the last bitter Percocet, and washed it down with a fresh Bud, wishing he had a quart of Stoli. He was thinking about how to get on top of this Tyler guy when he spotted Alice, dressed in her waitress uniform, smoking a cigarette and pacing on the sidewalk next to the inn.

He put the van in gear and rolled over, winding down the window. "Hey, Alice. You expecting someone?"

"I just worked a double shift, and that lazy good-for-nothing Wade was supposed to give me a ride home. Haven't heard from him, can't find Kent, and no one's answering the damn phone up to the house."

"I'll give you a ride."

"You got anything in there stronger than beer?" Alice flicked the cigarette into the bushes.

# CHAPTER 28

Connor leaned against the foot of the bed, watching Crystal administer Reiki to his mother, her hands hovering inches above Brooke's head. If it weren't for a little problem called a coma, he could almost swear the new-age voodoo was working. Brooke looked peaceful, like she was taking a short, well-deserved nap. But gazing at her inert form only reinforced the guilty feeling that this was his fault.

Dr. Willis moved to the bedside and checked Brooke's vital signs, Joanna at his elbow. "Everything looks okay. The intracranial swelling has completely subsided, so there's no reason she shouldn't regain consciousness. In fact, I'm a little perplexed as to why she hasn't."

Crystal paused. "She's fighting it. Almost like she doesn't want to wake up."

"That's not like mom. She's too stubborn to quit," Connor said with a hollow ache in his chest.

"I know it looks bad, but at least she's stable." Joanna placed a hand on Connor's shoulder and asked Dr. Willis, "Move her to Mass General?"

"If she was deteriorating physically, or having complications, I'd say yes. Given her current status, let's wait another twenty-four hours before making a decision."

Joanna's cell chirped; she checked the screen. "It's Dad." She swiped the screen. "Hi, Dad. You got my email? We're at the medical

center right now. No, no changes. Still stable, but no improvements
. . . I don't agree with that. Yes, I am a doctor— Your choice, but I
think you're making a big mistake."

Joanna ended the call.

"He's not coming, is he?" Connor asked.

She shook her head, fighting tears. "Selfish."

"His middle name." Connor put an arm around his sister's
shoulders. "Probably said that since you're here, there's nothing he
could do. So why fly halfway around the world?"

Joanna nodded. "Yup. Exactly."

"Wow, that's cold," Crystal said.

Willis closed the chart. "They need me back in Portland
tomorrow. So if she's showing no significant improvement by
morning, I suggest arranging a medical flight and transferring her
down to Boston. I've already alerted my boss, the head of Neuro.
We're much better equipped to look after her there."

"Why don't we take a break?" Connor said. "Maybe get some
lunch and talk through the options."

"Good idea. I've seen family members drive themselves crazy
waiting in hospital rooms all day. Is the White Swan open for lunch?"
Joanna asked.

"Yes. You and Crystal head over in the rental, and I'll follow in
few minutes." Connor headed for the door. "There's someone here I
need to see before he flatlines."

**CONNOR STEPS INTO** the hospital hallway, looks
right and left, stares directly into the camera.
"I figured you guys would show up here sooner or
later. Two rules. Stay out of my way and stay
out of my mother's room."

The Steadicam follows Connor as he heads off
down the hall, corners Kent. "I need to get the
*Nu B* out of Camden as soon as possible."

Kent glances into the camera, looks away. "I'm headed over there right now. Two hours to finish. You can run her this afternoon."

"No excuses." Connor turns, steps through a doorway, stops at the foot of a bed. "Sorry, the flower shop was closed. But I'll remember to bring a bouquet tomorrow. Tulips or pansies?"

Wade lies in bed, slurps chocolate pudding from a small plastic cup, a dreamy expression stuck on his fat face, pauses, wipes a glob of pudding from his beard. "The fuck you want?"

"Still looking for your pirate buddy."

Wade spoons pudding into his mouth. "Told you. Evan's no friend of mine."

"He the one that put you in here?"

"Jesus, what are you, a cop?" Wade cuts a look at the camera.

"I thought you might be ready to give up the little snot." Connor moves to the side of the bed. "I'm going to find him one way or the other."

"Good luck then." Wade licks his fingers.

"Don't worry, I'm not going to hurt him."

"Like I give a shit."

Connor scoops up a document lying next to Wade's lunch tray. "What the hell? What is this? A contract?"

Wade grins and opens a second pudding. "What's it look like, college boy?"

Connor fans through the contract, quickly goes to the signature page. "I can't believe that asshole double-crossed me!"

"I was the right man for the job all along." Wade grins at the camera. "It just took them a bit to figure it out, is all."

"I'm sure working for Tyler will be much better than fishing lobster. A lot easier and way more money. Especially since your pirate buddy swiped your boat."

"My boat?"

"I wouldn't be so quick to cash that check." Connor slams the contract down on the table and turns for the door.

Wade chokes on the pudding. "Boat? Check?"

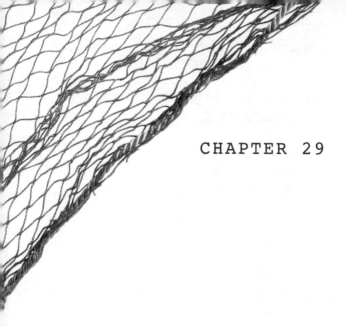

# CHAPTER 29

N ichols's visit jolted Wade's morphine-soaked brain. He didn't want to explain what happened to the *Sweet Tail*, especially to Tyler, so he needed to get his hands on a lobster boat and fast. And what was this shit about a check? Tyler didn't give him a check.

It took almost two hours to get released from the medical center because they insisted on fitting him with a toeless plastic-and-foam bootie so he could walk. Halfway to the lobby, he ducked into the bathroom and used his pocketknife to slice the toe off his old leather work boot, ditching the plastic gizmo in the trash can. At least the doc had written a script for OxyContin that he filled at the medical center's pharmacy.

On the way back to Tranquility, driving with one hand, he fumbled open the pill vial and gulped a double dose. Now the little narcotic bastards were beginning to work their gauzy, faraway magic.

Wade turned into his driveway and, son of a bitch, there was Evan's van. Un-fucking-believable. He slid out of his truck and hopped over, peering in the back—empty. Then he looked in the driver's window and spotted a big black shotgun lying on the floor between the seats. Wade reached in the through the open window and wrapped his hand around the gun. With the TV people arriving and the deal with Tyler in place, there was no way he was going to . . . well, there was no way he was going to . . . *Ah, fuck it*. He had to kill Evan first.

Wade shuffled into the kitchen and pointed the shotgun's muzzle directly at Evan's face and said, "Motherfucker."

Evan and Alice were seated at the table, Evan right in the middle of filling two glasses with Stoli. He smiled at Wade. "Hey, matey."

Alice whined, "I waited an hour for you at the inn."

Wade pulled the trigger.

*Click.*

No booming sound followed by the satisfying sight of Evan's brains splattered across the kitchen cabinets.

"If you got that out of my truck, it ain't loaded." Evan squeezed a lemon slice into Alice's glass.

Wade racked the slide, pulled the trigger.

*Click.*

Evan reached into his pocket and produced three shells, holding them for Wade to see. "I mean not loaded. Like, at all."

"Why don't you stop playing with that gun and join us for a drink?" Alice tipped the glass to her lips.

Evan stood, pulling a vacant chair away from the table. "Yeah. You don't look so good. You need to—"

Wade jammed the shotgun's muzzle into Evan's stomach. "Motherfucker."

"Ahhhhh!" Evan folded in half, dropping hard into his chair. "My ass! Shit!"

"Blow your ass to hell if that fucker had a been loaded." Wade leaned the Remington against the counter, sat in the empty chair, and picked up Evan's drink.

Evan gulped air and worked himself upright. "Okay, okay, I guess I had that coming."

"We're not close to even."

"Well, shit, Wade, you did try to drown me. What'd you expect?"

"I expected you to drown."

"You two grow up." Alice grabbed another glass off the counter and filled it with Stoli, handing it to Evan. "I've got some information for you."

Alice explained about the contract and fifty-thousand-dollar bank check Tyler had waved in front of Nichols.

"How do you learn this shit?" Evan asked.

"Told you before, I'm waitin' tables and cleanin' rooms. Nobody pays attention to the help. You wouldn't believe the shit I see and hear," Alice replied.

Evan gulped some Stoli. "So, if Tyler didn't give the check to Nichols, he must still have it."

"Ayuh. Like Alice said," Wade mumbled, staring down at his drink. Tyler sure didn't offer him any up-front money. Probably thought he could get a guy like Wade for cheap.

"That's like walkin' around with fuckin' cash," Evan said.

"Ayuh, but what can you do about it?"

"Cash," Evan repeated.

"I'm gonna lay down, get me some sleep." When Wade rocked forward, about to stand, the folded contract in his back pocket caught on the chairback and flipped onto the floor.

Before Wade could grab it, Evan snatched it from the floor. "What we got here?"

"Nothin'." Wade held out his hand.

Evan fanned the pages. "Don't look like nothin' to me."

"Looks just like the contract Tyler was showing to Nichols," Alice barked.

She and Evan stared at the contract and then at Wade.

"The bastard didn't give me no check."

Evan picked up Alice's cigarette lighter and flicked it, staring at Wade over the blue flame. "You sure?"

"Fuck you," Wade sputtered. "I'd fuckin' know if someone gave me a fuckin' check for fifty thousand fuckin' dollars. He didn't."

"Why, you think?" Evan asked.

"I don't know how this shit works. Guess he thought he could get me to sign the contract without no money."

Alice laughed, slopping vodka on the table. "Looks like he was right."

"So, he's still got the check?" Evan refilled her glass. "Wonder why he didn't give it to Wade."

"Rich guys don't get rich giving people money for no reason," Alice cackled.

Tyler's check would go a long way to solving his boat problem. Maybe he could go visit the guy and ask. But Wade could see a plan forming in Evan's mind, and he wanted no part of it. He grabbed the contract from Evan and headed for his room. "Forget it. No way. No fuckin' way."

"Ah, come on, matey," Evan called after him. "I'll even drive this time."

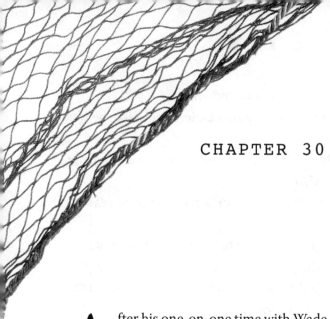

CHAPTER 30

After his one-on-one time with Wade, Connor was no closer to getting his hands on Evan, but at least now he knew where he stood with Tyler—so much for stock options and a cushy leather interior. Tyler hadn't even made a counteroffer. Just blew him off for Wade. He had heard of similar dealings from his father. In fact, duplicity seemed like standard behavior in the business world. Connor preferred enemies that were easily identified—like the guy cutting your lines or putting rocks in your traps.

He arrived from the medical center and found the two women in the White Swan's dining room. They were leaning close, shoulders touching, all big smiles and hushed whispers as he walked over to the table. "You know, maritime law gives the captain absolute power over the entire crew."

"I don't think that applies to the dining room of the White Swan," Crystal replied.

Joanna giggled, "My little brother thinks he's Captain Ahab."

He pulled out a chair and sat down. "I just saw Jeff Russell in the lobby; he's going to join us for lunch."

"Who's that?" Joanna asked.

"Assistant producer or something for the TV show. You'll like him. Nice guy," Connor replied.

"He's sweet, for a TV person," Crystal added.

"I don't get it, Connor. A reality TV show doesn't make sense to me. Especially the way we were raised."

"Reality TV shouldn't make sense to anyone." Crystal neatly arranged the napkin in her lap.

"I consider it more of a documentary. It's an opportunity to memorialize the lobster fishing industry and its importance to the livelihood and prosperity of a small town." Connor tried to look sincere. "It's really a slice of classic Americana."

"Was he always this thick? Or is it a recent condition?" Crystal asked Joanna, then to Connor. "You *can* walk away."

"I've got too much time and money invested," Connor replied.

"I think Crystal meant the TV show, not lobster fishing. Why bother with the show? Isn't it just a distraction?"

With Tyler's deal in the tank, Joanna's question hit home. And with Brooke in the medical center, Connor was beginning to feel like everything was falling apart. But he wanted to take one more run at Tyler before making any decisions. "It's all connected."

"You're saying they can't do the show without you?" Joanna asked.

"There is no show without Connor." Russell walked up and smiled at Joanna. "*Hello.*"

"Jeff Russell, meet my sister, Joanna Nichols—*Dr.* Joanna Nichols."

Russell grinned and shook Joanna's hand. "Wow, it's nice to finally meet a beautiful woman who's not in love with Connor."

"But I am in love with Connor," Joanna teased. "Which is why I'm wondering about his participation in your TV show. Aren't there enough people in the entire town of Tranquility? Why do you need Connor?"

"I bet you don't watch much reality TV."

"I'm a cardiothoracic surgeon at Mount Sinai. I spend my days up to my elbows in bloody chest cavities. That's enough reality for me."

"Interesting visual," Russell said. "Might be an idea there. You live in New York, huh?"

"Joanna's right," Crystal said. "If you've got the entire town and all the other lobstermen, what do you need Connor for?"

Russell paused briefly before ticking off the points on his fingers. "Good versus evil. Winners versus losers. Nichols versus Baxter."

"It's not about lobster fishing?" Crystal asked.

"The lobster fishing is only a metaphor," Russell laughed. "Because truthfully, no one gives a crap how many they catch."

"It's a classic formula for a drama," Connor added. "One character you love to hate versus one character you hate to love."

"So, you actually *did* attend some classes at Bowdoin," Joanna observed.

"But your brother's wrong on one important point." When he had their attention, Russell eased back in his chair, crossing his arms over his chest. "Handsome. Hunky. Heroic. The viewers love to love Connor."

Connor's face flushed red.

Joanna rolled her eyes. "I've noticed nurses sure do."

Evan angled his putty-brown van up to the service entrance of the White Swan. No amount of pleading, begging, or threatening would convince Wade to help him, so he was on his own. At least he had the shotgun, a handful of Wade's OxyContin, and a vague idea of the layout. He gobbled the pills and then grabbed the Remington, shoving three shells into the magazine. Just in case.

He used Alice's master key to unlock the outer door of suite 210, and then, leading with the barrel of the Remington, Evan tracked voices into the main room. Tyler and his crew were gathered around a table covered with papers, having some kind of meeting where everyone talked at the same time. Nobody even looked up. He followed the action, finally clearing his throat.

They kept talking, shuffling papers, and working.

"Yo, hey . . . over here."

The dark-haired girl finally glanced his way, her eyes going wide, then put a hand on her boss's shoulder. "Uh . . . Tyler."

"Yes." Tyler looked up from his document, turned toward Evan, and recoiled at the sight of the shotgun.

Evan blinked and tucked a hank of greasy hair behind his ear, trying to keep his head straight and focus on the mission. He leveled the shotgun. "I came to make a withdrawal. Where's that check you've been waving around?"

"You're the lowlife punk that put Brooke Nichols in the medical center," Tyler replied.

Evan spotted the big shiny gun, nestled in its shoulder harness, hanging from the back of a chair on the other side of the room. "Yeah. You shot me in the ass. So we're even."

"How do you figure?

"Well, uh, uh . . . I figure fifty K makes us even. Now, where's that check?"

"What check?" Tyler asked.

Evan waved the Remington. "I want that check. Now."

"Check? Why do you keep asking about a check? I have no—"

Evan impatiently racked the slide. "You were saying something? I can't hear you. Talk into the big black hole."

As Connor jogged up the stairs to the second floor, he realized there was a big difference between grubbing enough cash for a new truck and demanding options. He may have overplayed his hand with Tyler. Time to work on his negotiating skills.

Connor pushed through the unlocked door and followed the voices. He was not all that surprised to see Suzanne and Ronald, but he was surprised to see Evan Pratt twitching and sweating and pointing a nasty black shotgun.

Connor stopped in the doorway and said to Tyler, "I was hoping we could discuss our deal. But I can see you're busy, so I'll come back later."

Evan swung the shotgun. "Nah, you stay put till we get our business done."

"That thing loaded?" Connor hated guns, had seen too many nasty accidents in logging camp, especially when booze and drugs were involved. Right now, Evan twitched like a junky trying to ride a unicycle.

"Goddamn right it's loaded. Now shut up." Evan turned to Tyler. "Where's that check? Don't ask me again which check."

"I'm sorry, you're going to have to be more specific."

Evan shifted his weight and grimaced. "Didn't I say not to—"

"Tyler, I think he means the check you were going to give me," Connor offered. "You know, for our deal. Which I was thinking—"

"Yeah, yeah, yeah. The check you were going to give this guy."

"Oh, *that* check," Tyler replied.

"Uh-huh. *That* check, smart-ass."

Tyler pointed and began to stand. "It's in my briefcase on the table in the corner."

"No. You stay there and let Nichols get it."

Connor walked over to Tyler's briefcase, opened the lid, and pawed through its contents. He spotted a big handgun hanging from a chair but didn't want to stand there searching for the safety, trying to make the thing work while Evan blasted away with the shotgun. He shook his head. "Can't find it."

Tyler said, "Bring me the briefcase."

Connor carried the briefcase over to Tyler. "I was thinking we could table the idea of options for now. You know, until we're past the start-up phase."

"Temporarily forgoing options would make things easier." Tyler pulled the check from the briefcase, handed it to Connor. "Here it is."

"Okay. Give it over." Evan impatiently held out his hand.

"Then maybe we should get the lawyers together." Connor

extended his arm, waving the check at Evan. "Here."

"Bring it to me, damn it." Evan had backed over to the window, glancing outside, looking down at the street.

Keeping a very close eye on the shotgun's jittery muzzle, Connor tamped down his fear and offered the check. "Come and get it, asshole."

"Fuck you. Bring it here." Evan motioned with the shotgun, his eyes flicking back to the window.

Connor slowly walked over, arm outstretched, the check pinched between his thumb and forefinger. "Here you go, dickweed."

"Yeah, who's the dickweed now, asshole. I just made me fifty K." Evan reached out to grab the check, his dilated pupils fixed on the slip of paper.

Connor opened his fingers, and the check fluttered to the floor, landing at Evan's feet. "Oops, sorry. I'll get it."

Before Evan could react, Connor dropped below the gun and, lunging forward, wrapped his thick arms around Evan's legs, right behind his knees. In one quick motion, he exploded upward, tossing Evan through the window. Evan's yelp could barely be heard over the sound of shattering glass and snapping wood.

Connor leaned out of the broken window in time to see Evan land on the sloped roof of the inn's first-floor porch, roll six feet down the steep pitch, pinball onto the roof of a tan van, denting it, then ricochet off, slamming onto the hard street. "Ouch. That's gotta hurt."

Tyler snatched up the shotgun, joining Connor at the window.

The two men watched while Evan stumbled to his feet and dove into the van.

"Little guy's hard to kill," Connor said. "So, about getting the lawyers together—"

"Maybe this will help." Tyler threw the Remington to his shoulder. As the van cut a quick U-turn and began to speed off, tires squealing, he peppered the driver's side with three quick shots.

Connor bent and plucked the check from the floor, handing it to Tyler. "The lawyers?"

Tyler was inspecting one of the spent shotgun shells that had landed on the windowsill. "Number 8s, light loads, hardly do any damage at this range. Too bad."

Ears ringing, an aftershock of adrenaline flooding his body, Connor lurched down the staircase on rubbery legs and spotted Crystal waiting for him in the lobby. Which made sense since he had asked her to accompany his sister back to the medical center. He vaguely believed that most women occasionally visited opposite land, but Crystal seemed like a permanent resident.

He grabbed her arm, partially for support, and ushered her toward the lobby door. "Time to go back to the medical center."

"I heard shooting. Did you hear shooting? It sounded like a war upstairs." She looked down at his hand on her arm. "Your hand is shaking."

"I had an unscheduled meeting with Evan Pratt." Connor quickly guided her down the front steps in the direction of the Land Cruiser parked by the sidewalk.

"The guy that hurt your mother? Did you kill him? It sounded like you killed him," Crystal asked as she slid into the passenger seat.

"Nobody killed anybody."

"What about the shooting?"

"Tyler did all the shooting. If anyone asks, I was with you the entire time."

"But that's not true."

"Then tell them the truth. You didn't see anything." It took three tries to fit the key into the ignition, but Connor finally clicked the engine to life and pulled away from the curb just as a state police cruiser, lights flashing, rolled up to the White Swan. In the rearview mirror, he could make out Trooper Mack fitting his Smokey the Bear hat in place as he climbed out of his vehicle.

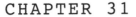

# CHAPTER 31

Connor paced at the foot of the bed, watching Crystal dab essential oils on his mother's wrists. Brooke's room had the syrupy look of a Hallmark store dipped in a flower shop. Since she had shown no improvement, Joanna and Dr. Willis were finalizing plans to transfer her to Mass General in the morning.

"Connor, please explain why your first mate is dripping that cloying oil on my hands," Brooke said in a dry whisper.

Dr. Willis looked up from his chart. "Ah, Mrs. Nichols, you're awake. Excellent."

"Of course I'm awake. Why wouldn't I be?"

Joanna dashed over to Brooke's bedside, cradling her mother's hand. "Mother. We've all been so worried."

"Joanna, what are you doing here? Why am I in the medical center?" Brooke looked around. "All these flowers. Who died?"

Connor answered from the foot of the bed. "You walked in on someone robbing the house and he hit you on the head. You don't remember?

"No."

"But you remember Crystal?"

"Welcome back." Crystal smiled and waved.

"How long have I been here?" Brooke asked, her voice gaining strength.

"Less than twenty-four hours. It all happened the night of Kent's showing," Connor answered.

Brooke closed her eyes. "Ah, that pleasant Mr. Lane."

Dr. Willis checked Brooke's vital signs. He addressed his comments to Joanna. "Everything looks okay. A little selective memory loss is not unusual. The mind tends to repress the specific traumatic event. We'll run some tests, but everything should come back over time."

Brooke tugged on Dr. Willis's sleeve. "Young man, please address your comments to me."

Dr. Willis smiled down at Brooke. "We were planning to transfer you to Mass General. But given this turn of events, I think you're better off staying here, close to your family."

"Very well." Brooke addressed Connor and Joanna. "I assume you've been in touch with your father and apprised him of the situation?"

Joanna replied vaguely, "We've spoken several times."

"I see. When will he be arriving?"

Connor caught Joanna's eye, cleared his throat to speak.

"Let me guess." Brooke cut to the quick. "He's not coming."

"Well, uh. Dad thought—" Connor stalled.

"I understand." Brooke reached for Connor's hand. "He's very busy."

While Brooke slept, Connor slumped in the guest chair, struggling to keep his eyes open, drifting on the ebbing tide of stress. Crystal and Joanna had taken the rented Camry out to the Shaw's on Route 1 to stock up on groceries. Then Joanna was going to drop Crystal at the boatyard, and everyone was going to meet later at the house for a little celebration in honor of Brooke regaining consciousness. With a poorly concealed wink at Crystal, his sister had even mentioned inviting Jeff Russell, just to keep the male–female ratio balanced.

Brooke stirred, and Connor rocked forward in the chair. "Can I get you anything?"

"Some water, please."

Connor filled a cup and steadied Brooke's hand while she sipped. "I'm sorry Dad's not coming."

"It's not your fault. Stop making excuses. Everyone's always making excuses for him."

"Including you?" Connor instantly regretted the question.

"I was wondering when one of you would finally work up the nerve to ask." Brooke paused for another sip of water.

"I'm sorry. That was insensitive. Maybe we should save this conversation for when you're back on your feet."

"No. Now is good. This family always puts off the difficult discussions. I'd never expect that question from your brother or even your sister. You're right, of course. I've made excuses for years." She sagged against the pillows with a formless smile. "You're too young to remember, but it was all very different at first. *He* was very different."

"And then things changed," Connor prompted.

"I was an angry poet with a political agenda. Practically a socialist. Your father was a brilliant engineer with an idea. And don't forget handsome. But when an idea becomes a plan and the plan works, it can be very seductive." Brooke gave a dry laugh. "Do you know how much a poet earns? Even a successful one?"

"Less than a lumberjack?"

"Hah, less than a lobsterman." Brooke winked. "Especially one who stars on a reality TV show."

"But does it always have to be about the money? The judging? The measuring? Keeping score?" Connor asked.

"At first you think, *No. That's not me. It won't affect me.* But it has a way of sneaking up on you, catching you by surprise, compromising you. One minute, your passion is ideas and concepts. The next, you've got responsibilities, obligations, children and you're worried about things, possessions . . . *assets.* "

"But you aren't angry anymore?" Connor asked.

"Oh, I'm still angry, all right." Brooke paused. "But for all the wrong reasons."

"Should I feel sorry for you?"

"God, no, Connor. Coming from you, that borders on pity."

"Sometimes I wonder about my agenda," Connor admitted. Even with Brooke regaining consciousness, he still had that tearing-at-the-seams feeling.

"What became of those 'various opportunities' you were entertaining?" Brooke asked.

Connor grinned. "My plans seem to have run aground."

"I'm certain things will work out. I know you'll find this hard to believe, but you're the one I worry about least." Brooke touched the side of her head. "Besides, I'm afraid I'm out of the advice business."

# CHAPTER 32

G roggy from his nap, Wade wandered into the kitchen to
find Kent and Darlene eating lunch. It smelled like takeout
from the market. His toe ached from the torch burns, his
jaw still throbbed from Nichols's punch, and a residue of booze and
narcotics echoed in his head. But Tyler's contract was safely tucked
away in his room, so life was pretty damn good. He pulled a cold
Busch from the fridge and sat down.

Kent glanced up. "You look like shit."

"Thanks." Wade gulped beer.

"Want some meat loaf? Mashed potatoes? Gravy? We've got
extra." Darlene went for a plate and silverware.

Wade gently probed his tender jaw with his fingertips. "Ayuh,
put it in a blender."

Kent said to Darlene, "After lunch, we got to load those pieces
and get them to the gallery."

"Let's not take all of them. Hold back a couple." Darlene fixed a
plate of meat loaf and mashed potatoes in front of Wade. "It seems
these rich art folks like to believe they're getting something no one
else can have."

"If you think so."

Darlene nodded. "Pick the best two and leave them here for now."

Kent speared a piece of meat loaf and dredged it through the
gravy before popping into his mouth. "Mom said you cut a deal with

Tyler. Congratulations."

Wade thought his brother looked happy. Maybe it was Darlene.

"But tomorrow Tyler wants to film some kind of TV commercial on the *Sweet Tail*." Wade grabbed the fork, tried a small bite of mashed potatoes.

"So?"

"A minor problem with the boat."

Kent wiped his mouth with a paper napkin and pushed back from the table. "I'll get my tools."

"Don't forget your scuba tank," Wade laughed bleakly. When Kent shot him a look, Wade decided to come clean. Not completely clean; he skipped the part about helping Evan rip off Nichols's mother. "Sank her the other night trying to run Jaws in the dark."

"You're shittin' me." Kent stared at Wade. "I don't even want to know what you were doing."

"I bet it had something to do with Evan." Darlene carried Kent's plate over to the counter for seconds.

"Ayuh. Worse than when we was kids," Wade replied. "If I don't get my hands on a boat, I'll have to make up some excuse, and Tyler don't seem like the kind of guy who likes excuses. He seems like the kind of guy who gets his way. I could lose everything."

"Can't you borrow one?" Darlene asked.

"Are you kidding? No one will loan Wade a boat," Kent snorted and slapped the table.

"But what can he do?" Darlene leaned against the counter, crossed her arms over her chest.

"There're two used ones sitting in the yard. One's in pretty good shape. Could probably have it in the water with half a day's work," Kent replied.

"I got no money to buy a boat. Not even a down payment," Wade said. "I got no credit at the yard. You know that."

"Maybe we can help." Darlene placed a hand on Kent's shoulder.

"We?" Wade asked.

"Turns out Tyler's a well-known collector of conceptual sculpture, and after he bought those pieces, word got out, and there's a lot of interest. The gallery's even getting calls from people in other countries. Darlene's going to be my agent." Kent smiled. "She's got a way with people."

Wade eyed Darlene's yummy rack. "I'll bet she does. But how much money we talking about?"

"The yard's asking one-eighty for the better boat. I think we can get 'em down a little, maybe one-seventy-five. And I'm sure they'll take twenty-five K for a deposit if I sign for the rest."

"Who runs the boatyard?" Darlene asked.

"Crotchety old bastard, tighter than a cat's ass," Kent replied.

Darlene smiled at Kent. "Let me handle it."

"You say so." Kent shrugged, picked up his fork.

Wade couldn't believe what he was hearing. Kent throwing around numbers like a fucking banker. How much did Tyler pay? How much did Kent think Darlene could move? There had to be more to this art business than deep-dish cleavage.

"You'd do that for me?" Wade was almost afraid to ask.

"Shit. You was the one loaned me the money for welding school." Kent pointed. "Pass the ketchup."

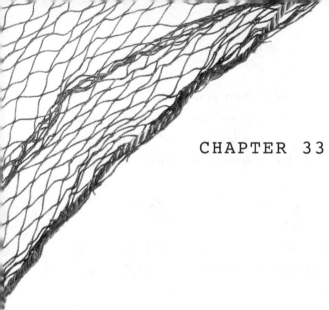

# CHAPTER 33

Tyler dropped the sheet of paper onto the table. "The TV spot looks good. After it's finished, we can add it to my presentation for the board. What did Legal say?"

"Same as last time." Ronald shrugged, plucked the page off the table, and fed it into a small shredder. "Let them do all the talking."

"I don't understand why that state trooper was so angry. The guy tried to rob me in broad daylight. He walks into *my* suite with a goddamn shotgun, right when *I'm* in the middle of an important meeting, and the cop made it sound like it was my fault." Tyler had to raise his voice to be heard over the high-pitched whine of an electric saw as the carpenters labored to repair the broken bedroom window.

"I think he was a little put out over you firing off three shots in the center of downtown Camden," Ronald replied.

"Then he should do his job and find the guy before someone else gets hurt. At least I got a good look at him this time." Tyler turned to Suzanne as she walked into the suite. "What's the latest?"

"Pelly's people have called six times to confirm for Friday. When you blow them off, they're going to have a fit. I have no idea what they'll do. But there will be repercussions. I promise."

Tyler stood. "Can't be helped. You'll come up with something. What about the board meeting?"

"It's scheduled for 2 PM on Thursday."

Tyler straightened his tie in the mirror over the fireplace. "Captain

Baxter Lobster Shacks. That's the big idea the board's looking for. Plus, a new chain of healthy-alternative restaurants will blunt any negative publicity from the *Sixty Minutes* piece. Or at least give us some leverage with damage control. We may take a short-term hit on the stock price, but if profits stay up, the price'll bounce back. Where do things stand with the production?"

"Ready to roll. Only I can't find our star."

Tyler grimaced. "The medical center?"

"Released."

"His house?"

"No answer," Suzanne replied.

"The docks?"

"We checked. One of the other lobstermen said he hasn't seen Baxter's boat. So he must be out on it. After all, he is a lobsterman. I'm sure he'll turn up."

"Good point. Both of you go down to the docks and wait for him. Babysit him until we get a couple of handlers in place. I don't want another Rowdy Robby on my hands." Tyler consulted his watch as he slipped into his suit coat and headed for the door.

Ronald looked up from his laptop. "Where will we be able to find you?"

"I'm pretty shaken up by the whole incident. I'm going for a massage."

# CHAPTER 34

**THE STEADICAM PARALLELS** Connor as he moves quickly down the hospital hallway, toward the lobby. "Having my mother regain consciousness is a major relief. I was pretty rattled, but it looks like everything's going to be okay. I can't say the same for the guy who hit her. If I get my hands on him before the cops, well . . ." Connor pauses, looks at the camera, winks.

Connor pushes through the lobby door, crosses the parking lot. A state police officer steps out of a cruiser and blocks his path.

Connor stops, addresses the policeman. "Trooper Mack. Any arrests?"

The trooper swivels his head between Connor and the camera, finally settles on Connor. "Did you eat lunch at the White Swan today?"

Connor takes a half step toward the trooper. "Someone sets fire to my truck, sets fire to my boat, robs my mother and sends her to the hospital. And you're asking questions about my dining habits?"

Trooper Mack scowls. "There was a shooting in suite 210, and you were seen leaving the second floor."

"Isn't that Tyler Lane's suite? Ask him."

"Just like last time, he's hiding behind his lawyers. Mind telling me what you were doing on the second floor?"

"I was looking for the men's room."

"Then you don't happen to own a Remington Model 870 Pump?"

Connor shakes his head. "I'm afraid of guns."

After slipping the Land Cruiser into its space in the garage, Connor found Crystal, Joanna, and Jeff Russell crowded around the kitchen's center island, joking and chatting while they prepped dinner. Crystal worked on the salad as Russell organized a plate of cheese and crackers. Joanna was filling a big pot at the sink but mostly giving orders and directing traffic. Everyone looked pretty damned comfortable.

An almost empty bottle of white wine rested on the counter. Connor fetched a glass from the cabinet. "Hope this isn't the last bottle."

"Unless you can find the key to Dad's wine cellar." Joanna raised her wineglass. "To Mom."

They all paused and touched glasses.

"He put a lock on it? On the damn wine cabinet?" Connor set his glass on the counter. "Now, that's taking obsession to a whole new level."

"How's your mother?" Russell asked.

"She was in good spirits when I left. Looking forward to coming home." Connor rummaged in one of the drawers.

"That would make some great footage. Really show your soft side. Really humanize you," Russell offered.

"I'm human enough," Connor replied. "You don't want to tape my mother's opinion of reality TV. Even if you got her to sign a release, you'd never be able to air a word of it."

Crystal said, "Your mother does have a strong spirit. But her chakras are certainly blocked, and they need alignment. Connor's are also blocked. His first, second, and fourth need clearing." She returned her attention to the salad. "Does anyone mind if I add some beets and fresh figs? Maybe crumble some goat cheese?"

"Goat cheese? Figs in the salad? I thought we were in Maine, not California." Connor pulled a hammer and a screwdriver from the drawer, laying them on the counter.

"Hey, I'm from California," Russell said.

"My point precisely," Connor replied.

Joanna eyed the tools suspiciously. "Those don't look like the key."

"I'm not driving all the way back into town for a couple of bottles of vino." Connor inspected the glass-fronted wine cellar built into the wall next to the Sub-Zero.

"I'll make a liquor run," Russell offered.

"No need." Connor fitted the screwdriver's blade into the key lock, struck the end of its handle with the hammer, and the door swung open.

"Dad's not going to like that."

"Then he should have gotten his ass on a plane." Connor opened the glass door and surveyed the collection. "Looks like *Edwin* has been investing heavily in wine futures. No wonder he locked the door. I think we're going to have to do some damage here."

"Goat cheese?" Crystal asked.

Joanna pointed. "Sub-Zero. Second drawer."

"Any requests? Don't be shy," Connor asked.

Russell stepped up to the wine cellar and looked in. "Whoa. Your father has some awesome stuff."

"You know about wine?" Joanna asked.

"I grew up right outside Napa." Russell reached in and pulled out a bottle. "How about we try a Kistler Chardonnay?"

Connor pointed. "You missed the 2009 Batard-Montrachet from Ramonet-Bachelet."

"But that's like three hundred bucks a bottle."

Connor pulled the Batard from the rack. "Life's too short to drink shitty wine."

"We should put that on a T-shirt." Russell pulled a waiter's knife off the counter and began to uncork the bottle.

"This should clear my chakras," Connor said.

Crystal threw him a look as she tossed the salad.

"Connor, can you help me with the pot?" Joanna pointed to the large pot sitting in the sink. "Just put it on the back burner."

Connor lifted the pot into place. "I'm starving. What's for dinner?"

"You're joking, right?" Joanna accepted a fresh glass of wine from Russell.

"Oh no. Are you serious?" Connor asked.

Russell looked up from his wine. "Am I missing something?"

"Dad's favorite family tradition. We *always* have the same thing at the beginning of the season." Joanna turned up the flame under the big pot.

"From halfway around the world, he still manages to pull our strings." With his boot, Connor flipped open the lid of the large cooler sitting on the floor next to the stove.

Russell peered in. "Lobster."

Two hours later, Connor leaned back from the table and

contemplated the damage—six lobsters and three bottles of the Batard. He watched Crystal and Joanna chatting, comfortable, like peers or good friends. Now that Crystal's boat was repaired, he realized that he was going to miss her, that he enjoyed her quirky company. It might be nice to pull back from his current problems and focus on her.

Connor turned to Crystal. "When are you leaving?"

"Why?" Crystal asked.

"Just wondering." Connor watched the two women exchange smirking glances.

"I already picked up supplies at the grocery store, so I just need to get organized." Crystal smiled. "Maybe midmorning."

"Tomorrow?" Connor shot his sister a *mind-your-own-business* look.

Joanna placed a possessive hand on Russell's shoulder. She announced, "Did you know that Jeff's passion is making documentaries about environmental and social issues?"

"Well, I've only made one. About the effects of strip-mining. It was a bear to produce," Russell said with a tinge of pride. "But it was well reviewed, and I did win a Golden Oak Leaf."

"You must feel very strongly about that," Crystal said.

"I've seen firsthand the impact on the environment. It's sickening."

Joanna winked at Connor. "My little brother seems to be under the impression that *Lobster Wars* is a documentary."

"*And* a slice of classic Americana," Connor added.

Russell snorted. "Yeah, in a car-wreck sort of way."

"If documentaries are your passion, why work on a reality TV show?" Crystal asked.

"Have to pay the bills. I'm not Michael Moore or Al Gore. Yet. Funding for documentaries is tough. Even popular docs don't turn much of a profit. The money either comes from private sources or corporate. And believe me, corporate America is very sensitive about exposing themselves, so they demand a lot of input. Their money comes with strings."

"How about a documentary on obesity? I know exactly where you can get your material." Crystal gave Connor a frank stare.

"I know the big restaurant chains and agri-business are on the hot seat over the obesity and health issues. But it's been done, and I'm not sure it had much impact. Remember *Super Size Me*?" Russell paused and when no one responded said, "I didn't think so."

"But why?" Crystal asked.

"Think cause and effect. Showing the cause is tricky. Hidden calories, slightly oversized portions on big plates, charts and graphs, are all really boring visuals. And the effect? Well, fat people waddling around the mall doesn't make for exciting video. Not like strip-mining. Or clear-cutting. Now, those are visuals a cinematographer can sink his teeth into."

Crystal asked, "So, you're saying it's a tough sell with the audience?"

"Yup, afraid so."

"Plus, I think obesity is perceived as a self-inflicted wound," Connor added. "In other words, if you don't like being fat, just shut your pie hole."

"*Exactly*," Russell agreed, then glanced at his watch. "Hey, it's almost eight o'clock. Who wants to watch *Lobster Wars*?"

**ON-SCREEN IMAGE:** Long shot of a line of weather-beaten lobster boats chased by dipping, banking seagulls as they steam out of the harbor into the cold sunrise. Dark-green waves break over the boats' sharp bows. Red channel buoys rock and clang. Surf crashes on a rocky shoreline in the distance.

**VOICE-OVER:** It's the halfway point in the season, and the lobstermen of Tranquility are working hard to make their numbers, but tensions are mounting. The new guy, Connor Nichols,

hasn't given up, while the old guard, led by
Wade Baxter, grumbles and fumes. And rumors of
conflict are circulating around the docks.

**CUT TO:** Wade pushes a baited trap over the
side, the line snakes over the gunwale, then
he throws the orange-and-black buoy. "That was
a good string, almost a hundred pounds. Prices
edged up a few cents over the weekend. Gonna
be a money week. Ayuh. Which I need, paying
alimony to two women. One's already shacked up.
Still taking my checks, though. Guess I could do
better workin' construction or drivin' a truck.
But then I'd have some a-hole boss lookin' over
my shoulder."

**CUT TO:** Connor, dressed in yellow storm bibs and
a gray sweatshirt, quickly measures a lobster
and tosses it over the side. He smiles at the
camera. "Too small. But I'm finally getting the
hang of this. My average per trap is way up. So
far today about forty keepers out of my first
ten traps. About eighty, ninety pounds. I'll
re-bait this one and send it back down. Then
move on to the next string."

**CUT TO:** Wade puts the *Sweet Tail* in gear,
pushes the throttle, spins the wheel. "If prices
hold and the yield stays up, might even have
enough left over to get back into my own place.
But either way, I'm done with that marriage
bullshit, ayuh."

**CUT TO:** Connor throttles down the engine, steps
over to the side, grabs the boat hook. He waves
at the bobbing red-and-white buoys. "This is a
good sign. It always helps my yield when nobody

cuts my lines."

**CUT TO:** Connor at the wheel. "It's bad enough that I come out here every day and get my butt kicked trying to make a go of lobstering. But when I got back to the dock last night, all four tires on my truck were flat. The truck sat in the parking area all day, and of course, no one saw a thing."

**CUT TO:** Wade on the *Sweet Tail*. He grins and works the wheel, pushes the throttle forward. "College boy thinks I slashed his tires. But there's a dozen other guys could have done it. Just like there's a dozen other guys might cut his buoys or put rocks in his trap."

**CUT TO:** Connor pulls back on the throttle, slows, enters the channel. "Baxter claims he didn't do it, but I'm pretty sure it was him. The season's half over, and I haven't given up, and I'm not going to. If it wasn't for all the money I'm losing, I'd just laugh at their bullshit. But I'm afraid someone's going to take things too far and end up getting hurt. Bad." He grins at the camera. "I just hope it's not me."

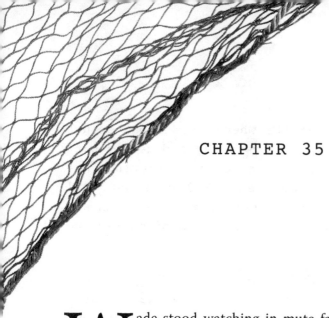

# CHAPTER 35

Wade stood watching in mute fascination as Darlene negotiated with the crotchety old bastard that ran the boatyard. Each time she leaned over his desk and touched his arm, he dropped the price ten grand.

Finally he shook his head and bolted out of his chair. "One-forty. That's the best I can do."

"And you'll carry the note?" Darlene asked.

"Ayuh, sure. At ten percent."

"Eight."

"Okay, okay. Eight." He waved his hands in surrender.

Darlene glanced at Kent, who nodded, and then she kissed the old fart on the cheek. "Done."

He blushed and stumbled backwards into a filing cabinet.

She *did* have a way with people.

Next, Kent wrote out a check for twenty-five thousand dollars to cover the deposit, like he was buying a tank of gas. Signed the note for the balance, too. They were going to spend tomorrow morning getting it in the water, just in time for Tyler and his people to tape their commercial.

After wrapping up the paperwork, they decided to hit the market on the way back to the house. Darlene grabbed a cart to work the aisles for dinner fixings while Kent wandered back to the liquor display. Wade stepped up to the deli counter.

"Hey, Wade." Phil grinned as he sliced bologna for another customer. "Be sure to tell your mom I've got that special cut of meat she was wanting. She can come in anytime."

"I'm headin' back to the house; just give it to me."

"It's in the walk-in, back of the store, and I can't leave the counter. Just tell her to stop by," Phil said as he finished wrapping the bologna. After the customer walked off, Phil leaned over the counter, speaking under his breath, almost whispering. "You seen Evan lately?"

"Why?"

"State Police was in here about two hours ago asking if I knew his *whereabouts.* Said they was investigating a big robbery in Camden where someone got hurt and an attempted robbery at the White Swan where there was a shooting. Plus, the statie said Evan jumped parole in Arizona."

"No shit. News to me. Don't know a thing about any of that."

Phil stared hard at Wade. "Don't bullshit me. I see you and Evan together, like old times."

Wade snorted, pointed at Phil. "You stay out of it. What I do is none of your fuckin' business. Stick to slicing bologna."

"It makes me nervous." Phil wiped his hands on his apron. "We got a good thing going here."

Grinning, Kent ambled over and placed two bottles of Stoli on the deli counter. "Hey, Phil. What're you guys talking about?"

"Food," Wade grumbled. "Phil's pushin' his damn lobstah rolls."

Wade pulled up to the market's gas pumps to top off before joining Kent and Darlene back at the house for dinner. He was leaning against the truck's fender, watching the numbers tick by on the pump, contemplating Phil's comments, when Evan lurched out from behind a tow truck parked in the shadows.

Wade jerked at the unexpected sight. "Wondering where you got off to. But I figured you'd show up sooner or later."

"Keep your voice down. Cops are looking for me." Evan scanned the tiny parking lot.

"The hell happened to your face?"

"Fucker shot me. Again." Evan touched his cheek and grimaced. The left side of his face was covered with small, angry red bumps. "You got any more pills?"

Wade pulled the bottle of OxyContin from his pocket. "Not many left. My foot's gonna be killing me later."

Evan snatched the little brown bottle from Wade's hand, gobbled two dry, and then quickly shoved it into his jeans. "You can get more, but I need these. I'm out of here tonight. But I need your help 'cause I don't want to use a stolen car." Evan waved at a broken-down Ford Taurus squatting at the dark edge of the parking lot.

"Whatever you're plannin', count me out." Wade fixed the pump handle in the bracket.

"No, listen. It's simple. We drive to Camden in your truck, me hiding in the bed under the tarp. I'm gonna swipe one thing out of that fuckin' house. It's a little cowboy statue. Worth like a hundred K. We meet my guy down to the harbor in Tranquility, where it's quiet. He pays me, and then he's giving me a ride to Boston. I'll even split the money."

"Didn't you hear me?" Wade clicked the gas cap in place.

"But I can't drive around in a hot car. Not with the staties lookin' for me," Evan whined. "Besides, *matey*, I thought you needed the money to replace the *Sweet Tail*."

"Well, uh . . ." Wade was about to tell Evan that his boat problem was solved thanks to Kent when he spotted the dilated greed shimmering in the man's eyes. "Fuck the money. Ain't worth it."

Wade walked around the nose of his truck, making for the driver's door as Evan clambered into the truck's bed and pleaded, "Okay, okay. Then just give me a ride to Camden."

Wade paused, his hand on the door latch, and shook his head.

"Told you, I'm out of it."

"Okay, okay. Leave me off at the house."

"I'm not waiting for you. How're you going to get back to the harbor to meet your guy?"

Evan lay down, covering himself with the grimy tarp. "I'll think of something."

Giving Evan a ride seemed like the only way of getting rid of the little shit. And maybe this time he would actually go. But they were having a tough time finding the Nichols place. Evan hadn't paid much attention the day of Kent's art party. Lying under the tarp in the truck's bed, he offered Wade directions through the truck's open back window. "I think to the left."

"We already went that way, and it just circled around back to here." Wade spun the steering wheel to the right. The roads in Maine were twisty and curvy, and many of the oceanfront houses shared driveways that branched off like gnarled tree limbs. "What was the number?"

"Told you, I don't remember the number. There was a bunch of numbers and like a dozen mailboxes. But it was on Shore Road."

Wade slammed the brakes in frustration and peered at Evan through the back window. "You dumbass. You know how many fuckin' Shore Roads there are in Maine?"

"Shit. It's been so long since I lived here. But aren't we on Shore Road now?'

"Ayuh, Shore Road South. In Camden there's Shore Road North, Shore Road East, *and* Shore Road West."

Evan stammered, "But . . . but . . . there was a sign, too."

Wade crept along in the dark. "What kind of sign?"

"You know a sign, with the family's last name on it. Carved outta wood, nailed to a tree."

Wade finally stropped the truck and pointed. "You mean like that."

Directly across the street was a narrow driveway flanked on one side by six mailboxes and on the other by a neat column of wooden signs. The top sign read, *The Nichols*.

"Yeah, yeah, yeah. That's it. That's it. Turn down there. I'll grab the little statue quick and we can get back to Tranquility."

"No way I'm going down that driveway. It's practically one-way." Wade shook his head as he climbed out of the truck's cab. "Besides, I told you, I'm out of it. You're on your own."

"But how do I get back to the harbor?" Evan whined.

"Thought you said you'd figure something out. Steal a car. Steal a bicycle. Steal a fuckin' boat for all I care, *matey*."

Evan leaned over the side of the bed, right in Wade's face, pointing wildly across the street at the driveway. "But, goddamn it, we're *here*. Right *here*. Five more minutes and we split a hundred K."

"You better start walking then."

"You'll wait for me?" Evan asked hopefully.

"No, but I'll help you out of the truck." Wade grabbed the front of Evan's jacket and launched him over the side into a ditch.

# CHAPTER 36

After an hour of watching himself on *Lobster Wars*, plus a bottle of his dad's finest port, Connor wandered down to the dock to check the boats, get some fresh air, and clear his head. The gentle onshore breeze tasted of salt and seaweed, and the spring sky was clear with a bright full moon hanging just above the watery horizon.

Crystal appeared as he finished retying one of the *Nu B*'s lines, and she walked over to her sailboat, now tied to his family's dock. It was a sleek, black-hulled, single-masted ocean cruiser with a raised salon.

Connor followed. "Beautiful. It looks like a Morris. Maybe a forty-eight?"

"It's a forty-five. I don't feel comfortable sailing solo on anything larger."

Connor looked at the boat's name painted on the transom. "The *Prana*. Why am I not surprised."

She grabbed his hand and led him over. "Come on, I'll give you a tour."

They went down a short gangway into the main salon. It reminded him of the Hinckley, all teak and leather and hand-fitted craftsmanship. She led him around the interior—owner's berth, galley, head, guest quarters—and then they settled side by side on a thickly padded couch in the main cabin.

Connor waved at the interior. "It looks like you *were* running a yoga empire."

"I did okay." Crystal pulled her legs onto the sofa and curled into his side.

"That's an understatement." Connor wrapped his arm around her and was pleased by how comfortable he felt.

"It wasn't just about the money."

"You say so."

"Believe me, I could have made a lot more if I was willing to keep compromising my beliefs."

"So, where are you going tomorrow?" Connor asked, but what he really wanted to know was where this was going tonight.

"Depends on the weather, but my plan is to head toward Bar Harbor. I haven't been there since I was a little girl. Then maybe up to the Maritimes."

"You know, you could stick around *here* for a while. No one will mind."

"I think that's the port talking. Besides, there's a big difference between 'not minding' and actually wanting someone to stick around." Crystal shot him a frank, green-eyed stare. "Which is it?"

"I'd formally invite you, but I don't feel like being called 'clueless' again," Connor replied with as little petulance in his voice as possible.

"You know, for a guy your size, you're pretty sensitive." Crystal rested her head on his shoulder.

"Sticks and stones . . ."

"At least you're cute." Crystal turned her face up, lips slightly parted.

Connor gave her a soft kiss. Her lips were warm, and he felt the heat coming off her body. "But I'm still clueless, right?"

"You're making progress. There may be hope for you. Now that the deal with Tyler isn't going forward, what are *you* planning to do tomorrow?"

"I'm moving the *Nu B* back to Tranquility first thing in the morning. Then I'll start hauling traps and get on with my career as a reality TV star."

"So, you're going back to war with Wade?"

"The show makes it look worse," Connor replied, now on the defensive—again.

"I don't think slashed tires are an editing trick."

"Well, no, but—"

"How about a firebombed truck and sabotaged boat? And the TV crew hasn't even started taping."

"I know the other guys don't like me fishing, but at least they've backed off. Wade's not getting the message."

"But what message are you trying to send?" Crystal asked.

"Same as last year."

"It seems like you're living last year all over again. Have you ever talked to Wade?"

"All the time."

"I don't mean trading insults while you play chicken in the harbor. I mean communicate. And do it with intention," Crystal paused and placed a hand on his chest. "From here."

"Lobstermen don't have that kind of relationship. We're not all touchy-feely." Connor thought about his confrontation in Wade's front yard.

"It might be easier than repeatedly banging your head against the wall."

Connor looked at her in the gathering darkness of the cabin. She just wouldn't cut him any slack. "You seem to have all the answers. What do you think I should do?"

"Oh, I can't *tell* you what to do. Besides, I think you already know." Crystal kissed his cheek, slipped off the couch, and headed toward the forward cabin. "I'll see you at breakfast."

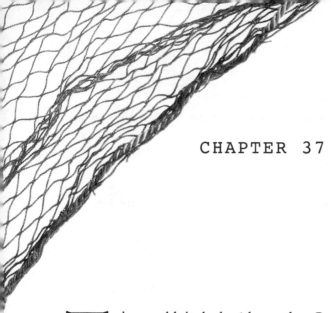

# CHAPTER 37

Tyler couldn't deal with another Rowdy Robby, so when Ronald and Suzanne got word that Wade was at home, he took matters into his own hands. He stared out of the limo's window at the overgrown bushes and weeds threatening the small, swaybacked Cape. "Driver, are you sure this is the right address? It looks abandoned."

The uniformed limo driver tapped his finger on the dash-mounted GPS, answering over his shoulder, "I'm not from around here, sir. But this is where the GPS brought us."

Ronald hit the button to lower the window and peered out, his nose wrinkled in disgust. "It matches the address he put on the contract. Matches the guy, too, if you ask me."

"Don't forget, this was *your* idea." Tyler pinched the crease of his freshly pressed, navy-blue suit pants and studied the shine on his black cowboy boots. "A lot's riding on this. I hope I didn't make a mistake trusting your judgment."

"Well, uh, I think—" Ronald fidgeted in his seat.

"What's the matter, boy? No snippy comeback?" Tyler swung open the door, staring at Ronald in the weak dome light. "Guess there's only one way to tell for sure."

Wade was surprised to find Tyler and the little homo standing on his stoop at eleven o'clock at night.

"Welcome to the party." He waved them in with a half-empty bottle of Stoli. "Where's the girl?"

After spending the last three hours celebrating his new boat with Kent and Darlene—but mostly watching Darlene shake her ass while she bopped around the kitchen—he would have liked to take a shot at the hot business chick with the nice legs, even with her pushy attitude.

"You mean Suzanne?" Tyler asked. "She's preparing for tomorrow's taping."

"Too bad." Wade ushered them down the hallway and into the kitchen. Darlene and Kent had disappeared. From the thumping sounds seeping through the walls, he knew their location. He placed two glasses on the table, slopped in some vodka, and jabbed a finger at the refrigerator. "Ice in the freezer, you want it."

"Neat's fine." Tyler grabbed his drink.

Ronald paused and then picked up the glass with his fingertips, examining the surface. "No ice for me, thanks."

Wade raised his vodka in a drunken toast. "To lobster fishing. The best goddamn job in the world."

Tyler countered, touching glasses, "To the Captain Wade Lobster Shacks."

The two men threw back their drinks while Ronald squinted and sipped, then coughed.

Wade poured refills and then slumped into a chair. "Have a seat."

"Where's your boat? My people have been looking everywhere for you."

"My boat?" Wade stalled. "Uh . . . took it up to Camden for some work. Rudder's sticking."

"Will it be ready for the TV shoot tomorrow?" Tyler asked. "This is very important. Your boat, in its working environment, is crucial to the message we're crafting. Image is everything."

"For sure." Wade took another gulp of Stoli. "Nooooo problem. That good-looking chick gonna be there?"

"Maybe you should spend the night in Camden. It'll make everything easier tomorrow." Tyler turned to Ronald. "Why don't we get Wade a nice comfortable room at the inn."

"The rest of TV crew arrived today. Every room's taken. We even had to put Suzanne's people somewhere else," Ronald sniffed.

"Never stayed at the fuckin' Swan."

"You can use Ronald's room," Tyler offered.

"My room? Where will I sleep?" Ronald whined.

"Work something out with Suzanne. Call the inn and tell them to have housekeeping get the room ready." Tyler stood. "Come on, Wade. Might as well get used to riding in a limo."

Wade's toe ached, sending a constant stab of pain all the way up his leg. He finished his Stoli in a single gulp. "Think we could stop at the medical center first?"

# CHAPTER 38

Sitting on the patio facing the water, Connor snugged the blanket around his shoulders, breathing the cool night air, trying to organize his thoughts. He felt like he was trying to solve separate little puzzles that were all missing the same piece.

Was Crystal one of the puzzles or the missing piece? Or both? Every time Connor felt like he was getting close to the answer, she tripped him up, constantly knocking him off balance. He wasn't used to that. His relationships with women were usually much simpler. She was really making him work. But she was sailing away in the morning, so it looked like he'd never figure her out, and quite possibly, that was okay—one less thing to worry about.

Connor continued to breathe deeply, letting his mind drift, until his gaze finally settled on the water's taut surface. The incandescent moon was chasing the tide into full retreat, and he felt himself pleasantly pulled along on the ocean's outgoing current.

"Connor. Connor. Wake up." Joanna shook Connor's shoulder.

"Huh? What?" He didn't realize he had fallen asleep. In fact, he felt wide awake as he looked up at Joanna, wondering vaguely where she got an oversized *Lobster Wars* T-shirt.

"The medical center called. It's mother. They think she may have had a stroke."

Connor scrambled to his feet and followed Joanna into the house. His sense of serenity quickly evaporated as a hard knot of fear settled in his gut. He checked his watch—almost midnight. "When did they call?"

"Few minutes ago," Joanna answered. "What about Crystal?"

"What about her?"

"Do you want to tell her? I might be good to have her along."

Connor felt a flash of frustration and shook his head. "No. Leave her."

"You say so." Joanna slipped into the coat held for her by a red-faced Jeff Russell.

"Guess that explains the T-shirt," Connor muttered as he grabbed his canvas jacket off the wall peg in the mudroom.

From behind the corner of the garage, Evan watched Nichols and two other people sprint out of the house, quickly pile into the two cars sitting in the driveway, and tear off into the night. He cradled his aching ribs and wondered briefly what was the big damn hurry.

Evan leaned against the garage's wall, waiting to see if anyone else came running out of the house. After about ten minutes of nothing, he felt pretty good about his chances. In fact, if the house was now empty, why not stop in for a little something to ease his aching ribs?

Hanging in the shadows, Evan made his way toward the front door. When he grabbed the knob, he was surprised to find the door unlocked. He made straight for the bar, hoping for another bottle of Kettle. But they hadn't replaced it. How inconsiderate. He contemplated leaving an angry note. But he finally settled on a fresh two-liter bottle of Dickel, cracked the paper seal, took an eye-watering swig, and wandered into the kitchen.

He couldn't remember when he had last eaten as he jerked open the door of the giant silver refrigerator and rummaged through its packed shelves. He piled cheese, cold cuts, and two boiled lobster on the center island and went looking for an empty grocery sack, which he found in the pantry, along with a big unopened bag of potato chips and several cans of salted nuts.

Dickel in one hand, groceries in the other, Evan lurched into the living room, and there was the Remington sitting on a small table. He took another big slug of Dickel, slipped the bottle into the grocery bag, and scooped up the statue. He opened the French doors, walked across the patio and down the gently sloping backyard toward the dock and his hundred-K payday.

His plan was simple. Even though the staties were looking for him, Evan doubted the Coast Guard had much interest. Since Wade had turned pussy and bailed on him, traveling by water seemed like the slickest way back to Tranquility and to meet his fence.

He entered the *Nu B*'s small wheelhouse, wedged the bottle of Dickel under the armrest of the captain's chair, and dropped the grocery bag onto the console. It had been ten years since he'd last piloted a boat. He studied the controls, trying to concentrate through a haze of throbbing pain and prescription narcotics. After a few minutes of randomly flipping switches, pressing buttons, and turning keys, the big diesel finally roared to life with a belch of black exhaust smoke.

While the engine warmed, Evan carried the Remington down into the cabin. He opened a small door and slipped the statue deep inside a storage locker built into the boat's hull. He wanted to stow it someplace safe and out of sight, just in case he was stopped and searched.

Evan grinned to himself as he settled his throbbing ass into the captain's chair, giving the engine a few minutes to warm. After a big hit of Dickel, he rummaged in the grocery sack and came up with the bag of potato chips. He was chasing a big mouthful of chips with the Dickel when a small woman materialized out of nowhere, a look of surprise on her pretty face.

"Who are you?" she demanded.

"The fuck?" Evan choked, spraying the console with whiskey-soaked potato chips.

"Do you know how much trans-fat is in commercial potato chips?" she asked.

Still gagging, Evan spit into his hand. In the thin light of the gauges, he stared at the dark-red blood. "That ain't good."

"You *may* have a problem," the girl agreed.

"No shit. You think," Evan replied, probing his aching ribs after wiping his hand on his jeans.

"I thought you were Connor."

"Do I look like fuckin' Connor?" Evan snapped. "Who are you?"

"Crystal, his first mate. What are you doing on his boat?"

"What's it look like I'm doing?" Evan hated stupid questions.

Crystal answered, "Stealing it."

"I'm just borrowing it," Evan corrected her.

"Did you ask permission?"

"Fuck no."

"Then it's stealing." Crystal reached for the radio handset.

"What are you doing?"

"Calling the Coast Guard." Crystal punched a button and twisted the dial. "I wonder if they still hang pirates?"

"Pirates?" It took Evan's brain a few slow beats to react. Finally, he launched out of the chair, swinging his fist, and caught Crystal in front of her ear. She dropped to the deck.

# CHAPTER 39

Connor held Brooke's hand, trying to keep clear of the staff bustling in and out of the room. The look of fear in her eyes was contagious, and the hard knot in his gut pushed out, crowding his chest. He felt like a third-person witness to his own nightmare. Joanna was huddled in the corner with Dr. Willis, talking doctor speak in hushed tones, but Connor occasionally picked up exotic medical terms like *ischemic* and *hemorrhagic*. However, it was the familiar words that stoked his fear. Words like *irreversible* and *paralysis*.

Russell offered him a cup of vending machine coffee. "Thought you might need this."

"Thanks." Connor reached for the cup but was distracted by his mother's grip. He forced a smile for her. "They're doing everything they can. Joanna's here, so you're going to get first-class care."

"Ma rain. Ma rain. Sav ma rain," his mother whispered.

Joanna and Willis scurried over to the bed. Joanna asked, "Please, say that again, Mother. Slowly."

"Ma rain. Ma rain. Sav ma rain," Brooke said with increasing agitation.

Joanna and Willis stared at each other, obviously lost.

Connor leaned over, his ear close to his mother's mouth, and nodded. "Once more, Mom, please."

"Sav . . . ma . . . rain . . . sav . . . ma . . . rain." Brooke's body twisted and convulsed as she forced out the words.

Connor straightened, looking at his sister with moist eyes. "She's saying, 'Save my brain.'"

While Willis and the medical center staff continued to work on Brooke, out in the hallway Joanna faced Russell and Connor. "Okay. Simple explanation, she's showing all the symptoms of a stroke. Most likely precipitated by the head trauma."

"But why now?" Connor asked. "She was awake and getting better."

"We're probably looking at a dissection, a torn blood vessel. In those cases, a delayed occurrence is not uncommon, even days or weeks after the traumatic event."

"So, what's the plan?" Connor asked.

"Willis wants to run more tests before recommending a course of treatment."

"Tests? He needs to *do* something. *Now*. Before it's too late," Connor growled.

"Like what?" Joanna asked.

"I don't know. You're the doctors."

"I don't like waiting any more than you, but Willis needs more information. In the meantime, they're following the standard protocol."

"You mean standard doctor bullshit. Always covering your asses." Connor watched Joanna flinch.

"That's not fair, Connor. She's *my* mother, too." Joanna crossed her arms over her chest, fighting back tears.

"Yo, dude, really," Russell chided.

"You're right. I'm sorry." Connor's shoulders sagged. "This situation is out of control, and I'm scared and I hate feeling useless. I want to do something."

"Me too. It's very different when the patient is a family member." Joanna placed a warm hand on his arm. "But I'm afraid there's not much else we can do."

Connor looked down the long hallway and spotted Wade and Tyler, trailed by Ronald, coming in their direction. The needle on his frustration meter pegged, and he broke away from his little group. "Maybe there's something I can do."

Connor faced the two men. "Kind of late. Visiting hours are over."

"Is it your mother?" Tyler gripped Connor's hand.

"They think she's had a stroke." Connor hated even speaking the words.

"I'm sorry." Tyler frowned. "Is there anything I can do? Make some calls? Private plane? Anything? You name it."

"No, but thanks. My sister's here, and she's a surgeon and keeping an eye on the situation." Connor turned to Wade. "Remember what I told you about keeping your head above water?"

"Look, Nichols. Sorry about your mom, but wasn't my doing. This is 'cause of Evan," Wade replied

"Is that the guy who's been causing all the problems?" Tyler asked. "Do you know him?"

Wade replied, "Everyone knows him. He's a townie, like me. But we ain't friends."

"That's not what I heard," Connor said.

"We was, back in the day. Not now. We had a couple of drinks lately, but he's too much of a troublemaker. And I'm afraid he ain't done."

Connor asked, "What are you talking about?"

"I don't know for sure. Just a feeling." Wade studied the floor, avoiding Connor's stare.

"Bullshit. You know or you wouldn't say anything."

Wade hesitated, then replied, "He needs money. Doesn't care how he gets it. He might be planning to steal something."

"Where, from our house?" Connor asked.

"Ayuh."

Joanna and Russell had joined the group.

"Why? What?" Joanna asked.

"Said somethin' about a cowboy statue. I don't know."

"The Remington?" Connor demanded.

"Ayuh. Like the gun. And I think he's going to head for Tranquility, but not until morning. Staties are looking for him. The best way might be by boat. I think he might take the *Nu B*."

"The *Nu B*?" Connor stared at Wade.

Tyler asked, "What makes you think so?"

"I heard, okay. You know, around the docks, like a rumor. But Connor here should go check."

"Rumor my ass." Connor edged forward. "Crystal's sleeping on her sailboat right next to the *Nu B*."

"You think she'd try to stop him?" Russell asked.

"What do you think?" Connor replied.

Wade searched their faces in confusion. "Who's Crystal?"

"Isn't that the young lady who joined us for dinner?" Tyler asked. "Your first mate?"

"Yes. And she's sleeping on her boat tied to my parents' dock," Connor answered.

Wade shook his head. "He's not interested in no girl, unless she gets in his way. That happens, no tellin' what he'll do. He's really losin' it."

Tyler shot Wade a suspicious look. "How do you know all this?"

"He gets drunk and shoots off his mouth. Okay?" Wade snapped.

Connor glanced at his watch. "Almost dead low. Bad time for finding your way in the dark."

"Especially for an asshole like Evan," Wade replied. "He can barely pilot a boat during the day."

"What about Mom?" Connor asked Joanna.

"There's nothing you can do here. I'll stay and monitor her treatment. You need to make sure Crystal's safe."

Pulling his cell phone from his pocket, Connor turned to Russell. "Here's my number. Go to your production trailer and fire up the cameras. Take Wade. He knows every inch of water between here and Tranquility better than anyone.

"What can we do?" Tyler asked.

"Shouldn't we call the police? Let them handle this? I mean, this guy's dangerous," Ronald asked.

Tyler cringed. "The police haven't been much help—nothing but questions and accusations, and this Evan guy's still running around, causing problems."

"Keep them out of it for now," Connor said.

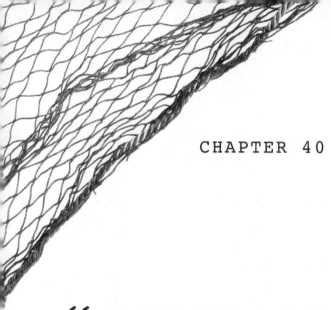

# CHAPTER 40

"Shit. Shit. Shit." Evan jammed the throttle into reverse, backing the *Nu B* out of another dead-end cove. Despite the full moon, all the inlets and coves looked identical—jutting, craggy rocks guarding openings made even more narrow and treacherous by the falling tide. You couldn't tell where the fuck you were. He squinted with frustration at the swinging compass needle, trying to recall the heading Wade had followed on their way back to Tranquility.

The green-eyed chick with the sandy hair claimed she was Connor's first mate, so she must know her way around. Maybe he could ask her. But she was tied up below, either still unconscious or keeping very quiet.

Right after he whacked her on the side of the head, he had dragged her limp body down into the forward berth, copping a quick feel as he loaded her onto the bunk. Nice ass, but not much in the tit department. Not like Darlene, who had a world-class pair of hooters. Which were now being fondled by that pus-nut, Kent.

After he did this deal and was flush with cash, maybe he could convince Darlene to give him another chance. Take her someplace nice, like one of those spas she was always talking about. Buy her a new outfit and some earrings or a bracelet, something shiny. Show her he could change and be the kind of guy she wanted.

In the meantime, he wasn't meeting his fence until 10 AM, so it was tempting to drop anchor in one of these inlets and wait until first light. Just to pass the time, he could even imagine giving the pretty first mate a poke or talking her into a blow job. If her jaw wasn't too sore.

While he glanced at the doorway leading to the small cabin, pondering his options, Evan coughed into his hand. He stared with unease at the dark-red, almost black blood staining his palm. Not good.

Russell fired up the console in the production trailer, and Wade shifted in the tight space, trying not to bump any of the expensive-looking equipment. He watched with interest as the six monitors flashed to life, noticing that each image was labeled with its location.

Russell talked over his shoulder. "I heard you cut a licensing deal with Tyler."

"Ayuh. Gonna open a bunch of lobster shacks with my name on 'em."

"Reality TV. Got to love it," Russell chuckled.

Wade gestured at the screens. "I thought you had way more than six cameras set up."

Russell replied, "Between lobster boats, pickup trucks, and fixed locations, we've got thirty-two cameras, not counting the two Steadicams that the crews use. But we can only watch six at a time, even though they're all recording."

"Always watch the same six locations?"

Laughing, Russell shook his head and began flipping switches, and the images jumped from location to location. "Are you kidding me? We'd die of boredom watching the same six cameras all day. Even with the crazy shit you guys do to each other. At night, it's even worse, except for camera number fifteen. Sometimes the whole production crew sits in here and drinks beer and watches the show."

"What's so special about that one?"

"See for yourself." Russell looked at his watch and pointed. "It's just about time. Check out monitor five."

The image on monitor five was labeled *Tranquility Market* and showed a dim black-and-white shot of the unlit deli area.

"Phil's deli. Big deal," Wade said.

Russell reached for a small knob. "Can't do anything about the light, but let me turn up the volume."

THE SOUND OF KEYS JINGLING, followed by the squeak of a door opening, and then Phil's voice booms through the speakers. "Hello, ma'am, welcome to my shop. What can I do for you?"

"I understand from the other ladies that you have the best meat in town," a woman's voice replies.

"Nothing but Grade A, prime. Better than that fancy butcher shop up to Camden."

"I don't know. I hear them rich folks like their meat."

"If they tasted mine, they'd never go anywhere else."

"Is it tender and juicy?"

"My meat is bursting with flavor. What cut were you looking for?" Phil asks.

"I'm very, very hungry. What would you recommend?"

"How about a nice rib eye? It's my specialty."

"That sounds delicious. But do you think I'll be satisfied?"

"Oh, I'll guarantee it, especially if you take

the bone in.

Russell adjusted the volume. "Oh, good, tonight they're playing butcher."

"What the fuck?" Wade leaned in. "That don't sound like Irene."

**THE WOMAN GIGGLES.** "Of course, my big strong butcher, always with the bone in."

"Then why don't you come with me and we'll find you a nice, big, tasty cut."

Phil's image appears, leading a thin, angular middle-aged woman by the hand, her face obscured by the shadows of the darkened store. He is naked except for a stark-white butcher's apron, severely tented in the front, as he ushers the woman around behind the glass display case, and with his back to the camera—ass cheeks playing peek-a-boo—helps her climb onto the counter.

Wade groaned and shook an angry finger at the monitor. "He makes my sandwich on that counter."

"Always kills my appetite," Russell responded dryly.

"**THERE YOU ARE,** my dear. Why don't you make yourself comfortable while I get your steak ready."

"Thank you, kind butcher. And please don't forget the bone." Her face hidden by the back of Phil's head, she hikes up her skirt and wraps her bony legs around his thick waist.

"I never forget the bone." Phil pulls up the apron, spreads his legs, and his cottage cheese butt puckers rhythmically with the staccato exertions of delivering bone-in rib eye.

The woman leans forward, resting her chin on
Phil's humped shoulder, and her face comes fully
into focus.

"Good old Phil. A different lady practically every week," Russell
commented.

Wade roared at the screen, "Goddamn it! He's fuckin' my
mother!"

# CHAPTER 41

Since Wade had practically guaranteed Evan was going to steal the *Nu B*, Connor wasn't surprised to find it missing. Or Crystal. Most likely she had tried to stop Evan or at least got is his way and he grabbed her for insurance.

He pushed the Hinckley through the light chop, running without lights, hoping to spot the *Nu B* in the bright moonlight. The going was slow as he traced the tortured coastline, realizing that Evan could be hiding anywhere in the maze of coves and inlets between Camden and Tranquility.

Over the last two hours he had spoken with Russell several times, and despite Wade's knowledge of the area, they had come up empty handed. He flipped open the cell phone and thumbed Russell's number. "Yo, Russell, talk to me. I'm burning holes in the ocean, and Crystal's odds aren't getting any better."

"Hang on. Wade's checking the screen. We might have something."

Even with the full moon, the little camera mounted on the *Nu B* had very limited range at night. So far, spotting any identifiable landmarks had proved futile. Daylight would make everything easier, but sunrise was still five hours away.

"That's what you said last time."

"Okay, Wade figured out where he is and we can see him. But no Crystal."

"Not good. I'm sure he's got her."

"He's passing Spruce Head point right now, heading north toward Tranquility."

Connor pounded the wheel in frustration. "Assuming that's where he's going, he's only ten minutes from the mouth of the harbor."

"That's what Wade claims. Where are you?"

"Fifteen minutes behind him." Connor mashed the throttle, and the Hinckley surged forward, jumping up on plane.

"So what's the problem? Wade and I can go down there. You can bottle him up with your boat. When he ties up, we've got him cornered."

"Too dangerous. I want to keep him moving. And I need room to maneuver."

"Maneuver? What the hell are you talking about?"

"You guys stay in the trailer and keep watch. I need to think. I'll call you back." Connor ended the call, and when he slipped the phone into his front pocket, his fingers felt the stiff edge of a business card. His original plan was to use the faster, more maneuverable Hinckley to track Evan down on open water and talk him into handing over Crystal. Evan could keep whatever he stole from the house. Hell, he could keep the *Nu B*, too. But given Evan's track record for violence, Connor certainly didn't want to corner the unpredictable bastard at the docks. He pulled Trooper Mack's card from his jeans, studied the number, and dialed.

"Bob Mack."

"It's Connor Nichols. Are you on duty?"

"Kind of late, Nichols. What can I do for you?"

"Evan Pratt stole my lobster boat and robbed my family's house. Again. He's on the *Nu B* right now and about fifteen minutes from Tranquility Harbor."

"How do you know this?"

"Baxter."

"How does he know this?"

"I don't have time to play twenty questions. You'll have to ask him."

"Where are *you*?"

Connor pulled the phone back from his mouth. "Huh? Say again. I'm losing the signal."

"Can you hear me? I asked, 'Where are you?'" Mack's voice grew weaker.

"Huh? What? You're breaking up." Connor broke the connection. He tweaked the throttle and made a small adjustment to the Hinckley's trim, trying to squeeze every knot out of the boat. Evan should be entering the harbor's mouth right about now. Connor had closed the gap and estimated he was only a few minutes behind.

He powered up the radio and set the channel to seven. Holding the mic to his lips, he keyed the transmit button. "Evan, can you read me? Evan, do you copy?"

Nothing.

He tried again. "Hey, dipshit, pick up the microphone and press the little red button."

Evan's response finally crackled through the radio's speaker: "I hear you, asshole."

"Where are you?"

"Wouldn't you like to know."

"Better watch out for Jaws," Connor said.

"Fuck you, I grew up here. Everyone knows where Jaws is. Besides, it ain't my boat." Evan's brittle laugh echoed in the Hinckley's cockpit.

"Let me speak to Crystal."

Evan came back on the radio. "She's busy. Can't come to the phone."

"Bullshit. Let me talk to her."

"She's quite the first mate." Evan paused. "A little talky, but the chick does have a sweet tush. Not much in the tit department, and I ought to know, being a tit man and all, but that's no reason to kick her out of bed."

"You know I'm going to kill you, right?"

"Says you."

"No, seriously. You're dead."

"You already tried once. What are you going to do this time, throw me out of a fuckin' porthole? Take a number."

Connor slowed and entered the harbor's mouth, spotting the *Nu B* about five hundred yards ahead, making for the docks. He swung the Hinckley wide to the left, picking his way carefully along the rocky shore for about two hundred yards, and finally throttled down the jet drive, using only enough power to maintain position. The boat's black hull would make it very hard to spot against the mottled gray-and-black shoreline. On the far side of the harbor, three state patrol cars burst out of the tree line, snaking down the access road to the docks.

Connor keyed the mic. "Take a number? Okay. How about the number three?"

"Three?" Evan answered.

"Yeah, like the three state cops hammering down the dock road right now. Piracy, kidnapping, robbery, assault. You're screwed."

Connor watched as the *Nu B* spun 180 degrees and headed for open water at full throttle. At dead low tide there was barely enough room for two boats to run the channel side by side. You had to know the exact location of every hull-gouging rock, and lurking just outside the markers was always Jaws. You had to take it easy. Use a light touch. However, from the way Evan was running the *Nu B*, Connor could tell he had no intention of taking it easy. He got the Hinckley up on plane and set a direct course for the harbor's mouth. Connor keyed the mic. "I told you there were cops on the dock. Didn't you believe me?"

Evan spit back, "Screw you. I'm out of here."

"Says you."

"What's that supposed to mean? You gonna try and stop me?" Evan asked.

"Not *try*, asshole."

"Fuck you and fuck Maine and fuck everyone in Maine. I never should'a left Arizona. But I got what I came for, plus a little something extra. A tight little something. If you know what I mean."

"Don't you even want to know how I'm going to kill you?" Connor made a small course correction and tweaked the throttle, vectoring the Hinckley on a forty-five-degree intercept. The key was timing. Not a light touch.

"Kill me? You've got to find me first."

Connor keyed the mic. "I know exactly where you are."

"Bullshit. You're bluffing."

"Was I bluffing about those staties?"

"Lucky guess."

Connor estimated Evan was now about three hundred yards from the harbor's mouth, making about twenty-four knots, the *Nu B*'s top speed. Turning at thirty-five knots, the Hinckley was closing quickly from behind and to the starboard side, exactly in Evan's blind spot. Right where Connor wanted it. And both boats were about sixty seconds away from occupying a very small patch of water.

Connor needed to keep up the distraction, make sure the little weasel had his hands full. He keyed the mic again. "So, what's your plan? Hit the open ocean? Go for a cruise? Because I doubt you're carrying enough fuel to make it back to Arizona."

"I'm carrying enough fuel to get out of this shithole, that's for sure."

"You might want to take it easy in the channel. You know, slow down a little."

"Why? Worried about your boat?"

"I am behind a few payments, now that you mention it." Connor could see Evan's silhouette in the dull glow of the *Nu B*'s instruments. The guy looked busy, his head darting around, one hand sawing on the wheel, trying to keep the boat on course, the other holding the radio mic. Connor couldn't see Crystal, and he didn't know if that was good or bad. "But you're carrying a lot of speed, and boating accidents are nasty."

"I thought you wanted to kill me."

"Oh, I'm going to kill you, but with my bare hands." Connor slightly eased off on the throttle, matching speeds as the two boats closed. The Hinckley was now only ten feet behind and five feet off the *Nu B*'s starboard side—both boats bearing down on the harbor's granite-clogged opening.

"This is bullshit. I don't got no more time to talk." Evan clicked off, but then, a second later—"Where the fuck *are* you anyway?"

"Right here." Connor jammed the throttle, and the Hinckley jetted forward, ramming the *Nu B*, the heavier, more powerful Hinckley driving the lighter boat forward and to the port side as they plowed through the treacherous water, hull to hull.

**EVAN WHIPLASHES** off the captain's chair, yelps in pain as the big stainless wheel slams into his gut. Coughing, hacking up a fine mist of dark blood, he fights the wheel with both hands, barely able to stay upright, battling the bucking, lurching boat as it slaloms through the dark, greasy water.

He cuts a quick glance over his right shoulder, and there's Nichols, grinning. Evan sputters, "The fucker. Where the hell did he come from?"

Nichols blatts his horn and points. Evan follows the gesture; the remnants of an old seawall loom to his left. He wrenches the wheel hard right, and a tiny gap opens between boats. "The fucker's just trying to scare me."

Evan steers into the other boat.

The tiny gap widens.

Then Nichols's bow falls off a few feet, keeps pace, but opens a bigger gap.

Evan says to himself, "Not really up for a game of chicken after all, huh? What a pussy."

He straightens the wheel and mashes the throttle full forward, eases his ass cheek against the edge of the captain's chair. "Full steam ahead. Smooth sailing all the way. Next stop. Next stop. Well, let's get clear of this shithole."

Evan licks his lips. "Where's that goddamn Dickel?" His head swivels around, stops. "There it is. Exactly what I need."

Keeping one hand on the wheel, he leans over, stretching, straining, trying to snag the bottle with his free hand without pulling his eyes away from the slice of ocean right off his bow.

Nichols's voice pops out of the radio. "Tricky bit of water coming up. Not sure you've got the draft to make it."

Evan looks over at Nichols standing in the wheelhouse of the other boat. He keys his own mic. "Draft? The fuck you talking about?"

From below, Crystal says, "He's talking about how much water you need under the boat, Mr. Pirate."

"I'm talking about Jaws tearing a big goddamn chunk out of your hull," Nichols echoes from the speaker.

"You mean your hull." Evan laughs and then squints through the windscreen at the flat water ahead, sparkling in the moonlight. "Besides, the tide's turned. Plenty of water."

"You better hope so," Nichols says.

The other boat edges up, crowding him.

Evan keys the mic, says, "There's enough water and enough room, and if you want to play chicken, then fuck you. I'm up for it. Hell, I grew up here. I know exactly where Jaws is. Plus, there's the line of red channel markers. All I have to do is keep them on my right. Just like when I came in."

Evan bears down on the first red marker, keeping it to his right.

The other boat matches speed, shadows him, but no contact.

Evan grins, makes a fast stab for the Dickel, and gets his fingers around the bottle's neck, snatching it off the deck.

He's raising the bottle to his mouth when Nichols's voice fills the wheelhouse. "Hey, asshole, sure you want to be on this side of the red markers?"

Evan lowers the Dickel and keys the mic. "Red right, dipshit."

"Maybe in Arizona," Nichols answers.

"Fuck you." Evan knocks back a big slug of bourbon, his eyes water, and he coughs blood into his hand. "Why are you so worried about the fuckin' channel markers?"

"Because it's red right returning," Crystal answers from the cabin.

"Bullshit," Evan snaps. "Since when?"

Nichols replies, "Christopher Columbus."

"Shit!" Evan drops the Dickel and wrenches the wheel. Desperately working to pull left of the marker, he slams against Nichols's boat.

But this time, it doesn't give.

The two boats flash by the first red marker. From below deck an explosive banging sound echoes violently through the hull. The whole boat shudders and flexes as the bow launches out of the water, porpoises down in a slap of spray that washes up and over the bow, momentarily blocking out the moonlit horizon.

But when the windscreen clears, the *Nu B* is still moving forward smartly. Evan relaxes against the captain's chair, glances smugly over at the other boat, still right off his starboard side, still keeping pace. "Fuckhead."

He's reaching for the mic when Crystal calls from below, "Hey, Mr. Pirate, we're taking on water."

CHAPTER 42

Connor trailed the foundering *Nu B* all the way from the mouth of Tranquility Harbor and into Seal Cove and watched Evan run it aground in about eighteen inches of water. High and dry. Then he disappeared, which wasn't easy on a thirty-six-foot lobster boat.

Not exactly the outcome he was looking for. Connor backed the Hinckley off several feet, hoping to relieve the pressure, give the guy a chance to sort out his limited options before he did something irreversibly stupid. However, Connor wasn't too optimistic. He was afraid that Crystal was in a bad place.

He punched up Russell's number on the cell. "Talk to me, Jeff."

"We can see you from the *Nu B*'s deck camera. Wave for the audience."

Connor asked, "What about the unit in the wheelhouse?"

"Nothing. He's not there. Can't see Crystal either."

"He either jumped overboard or he's hiding below."

"You should have let me put a camera in the forward berth."

"Yeah, that would have made you and the pervs on your crew happy. Hang on while I call him on the radio." Connor keyed the mic. "Yo, Evan, can you hear me? Pick up the mic, dirtbag. Might as well talk to me; there's nowhere to go."

No response.

Connor set down the mic and spoke into the cell. "I still can't see him or Crystal and the guy's not answering. I'm going to slide over and board her."

"Anything we can do?"

"No, sit tight and wait to hear from me." Connor was about to break the connection, but changed his mind and said to Russell, "Yeah, there is one thing. Turn off all the cameras."

Evan sloshed down into the small cabin and was surprised when the water came up to his knees. The first mate was tied facedown on the lower bunk. In the weak light generated by the boat's battery, he could see she was almost fully submerged as she frantically arched her back, struggling to keep her face clear.

Crystal looked over and asked, "Aren't you going to untie me?"

Ignoring her, he waded over to the storage locker built into the side of the hull.

"If you don't cut me loose, I'm going to drown," Crystal pleaded.

"Boat's grounded. Don't worry about it. Got to get something out of here; then we'll see about you." Evan knelt down in the cold water, twisted the latch, and pulled the locker door open.

Empty. *Where is the little cowboy statue? Gone? How is that possible?* Wouldn't that be a bitch. His whole trip a total jerkoff.

Evan squinted, trying to peer into the black water, past the surface glare from the flickering, dying lights. But the locker was almost fully flooded. He leaned forward, water up to his chest, and snaked his skinny right arm inside. Stretching, straining, his fingers finally touched cold bronze, and he thought he felt the horse's rump and tail. But he couldn't get a decent grip on the slippery thing.

Crystal repeated her request with more urgency. "I'm getting weak. I can't keep my head up much longer. You have to help me."

"Told you, there's nothing to worry about. The boat's sitting on the bottom," Evan replied.

Grunting and straining, he jammed his arm deeper into the narrow locker. The water now covered his shoulders, but he finally slipped his hand between the hull and the statue, wrapping his fingers around what felt like the horse's hind end. He pulled, but nothing happened. The Remington was stuck good.

"Just because the boat's run aground doesn't mean I won't drown."

"You talk too much. Stop interrupting me. This is my goddamn payday. I got to get this fucker out."

The water now lapping at his chin, little by little Evan snaked his arm deeper into the locker, inching his fingers tighter around the metal. As he pulled with all his strength, the Remington shifted slightly, like it was coming free.

"Ah, come to Daddy," Evan groaned.

Crystal thrashed against the ropes. "You don't understand."

"Shut up, goddamn it. You're not getting out of here until I get this fuckin' thing loose," Evan snapped.

As he tensed his shoulder for another effort, there was a heavy thump on the deck. The entire boat rocked on its keel. The Remington shifted again. This time his hand was wedged against the *Nu B*'s hull. Like one of those goddamn Chinese finger puzzles, the harder Evan pulled, the tighter he was trapped.

He paused in his struggle to free himself and shot a frustrated look at Crystal. "All right, smart-ass, what is it you think I don't understand?"

"High tide," she whispered as the boat lights finally winked out.

Connor stooped into the tiny cabin and swept the flashlight's tight beam across a bizarre scene: two heads poking above the slick, dark water. "Boy, the people at my bank are going to be pissed."

Crystal struggled on the lower bunk. "Get me out of here."

"Yes, ma'am," Connor replied.

Evan, slumped against the hull with the beady-eyed expression of an opossum caught in the headlights. He nodded stupidly toward the submerged locker. "Arm's stuck."

"Stuck, huh?" Connor waded down into the cramped cabin. "Forgive me if I don't take your word for it." He grabbed Evan's shoulder with both hands and pulled.

"Ow, shit! Told you. Arm's stuck," Evan complained. "You got to get some kind of tool. A saw or something. Cut me out."

Connor turned to Crystal. With his left hand, he cupped her chin for support and went to work on the ropes with his right. After several tries, he said, "Knots are pretty tight, especially now that they're wet. I'm going to need both hands. Can you hold yourself up a little longer?"

"Yes, but make it quick," she replied.

Connor reached into his pocket and pulled out a small Swiss Army knife. Biting the flashlight with his teeth, he opened the knife and quickly sliced the ropes from her hands and feet. He closed the knife, slipped it back into his jeans, and gathered Crystal into his arms.

Talking around the flashlight, Connor said to Evan, "Don't go anywhere. I'll be right back."

Holding Crystal to his chest, Connor made his way topside and with a few strides crossed over to the Hinckley, which he had left bobbing in the shallow water, tied alongside the grounded *Nu B*.

She was shivering and shaking as he carried her below. He laid her on the bunk, stripped off her wet clothes, and covered her with a heavy blanket.

Crystal spoke through chattering teeth. "Thank you. I don't think I could have kept my head up much longer."

Connor knelt next to the bunk and pushed a strand of damp hair out of her face. "Any injuries?"

"The side of my face hurts from where he hit me—otherwise nothing but some rope burns. I'll be fine once I warm up."

"I'll get you to the medical center to get checked out."

"What about Evan?"

Connor stood. "I'll take care of him now."

"Oh, good, you're still here." Connor smiled in the dark. "Let's make this quick."

"Yeah, yeah, no shit I'm still here. Now, get me loose. That girl said something about high tide." Evan craned his neck, working to keep his chin clear of the water.

"Yup, eight feet this time of the month." Connor wedged the flashlight under the edge of the mattress on the top bunk, angling it toward Evan. Then he wrapped his big arms around the man's skinny chest. "This might hurt a little."

"You mean eight feet, like out in the open water. Right?" Evan asked with a touch of apprehension.

"I mean like eight feet everywhere. The tide doesn't know the difference. It comes in, it goes out." Connor adjusted his grip. "Now hold still."

"Yeah, but not back here in the cove."

"Everywhere." Connor planted his feet and wrenched and felt Evan's shoulder pop.

Evan screamed, "Ah, ah, ah, ah, ah, ah!" He paused, sucking in a lungful of air. "Motherfucker! You dislocated my goddamn shoulder!"

"Apparently so," Connor replied, heading for the cabin's small doorway.

"I can't move my arm. I can't feel my fingers." Evan gave a frightened nod toward open ocean. He whined. "This ain't right."

# CHAPTER 43

Connor felt like he was sitting inside a giant ball of cotton as he steadied two coffee cups while Joanna filled them from the thermos she had brought from the house. Then they both settled back onto the padded bench in the *Prana*'s cockpit. A thick layer of fog blanketed the harbor. Its smoky tendrils, pulsing and drifting on the light breeze, teased their way up the shoreline but never strayed far from the water.

"Thanks for bringing the coffee. I really needed it," Connor said.

"You look like crap, little brother," Joanna offered.

"Tough night." Connor ran a hand over his heavy blue-black stubble, tugged at the front of his dirty hoody. "I wish you and Willis could have convinced Crystal to stay at the medical center."

"He said it looks like a minor concussion. But she still needed observation."

Connor waved in the direction of the cabin. "So I end up watching her for the rest of the night while she sleeps."

"I didn't think you'd mind. The way you shot out of the medical center last night—"

"Well, uh . . . I was worried about my boat. I've put a lot of money in that boat."

"I know. And she's not even your type." Joanna smiled.

"Exactly," Connor declared.

"You sure did a number on Daddy's precious toy." Joanna looked at the Hinckley. "Do I even want to know what happened to the *Nu B*?"

"The less you know, the better."

"Funny, that's almost the same thing Jeff said this morning. You must have been a very bad boy."

"Where is Russell?"

"Something called a preproduction meeting at the White Swan. I might see him tonight, not sure."

Connor sipped his coffee and tried to work the kinks from his neck. "What's the plan for Mom?"

"Now that the event has passed and she's stable, Willis wants to begin therapy as soon as possible. He sees no reason to move her, and she indicated that she prefers to stay here. So we'll grab a pile of money from Daddy's bank account, which he won't even miss, and set her up with the best. I'll hang for another day to put everything in motion, but I've got to get back to New York. The chief of surgery is screaming."

Connor looked over his sister's shoulder, in the direction of the house, as Trooper Mack appeared out of the fog. His spit-shined boots marked a dark trail through the dew-covered grass as he stalked across the yard, looking very unhappy. "Like I said, the less you know . . ."

Joanna followed Connor's gaze. "Oh boy, I don't want any part of this." She slipped off the bench. "I'll call you from the med center."

Connor watched Joanna stop and exchange a brief greeting with Trooper Mack. As they talked, she placed a hand on his upper arm, and Mack removed his Smokey the Bear hat, smiling broadly, practically melting from her attention. When she broke away and continued toward the house, Mack eyeballed her retreating figure. Then he fixed the hat low on his brow, clicked his scowl back in place, and continued toward the dock.

Coffee cup in hand, Connor addressed the trooper from the deck of the *Prana*. "What, no big smile, no snappy hello?"

Mack cut a guilty glance in the direction of the house, quickly composed himself, and then pulled a small notebook from his shirt pocket. "You're screwing with me, and I'm getting tired of it."

"Coffee?" Connor held up his cup. "Sorry, no donuts."

The trooper pointed at the damaged Hinckley. "Looks to me like you ignored my advice about taking matters into your own hands. Mind telling me what happened?"

As if noticing the damage for the first time, Connor squinted at the scarred and gouged hull. "Your guess is as good as mine. Found it like this when I came down here this morning. A real shame, but it's like a new car: that first ding is always the worst. Maybe you should talk to Pratt."

Trooper Mack shifted his weight in frustration. "Now you're telling me he stole *your* boat and smashed the side of *this* boat? The side that's tied against the dock. That's bullshit, and you know it." He consulted his notebook, and said, "Plus the Coast Guard reported some crazy cross talk on channel seven last night. They said it sounded like two guys threatening each other. Care to explain?"

"All the lobstermen talk on channel seven, and I'm afraid the language can get pretty salty. I'll bring it up at the next meeting."

Mack fixed Connor with a disbelieving stare before continuing, "After you called me, we sent three cars to Tranquility Harbor. One of the troopers thinks he spotted the *Nu B*, but it turned and ran before docking. We may have spooked him."

"So, no Pratt."

"The Coast Guard's pitching in. Pratt's got a reputation as kind of a screwup. We'll find him. In the meantime, I interviewed Wade Baxter this morning."

"I'll bet he was a wealth of information." Connor sipped his coffee.

"He's not saying much. Confirmed your statement about Pratt stealing the *Nu B*. But he was kind of vague on the details—said he heard something from someone but couldn't remember who. These old boys can clam up when they don't want to get involved. But I think he knows more about what's going on around here than he's letting on. I've seen it before."

"Why don't you ask him about my truck?"

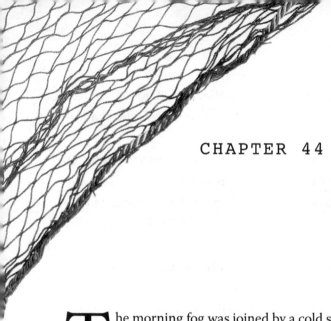

# CHAPTER 44

T he morning fog was joined by a cold spring rain that slanted against the windows of Tyler's suite in the White Swan. He sipped coffee and focused on the spreadsheet in his hand, preparing for tomorrow's board meeting. "Ronald, tell the team that the plan and the projections look good. Add them to the presentation."

Ronald nodded silently and typed on his laptop.

"Let's see the preliminary location list." Tyler exchanged papers with Ronald and studied the list. "So, we open with three in Maine, work out the kinks, and roll from there. That'll mitigate the downside risk of a failure. But if it hits, originating in Maine will help create the right image. Good, makes sense. This goes in too."

Again, Ronald nodded silently and tapped some keys.

"Okay, how about the test menu?" Tyler handed over the location list and refilled his coffee cup from a silver carafe. The remnants of a room service breakfast littered the table.

Ronald dug through a stack of papers.

Tyler sipped his coffee and waited.

Ronald switched to a different pile of papers and continued his search.

Tyler placed his coffee cup on the table, checked his watch, and cleared his throat.

Without looking up, Ronald frowned and attacked some loose file folders.

"Damn, boy, are you lost?" Tyler finally barked.

Ronald's head snapped up. "No. Just tired. You made me give up my room to Baxter, and I had to spend the night on a cot in Suzanne's room, and I didn't get any sleep."

"What happened, she try to recruit you for the home team?" Tyler laughed. "If that little gal can't turn you into a switch hitter, no one can."

Ronald squirmed in his seat, refusing to make eye contact. "It's not like that."

"It's not like what?" Suzanne asked as she entered the suite, heading straight to the room service cart.

"Ronald here was about to explain why he didn't get any sleep last night."

"I wasn't about to explain anything." Ronald produced a copy of the test menu, thrust it at Tyler, and bolted from his chair. "I'm going to find someplace to lie down. I can't function without sleep."

Carrying a plate of scrambled eggs, fresh fruit, and toast, Suzanne slipped onto the chair vacated by Ronald. "You shouldn't pick on the guy. He's got your back more than you realize. Way more. Besides, all we did was talk."

"Talk, huh?" Tyler gazed at Suzanne's legs and smiled. "I know we never could have spent the whole night in the same room and just talked."

"Ancient history. Want an update?" Suzanne dug into her eggs.

Tyler flicked the menu onto the table and settled back in his chair. "Update me."

"The team's working on Baxter now. Hair, beard, clothes, everything. I mean everything. The guy's pretty rough, but once we exfoliate a lifetime of barnacles, he'll be presentable."

"I love it. We're turning a real lobsterman into a corporate lobsterman."

"No choice. The public can only take so much reality." Suzanne nibbled on a corner of toast. "We're all going down to his boat in

Tranquility to walk through the setup. That way, when we start taping this afternoon, everything runs smoothly."

"Do you need me for that?" Tyler asked.

"It's Baxter that the director is worried about. He says there's a big difference between mugging for the camera on a reality program and taping a slick promotional spot."

"Any word from Pelly's people?"

"They're circling. I think they're nervous you might not show Friday."

"I'm not going to help *Sixty Minutes* savage my company on national TV."

"Oh, I don't think they need your help."

"You know what I mean. Why doesn't Pelly go after Olive Garden or Pizza Hut or, or . . . Friday's? Talk about a calorie pusher. Their customers are practically fat junkies. Why pick on us?" Tyler stood and adjusted his shoulder rig. "I'm going for a ride."

Suzanne carried her plate and coffee cup over to the room service cart. "Will I be able to reach you?"

"Call my cell," Tyler replied. "This Baxter character worries me. I didn't want to tell Ronald, but after we split up at the medical center, the guy never even showed last night. We kicked Ronald out of his room for nothing. Feels like another Rowdy Robby. I wish we had a backup plan, something else to get the board off my ass."

"What are you thinking?"

"Ernie's the weak link. Something Ronald said gave me an idea. I've got a call into a friend at Goldman. I'll let you know."

# CHAPTER 45

After last night's aquatic insanity, Connor planned to keep playing dumb regarding the *Nu B* until someone like the Coast Guard found her. Meanwhile, his whole lobster business plan required some serious thought. Particularly the sunken boat part.

Dressed in jeans and a flannel shirt, clean shaven, hair still damp from the shower, he marched into the kitchen and went straight for the coffee pot, pouring himself a fresh cup. He sat at the center island and watched Crystal working at the Viking.

"I know you were planning to leave today, but I think you should see Willis first, just to make sure you're okay."

"Can you drive me? I'm still pretty shaken up from last night." She had showered first and was wearing black yoga pants and a lightweight green fleece jacket over a tank top.

"I'm going to visit Mom, so sure. That was some scary shit. That nutjob could have really hurt you." Connor wrinkled his nose. "That doesn't smell like bacon and eggs. I thought you said you were going to make us breakfast."

"I am making us breakfast." She turned from the stove and placed two steaming bowls on the counter.

Connor stared. "Doesn't look like bacon and eggs."

"That's because it's oatmeal with blueberries and walnuts." She pulled four pieces of bread from the toaster and arranged them on a plate. "Spelt bread."

"What kind of bread?"

"Spelt. It's a grain, but better than wheat. More protein. But it still has gluten. So it's not perfect." She offered the plate.

Connor examined a piece, turning it over in his fingers, finally taking a small, hesitant bite. He chewed for a few seconds before swallowing. "Disgusting. Tastes like cardboard."

"The fiber's good for your colon."

"You spend way too much time thinking about my colon. Can't we eat a real breakfast? You know, eggs, bacon, ham, home fries, buttered rolls. I'm starving."

"I'm just trying to do something nice for you."

"By fixing my colon?"

Crystal slammed the plate on the counter and blurted, "You're so dense!"

She bolted from the kitchen.

Connor trailed her to the doorway and watched as she ran down the lawn toward the dock, her small shape finally swallowed up by the thick fog.

Maybe he was dense. He knew enough about women to realize that they didn't come with an owner's manual. But a short set of instructions sure would make things easier. Even a label or a small tag—*dry clean only.*

He took a deep breath and followed.

Crystal was standing on the *Prana*'s deck, wiping her eyes with a tissue, when he crossed over from the dock. He searched her face for a clue that would explain the outburst, finally asked, "I get the feeling that this isn't about breakfast."

She dabbed at her eyes and shook her head. "Of course this isn't about breakfast."

"Then what? Did I do something?" Connor asked.

"No." Crystal paused. "Well, yes."

"Thanks. That clears things up." Connor wished for that set of instructions.

"This is about last night," Crystal explained.

"Oh."

"You could have gotten hurt. Or even killed. What were you thinking?"

"I just reacted. But everything worked out."

"And you sacrificed your boat to save me."

"Yeah, I guess the *Nu B* didn't make out so well. I'm going to miss her."

She leaned against him, resting her head on his shoulder. "You don't care about that boat."

"I put a lot of money into that boat." Connor wondered if this fact was only important to him.

"You can always get another one. If you really want to." She began to unbutton his shirt, lightly kissing his bare chest.

"I am . . . I will . . ." A lame response, the best he could come up with.

"Even though you don't like lobster fishing all that much." She slipped off the fleece jacket. Her nipples were hard against the thin tank top.

"Yes, I do. I love lobster fishing."

"For all the wrong reasons." Crystal began to unbuckle his belt. "Are you going to argue or take me into the cabin?"

"I thought I wasn't your type."

"I've been known to make exceptions."

"You think this is a good idea?" Connor asked.

"Absolutely not," she whispered

Connor scooped her into his arms. "Then I'm glad we finally agree on one thing."

An hour later, they were lying under a blanket on the bed in the main berth, Crystal nestled into the curve of Connor's side, her head resting on his chest. Maybe he did need to change his diet. Or go to the gym. Take up running. Something. One round and he was exhausted. He wondered how a girl who barely weighed a hundred pounds sopping wet could generate so much *leverage.*

Crystal propped herself on one elbow and said, "You never told me what happened to Evan."

"Evan? Nothing. He decided to stay on the boat."

She gave him a disbelieving look. "What are *you* going to do now?"

"Get some real food and then go visit my mom."

She poked him in the ribs. "No. I meant about fishing, the show—you know, everything."

"Get back to my agenda. Patch up the *Nu B.* Start hauling traps. Kick Wade's ass."

"You could make a career of it." Crystal slid on top of Connor.

"Not to mention the TV show. Maybe I can get an agent and land some movie roles. I could play myself when they make a movie about *Lobster Wars.*"

She straddled him, and the heat between her legs began to make him hard. "And how does that feel."

"A little to the right."

"No, I meant when you talk about going back to everything you were doing before. How does it make you feel?" She reached between her legs and grabbed him.

"I'm done screwing around. Time for a new plan." And he hoped the conversation was over too.

Connor's eyelids clicked open. He must have dozed off.

Crystal was lying on her side, staring at him with those soft green eyes. "You were snoring."

"At least I was breathing." He contemplated the potential effort required to swing his legs over the edge of the bed and work his way into a sitting position. "Were you *trying* to kill me?"

"Once we get your diet rearranged, you'll definitely have way more energy. Plus throw in a little yoga. You know, for flexibility."

"No one's complained before."

"Maybe you're just out of practice." Crystal smiled. "How long has it been? A month? A week? Three days?"

"Look who's talking." Connor struggled upright. "What would Thich Nhat Hanh say about your vow of celibacy? He must be rolling over in his grave."

"A little backsliding is to be expected. Besides, I understand he was very forgiving."

"Not like my mother." Connor swung his legs over the side. "She's expecting a visit."

"Then we should probably leave for the medical center."

"You don't have to come. She's my responsibility, not yours." Connor noticed a small tag on the inside of his flannel shirt—*cold water wash, tumble dry, low heat.*

Crystal sat up and sorted through the tangled pile of clothes. "You still don't get it, do you?"

# CHAPTER 46

Wade limped into the kitchen and was relieved to find Kent and Darlene huddled around the table, giggling and laughing. "We got to get the new boat in the water and down to the harbor."

Kent rocked back in his chair, eyes wide. "You look like that guy on the box of fish sticks."

Darlene squealed with delight and clapped her hands. "Don't listen to him. I think you look great."

Wade ran a hand over his neatly trimmed beard. "Screw fish sticks." He was wearing a new flannel shirt and new jeans picked out for him by a hot little number that Suzanne, the business chick, had called a *stylist*. "Come on, we don't got much time."

"We've been waiting on you," Kent said. "But I did some work on the boat yesterday. Won't take much to get her going."

"Good, because they want to practice the TV commercial in a few hours. You know, before the real thing later today." Wade rummaged in the kitchen cabinets.

"This is exciting. Can we watch?" Darlene asked.

"Sure, why not." Wade searched the pantry. "What's with all that crap in your truck?"

"We're moving in together," Kent replied.

"We rented a cute little house just outside Camden, and it's got a big barn Kent can make into a studio." Darlene placed a hand on

Kent's shoulder. "So he'll have more space to work his art. And I'm gonna take me some business classes up to the community college."

"Business classes, huh?"

"Yeah. That way I can keep the books for Kent, make sure nobody is ripping him off, and he can concentrate on his work."

"Good for you." Wade finally spotted the nearly empty bottle hidden behind a box of cornflakes.

Kent asked, "What are you looking for?

"Vodka," Wade answered as extracted his prize from the pantry. "Mom needs to find a better hiding place."

"A little early?"

"Big toe's killing me. Had 'em change the bandage last night, but the fucker still hurts like a bitch." Wade shook out two OxyContin and slugged them down straight. He wiped his beard with the back of his hand and grinned at Kent and Darlene. "Ayuh, everyone's getting what they want."

Darlene frowned. "Just long as Evan don't come around and spoil things."

"Yeah, that would suck," Kent added.

Wade leaned against the counter, feeling the vodka rush on an empty stomach. During last night's limo ride to the medical center, the idea of getting everything he wanted had finally hit him. Sure, he would still have to put up with Nichols running his goddamn lobster boat and horning in on the TV show, and maybe Wade *had* taken their war a bit too far, but it was Evan who was the real problem. College boy was keeping his mouth shut about what happened after Russell turned off the cameras, but Wade had a pretty good idea. "I wouldn't worry about Evan."

The new *Sweet Tail* was solid and fast. Much nicer than the old *Sweet Tail*. Kent had worked his ass off, getting her ready in only four hours. But right before the crane lowered her into the harbor, Darlene had insisted they paint the old name on the new boat. Despite the added time, Wade realized it was a better idea than Darlene could even know. Tyler had never seen the old *Sweet Tail* in the daylight, so now no explanation was needed. As for the other lobstermen asking questions about what happened to his old boat, fuck 'em. Wade was a reality TV star and restaurant big shot.

Wade nudged the throttle forward, squeezing a few more rpms out of the big diesel. He glanced at this watch. If he was going to make the docks in Tranquility in time for the practice session, then he really needed to pick up the pace. He had the wind in his favor, but he was bucking an outgoing tide that would only get worse once he turned directly into the harbor's entrance. Even though the morning fog had thinned, it was now mixed with a cold spring rain, keeping visibility under one hundred yards.

He pulled the little brown pill bottle out of his pocket and squinted at the label. The instructions said one every eight hours or as needed for pain. He couldn't remember when he last took one, but his jaw ached and his big toe hurt like a mother. And that counted as pain. So he doubled up, washing down two with a slug of vodka.

Faster than he could have hoped, the vodka and narcotics kicked in, and Wade's head disconnected. It snapped right off at the neck, hovering above his shoulders, receiving no signals from his body. He might have an aching jaw and roasted big toe blackened with third-degree burns, but his brain didn't give a shit. Which was better than fine.

He looked down from his floating head, watching his hands on the wheel, guiding the new *Sweet Tail*. Wade marveled at how his body could perform such a difficult task as finding the mouth of Tranquility Harbor with almost zero visibility, in fog and rain, and a falling tide that was quickly exposing every hull-eating rock that guarded the harbor's entrance. *Piece of cake. Nooo problem.*

Wade actually placed one hand on top of his skull and tried to push his head back down onto his neck, to reconnect his fuzzy brain with his aching body. Something wasn't right. He needed to focus. Sort things out.

Evan was definitely off the board. The staties were clueless about everything—the robbery, the shooting at the White Swan, even torching Nichols's truck. *Lobster Wars* was about to start up again, and his deal with Tyler was going to make him rich.

So what was the problem?

As he plowed on in the crappy conditions, Wade's brain pondered the issue while his hands continued to mind the controls. Whatever was bothering him remained just out of reach, repeatedly slipping from his mental grasp.

He had all but given up when out of the fog and rain a dull-red channel marker materialized directly off his bow. Acting purely on instinct, Wade wrenched the wheel hard left, squeezing past the bobbing marker with only inches to spare.

As he watched the red buoy silently glide past his starboard side, he pounded the wheel and roared with laughter until tears leaked down his cheeks.

Twenty minutes later, Wade carefully backed the new *Sweet Tail* into his slip. He put out the bumpers and then grabbed the lines and moved quickly to make the boat fast to the dock. Once he was satisfied the boat was secure, Wade rewarded his efforts with a healthy shot of vodka, killing the bottle.

He had made good time after all, beating the production crew by forty minutes. But the booze, pain, and stress were finally getting to him. Wearing him down. The bunk in the small V-berth looked pretty cushy. Very cushy, in fact. So a little nap before his big moment seemed like a great idea.

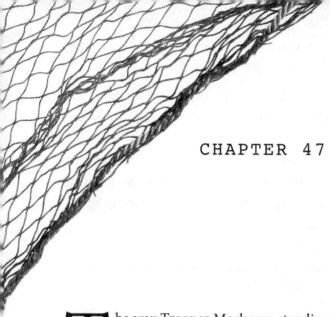

## CHAPTER 47

The way Trooper Mack was standing in the medical center lobby—feet planted, spine rigid, one hand resting on the butt of his sidearm—Connor could have sworn the guy was about to arrest him. Or shoot him. He nodded a silent greeting and tried to usher Crystal past the officer without a conversation, but Mack moved to his left, blocking their path.

"A word, Connor." Mack fished a small notebook from the breast pocket of his uniform shirt.

Connor turned to Crystal. "You go ahead. I'll be there in a minute."

"I can wait." Crystal smiled at Mack. "This won't take long, will it?"

"Depends," Mack replied without returning her smile. "The Coast Guard found your boat."

"I'm not surprised. Those guys are superefficient, especially when it comes to solving crimes. Where is it?"

Mack frowned at his notebook. "Run aground in Seal Cove. And no sign of Pratt. But I'm sure he'll turn up."

"I wonder why the tide didn't float it out to sea," Connor replied.

"There's a big hole in the bottom of the hull."

"Ah, well, that surely explains everything. Doesn't it?" Everything except one tiny nagging thought that now began to form in Connor's mind; maybe it had been a mistake to rely on the tide to do his dirty work.

"Not everything." Mack eyed Connor suspiciously. "Here's the part that's got me scratching my head."

"Yes?" Connor replied, imagining the handcuffs.

"There was also damage to the *right* side of your boat. And it looks like it would match what I saw on the *left* side of the Hinckley."

Connor shrugged. "Evan could have smashed against anything."

"True. But whatever he hit left black paint on *your* boat," Mack paused. "Isn't the Hinckley's hull black?"

"I have a confession to make," Crystal interrupted.

Both men stared at her.

Connor could almost hear the cuffs snick into place, feel their metallic pinch.

Officer Mack tilted his head toward her. "Go ahead. I'm listening."

She faced Connor. "I'm sorry. It was me. I scratched your dad's boat. Even though you told me not to take it out, I did. I couldn't resist. Just for a short ride. But when I came back, I misjudged the wind and banged against the *Nu B*. I hope you'll forgive me."

"Joyriding in my father's brand-new Hinckley. After I explicitly instructed you not to. That's a flagrant disregard of your captain's orders," Connor scolded. "I'm very disappointed in you."

"I understand." Crystal nodded and hung her head.

"This is completely unacceptable. I may have to find a new first mate."

"Can you please keep me on long enough to work off the cost of repairs?"

"I'll think about it. But I'm very upset." Connor scowled and pointed down the hall. "Now go wait in my mother's room."

Officer Mack glowered, his lips pressed into a hard line, the corner of his mustache twitching.

Connor paused in the doorway of Brooke's room. The volume of flowers had doubled. His mother was propped up in the bed, Crystal leaning over the side rail with her ear next to Brooke's mouth, writing on a tablet of paper while Brooke spoke quietly.

"I like what you've done with the place. Very cheery." Connor kissed her forehead.

Brooke gamely worked half of her face into a smile and gestured at the room. "Mah fends on da auts consal. Dey worreed."

"They love you, Mom."

Brooke tried to roll her eyes. The effect was comical and sad at the same time.

Crystal tore a page from the tablet, folded it, and slid it into an envelope, which she sealed and said, "Can I get you anything else?"

Brooke nodded. "Nu fends."

"Your mother wants you to deliver this to Tyler." Crystal handed the envelope to Connor.

"What is it?" Connor asked.

Brooke replied, "Ah . . . ah . . . poum."

"Good news, Mom," Joanna said as she and Russell entered the room. "I've set everything in motion for you to rehab at the house. If nothing changes, Dr. Willis plans to release you tomorrow."

"Much better energy at the house," Crystal offered. "Much more peaceful environment."

Joanna looked from Crystal to her brother. "Speaking of energy, what have you two been up to? I was expecting you hours ago. It's almost one o'clock."

"Nothing," Connor replied. "Having breakfast. Taking care of a few things. You know, organizing."

"Getting some rest," Crystal added.

"Connor doesn't look very rested," Joanna observed. "He looks worn out."

Brooke interrupted, "Fust mate, ah? Oly en da naticul sens, ah?"

Russell grinned. "Dude, you look like crap."

"It was a long night, *remember*?" Connor grabbed Russell by the arm, herding him toward the doorway. "Out in the hall, we need to talk."

Connor pulled a sheath of papers from the back pocket of his jeans and slapped them into Russell's hand. "Contract and release for this year's production."

"Great. It's about time." Russell studied the pages, looking confused. "These aren't signed."

"Very observant. I'm done. I quit."

"You're kidding, right?" Russell asked.

"Never been more serious in my life. I don't know what I was thinking when I agreed to do it. Should have had my head examined."

"But what about the show? The exposure? The fame?"

Connor fixed Russell with a cold stare.

"I know. I know. Who am I kidding? I'm only doing it to pay the bills."

Connor poked a finger at Russell. "At least there's something positive in it for you."

"The executive producer and the network are going to go ballistic." Russell paused. "So I have to ask. Sure you won't reconsider? You know, take one for the team?"

Connor pointed at Brooke's room. "The show's caused me nothing but grief."

Russell nodded. "Fucking reality TV.

**THE STEADICAM FOLLOWS** Connor as he climbs the stairs. "Didn't you get the memo? I quit. Your foul-mouthed little munchkin boss can yell and scream all she wants. It's not about her life. It's about mine." He pushes open the door to suite 210. "And no, I'm not 'still' under contract. So I don't know what you're planning to do with this footage."

Tyler is sitting in a straight-backed chair,

suit jacket off, sleeves rolled up, reading a document. Ronald and Suzanne are each jabbering on their cell phones, holding separate conversations as they wander around the room.

Tyler looks up and gives a wicked smile. "Connor, you sure set a fox in the henhouse."

"You heard?"

"Shit, boy. I could hear the screaming through the floorboards." Tyler replies. "Can't say I blame you, but it does potentially scramble my plans."

"Your plans?"

Tyler points at the camera. "That's not the news media?"

"Confused cameraman." Connor shakes his head.

Tyler stands and takes a half step forward but stops when Evan stumbles out of the suite's bedroom, holding Tyler's big, nickel-plated .45 in his left hand.

Evan's limp right arm is wedged under his belt, held immobile against his body. His clothing is damp, the knees of his jeans shredded and bloody, the shoulder of his jean jacket ripped at the seam. His greasy hair is slicked back, and his dilated eyes stare without blinking.

The giant black hole in the end of the .45's barrel wavers and jumps.

Evan sniffs and shoves the gun at Tyler. "You think I'd forget about that check?"

"How did you get here?" Tyler asks.

"Swiped a fuckin' moped."

"No. I mean in my room."

"Contractor left a ladder outside. Must still be working on the window that asshole pitched me out of." Evan swings the .45 at Connor.

"That's the last time I count on the tide to wash out the garbage," Connor says.

"Should'a killed me proper when you had the chance. You'd be surprised how much pain a guy can take, he's got a head full'a Oxy." Evan touches the barrel of the .45 to his damaged right shoulder, then swings the big gun back to Connor and jerks the trigger, and the .45 booms.

The camera angle goes crazy—floor, ceiling, walls, furniture—and finally steadies.

"Shit!" Connor doubles at the waist, drops to his knees, and grabs at the bicep of his left arm. Blood flows from between his fingers. "That hurts like a bitch. I hate guns."

"Damn, I can't hit nothing with my left hand." Evan tries to line up the sights. "Hold still."

Tyler shouts. "Wait! I'll pay you."

Evan lowers the pistol and stares.

"Ronald, get the check from my briefcase."

"Me?" Ronald whines.

"Yeah, Ronald, get the check," Evan mimics in

a squeaky voice.

Suzanne asks, "You think this is the best idea, Tyler?"

"Never argue with a loaded gun. Besides, it's only money." Tyler accepts the check from Ronald and waves it at Evan. "Fifty grand. Happy?"

"Shit, yeah." Evan laughs, cuts a glance at the camera. "That thing on?"

Connor sputters. "You're going to give this asshole fifty thousand dollars?"

Tyler holds it out to Evan. "Here, take it."

Evan takes half a step forward and pauses. "Goddamn it." Points the .45 at his limp right hand pinned under his belt. "Stick it between my fingers."

Tyler steps forward and complies. "There. Now get the hell out of here."

Evan hits Tyler between the eyes with the gun's barrel. Tyler drops to the floor with a grunt, and a gash opens on the man's forehead. Blood streams into his eyes and down his face.

"Why'd you do that?" Ronald screams and moves to help his boss.

Evan levels the .45 at Tyler. "Too many rich fuckers always calling the shots."

"No!" Ronald snarls and lunges at Evan.

The big gun booms again as both men crash to

the floor.

Image jerks, levels, steadies.

Ronald rolls away, clutching his side. A red bloom appears on his light-blue dress shirt, his face ashen with shock.

Suzanne cries. "Oh, Ronald, no, no, no!"

"Dumbass." Evan lurches to his feet, looks around. "Now, where was I? Oh, yeah." He swings the .45 back toward Connor. "Like I said, should'a killed me for real when you had the chance."

The gun booms again, but Connor ducks, and the shot buries itself in the plaster wall.

Evan works to steady the heavy pistol, complains. "Goddamn it. Hold still. I don't got all day."

He jerks the trigger. Nothing.

He jerks the trigger again. Nothing.

Evan glares at the .45. "Fucker's jammed. Piece'a shit."

Connor inches forward.

Evan attempts to clear the jam by pinching the slide between his knees.

Connor sucks in a deep breath, gathers himself.

Evan turns the .45 around and wedges the slide between the heel of his dead hand and his hip.

Connor rocks forward, pulling his legs under,

tenses.

Holding the pistol's grip with his left hand,
Evan pushes down, and a shiny brass cartridge
pops free. The slide clacks home; the big .45
flashes and booms again.

The gun recoils from Evan's hand, his legs shoot
out from under him, and he slams to the floor.
"Ow! Fuck! Shit!"

Connor freezes, staring, as blood begins to
spurt from Evan's right thigh. "That's got to
hurt."

"Huh?" Evan's eyes flick down. "This ain't
good."

"I wouldn't worry about it." Connor crawls
forward and plucks the .45 from the spreading
pool of blood. "It's only a flesh wound. Relax.
You'll be fine."

Evan stares into the camera. "That thing on?"

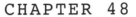

## CHAPTER 48

Wade rolled over and scrubbed his crusty eye sockets with the heels of his hands. Tight shafts of bright sunshine beamed through the small starboard portholes, bathing the little cabin in a friendly light. He heard the cheery morning sounds of a working harbor—the idle chug of warming diesels, the thump of bait boxes, the off-color greetings of fellow lobstermen.

He swung his legs over the edge of the bunk and pushed himself upright. His head pounded, and when he tried to swallow, the inside of his mouth felt like it was packed with cotton. His big toe throbbed.

The wristwatch strapped to his arm read 7 AM. He'd slept for almost eighteen hours. What happened to taping the commercial? They couldn't shoot it without him. Could they? Tyler must have made a last-minute decision to do it today and had no way to reach Wade, to let him know. Surely one of the production flunkies would show up any minute, probably bring Wade a hot coffee and an apology for the delay. After all, he was their big star, their meal ticket. Captain Wade Lobster Shacks couldn't move forward without him. That was the only logical explanation. But just in case, he thought it was a good idea to head down to Camden and check in. Make sure everything was still on track, business-wise.

Wade limped across the White Swan's lobby and found what looked like the inn's entire staff crowded around the bar, chatting with the animated, upbeat energy of a party. But Wade spotted his mother off to the side, sitting alone and sipping clear liquid from a short glass, a smoldering cigarette dangling from her thin lips.

"What the hell's going on? Why all the cop cars out front, and what's with the yellow tape across the stairs? They won't let me go up to see the restaurant guy."

"Never seen nothing like it in my whole life." Alice sipped from the glass without disturbing the cigarette. "Won't never get those images out of my head neither."

"What are you talking about? I thought you was working nights?"

"Picked up the dinner shift. Was gonna work the dining room, but they sent me upstairs with room service." Alice gestured in the general direction of the guest rooms.

"Upstairs where?"

"Two-ten."

"Tyler's room?"

Alice nodded. "Heard a *boom, boom* sound. Thought it came from outside, like kids lighting M80s or something."

"M80s?"

"At least cherry bombs." Alice shook her head. "But that dark-haired gal was screaming into her phone for the emergency people. Mr. Lane standing there with a towel to his head." Alice paused and drained half the glass. "The other three laying on the floor. Goddamn blood everywhere."

"Which three?"

"The young fella what works for Mr. Lane. And Nichols. And—"

Wade cut her off. "Connor? Connor Nichols?"

"Ayuh. And your buddy Evan, what was left of him."

"Evan?"

"Dead as a goddamn doornail. They say the fucker shot hisself. But I don't know." Alice shuddered. "Hard to tell with all that blood."

"Where's Nichols?"

"They took him and the young fella to the medical center."

Wade asked, "Tyler?"

"Gone. Him and the gal. Left first thing this morning."

"Where?"

"No idea." Alice shrugged. "The TV people, too."

"Why would the TV people leave? They were gonna begin taping. None of this makes any sense," Wade argued.

"Manager said they went back to New York City 'cause of some problem with the show. I been up all night talking to the police." Alice killed the drink, took a big pull on her cigarette, and blew a jet of smoke over Wade's head. "I can tell you one thing for sure. I ain't cleaning it up."

"Back to New York? Problem with the show?" Wade stuttered and looked away.

Alice leaned forward. "Why don't you look me in the eye when I'm talking to you?"

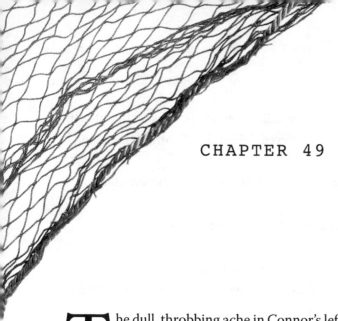

# CHAPTER 49

The dull, throbbing ache in Connor's left arm was only thinly masked by the morphine drip. But there was some good news. Breakfast. Scrambled eggs, hash browns, and toast. Plus, the pretty nurse who delivered this feast, with zero discussion of his colon, also hinted that he might get released tomorrow.

He leaned forward and peered around the curtain that partially separated the room's two beds. "How you doing over there?"

Ronald's response was weak. "Okay, I guess. Considering I was shot. That doesn't happen often in the corporate world. Lots of yelling and screaming but not much gunfire."

"Yeah, that was a little crazy even for Maine. Jumping on Evan to protect your boss took a real pair of stones. When you get on your feet, I owe you a boat ride."

"As long as it's not too rough," Ronald mumbled.

"Smooth as glass. Promise." Connor forked egg into his mouth.

Crystal and Joanna sailed into the room, taking up positions on each side of Connor's bed. Crystal grabbed his breakfast tray.

"Hey, I was eating that." Connor waved his plastic fork.

"We're going to use this as an opportunity to straighten out your diet."

"Gunshot wounds are not a dietary issue." Connor licked the last bit of egg from the fork's tines.

Joanna studied his chart. "You big dummy. You were lucky.

Missed the artery, missed the bone, minimal blood loss, and so far, no sign of infection. What the hell were you thinking?"

"Honestly, Joanna, I didn't plan to get shot delivering Mom's poem."

"Says you," she replied skeptically.

Crystal turned to other bed. "Poor Ronald. Can I get you anything?"

"No thanks, I'm just tired."

Joanna grabbed Ronald's chart. "*You* weren't so lucky. They had to take out a small part of your stomach. But everything looks good. Stable." She replaced the chart and headed for the doorway. "Willis discharged Mom yesterday. I'm finalizing arrangements with the home care service and then heading back to New York. He's all yours, Crystal. Good luck."

Crystal opened her bag of oils. "Even with two good arms, he can't keep up with me."

Ten minutes after Joanna left, Trooper Mack sauntered into the room, tugging at the corner of his brushy mustache. He tipped his hat at Crystal before addressing Connor from the foot of the bed. "A pacifist with a bullet hole in his arm. Ironic. But I told you Pratt would turn up."

"At least you cracked one case," Connor replied.

"We're still trying to determine how he got from your boat all the way to the Swan. And we want that tape, but the TV people are hiding behind the First Amendment. So our lawyers are fighting with their lawyers. But it doesn't really matter much at this point. Pratt's future movements, as they say, will be limited."

"Any word on my truck?" Connor asked.

Connor was just waking from a short nap when Phil walked into the room. The man looked drawn and tired and agitated all at the same time. Holding a white lunch sack, he stopped next to the bed, shifting his weight from foot to foot.

Connor yawned. "Let me guess."

"Grindah." Phil placed the sack on Connor's tray table. "Listen, I talked to the producer, and there's still a chance."

"No way. I'm done. Forget it," Connor replied while he peeked into the bag.

"But . . ." Phil whined, and moist tears formed in the corners of his eyes. "But the show . . . the money. It's our chance . . . *your* chance."

Connor shook his head. "Sorry."

"You won't even consider it? You know, for the good of—"

"No."

Phil placed his elbows on the bed rail and buried his face in his hands. His shoulders heaved and his body shook as he cried.

Later that afternoon, Connor perched on the edge of the bed, wearing blood-free jeans and new sneakers, while Crystal helped him finish dressing. They wanted him up and moving, but no way was he walking the halls with one of those butt-crack hospital gowns. She gently pulled a clean sweatshirt over his head and left arm, which was resting in a sling, and said, "After your walk, I'm getting a ride to the *Prana*. I can't think of any reason not to restart my trip. Can you?"

"Well, uh, I thought you were going to stick around," Connor replied.

"Only if I'm invited. And that doesn't sound like much of an invitation."

"Okay, okay." Connor waved his good hand in surrender. Damn, she was making him work for every inch. He didn't know where this was going, but clearly, there was only one way to find out. "Please stay."

Before Crystal could answer, Wade came limping into the room. "Heard you quit the show."

Connor replied, "Yup. Isn't that what you wanted? Now you're the big star of *Lobster Wars.*"

"But the TV people bailed. All of them. Went back to New York City. Not a word."

"I guess Russell knew what he was talking about," Connor replied.

Wade turned to Ronald. "Your boss left too."

"I'm not surprised. He has a very important board meeting today. In fact, it starts in about five minutes. I think," Ronald replied. "My brain's kind of fuzzy. Yeah, five."

"What about my deal? The restaurants? The TV commercial?" Wade asked.

Ronald pulled the blanket up to his chin. "I believe Tyler changed plans."

"But everything's all set. Maybe he's going to come back?" Wade asked hopefully.

Ronald giggled, "I seriously doubt it."

"But I've got a contract. It's all in writing."

"You'd have to speak with our legal department. But I'm sure there's an out clause." Ronald paused. "Like if *Lobster Wars* gets canceled."

"Canceled?"

"Or delayed," Ronald added.

A nurse came in to check Ronald's vitals.

"What's that got to do with the Captain Wade Lobster Shacks?" Wade asked, practically whining.

"Everything," Connor laughed.

Wade looked at Connor and then turned back to Ronald. "Is he right?"

"Afraid so," Ronald replied.

Before leaving, the nurse handed Ronald a long white envelope. "A messenger delivered this to the nurses' station right before I came in to check on you."

Ronald studied the envelope and then placed it unopened on the nightstand.

"Aren't you going to open it?" Crystal asked.

"I'll look later," Ronald sighed.

"Not curious?" Connor asked. "Probably your bill from the White Swan. I hear they have a very stringent no-gunfight policy. I bet they tacked on some serious extra charges."

"It's from Tyler."

Wade scowled. "Boss sends you a letter and you don't look?"

"I've got a pretty good idea what it says. Tyler always terminates people in writing." Ronald looked at his phone. "His meeting must have started."

"Your boss cans you for getting shot?" Wade snickered. "What a shit."

Crystal frowned. "That's cold."

Tyler glanced at his watch and pushed the intercom button on his desk phone. "Are all the board members here?"

His secretary replied, "We're waiting for one more. His limo is stuck in traffic. Maybe fifteen minutes."

"Has Ernie arrived?"

"Yes, sir."

"Please ask him to come to my office."

"Right away."

Tyler tore a small sheet of paper from a notepad and began writing. A minute later, his secretary escorted Ernie Peltz into the office. The man was short and pear shaped, with a bad combover and a very expensive, dark-blue suit that did little to hide his bulk.

Tyler made his way around the desk, right hand outstretched. "Ernie, good to see you."

"Tyler." Ernie nodded. "Sorry about all this business with the board, but they're really pressing. I didn't know what else to do."

"I understand." Tyler placed the slip of paper into Ernie's fat hand. "That's the direct line for my guy at Goldman. They're working on a deal that could lead to a major IPO. I thought you might find it very interesting. He's expecting your call."

Tyler's intercom buzzed. "Mr. Lane, everyone's accounted for and seated in the boardroom."

Tyler clapped Ernie on the shoulder and gestured toward the doorway. "Shall we?"

Connor was thinking about the second half of Phil's grinder, which he had carefully wrapped and hidden under his pillow, when Ronald's cell phone chimed.

Ronald said to Crystal, "Can you put it on speaker? I don't feel like holding it."

"Certainly." Crystal hit the icon and placed the phone on Ronald's tray table.

"Ronald?" Suzanne asked. "Can you hear me? How are you?"

"I've got you on speaker. I'm okay, but tired and weak, and everything aches. What happened at the meeting?"

"The whole thing lasted fifteen minutes. Ernie Peltz made a motion for the board to unanimously endorse Tyler, and when they balked, he and Tyler combined their votes to remove the entire board. There's still some legal maneuvering, but they're out," Suzanne paused. "Listen, Tyler's waving me into a meeting. Got to run. Feel better."

Ronald broke the connection and relaxed into his pillow with a giant smile. "That was *my* idea."

"What about the restaurants?" Wade asked. "She didn't say anything about the restaurants."

"Tyler's real problem was with the board, but now he's taken care of it."

"This is all bullshit. I'm not getting *my* deal because of a bunch of rich business guys voting at some fuckin' meeting. I'm done with all of you." Wade stormed from the room.

"It's not bullshit to Tyler." Ronald plucked the envelope from the nightstand and turned it over in his fingers like he was trying to decide what to do. "Rowdy Robby's his life."

"Now you're going to open it?" Crystal asked.

"Might as well get the bad news over with." Ronald slit the flap with his finger, pulled out several sheets of paper, and read.

Connor asked, "Well?"

Ronald lowered the pages, a look of surprise on his face. "Tyler's awarded me fifty thousand stock options at three dollars each."

"Stock options?" Crystal asked. "That's a deal with the devil."

"Not bad," Connor said. "What does Rowdy Robby trade at?"

"It closed yesterday at forty-five a share. That's a forty-two-dollar spread." Ronald paused, frowning, obviously trying to do the math in his head. "Holy shit!"

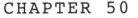

# CHAPTER 50

C onnor knew that it was going to take a lot more than a stroke to break Brooke Nichols. He was looking forward to seeing his mother back in her home. But the first thing he noticed when he and Crystal pulled up to the house was the long black limo wedged in the turnaround. Edwin must have finally surfaced.

Connor bailed out of the Land Cruiser's passenger seat. "Why don't you take the gear down to the boat. This is a family matter."

Ignoring his instructions, Crystal entered the house right on Connor's heels. "Let me help you."

"I don't need two good arms to deal with my old man." Connor adjusted the sling as he stalked across the foyer.

"That's not what I meant and you know it." Crystal tugged on the back of his shirt, trying to slow him down. "You need to calm down. Find your center. Breathe. Breathe."

Connor entered the living room and was brought up short by the sight of his mother sitting on the sofa, surrounded by three men in dark business suits, none of whom were his father.

Brooke offered a crooked smile. "Hallo, Cahner."

"What the hell's going on?" Connor demanded.

The oldest of the three men—salt-and-pepper hair combed straight back, gray flannel corporate uniform, golfing tan—stood and offered his hand. "Jennings Wilson of Simpson, Donnelly and Wilson."

"You're lawyers?" Crystal asked.

Connor ignored Jennings's hand. "Of course they're lawyers. The question is what kind."

"Our firm handles a wide range of clients. But I specialize in divorce. These two young men are associates of—"

"That's what I figured." Connor turned to Brooke. "Unbelievable. Dad doesn't even bother showing his face. Instead he sends these guys—vultures in five-thousand-dollar suits."

Jennings cleared his throat. "Mr. Nichols, I don't believe you understand—"

"This is intimidation, pure and simple. You three roll in here when my mother's recovering, trying to badger her into signing—"

"But, Cahner," Brooke tried to interrupt.

Crystal touched his sleeve. "Breathe, Connor, breathe."

"Enough bullshit. Time to go before I get really pissed." Connor grabbed Jennings by the arm and dragged him toward the front door. Jennings's associates began to stand. "Tell my father—"

"But, Cahner!" Brooke fought to spit out the words. "Dey're ma lawurs!"

"Huh?" Connor paused and stared at his mother.

Brooke pounded the sofa in frustration. "Ma lawurs! Ma lawurs! Ma lawurs!"

The next morning Connor walked out onto the patio and stopped next to Brooke's wheelchair. The sun was bright and warm, but she was wrapped in a light cashmere blanket, an open spiral notebook and pen resting on her lap. Connor dropped to one knee and gently folded Brooke's hands in his own. "I'm very happy with the progress you've made in such a short time. But are you sure you're going to be okay by yourself?"

"Joanna's got more peepol working here than in ah hospatal."

"I meant Dad."

"That waas ova ah long time aago. I waasn't willing to admit it. Now it's jus lawurs fightin. Wha about you? Whas your plaan?"

"I need to borrow the boat."

"Da Hinckley?"

"Dad will never be satisfied with the repairs. Have your lawyers put it on the list." Connor grinned.

"Then wha? That's not much of ah plaan."

"I'll figure out something by the end of the summer." Connor shrugged. "I thought I was the one you worried about least."

"You're right. I'm out of da advice business." Brooke squeezed his hands with remarkable strength.

They were both distracted by the sound of the Hinckley's motor burbling to life. Crystal moved around the deck, storing gear, preparing to leave.

He turned back to find his mother sporting a lopsided grin. She said, "First mate, ah?"

Wade wiped his beard with the back of his hand and passed the Wodka to Kent. They were sitting side by side on the lobster tank of the new *Sweet Tail* while Darlene leaned against the gunwale, arms crossed, hugging herself. Wade had just finished explaining the events of the last forty-eight hours.

"So, all that bullshit for nothing." Kent laughed and knocked back a heavy slug of the clear liquor, then offered the bottle to Darlene.

Wade nodded. "Go figure."

Darlene shook her head at the bottle. "At least we don't have to worry about Evan coming around and spoiling things for us."

"He was the one robbed Connor's mother and hit her on the head?" Kent passed the bottle back to Wade.

"Ayuh. I assume so, but he never admitted it straight out."

Darlene said, "I bet it was him, the way he was eyeing Brooke's place the day we worked Kent's showing."

"I wonder what he did with the art he stole. Stuff must be someplace. Those were some very special pieces. They're worth a lot of money." Kent retrieved the bottle from Wade.

"Asshole probably sold it down to Boston," Wade said.

Kent shook his head. "I guess we'll never know."

"Took the answer to his grave." Wade looked out over the placid water.

"Maybe he buried it somewhere," Darlene said. "You know, like a pirate."

Wade decided to change the subject. "Guess I'm stuck livin' with Mom for a while longer. What'd she have to say about you moving out?"

"Not much. But she's been acting stranger than normal." Kent sat the bottle on the lobster tank. "I was coming out of the market late the other night. Right when Phil likes to close down, and here comes Mom all dressed up in her church clothes. And no shit, he unlocks the door for her."

Wade shuddered as he grabbed the Wodka. "Gimme that."

"What do you think Connor's going to do?" Darlene asked.

"The salvage guy brought the *Nu B* to the boatyard. I'm not sure it's worth fixing, most likely sell it for parts," Kent replied. "He could settle with his insurance and buy another boat."

"Ayuh. Whatever," Wade said. "Don't care."

"So, what are *you* going to do?" Darlene asked.

Wade swished the remaining vodka around in the bottle and paused before raising it to his lips. "Got a new boat. Might as well go fishing."

Connor guided the Hinckley through the early-morning swells, heading for his first string of buoys. The late-September air was crisp, the water temperature was falling, and soon the lobster would move offshore. But he had a few more weeks of hard fishing before Maine's long, cold winter brought the season to a close.

"Five minutes to the first string. Bait bags ready?" Connor called over his shoulder.

"I've made at least three dozen," Crystal replied. She was wearing yellow bibs over a heavy white hoody. Standing at the bait station, her gloved hands were a blur as she filled and tied bait bags.

"We'll try to pull ten strings today. That should put us back at the dock by three at the latest."

"Good. Darlene and I have a meeting at five with the real estate agent to sign the lease for that second space. It's going to make a very nice yoga studio."

"Splitting her time with Kent isn't a problem?"

"Not at all. She's very organized, probably the best manager I've ever had. And the clients love her."

Connor approached the string of ten red-and-white buoys, threw the motor into neutral, stepped away from the wheel, and grabbed the boat hook. He leaned over the side and, in one swift motion, snagged the line, looped it over the block and around the hauler, and started it spinning. The line snaked over the rail and coiled onto the deck. When the wire trap broke the water's surface, he stopped the hauler, grabbed the trap, and heaved it onto the flat wooden workstation mounted on the Hinckley's gunwale.

"Nice," Connor said.

He opened the door and began pulling out lobster, measuring each. One, two, three, four. All legal. After he tossed the last one into the holding tank, Crystal darted forward, removed the old bait bag, and re-baited the trap with a fresh bag. That done, Connor tossed the trap and buoy back into the water, keeping clear of the line flowing over the side, pulled by the heavy trap.

They repeated the procedure nine more times, and thirty more lobster were added to the holding tank.

"That was a good string. We may haul some good numbers today." Connor stepped back into the wheelhouse, threw the motor into gear, and headed for his second string. "Now that the summer's over, Mom is going back to Darien, and she wants to know if we'd like to stay at the house. What do think?"

"We'd have to drive back and forth from Camden on days we run the boat, but only until the season's over. I like staying on the *Prana*, but I don't want to leave it in Tranquility Harbor for the winter."

"Probably a good idea to spend the winter in Camden. Some of the folks in town are still pissed about the show. Phil barely talks to me. I have to keep an eye on him when he's handling my food." Connor backed off on the throttle as he approached the first buoy of his second string. "So, I'll tell her yes."

The next eight strings were as productive as the first, and Connor estimated the day's haul at close to five hundred pounds. So far, so good. But they had worked hard, and he was looking forward to hauling the last few traps and making for the docks and a cold beer. As they headed for the last string, Connor caught sight of the *Sweet Tail* cutting across the late-afternoon chop, moving in the same direction.

When Connor arrived at his first buoy, he noticed that Wade's orange-and-black buoys were set in a line parallel to his and not more than twenty yards away, which was very, very close. The two lines of buoys bobbed and rolled, wobbling off into the distance like twin columns of drunken sailors.

Wade pulled up in the *Sweet Tail* and stepped out of the small wheelhouse. He waved his gaff and hollered, "What do you say, college boy? Last one to haul his traps buys the beer. And to make it fair, you can even use your stern *girl*."

Connor glanced at Crystal. "What do you say? Up for a little competition?"

"As long as it's friendly." She nodded at Connor and stepped away from the bait station, facing Wade across the open water, raising her voice to be heard over the sound of the diesels. "And it's *first mate*."

"Ayuh. Sure it is." Wade snagged his first line, and the race was on.

Connor and Crystal worked well, with few stumbles as they hauled trap after trap—counting, measuring, re-baiting, and sending the traps back over the side. But damn was Wade quick, doing the job of two people.

Shoulders burning from the effort, Connor finally hooked his last trap, looped the line over the block, around the hauler, and started it spinning.

Crystal clapped her hands and bounced on the balls of her feet. "Hurry, hurry, hurry."

"We'll make it." Connor looked over.

Wade laughed as his final trap broke the surface. "Ayuh. I can already taste those beers."

Connor jammed his fingers into the green wire and started to lift, but the trap's unexpected weight almost pulled him over the side. Straining, he finally muscled it onto the workstation.

"Son of a bitch," Connor wailed. "Rocks!"

## ACKNOWLEDGMENTS

Writing a novel is really hard. Not digging ditches hard. Or fighting fires hard. But hard. And it's virtually impossible without getting all kinds of help. Which really means imposing your crazy writing obsession on perfectly innocent bystanders. So when your novel finally does get published, it's a very good idea to thank the people who helped you. Otherwise, next time, well, you're screwed.

So, here goes.

First, my wife, Nanette, who is way-big smarter than me and believes in me more than I believe in myself. Without her unflagging support, I would be the proud owner of about a hundred reems of blank paper. Next is Patrick McCord, who read some of my early scribblings and saw something he could work with. And Meryl Moss, who finally convinced me that I needed an audience and showed me how to get one. And my friend Peter Matton, who took me out in his Boston Whaler so I could witness firsthand the craziness that is Maine lobstering. And finally, Troy Hayes, one of those very same lobstermen, who let me spend the day on his boat and graciously complimented the fact that I didn't puke. I'm certain that I left out someone, so please don't be pissed. I'll get you next time.

Printed in the USA
CPSIA information can be obtained
at www.ICGtesting.com
LVHW091548290923
759455LV00007B/775